Corin & Angelique

Book 1

After the Fall of Night

S.L. CLAYTOR

Darter Lane Books

Darter Lane
Books

ISBN-13: 978-1-950900-00-8
ISBN-10: 1-950900-00-2

CONTENTS

PROLOGUE

Corin von Vadim walked amid the stones, fog rising around him in a silken veil. He looked down at each crumbling, mold-covered headstone and read what remained legible on the aged epitaphs. Many had decayed so much with the passing of time that all visible record of whose earthly remains rested within had been lost, yet he knew who each one of them had been in life. This was the place of the dead, but Corin possessed a gift that allowed him to visit the past lives of the deceased just by touching the sacred ground where dust and bone rested. His power often served as a cure for boredom in his solitary life.

He pulled the collar of his dark, knee-length cape tight against his jaws and tilted the brim of his black Stetson back while gazing at the chaos building in the sky. Lightning cracked across the heavens with avid ferocity. Heavy rain followed, the water almost immediately running down the brim of his hat and onto his shoulders. He stood calmly in the deluge, getting soaked nothing more than a nuisance, for no illness caused by the cold, damp night could harm him. The undead did not so easily die.

Then, sensing the nearness of another presence, Corin cocked his head and scanned his surroundings, his view diminished by the torrential downpour. Luckily, each bright flash of lightning illuminated the graveyard, and with the next fierce arc, Corin's gaze froze on the silhouette of a man—comparable to his own height—standing at a near distance.

"Tomes Jaffler," Corin called out, staring into the individual's featureless face, knowing, without question, his identity. "What is it you hope to gain by following me here?" Corin's voice floated over the turmoil of the storm.

"Justice, Corin von Vadim. I seek justice!" Tomes yelled back. "And it's a fitting night to achieve it...monstrous!" Hatred emanated from Tomes—a devouring sickness seeping from his very pores. "I know what you are, Nightwalker."

"It sounds like you've made quite a discovery."

"Don't deny it," Tomes responded.

"I wasn't going to. But I didn't kill Louisa. I am not responsible for her death."

"I found her nearly drained!" Tomes disputed. "Isn't that what you do, von Vadim, drain your victims of all life—take their essence in order to sustain your own vulgar existence?"

Tomes pulled a wooden stake from beneath his coat and charged his enemy, but Corin, endowed with superior speed, had little trouble dodging the onrush, whirling as Tomes lost his footing in the sludgy muck produced by the continual downfall and took a nasty dive to the ground.

Covered in mud, Tomes pushed himself up and onto his knees, and with tightly clenched fists, he expelled a mournful wail that challenged the roar of the storm. He then slumped forward, his arms supporting his upper body, mud squishing up between his fingers, and there, bellow after bellow of anguish escaped him.

"I'm telling you the truth, Tomes. I did not take Louisa's life. Nor do I wish to take yours now." Corin moved closer, but he knew there would be no reasoning with his opponent.

"It had to be you." Tomes glared at Corin with hate-filled determination, his breath erratic, and his light-brown hair plastered to his head.

"No, Tomes, it wasn't me. I didn't take her life."

"Who else could it have been? All the evidence is there, von Vadim, and I found two puncture marks on her neck, left there by the fangs of a feeder of blood! What else but a monster would perform such a sickening, repulsive act of drinking human blood?"

"You're right." Corin arrived at an unexpected realization by fitting that fragment of information into a much larger picture. "There *must* be another."

"What?" Tomes swallowed hard.

"Could it be that I am no longer the only nightwalker residing in Hixton?" The wheels in Corin's mind reeled at an alarming rate.

"No! It can't be. More of your kind? What's to become of us all with such an infestation of filth overtaking Hixton?"

"I am different from you, Tomes, but I'm not filth," Corin protested his choice of words. "I was once mortal—human—living flesh and bone. I struggle daily with what I've become and what I must do in order to survive, but I'm no worm or maggot."

"That's all a matter of opinion. I would rather be dead than become what you are. I couldn't imagine drinking the blood of another creature—human or animal—in order to survive."

"You deplore us, but I think if you were to walk in my shoes for a time, you'd come to feel quite differently about our existence. The mortal man I once was, though a distant memory, would have upheld your same ideals. However, when I was turned, I developed a new understanding of life. Many call us cursed, and it's true, we are cursed, but we're still living, breathing creatures. Like it or not, we all share one thing—the natural instinct to survive and fight the reins of death. I only do what I'm cursed to do in order to accomplish that. All things must feed to survive."

"If you speak the truth, von Vadim, and there is another nightwalker roaming our community, what you're saying is that Louisa was nothing more than a quick feed?"

"I know it sickens you to think of her taken in such an inhuman manner. I truly am sorry for your loss, Tomes. And as for what seems to be a new addition to our community, well, I'll have to look into the matter and find out just what it is that's found its way among us...and why. We could very well have a real fight on our hands."

"I thought all you monsters would stick together...wolves in a pack. You mean you would fight this creature?" Tomes questioned with surprise.

"I fight for what's mine regardless of who, or what, it is posing a threat," Corin replied. "The people living here in Hixton, I consider them family. I knew your father and your grandfather."

"You've only been in Hixton for what, a month? My father died more than ten years ago. How is it you knew my family?"

"I've always been here, Tomes. This is my home. I've been around a long, long time. I'm more than five hundred years old. I've seen generations come and go."

"I do recall my father speaking of your uncle, Victor

von Vadim, but never of you."

"But I *am* Victor von Vadim, and Nevin von Vadim before him." Corin exposed his deepest secret.

Corin had the ability to appear to age as any mortal man, and after a sufficient lifespan had passed, he would fake his death and return to von Vadim Estate under the pretense of being a lucky heir. By claiming to be a blood relative, a resemblance would be expected, and up to present day, the process had never failed. He had always taken every precaution when making those vital exchanges, choosing precise moments with the least risk of discovery. Luckily, the passing of years had a magical way of wiping away faces and memories, like erasing writing on a blackboard, providing opportunities to start anew.

"I understand that you're immortal and don't physically grow old, but it's amazing how you don't look any older than my age of twenty-six," Tomes said. "So, tell me, Corin, am I now going to die because of my newfound knowledge? Is this conversation with you going to be my last?"

"I have no intention of killing you." Corin squatted next to Tomes. The rain had slackened to a drizzle, and the lightning passed, rendered into distant rumbles of thunder. "Do you want to know why I hold on so dearly to this little town? It's my refuge from affliction. An old friend. All creatures need a safe haven and Hixton is mine. This land and I go back a long way. It holds my past, helps me remember that I was once transitory with all the frailties of a mortal man. Once, I walked in the warmth of the day and felt the weight of a soul within me, and I must never lose that vital part of myself—the human part. Without it, I become nothing more than a monster."

"And who exactly were you when you lived as this mortal man?" Tomes asked.

"My given name is Luca…Luca von Vadim, son of Count Ramone von Vadim of Hungary. My father was an official there, a proud man of high position. When I was changed, I knew I couldn't remain. I didn't possess the control I now have, and I couldn't bear the thought of being responsible for the fall of the von Vadim house. In order to save those I loved, I set out for the Americas, leaving all that I knew behind. I settled here and started a new life. I was, in fact, the first non-native settler in this area—the true founder—long before it became Hixton. Although, I'm sure past records would not state that truth.

I chose this area for the solitude and concealment it afforded. It was then a massive forest, offering me adequate separation from the New World settlers. But I knew the solitude couldn't last forever, and eventually they encroached upon my territory and built their homesteads, making it increasingly difficult for me to remain hidden, forcing me to reinvent myself."

"I can't believe you've been able to keep your identity secret for so long."

"In five hundred years of existing here, only a handful have ever come to know the truth. You are one of a very minute number, Tomes," Corin replied. "Although, there is something different this time that leads me to wonder if the fates might have had a hand in your discovery of my secret."

"The fates…." Tomes sneered. "What is fate anyhow? And what does any of it matter? My Louisa's gone, and life no longer matters. If you killed me now, it would be a blessing."

"You'll find meaning again, in time. You can't give up on life. Louisa wouldn't want that." Corin offered Tomes a hand and pulled him to his feet.

"You sound like a shrink, von Vadim."

Corin's mouth drew up on one side. "Well, after the

scene I've just witnessed, I'd say you could use a session or two."

Tomes offered no comeback.

"Now, if we're settled here, I should head out and search for this new arrival before another life is taken."

Tomes grabbed his arm. "Remember, Corin, the one who took the life of my wife is mine for the killing."

Corin nodded, and then he quickly vanished into the night on the mist of the wind.

* * * *

Tomes stood alone in the darkness, surrounded by the dead. He collapsed to his knees and continued to grieve. In the somber aftermath of the storm, the night creatures sang their songs to the sullen man and wept with him in his state of perpetual sorrow.

He'd never forget Louisa, nor did he ever wish to. She'd meant the world to him and losing her left him to question what life could ever offer him again. For no matter how much time might pass, he feared his heart would never heal. How could he continue without her? And with that dismal thought, he gave in to his sorrow and fell back in the muck. Tonight, he would simply cry.

1

Murder at Jaffler Farm

Sheriff Allen Pierson sat at his desk, thumbing through the case file of Louisa Jaffler. Now day two after the murder, he had to admit the investigation had stalled. He'd just received the medical examiner's preliminary report, complete with the autopsy findings, but regrettably, the outcome hadn't told him very much.

A little after midnight on the night of the horrific crime, a 911 dispatcher transferred a call to the station from Angelique Jaffler—sister-in-law of the victim— who claimed Louisa Jaffler had been murdered. Upon notification, Sheriff Pierson headed straightaway to Hixton, where the Jafflers resided. At the junction of Old Denaud Road and the farm entrance, he spotted a patrol car. Officer Jake Strutherford waved him down with a flashlight.

"I'll show you to the site."

Sheriff Pierson followed him to the crime scene, just

past the farm near a wood-line of tall, white pines. He pulled off behind two more patrol cars that were sitting off to the right side of the road with their lights flashing. Officer Bob Tanner stood several feet in front of one of the vehicles, in the direct path of the headlights, staring toward the woods as if paralyzed. The sheriff followed the officer's gaze and realized what had made such an impact on him.

"Dear Lord." He'd not soon forget the heart-wrenching scene.

A man sat on the ground, wearing nothing but pajama bottoms, cradling the victim's lifeless body in his arms. His face devoid of emotion, he rocked her back and forth like a mother would a child.

Officer Strutherford approached.

"What do we know?" the sheriff asked.

"Her name is Louisa Jaffler. That's her husband with her. She was found by him and his sister." The officer pointed out Angelique's position and motioned for her to come over.

Pierson turned his attention to her.

"I'm Angelique Jaffler. Tomes is my brother. He's been this way since we found her," she told him, clutching a flashlight.

"Has he said anything?" Pierson asked.

"Only to go away. He refuses to let her go," Strutherford answered as Officer Tanner joined them next to the SUV.

The sheriff was worried that the husband might very well be in shock. "Did you call for an ambulance...EMS?"

"George has them on standby." Tanner pointed to another officer who appeared busy, on the phone in his patrol car. "Since she was already dead, we were waiting to get your input," Bob explained.

"Sorry Ms. Jaffler." Strutherford apologized for

Tanner's bluntness.

Tanner continued. "We knew you were on your way. And we'll only need them for transport."

"I'm thinking of the husband. I think we'd better get some paramedics out here. Taking care of Mr. Jaffler is our priority right now." He wasn't sure how to properly handle this sort of psychological issue and thought it best someone trained in the medical field tend to the delicate situation.

"I'll let George know." Tanner headed toward the car.

"Should we try to force him away from the scene?" Strutherford asked. "He's disturbing the evidence."

"No. I don't think so. Just leave him. We'll wait on EMS. We certainly don't want to cause more damage. It might take him some time to come to terms with what's happened."

With no further delay, Sheriff Pierson made a call to the station, making arrangements to alert the only crime team at his disposal. That small group consisted of Forensics, which also covered bordering counties, and Dr. Jason Berg—head pathologist at Black River Falls Memorial Hospital, who also served as the county medical examiner. Jackson County had never needed a homicide division, but with this unexpected murder, it seemed that times had changed in their tranquil little area of the globe. And not for the better.

When his call was done, he instructed Officer Tanner to head over to the farm entrance and direct the paramedics to the crime scene when they arrived. In the meantime, he and the others kept a close watch on Tomes Jaffler, but left him to his grief. This was, after all, the young man's wife lying dead in his arms. Pierson couldn't imagine what Tomes was experiencing. He wouldn't pretend to. But seeing him out there, suffering so cruelly, told him one thing—he was either very much in love or consumed by guilt.

The sheriff didn't think he looked the part of a killer, but a crime of passion still had to be ruled out. Looks, after all, could be deceiving, and quarrels could quickly escalate with tempers flaring from embers to a full-fledged roar in a matter of seconds. He'd seen such rage before. Not to the extent of murder, per se, but wildly out of hand all the same.

With matters what they were, he thought it best to personally handle the investigative responsibilities and took advantage of the opportunity to question Angelique Jaffler while waiting for EMS to arrive. A beauty in her mid-twenties with long, sable hair that fell down her back, she'd said very little up to this point. Left to deal with the authorities since her brother was understandably unable to, Sheriff Pierson could see that she held back her own breakdown.

He pulled a small notepad from his pocket and jotted down the date and time—July twentieth, 12:46 a.m.—and her responses, listening to not only what she said, but observing her reactions. Despite the tragic circumstances of the night, he found her very calm and collected.

"Tomes, Louisa, and I, we all retired to our rooms around eleven," she recalled. "I read for a while before falling asleep, waking abruptly at 11:42 to the sound of a woman's scream. I know the precise time because the first thing I did was look at the clock sitting on my nightstand," she explained. "I rushed out and met Tomes in the hall. He'd also heard the scream, telling me that Louisa wasn't in their room. He said her name...knowing."

"Knowing?" Sheriff Pierson needed clarification.

"I think he knew it was her scream and feared the worst. Anyway, Tomes grabbed a flashlight from his room, this one." She held it up. "And we hurried outside to look for her. We found her here five, or maybe ten, minutes later. It's hard to be exact. Everything happened so fast."

"What led you down the road, away from the farm?"

"Tomes was sure the scream had come from this direction, so we headed toward the road. We knew we were going the right way when he found her hair clip a short distance up the driveway."

"Is Tomes the one who found her?" he asked.

"Yes, as a matter of fact, he was. But I hope you're not suggesting he had anything to do with this. We both were—"

The glare of headlights alerted them to Officer Tanner's return with an ambulance following.

"That was fast. They must have been close by. I need to take care of this." Pierson excused himself to meet the paramedics and enlighten them on the sensitive matter at hand.

Allowing EMS full access to do their job, he, Angelique, and the officers stood in the background and watched while the paramedics managed to convince Tomes to release Louisa's lifeless body.

Acceding, Tomes reluctantly laid his wife on the ground. He was gentle, treating her body like a fragile china doll. Illuminated by the moonlight, her fair skin held a pale-blue hue. In contrast, her bright auburn hair spilled around her face in thick, lustrous waves. Dressed in nothing more than a sheer nightgown that left nothing to the imagination, it revealed the outline of what had been a fit, vivacious body.

"Let's get her covered up," the sheriff instructed Bob. It was the decent thing to do. Forensics would probably have a conniption, but the crime scene had already been disturbed, so he didn't see any harm.

He glanced over at the emergency technicians who were examining their patient at the back of the ambulance and started that way, but he was detoured by another vehicle arriving on the scene. He was glad to see his second in command, Deputy Rudy Wilkins, and relieved it wasn't the media. At any given moment, news crews might show up and throw the otherwise calm, and so far, controlled investigation, into utter chaos. And that worried him.

Touching base with Rudy, he brought him up to speed and finally made his way over to the ambulance where Angelique stood next to her brother, comforting him. He observed for a moment, finding Tomes upset, but alert and levelheaded.

"Are you up for answering a few questions, Mr. Jaffler?"

"I don't know, Sheriff," Angelique spoke for him. "He's not—"

"No, it's okay, Angel." Tomes cut her off. "I want to know who did this."

"That's what we're trying to determine. Can you tell me what happened, what led you out here?" Pierson opened his notepad, pen in hand.

"A scream woke me...Louisa's scream. I noticed she was gone and rushed out to find her, meeting up with Angel in the hall. We hurried outside to look for her and found her here."

"Ms. Jaffler stated you were the one who found her body...that you were sure the scream had come from this direction."

"That's right. I knew the sound had carried from the road, so naturally, that's the direction I headed. When I saw her clip, from her hair, I ran on up the drive and started this way. I was just about to turn back, thinking I'd gone too far, when I noticed her nightgown near the tree line."

"Just one scream?" the sheriff confirmed.

"Yes," Angelique spoke out. "Only one scream."

Sheriff Pierson had no cause to consider Tomes Jaffler a suspect, but the fact that he seemed to know right where to find the body, so far from the house, bothered him.

"We were too late," Tomes mumbled. "Just too late. She was already dead when I found her."

"Can't this wait till morning, Sheriff?" Angelique took a protective stand for her brother. "Can't you see he's not up for this right now? He's going through hell. If you don't mind, I really need to get him to the house."

"It can wait," the sheriff agreed. He asked the paramedics to escort the Jafflers to the farmhouse. He understood that they needed some time to absorb the shock and collect themselves, especially Tomes. This had to be a nightmare for him.

"I'm not going anywhere," Tomes stated. "I'm not leaving her."

"She's gone, Tomes, and we need to let the police do their jobs," Angelique urged.

"I'm staying. I need answers, who did this and why." Tomes held his position and remained on the scene until they took his wife's body away almost two hours later.

Bringing his thoughts back to the present, Sheriff Pierson leaned back in his chair and groaned, stumped by the whole ordeal. He scanned the medical examiner's report, stopping where it mentioned a chemical imbalance in the blood with unusual cell activity.

Strange. An illness wasn't mentioned.

His gaze then fell on the words *chronically anemic*—another mystery in itself—with no visible injuries to account for the substantial blood loss. The only marks found on the victim's body were two, three to four-millimeter puncture wounds on the left side of her neck. Dr. Berg had suggested needle insertions caused the marks, perhaps used to draw blood from the body, but Sheriff Pierson needed more than just speculation. He observed a notation the doctor had made in the margin: "inconclusive pending forensic analysis."

The sheriff knew Forensics had taken specimens of the surrounding tissue, but waiting on them could take longer than watching ice melt in the Arctic. He wouldn't hold his breath. The whole process dragged out even more with the shuffling of paperwork between the crime lab and the investigative offices. He just hoped that when the results did arrive, he would have a little more than supposition to go on.

Just one scream. He thought back to the Jaffler's claim of having heard a single scream. People had different reactions to fear, but he couldn't help questioning why, in a moment of terror, she'd cried out only once. However, he did have a hypothesis, which had led him to prompt Dr. Berg to check for any sign of head injury or chloroform use, thinking the killer might have knocked her out by striking her over the head, or by administering an anesthetic to sedate her. He'd hoped something might come of his conjecture, but according to the report sitting in front of him, the doctor had found no sign of head trauma or traces of chemical use.

He cursed to himself, his theory shot down. "Maybe she froze in shock...fainted," he speculated, trying to imagine all possible scenarios of what might have occurred that terrible night. He just prayed she was unconscious when the blood was drained from her body. To be conscious would have been torture of the worst kind. A torment fit for hell.

Sheriff Pierson massaged the back of his neck to loosen the tense muscles giving rise to a migraine. He pulled open the top drawer of his desk and rooted around until he found a bottle of aspirin. Popping the top, he shook out two tablets and tossed them back with a swig of black coffee that had turned cold after sitting too long, wrinkling his face at the awful taste. He took a deep breath and tried to expel his frustration. This case was impossible! *What purpose could the killer have had for draining the victim's blood?*

"O positive," he said. Someone might have needed that particular blood type for some critical reason, possibly emergency surgery.

He'd always been a "keep your feet planted firmly on the ground and your head out of the clouds" kind of man. However, he delved yet further into the pit of absurdity as he considered the possibility that Hixton might have even become an abode for a cult. Could Louisa Jaffler have fallen victim to ritualistic murder? It might be improbable, but not unheard of. He'd read about such occurrences happening in small, out-of-the-way places.

Releasing another groan, he lit a Marlboro, took a long, deep drag and slowly let it out. The smoke lingered in front of him for several seconds before dispersing. He rubbed at the twitch in his left ear, a signal that always alerted him something wasn't quite right. An inner alarm that, to date, had never failed him.

There hadn't been a murder in the Jackson County area for more than thirty years and news of the killing had the community stirred. Bigger than anything he'd ever faced during his career in law enforcement, the pressure to supply answers weighed heavily on his shoulders. His small force consisted of good, honest people, but they had no experience when it came to handling a homicide investigation. They normally dealt with less severe crimes, more along the lines of shoplifting, breaking up domestic disputes, or running down speeders. But like him, his team was dedicated and would never veer off a road just because it got a little rocky. They had a job to do, and with him personally overseeing the case, they would absolutely get it done. This was his county, and he was determined to do everything in his power to keep the residents here safe.

He wanted to believe this murder would be a one-time incident, but that nagging spasm just wouldn't let up, smothering him with an intense fear that more killing would follow.

Someone needing the victim's specific blood type for emergency surgery was a far-reaching scenario, but one he couldn't rule out. He refused to dismiss any possibility without at least some minor consideration. With that in mind, he grabbed his hat from the stand next to his door and set a course for Black River Falls Memorial Hospital.

* * * *

The sheriff approached the information desk and stated his position.

"I'm conducting an investigation, and I'd like to speak to someone in charge, anyone having the authority to relinquish information." He removed his hat revealing his reddish blond, recently trimmed, hair.

"I'll see if our hospital administrator, Patricia Watson, is available." The receptionist reached for her phone handset and tapped several digits on the dial pad.

Thanking her, Pierson took a seat, waiting no more than a minute when a tall, shapely brunette woman appeared in a doorway to his right. He held an unflinching gaze on her as she strode toward him. He loved a woman with a strong mind and self-assurance to match, and by the way this woman moved—shoulders squared, and head held high—she appeared to possess both qualities in droves.

"Sheriff, hello. I'm Patricia Watson, Hospital Administrator."

"Sheriff Pierson." He politely extended his right hand.

She shook it in return and proceeded to inquire on the purpose of his visit.

"I'm investigating a murder that occurred in Hixton two nights ago and I need to ask you a few questions."

"I don't understand what this has to do with the hospital, or with me."

"Oh no, this has nothing to do with you personally, ma'am, not at all. Or with the hospital. I guess you could say I'm here on a hunch."

"A hunch?"

"Yes. I should explain."

"Please."

"Well, first, I was hoping to find out if the hospital might be in short supply of 'O positive' blood, and in addition, whether you might have had—in the past two days—any patients in desperate need of that specific blood type."

"I don't think so. We should have plenty of O positive on hand, but I can contact the blood bank to make sure. Although, you must know, Sheriff, I can't divulge any confidential patient information without consent, or a court ordered subpoena," she informed him. "No matter how charming an official you might be," she surprisingly added.

"Oh, I'm aware of that Ms. Watson, and if necessary, I could have a subpoena here within the hour."

"One hour. You must have some clout."

"I *am* the sheriff."

Ms. Watson laughed.

"So, would it be possible to find out if someone made a deposit of O positive blood since the night before last?" Sheriff Pierson asked.

"Yes, it's possible. But if anything comes of it, I'll need that subpoena before releasing any files to you."

"Understood."

"Blood is usually drawn here, but sometimes it's sent in by an outside source. If you don't mind my asking, how does this relate to your murder investigation?"

"Well, it appears the victim was intentionally drained of blood, and this might sound absurd to you, but I was thinking that the killer might have been desperate to save the life of a loved one, in urgent need of her specific type blood. Crazy as it sounds, you get where I'm going with this. Who knows the lengths desperation might drive someone to, and for a person without a conscience, it could easily spell murder."

"I don't know, Sheriff," Ms. Watson said. "I hate to be the bearer of bad news, but O positive blood is a rather common type. I don't see there being any trouble acquiring it."

"Too preposterous, huh?" Sheriff Pierson sighed, feeling a little foolish.

"I wouldn't say that. Nowadays, more and more strange things happen than I would ever care to know about. But you've got me thinking. You still may be on to something. Maybe it's not so much the blood type, but rather something unique about the blood."

"There were some imbalances mentioned." He was relieved she hadn't laughed at his theory.

"Since you're here, Sheriff, there is something I should probably mention."

"What's that?"

"We've had a problem arise in our blood bank, not with deposits, but with unauthorized withdrawals.

Someone's been slipping in and taking bags."

"Stealing blood?"

"That's right. Over the years, we've had bags go missing from time to time, but never so much as what's been taken over this past week. I have security working on it, but we just can't seem to catch the culprit. Yesterday, I took even further measures and had a surveillance camera installed in the blood storage room."

"Do you suspect an employee?"

"I know most everyone working in the hospital, and I just can't imagine it being any of them."

"Who on earth would steal blood, and what would they be doing with so much of it?" He mulled over the act.

"Seems we have a similar problem on our hands, except, you're after a killer, and I'm after a thief."

"Let's just hope they're not one and the same."

"That thought just crossed my mind as well."

"About the information...?"

"Follow me, and I'll get that report for you." Ms. Watson led him to her office, motioning toward two chairs in front of her desk. She took her seat, reached for the phone, and placed a call to the blood storage department, asking the recipient of the call to check on the matter and get back to her "stat."

They continued talking while waiting for the information. The sheriff was not one for idle chitchat, but Ms. Watson had no problem keeping the conversation rolling.

"I was just reading about the murder in the morning paper," she told him. "Big news around here. I couldn't believe how the writer compared the killing to the myth of the vampire. They'll grasp at just about anything, won't they?"

"I've been so wrapped up in the case I haven't had

time to look at the paper today.”

“I have it right here, if you’d like to take a look.”

She retrieved the paper from her trashcan and held it up, so the article faced him. “Front page news, and your picture’s here too. Down the page a bit.” She placed a finger next to it.

He leaned forward, laid his hat on the desk, and took it from her.

“Wonderful,” he remarked with annoyance. “Man or monster?” He read the title of the article with sarcasm and laughed. “This is worse than yesterdays. These reporters sure come up with some real doozies.”

“They do embellish. But the hype sells papers.”

Her phone rang and she answered, signaling it was the information they were waiting for. “Great. Just fax it to me,” she instructed and hung up. “It’ll take a minute for it to come over the machine.”

He nodded and continued skimming the article, noticing that her eyes never averted.

“How do you feel about the way Terry Phillips used the vampire angle?” she asked.

“It’s ridiculous. Do you know anything about this guy?”

“No, I can’t say I do. Why?”

“He seems to know an awful lot about the case. Too much, in fact. And I don’t care for the way he portrays my department—making us look like a bunch of buffoons.”

“Oh, he’s just exaggerating a bit to create interest...draw in readers. Besides, you can’t go arresting Mr. Phillips just for writing something you don’t care for. He has a little thing called ‘freedom of speech’ on his side. ‘Freedom of press’ backing him.”

“Maybe so. But he’s a poor reporter in my opinion. I don’t hold much regard for someone who grabs his moments of fame at the expense of others.”

"If it helps any, Sheriff, I know you're no buffoon. And you have to keep in mind, this is probably the biggest story they've had to report on in years. You can bet they're going to exploit the situation...play it for all its worth. You'd best brace yourself for more."

"Oh, I know. The media can be a nightmare." He slapped the paper down in front of him. "The whole lot...they give me hives."

"You have an allergy to them, huh?" Ms. Watson laughed.

"I guess I do, especially this joker." He couldn't help but think she was flirting with him.

Ms. Watson laughed again, and this time there was no mistaking her flirtatious response when she reached out and lightly placed a hand on his sleeve. "You're not at all what I would have expected, Sheriff Pierson," she remarked.

Her fingertips grazed his wrist, generating a surge that caused him to shift in his seat. It had been a long time since he'd felt such instant attraction.

"That'll be the report." She got up and hustled over to the fax machine that rattled out several pages. "Well, we have plenty of type O blood." She glanced over the sheets. "Just as I suspected, I'm afraid there's not much to report. You can take this." She handed him one of the pages. "It shows the deposits we had yesterday...not many. They all came from our outpatient facility in preparation for upcoming surgery, and none match that blood type."

"I guess it's back to the drawing board." He reached for his hat. "You know, if I keep coming up empty-handed, I might just have to adopt Mr. Phillip's ideas and look into doing a little vampire research of my own," he said, prompting her to laugh once more. "I really do appreciate your cooperation, Ms. Watson, and I'm sorry to have taken up so much of your time."

"Patricia," she told him as she got up to see him out. "And you?"

"Allen," he responded. "Let me know what comes of your 'withdrawal' problem. You can reach me at the station."

"I'll do that. And, Allen, here's my business card, just in case you find you've forgotten something." She leaned close. "I work Monday through Friday, eight to five most days," she whispered seductively, and pointed to the exit.

He took her card, wishing the timing was better. He would have loved to ask her out to dinner. But in the midst of a murder investigation, he had to keep his focus on his work.

"I'll hold onto this." He slid the card in his pocket. "And thank you again Ms. Wa—"

"Patricia." She caught him mid-word.

Pierson nodded. "Patricia."

Glancing back as he left, he noticed that she continued to watch him. *The ol' dog's still got it going on.* He smiled.

He headed for the parking lot, climbed into his SUV, and scanned the report again, making sure he hadn't missed anything. But nothing on the page had any bearing on the case.

Having hit a dead end there, he decided to head over to the newspaper office to track down Mr. Terry Phillips. The newspaper journalist was just a little too well informed, and that made him a person of interest in his book. It wasn't much of a lead, but it was something, and he intended to follow every avenue available.

He'd leave no stone unturned.

2

Angelique

Angelique Jaffler took woodland walks each evening at twilight. Corin often followed her, lurking like a phantom in the cover of the trees. If he hadn't been a nightwalker, damned with his infernal curse, he would have chosen her to share his life.

Blessed with a smooth, olive complexion and long, dark hair that fell in fine strands along the sultry curve of her back, Angelique was lovely in beauty and heart. Her warm, hazel eyes were mesmerizing, ever-changing dependent on her surroundings and mood, a trait that Corin found captivating.

Since becoming aware of another nightwalker roaming the area, Corin refused to take any chances with her safety. Even though he knew she could never be his, he still couldn't let go of the dream. He'd developed an unexpected affection for her—a fondness that had grown into what he now feared was love

Although it was unlikely she'd ever know of his feelings, she would always be the angel of light in his world of darkness.

Over the years, Corin had remained conscious of those living in his vicinity. He'd watched Angelique blossom from a child into a stunning young woman. He'd met her only twice face-to-face, once recently in his present identity, and the other, years before while making a call on her father at the farm, when she was in her youth. During that period, he was under the persona of Victor von Vadim, who Angelique and Tomes knew to be Corin's deceased uncle. Their father, John Jaffler, had worked for him at the estate, but kept his family distanced. Even though they shared a friendship, John did not allow him to become acquainted with his children, something Corin had respected. His children's well-being was of the utmost importance to him, first and foremost in his life, as it should be.

Corin had decided it was time to transition into his current persona a month earlier, and he'd reinstated himself an heir—a lucky nephew of Victor. John was part of a life he'd now left behind, but his friend's spirit lived on in his children. Angelique possessed many of his great qualities. There were so many things Corin loved about her, but one chief attraction was the way she embraced the night, venturing out each evening just at the brink of dusk. Was she searching for something only found in the sunless hours, or was that just his fantasy?

The path she took led to a shallow creek where she stopped at the water's edge. Corin followed as a Great Horned Owl, the large nocturnal predator one of his favorite forms. Landing in a tree about ten yards away, his razor-sharp talons clasped a limb, offering him a steady perch.

A near-full moon commanded the sky, its light shimmering on the water's surface. He soaked in the sight of her, careful not to reveal his presence, wanting oh so desperately to capture just a small inkling of her pure, enticing essence—her beautiful soul. How he longed to touch her. Forced to admire her from afar, he gazed at her while she slipped off her sandals and stepped into the shallow water. Kneeling down, the hem of her sheer summer dress danced with the current.

With all the instincts of the large bird whose form he'd claimed, Corin cocked his head to the side at the unexpected crunch of underbrush in the woods behind Angelique. She looked back at the large trees and vines masked in shadows. He sensed her fear but couldn't go to her without compromising himself.

Being immortal, he possessed a keen awareness of other creatures around him, yet he was unable to see anything—man or animal. Perplexed, he scanned the area. Someone or something was out there.

Desperate to protect her and having no time to grapple over the risk of discovery, Corin was forced to make a decision. Quickly devising a course of action, he leapt from his perch and took flight, his massive wings beating the air, rampant in his urgency to get to her. The tree limb rocked in his wake. Well out of view, he dove through the trees and landed on the woodland floor where he shape-shifted into his human form.

"Who's there?" Angelique called out. "I know someone's there."

Hearing the distress in her trembling voice, he wished he'd assumed the shape of a smaller animal. Corin stepped out of the cover of the woods and revealed himself. Angelique's safety was all that mattered.

"Why hello. You probably don't remember me," he

said. "I hope I didn't scare you."

"Corin von Vadim?" she inquired with surprise. "You nearly gave me a heart attack."

"I apologize for alarming you. Are you all right?"

"I'm fine," she assured him. "You just startled me. What are you doing out here, so far from the estate?"

"I thought this was my estate."

"I meant from the mansion," she clarified. "It's quite a walk."

"I suppose it is, but it's a nice night. I was following the property line, getting a feel for the land. I believe our properties connect right here, along this very creek bed."

"That's right, but you seem to be standing on the wrong side," she pointed out.

"A little detail I was hoping you wouldn't notice."

"I see." Angelique flashed a smile.

The smell of lavender cascading from her stimulated an arousal he fought to keep suppressed, finding it hard not to act on his impulses when she was so close. But sweet and luscious as she was, he reminded himself that she was off limits—forbidden fruit.

"To tell you the truth, I really didn't expect to run into anyone out here, not at this time of evening. Acquainting myself with the land, I'm finding there's a lot of it to cover."

"More than two thousand acres," she replied. "I guess you've been here about a month now, so, what do you think of our small part of the world?"

"It already feels like home," he said, not able to tell her he'd actually resided there for hundreds of years. "This is a nice section of the creek. I believe it's my favorite part of the property."

"I've been coming here since I was a little girl. It's so serene. I love the way the meadow runs along the creek on the other side...your side. It's a beautiful view."

"Yes, it is. Absolutely beautiful," he agreed, but not referring to the landscape.

"And you're welcome to take a walk on my side anytime," he added with a devilish grin.

She looked away and twirled a strand of hair around her finger, the demure gestures telling him she'd caught the double entendre.

With her focus momentarily off him, Corin seized the opportunity to scan the woods around them. He didn't detect any other presence, but he couldn't be sure that whoever, or whatever, it was out there with them only minutes prior was now gone.

"Is there something wrong?" Angelique caught him looking around. Faint howls of crying wolves rode on the wind.

"No. Everything's fine," he replied nonchalantly, not wanting to alarm her. "That doesn't frighten you, knowing there are wolves nearby?"

"I hear one from time to time, but I don't worry much about them. What few wolves we have remaining keep to the denser areas," she told him.

"I was thinking, if you don't mind, I'd like to walk you home...see a bit of Jaffler land."

"It's a long walk from the farmhouse back to the estate. Are you sure?"

"What's a few acres more?" he teased. "The truth is I'd love the company."

"In that case, I must accept."

On their walk, Angelique reminded Corin of their first meeting on the night of his arrival in Hixton a month earlier. She confessed being tempted to pay him a visit at the estate, but that she'd decided against it, thinking their unplanned encounter hadn't acquainted them enough to warrant visiting him at his home.

As they approached the farmhouse, Tomes rose from the shadows of the wide porch stretching across the front of the structure. His gaze fell on Corin, staring him down. Corin felt the burn of his scrutiny and knew Tomes wanted to tear his head off for daring to come near his sister.

"What are you doing out with this guy, Angel?" Tomes demanded.

"Tomes, honestly, he just walked me home," Angelique answered.

"I don't want you seeing him...not him!"

"I don't know what's gotten into you, but you have no say when it comes to who I choose to spend time with. I'm not going to let you dictate who I can and can't see," she countered. "We may live under the same roof, but I'm a grown woman."

"You don't know what I know, Angel," Tomes argued.

Corin realized Tomes wanted to elaborate further, to make her understand.

"I think you should leave." Tomes shifted his focus back to Corin.

"Tomes! Don't be so rude!" Angelique scolded. "Corin, I apologize for my brother."

"It's okay," Corin assured her while passing Tomes a firm look. "Besides, I'd best be going." He let the matter slide, not wanting to upset Angelique any further.

"Thank you for the company."

"I should thank you for walking me home. I hate to own up to it, but I did get a little scared out there tonight. I sure was relieved when I saw you."

"What happened, Angel?" Tomes asked with concern.

"Your sister just got a little spooked, that's all," Corin told him. "Although, for the time being, you should try and dissuade her from going out into the woods alone after nightfall. It isn't safe."

Ending their conversation on that note, he bid them

goodnight and retreated into the darkness.

3

Marshal Jordon Black

Jordon Black sat in a booth at the Black River Falls Diner poking at the remains of his roast beef sandwich and fries. He pulled a newspaper article from his inside coat pocket and spread it out on the table. His bluish-gray eyes skimmed over the words. He circled several names of interest, stopping and looking up when a waitress appeared with his check.

"Where might I find the local Sheriff's Office?" he inquired.

"The police station is on Chester Street...two lights up." She pointed out the direction. "Just take a right when you pull out of here, then take a left on Chester. It's about a half mile from there, on the left."

Jordon had been with the U.S. Marshals Service for ten years, part of a special division established in association with the FBI in pursuit of the most dangerous individuals—the worst of the worst. He'd spent the last two years hot on the trail of a killer, and that continuing hunt had now led him to Jackson County, Wisconsin—a tranquil region of several close-knit, small towns. He took pride in his tracking expertise and was positive that the recent murder victim named in the article lying before him—Louisa Jaffler—was yet another of the many unfortunate souls left in the wake of his fugitive's killing spree. There were several instances when he'd come close to nabbing the monster, but the killer had proved himself to be of unusual intelligence and had slipped through his fingers each time.

In his mid-forties, Jordon was dauntless. Not at all the stereotypical image one might have of a Deputy U.S. Marshal. His predominantly brown hair held a scattering of gray. Long and untamed, he kept it pulled back and leashed behind him with a strap. He didn't own a suit, more comfortable outside the office, chasing down the bad guys. More often than not, his work attire consisted of worn jeans and cowboy boots. But just so no one could say he wasn't professional, he'd toss on a dress coat.

Gathering his things, he left a tip on the table and headed for the register to pay his bill. His Lucchese boots made a dull thud each time they struck the hardwood floor as he strode across it in a manner that told the world just how confident and determined a man he was.

Following the waitress's directions to the station, he arrived in mere minutes, parked, and went inside. Two officers talked behind a chest-high counter.

"I'd better get going." One officer got up to leave.

"I'll see you later, Bob," the other man said, then turned toward Jordon.

"Good day, officer. I'd like to see the sheriff in regard to the recent murder."

"Sheriff Pierson is out right now," the officer, whose nametag read 'Chuck Gantt,' informed him. "Hold on, and I'll take a message." He pulled a pencil from over his ear, breaking the lead the instant it touched the paper. "Dagnabbit." He fumbled for something else to write with, making a total mess of the paperwork on the counter.

Jordon, thinking the officer to be a simpleton by his appearance and clumsy actions, proceeded to pump him for information.

"So, Chuck," Jordon spoke as if he'd known the man his whole life. "I read about the murder...hear it happened nearby, in Hixton, I believe."

The man bit the first line he threw.

"Yeah, that's right, over at Jaffler Farm—the family raises thoroughbreds. The victim lived there with her husband and sister-in-law."

The officer blabbed away without the least bit of caution, having no idea who Jordon was. It apparently hadn't occurred to him to ask, proving Jordon's initial impression to be an accurate one.

The young man continued, "They found her body just past the farm entrance on Old Denaud Road, at the edge of the woods. We assume she was taking a late-night walk when the killer attacked her. However, there's some dispute on that theory."

"Dispute by whom?"

"The husband," the officer told him. "He claimed she never took walks after nightfall. To quote his exact words, 'she was afraid of the dark...never went out alone after the fall of night'."

"Really?" Jordon raised his eyebrows in interest. "Afraid of the dark?"

"That being the case, you can't help but wonder what led her out on that road all alone, and so late at night. It just doesn't fit."

"It sure doesn't," Jordon agreed. "Tell me, Chuck, were there any witnesses to the murder?" he pressed.

"Not a one. I personally don't know what to make of it. The poor girl's blood was drained, leaving her body blue as a dismal sky...or so I heard."

Jordon suppressed a laugh. Chuck wasn't the sharpest tool in the shed. *He* could have been the killer, and this nitwit would have been none the wiser.

"Did you happen to know the family?" Jordon asked.

"No, can't say I did. You'd have better luck with that inquiry over in Hixton."

"I'm sure you're right." Confident he'd learned all he could from Officer Chuck, Jordon was ready to head out. "Think you could you pen me some directions?"

"Oh, you won't have any problems. It's not far, just several miles north and to the west of I-94."

"Do you know the exit number?"

"105. Then turn right onto 95—it's also called Interstate Road. From there, it's less than a mile. You could also take County Road A, but the interstate is faster."

"I'm sure I'll find it. Thank you for the info, Chuck. You've been more help than you could ever know." Jordon's voice held a hint of belittlement.

"Well, that's what we're here for, to serve and assist," the officer replied in a chipper manner, seeming not to notice the derision. "What about a message...for the sheriff?"

"I'm with the U.S. Marshals Service. I just wanted to inform him that I'm here looking into the murder. I'd like to meet with him, but there's no need to take anything down. I'll stop back by later." Jordon gave a friendly nod and left.

What kind of a hillbilly hellhole have I wandered into this time?

He stepped outside the building and made a beeline

for his car, eager to get to Hixton. Visiting the murder site was his next plan of action. If Chuck was any indication of the rest of the force, the incompetent idiots running Jackson County just might have overlooked some vital clues.

Arriving in Hixton fifteen minutes later, he stopped at a local convenience store where a clerk gave him directions to Old Denaud Road. Following the course given, he found the two-lane byway with little effort. Traveling a little farther through dense, wooded terrain, he spotted a dirt drive to his right framed by two tall poles supporting a sign saying: Jaffler Farm. Several Thoroughbred horses grazed in a large pasture nestled between the road and the farmhouse that sat a distance back. Continuing past the farm entrance, he located the taped-off crime scene a minute later, at the edge of the woods.

Jordon pulled off the road and shifted the black Dodge Charger into park. His gator-skin boots had just hit the dirt when a white SUV pulled up behind him. By the dim view afforded him through the front windshield, he recognized the man behind the wheel from his picture in the paper—Sheriff Pierson.

The sheriff alighted from his vehicle, and Jordon heard him mumble, "Who the blazes is this beatnik?"

An imposing figure, he stared at Jordon in an obvious attempt to intimidate while pulling a pack of Marlboros from his shirt pocket and tapping one out. Cupping his hands to his mouth, he lit the cigarette and let out a plume of smoke that curled upward and drifted away on the light breeze.

"I prefer Camels myself." Jordon spoke first, reaching for his own gold-colored pack of cigarettes. He lit one up and blew the smoke out of the left side of his mouth in a cocky manner, letting the sheriff know he could not, would not, be intimidated. "You must be

Sheriff Pierson."

"I am. And who might you be?" Pierson asked and moved toward him. "This is an official crime scene."

"I'm well aware of that." Jordon bit his cigarette between his teeth to free his hands, searching his inner coat pocket for his badge.

In the process, Pierson caught sight of the 9mm strapped to his shoulder and immediately took defensive action.

"Put your hands up," the sheriff ordered, his gun trained on Jordon. "Where I can see them!"

"Whoa." Jordon raised his hands and spat out his cigarette so he could speak clearly. "Take it easy, Sheriff. I'm a Deputy U.S. Marshal."

"I'll be needing some proof of that."

"I have my badge right here in my coat. If you'll let me get it, you'll see this is just one, big misunderstanding."

"All right, but you make any sudden movements, and the next bullet's got your name on it," Pierson warned. "Now take it slow...real slow." The sheriff maintained a firm aim.

Jordon moved with extreme caution and reached into his coat. He located his badge right away, pulled it out, and flipped it open.

Sheriff Pierson lowered and holstered his Glock .45. "Sorry about that, Marshal, but you can't be too careful."

"No harm done. I'm Marshal Jordon Black. I stopped by your station to advise you of my arrival and spoke with Officer Gantt."

"I assume you've been sent to investigate the murder," Pierson stated.

"Not exactly, or I guess I should say I'm not quite sure yet." Jordon looked down and stubbed out his cigarette still burning on the ground at his feet. "The murder you had here is identical to those of a killer I've been tracking."

"So, you have a suspect, then?"

"Sorry, Sheriff, I wish I did. He's quite a mastermind, really good at covering his trail."

"What makes you think this is the same killer?" Sheriff Pierson reached for another cigarette, having lost the first when pulling his gun on Jordon.

"I'm not positive it is. But from what I've read it seems to be his handiwork. I've been after him for two years. He's cunning, never stays in one place for long. Killing comes easy as breathing to him. He's left a considerable number of blood-drained bodies in his wake, and the string of cases just keeps getting longer and longer."

"Blood-drained bodies?" The sheriff looked surprised. "I hadn't considered a serial killer."

"You don't know the half of it."

"I thought that was the FBI's job."

"I'm with a special division of the Service. We work closely with the FBI," Jordon told him. "Would you mind if I take a look around the site?"

"I have no problem with that. I'm here to take another look myself," Pierson replied and moved toward the taped-off area.

Jordon followed, sure that, sweep or not, the unqualified little force had missed something. And preferring to conduct his own search in private, he deliberately put some distance between them, scouring the tree line and underbrush about eighty feet away from Pierson, where he found something of interest. Squatting down, fearful the sheriff might confiscate his find, he smoothed out the crumpled piece of paper and gave it a quick skim. It was a receipt from the Black River Falls Inn.

"Have you got something there?" Pierson called over

to him.

Jordon slipped the receipt into his pocket before rising from his crouched position.

"Oh, no, I was just checking the underbrush for any tracks or clues your group might have missed," he lied.

"I know what I saw, so how about you just empty that right pocket of yours and prove me wrong."

"Happy to." Jordon pulled the pocket inside out, but with a bit of sleight of hand, transferred the receipt under his sleeve. "Nothing here but a pack of gum, a couple wrappers, and a lighter. What you saw was me retrieving a wrapper that fell from my shirt pocket when I was bending over. Like I said, I was just checking the underbrush for missed clues. I suspect you don't have the best forensics team at your disposal, am I right?" He went on with uncouth arrogance, not caring how his words came across.

"I'm rather proud of my team, Marshal, and I can assure you, they did a more than adequate job." Pierson responded, his irritation at Jordon's insult apparent.

"It's a small county, but we do know how to follow protocol. Everything was done by the book." He dropped his cigarette to the ground and pressed it into the dirt with the steel tip of his boot.

Jordon chuckled to himself, a mental image forming of the sheriff pulling out a large instruction book entitled *Homicide for Dummies* and attempting to instruct a group of inept deputies.

4

The Mansion

Corin rose from his dark sanctuary as the sun was setting. He usually waited for twilight before emerging, but being an older vampire, he could tolerate a small amount of sunlight. In the shadows of the forest, where he spent a great deal of time, he even dared to wander out in the earlier daylight hours. But that was a risk he wouldn't attempt often, for the burning rays could literally turn him to ashes.

Corin stayed in isolation at his estate—a sprawling and grand abode consisting of more than two thousand acres of lush woodlands running across a hilly terrain. The mansion had undergone numerous renovations over the last five hundred years, growing in size and value. It sheltered a host of treasures—just a taste of the vast wealth he'd accumulated over his many years of existence. A cunning businessman, he'd made many wise investments, ensuring his position. Money would never be a problem for him.

With his eyes shaded by dark glasses, he stood in a shadowed area near the lanai door, looking past the wall, toward the woods. This land had been his solitude from the very beginning of his changed existence, and if he had anything to say about it, it always would be.

"You're taking your walk, aren't you?" His thoughts were on Angelique, fearing she was venturing out alone, regardless of her recent scare. She had no idea of the danger lurking in the area.

Concerned for her safety, he disregarded his own well-being and braved the light. Twilight wasn't far off, but he refused to wait a moment longer for those last lingering rays to give in to the onslaught of falling night.

Sheltered under his cape and Stetson, he made a swift dash for the woods. Reaching the shady folds, he metamorphosed into a wolf and tore off in the direction of the creek, keeping to the cover of the woodland floor for protection from the dwindling light breaking through the shield of trees above him. He knew right where to find her—walking the path that led to the creek where their properties merged.

Making his way through the crowding of trees, he caught sight of another wolf running parallel with him. A bit to his left, the creature kept in perfect unison. Time slowing to a crawl, he watched as it moved in slow motion. Surmising this was no ordinary wolf, Corin veered toward it. But with his attempt to intercept, the animal suddenly dematerialized, confirming what he feared—another immortal walked the woods.

Why can't I sense you?

Corin picked up his pace, now more concerned than ever for Angelique's safety.

Relief suffused his body when he spotted her on the path. Careful not to be seen, he bypassed her in the woods, reached the creek ahead of her, and waited. He reclaimed his human form, clothes and all, having the exceptional power to shape-shift anything on his person. Fortunately, the sun had finally descended, but for the moment, he kept to the shadows and anticipated her arrival. Her scent carried on the air as she drew close. He inhaled deeply, a subdued groan emerging as he exhaled. Only a few feet away from him now, his gaze fell on her.

"Hello again." He stepped into view.

"Corin...hello." Her lack of reaction led him to believe she must have expected to run into him.

"We're going to have to stop meeting this way. We wouldn't want to subject ourselves to rumors." Corin's remark prompted her to laugh.

"Is that so?" Angelique played along, twirling a strand of hair in her fingers. "And who would ever know? I doubt anyone else is out here, traipsing around these woods."

"True," he responded, not able to tell her about the creature he'd just encountered in the form of a wolf, worried where it might be.

He could have offered to walk her home again, but she was an addiction—a sensual, dark-haired vision that haunted his every waking hour. Yes, he wanted to protect her, but he also longed to be with her even though he knew he shouldn't. Conflicted, he invited her to his house for drinks, but silently reprimanded himself for encouraging her affections.

"I'd love to. I never go beyond the creek, stemming back to a promise I made my father. But I'm not a child anymore, and it would be nice to explore your side for a change. The mansion is so secluded behind that wall. I've lived here all my life and have never seen it up close."

"Well, allow me to escort you, then."

The moon provided plenty of light as they made their way across a shallow area of the creek and through the winding woods. Corin kept a watchful eye out for any unwelcome company, but the trespassing immortal didn't show himself again.

"You must forgive my brother's behavior last evening." Angelique looked into his shadowed face. "I was so ashamed of his reprehensible conduct."

"There's no need to apologize. Considering everything that's happened, I can't blame him for being protective."

"He's under a lot of stress. And the sheriff pinning him as a suspect isn't helping matters any," she told him.

"That's just preposterous. From what I've seen, no man could have loved his wife more."

"He really did love her. They were a perfect fit. Made for each other," she responded in a low, remorseful tone. "They had something special. That once in a lifetime thing. The sort of love most of us spend our whole lives searching for and few ever find."

"They were soul mates, and he'll no doubt grieve for a long time to come."

"I just hope it doesn't destroy him. I'm afraid he's giving up on life."

"He's suffered a tremendous loss, but in time, he'll learn to live again."

"I pray you're right." Angelique suddenly halted as they rounded a corner, and a tall stone and mortar wall came into view.

"My uncle was a private man." Corin guided her to a gate and pulled a keychain from his pocket. Singling out the key required, he unlocked the gate and welcomed her inside. Passing through, the mansion loomed in front of them.

"Wow. It's breathtaking. I've only seen it once

before…a long time ago."

Corin was pleased with her reaction, almost relieved by her approval. He couldn't help fantasizing, envisioning her mistress of von Vadim Estate. He would have loved nothing more than to keep her there with him forever, but for the good of her soul, he would never be so selfish.

"I just see it as home." He guided her across the well-manicured back grounds to the house, watching her expressions. At the front of the structure, he motioned toward the entrance. "Shall we take company inside?"

"Listening to you, Corin, I'd think you were from another era."

He laughed to himself. *If she only knew how right she was.*

Past influences often crept into his speech. When living for hundreds of years, losing track of the changes in times and styles wasn't hard to do. Over the years, he'd observed the mortals living out their lives around him, rarely attempting to interact with them. He did form associations with a select few, those needed to maintain his personal finances and other necessities of living, finding that there was less chance of discovery that way.

"Maybe I am from another era, or was, in another life," he told her. Funny thing was, he spoke the truth.

* * * *

A dark-colored wolf raced across Old Denaud Road and prompted Tomes to stop. He hopped out of his truck and peered into the woods where the animal had darted, but the darkness and underbrush prevented him from seeing very much.

Mournful howls echoed, creating an eerie

atmosphere. It was unusual to hear so many of the animals, and he'd never spotted one so close to the farm before, giving him cause for concern.

"What is going on?"

The idling truck sputtered as he hopped back in. He contemplated going to von Vadim Estate to get Corin's thoughts but decided he should first locate Angelique and apprise her of the situation.

"You're out there in the woods...alone. Even after what happened to Louisa." He knew how much his sister enjoyed taking her nightly walk.

Figuring he'd best find her before she ended up face-to-face with one of the creatures, he hurried home, parked, and ran to the front door of the house. Stepping inside, he called out, receiving no response. She wasn't there.

"Darn it, Angel."

On foot, he headed for the woods. Dappled in shadows from the surrounding trees, the trail he followed wound its way to the creek. He expected to meet up with her at any moment along the way, but he saw no sign of her.

"Where are you?"

Standing next to the water, he looked around and sighed, growing more worried with every passing minute.

"Your cell phone."

He hurried back to the farm, hoping she had her phone with her. Bolting from the truck, he barreled into the house and dialed her number, expelling a held breath when she answered. He'd never been so glad to hear her voice.

* * * *

Angelique stared up at the massive three-story

structure in utter awe. She had seen it before, when she was a child, but only from a distance when Tomes coaxed her into exploring von Vadim land. They were curious about the recluse, Victor von Vadim, and why their father had so adamantly forbidden them from tarrying beyond the creek. She recalled how they found a tree overhanging the wall and climbed it, getting a view of the estate house. An unsettling dread befell her when her eyes gazed on the dwelling, as if it were reaching for her, trying to draw her in and capture her in its hold forever. It was so disturbing she never went there again.

Progressing toward the mansion now with Corin, that old eeriness crept back, but she chalked it up to being warned her whole life to stay away. But with Victor von Vadim deceased, she presumed any threat her father thought existed there was now gone. Thinking of the recluse, she recalled how he'd kept the gate at the main entrance chained, warding off anyone who dared attempt to enter. It had remained that way until Corin inherited the estate a month earlier and removed them.

"Wait." Angelique, growing disoriented, stopped and reached for Corin.

Suddenly inundated by past memories, she was unable to prevent a flashback, sweeping her back to a brief meeting she'd had with Victor von Vadim when she was eight years old.

Night had just fallen. She sat in the living room of their farmhouse reading a book when a knock sounded at the door. With everyone else preoccupied in other rooms, she answered, greeted by a tall, older fair-haired gentleman. Clutching her book, she looked up into his face with wide-open eyes, having no inkling of who he was.

"Hello," she managed to say before her father, John,

appeared in the room behind her. He rushed toward her as if intercepting her from some terrible danger.

"I want you to go to your room, little miss." He attempted to usher her away, but the visitor halted his attempt.

"Wait." The stranger knelt to her level and looked into her face. "What is your name?"

"Angelique. But my brother, Tomes, he calls me Angel. I'm no angel though. Just ask my dad." She looked up at her father.

"I'd wager that he'd disagree." The man laughed. "I certainly couldn't imagine an angel more lovely, not even in heaven." He brushed back a length of long, dark hair that fell across her face.

Angelique looked into his inky eyes. "Who are you?"

"I'm your neighbor. My name is Victor."

"You own the land next to ours?" She still held tightly to her book.

"Yes, von Vadim Estate," he replied, amused by his conversation with her.

"Don't you like people?" she asked candidly.

"Angelique!" Her father interceded. "It's rude to—"

"No. It's okay," Victor assured him. "I may not be the most sociable person in the world, but I don't dislike people."

"Then why do you try so hard to keep us all out? Your gate is always locked up with those big chains."

"That's a very good question, my dear, and all I can say in my defense is that I'm a very private person. I've never been fond of company, although, after talking with you tonight, I might consider leaving the gate open once in a while, especially if I knew I'd be getting a visit from a new friend."

"You mean me?" Angelique asked with enthusiasm.

"Yes, you." He tickled her under the chin before rising to greet John who was noticeably agitated by his interaction with the child.

"You'd better scoot on to your room now. Mr. von Vadim and I have business to discuss," John instructed, rubbing Angelique's head and sending her out of the room.

"She's a very special child," von Vadim said.

Angelique heard the remark from where she lingered just around the corner.

"I consider us friends, Victor, you know that, but there will be no visits to the estate by my daughter. When it comes to my children, I draw the line."

"I understand. I've overstepped my boundaries, and I apologize."

Both men grew silent when a thud caught their attention. Angelique, having accidentally dropped her book, quickly scooped it up and rushed to her bedroom. It wasn't like her to eavesdrop, but something drew her to Victor von Vadim. She just didn't know exactly what that "something" was.

At that point, the flashback ended, and Angelique blinked several times to clear her vision. Squatting, she rubbed her temples where pressure had built, gathering her bearings. Now remembering Victor von Vadim, she couldn't help wishing she'd known more about him. She presumed she'd never find the answers to the questions weighing on her mind—why she'd felt drawn to him. The man would forever remain a mystery. And her father. She didn't understand why he'd forbade her and Tomes from stepping foot on von Vadim land when all the while he spent his days there—the estate overseer. She always suspected that something deceptive was amiss, but since both men had carried their secrets with them to their graves, all she had was suspicion.

"Are you all right?" Corin bent in front of her, his face showing his concern.

"I'm fine. Just a little dizzy. Perhaps from the long walk," she lied, afraid he might think the flashback she'd just experienced was weird. She wasn't quite sure what to make of it herself.

"I'll get my car and drive you home." Corin helped her stand.

"No. I'll be okay. I just need to sit down for a few minutes."

"Let's get you inside." He reached for her arm and assisted her to the front entrance that stood wide and tall, making her think of a gigantic mouth ready to swallow them whole.

Corin opened the door and showed her into the foyer. She gasped upon first sight of the elaborate interior, grander than she'd imagined, more impressive inside than outside, lavished with fine natural stones and a number of tall marble columns. A mixed ivory and gray slate floor made the room appear to go on forever. Looking up beyond the second floor, centered on the third-floor ceiling was the imprint of a very unique-looking emblem.

"That must be your family crest." She commented on the rearing winged lion that had what appeared to be a cross marking its chest.

"Yes. Strong, noble, and God-fearing. The von Vadim creed."

"Three very strong virtues to live up to."

"I suppose, but I'm proud of my ancestors and what they stood for." He guided her to the sofa.

"You should be. And where are you from originally?" She got comfortable.

"I'm of Hungarian descent."

"But you're blond."

"It's not unheard of for Magyars to have lighter coloring."

"Magyars?"

"Hungarians."

"Ah. It must give you a real sense of completion, knowing your lineage so well. There's no question of who you are and where you came from. I don't think I could trace my family line beyond my grandparents."

"I'd be happy to help you do a little research if you'd ever care to tackle it."

"You might come to regret that offer," she teased. "This house, though, it is amazing. All I expected it to be and more."

"I'm glad you approve."

"I can't imagine anyone who wouldn't," she replied just as her cell phone rang. "Excuse me." She pulled it from her back pocket and flipped it open, looking at the display before answering. "Yes, Tomes. What?" She was surprised to hear him babbling about wolves. "Don't worry. I'll be careful. Besides, I'm with Corin. He'll see me home." She smiled at Corin, pointing to the phone. "Yes, I'm with him now." She couldn't believe how angry Tomes got at the mention of Corin's name. "I don't want to argue with you right now. I'll see you later." She cut him off and ended the call.

"Is everything okay?" Corin asked. "I take it Tomes is in a mood."

"He was letting me know he saw a wolf near the farm. One little animal and he's ready to confine me to my quarters."

"A wolf?"

"Not you too."

"He's right, you need to be careful. You shouldn't be going into the woods alone, especially at night."

"You two worry too much. Now, enough about the wolf, what do you say to a tour?"

"Are you sure you're feeling up to it? It's a big house...more walking."

"I'm completely rejuvenated. And I'm not about to

pass up this opportunity to see it."

"All right, then. It will be my pleasure to show the place off."

Corin led her from the living room to a smaller sitting room beyond, where from the clutter, it was easy to see he spent a lot of time.

"How many rooms are there in the house?"

"Including the library and scullery area, there are sixty-two rooms."

"You must get lost in here."

"Sometimes I do feel as though I'm wandering an endless maze." Corin removed his black Stetson and tossed it on a nearby table, reviving his ash-blond hair with a pass of his long fingers.

"Sixty-two rooms...wow! Who does your cleaning? Do you have a housekeeper...use a service?"

"I have someone come in periodically to give the entire place a thorough go over, but otherwise, I maintain it myself. I prefer it that way. Besides, I only have to upkeep the areas I utilize."

"You expect me to believe that a single man of your means does his own cleaning?"

"I do have skills, Angelique." He smiled. "And I don't use the whole house. With the exception of the library upstairs, I spend most of my time on the main floor, so there's not an awful lot to contend with. However, there are several rooms I avoid altogether."

"And what rooms would those be?"

"The kitchen and scullery areas. I'm not much of a cook, I'm afraid."

"You have to eat." Angelique giggled, unable to contain her laugh.

His expression told her that he had no idea what, in their conversation, had suddenly amused her.

"Honestly, Corin, who says scullery anymore?" She giggled again, finding herself feeling freer to speak her mind around him. "It makes me think of Cinderella. You know, from the fairytale. She was a scullery maid," she explained, repositioning several long, dark tendrils of hair behind her ear. "But life's no fairytale."

Corin continued with the tour, showing Angelique through the remainder of the first floor. She took in every inch of the place, admiring the décor of mixed eras, a treasure trove of valuables. The fascinating pieces showcased in every room ranged from furniture and art to breathtaking vases and fine collectibles—items of priceless value presumably passed down throughout the years from heir to heir. The estate was, after all, ages old.

"Just a little proof that I'm a modern man." He pointed out a desktop computer tucked away in one of the first-floor rooms. "World Wide Web connected and all that jazz."

"Impressive. Although, I never accused you of being old fashioned. Besides, I might be a modern woman, but I have an old soul."

Corin looked into her eyes. "Something I can completely relate to."

Passing through a lengthy corridor, portraits adorned both walls—paintings and old photographs—leaving little vacant space between them. Angelique slowed her pace, studying the faces, stopping when she came upon a large photograph to her left. The man held an uncanny resemblance to Corin. If she hadn't known it to be impossible, by the age of the individual in the picture—at least ten years Corin's senior—she'd have sworn it was him.

"The likeness," she spoke under her breath. "It's too much to ignore."

"My uncle, Victor von Vadim," Corin told her.

"This could be you in a few more years."

"Yes. We look a lot alike," he remarked

nonchalantly.

"You certainly do." Angelique's gaze traced the man's features, taken aback by several striking similarities.

"I'd say he was nearing forty in this sitting. Handsome man, don't you think?" Corin said with humor.

Angelique smiled but never pulled her eyes away from the portrait.

"Shall we move on?" Corin urged. "I'd like to show you the second-floor library."

Angelique reluctantly followed, feeling unsettled by the photograph. It was more than just a mere resemblance between the subject of that portrait and Corin. Everything was all so exact, even down to the dimple marking Corin's left cheek. And the thing alarming her the most were the eyes—those dark and piercing eyes—Corin's eyes.

The thoughts running through her mind were illogical and ridiculous, reminding her of the feeling she'd had when meeting Victor von Vadim all those years ago as a child. But she told herself that it was nothing more than a close family resemblance and pushed the troubling feeling aside.

What other explanation could there be?

* * * *

Later that night, Corin fed, taking nourishment from grazing cattle; a good alternative to human blood and readily attainable. Just like every other creature existing in the living world, he needed sustenance, and for him that meant acquiring fresh blood.

Black River Falls Memorial Hospital, where he'd been fortunate enough to treat himself to a pint of human blood from time to time, was no longer an option. The facility had suddenly heightened their security measures, making it much too risky for the steal. He, of course, had powers to assist him in accomplishing the theft, but it just wasn't worth the chance of exposure. So, for now, he would do without the occasional splurge and continue to satisfy his insatiable hunger with the blood of these mooing beasts. There were other options, but ones he chose not to pursue. Attacking innocent mortals for means of feeding was something he refrained from doing. He'd worked hard to conquer his cravings and hold the bloodthirsty monster at bay. He had no intention of backsliding now. It was crucial that he cling to whatever humanity there was remaining within him. His human part might have been the smallest part of him, but it was, without question, the most precious.

Corin sank his fangs deep into the animal's neck, drinking in the warm sustenance. In his haste to feed, a drop of blood trickled from the edge of his mouth, and he quickly wiped it away. If nothing else, he was a well-mannered eater. He might have been partial monster, but he wasn't devoid of etiquette.

When he finished, Corin closed the bite-wound with a pass of his hand and sent the beast on its way. The moon dominating the sky was magnetic, the force of its pull further enriching him. Along with the revitalization from the blood he'd just ingested, it built his adrenaline beyond measure, stimulating the wildness stirring within him. He would have loved to change to animal form and run freely through the woods, but he had pressing matters to attend to...a town to protect.

He headed for his Harley parked just outside the pasture fence-line running along a thick span of woods. Despite the fact that the boundary of woods cloaked the long running pasture in most areas, he hunched down as he moved across the field in the direction of his bike, just in case anyone should happen to be around.

He generally had nothing to worry about, but it was a bright night, which prompted a little extra precaution on his part. Over the years, he'd come to learn the importance of keeping an eye out for the occasional hunter or landowner.

Reaching the fence, he crossed the barbed wire and retrieved his motorcycle. With the fine weather, he enjoyed the open ride. Now sated, he was eager to get into town and do a little investigating. He wanted to make some inquiries, find out if any new residents might have moved in or around Hixton over the last few weeks. If he was dealing with a pup—a nightwalker of less than a hundred years—he knew the immortal might settle for just about any place offering protection from the daylight hours. On the other hand, he was more inclined to believe that the newcomer was an experienced nightwalker, maybe even an ancient—a nightwalker who'd been walking the earth for more than five hundred years. Corin was ancient, and like him, many of the older nightwalkers were wealthy. Having built their fortunes over many generations, they preferred elite estates with plenty of acreage capable of providing them the privacy and concealment they would require to keep their "condition" secret. These elders were the most powerful of his kind, making ruling out the new arrival an ancient his foremost concern.

Von Vadim Estate was the only fine estate existing in the area, but there were alternatives—farms and ranches that might suffice as an acceptable second choice. First thing first, though. He had to start by conferring with a real estate agent. He just hoped he'd find someone working late in one of the offices. For a nightwalker, trying to conduct business after nightfall could be a real hassle. When everyone else was winding down, his kind was just waking for the night.

* * * *

All the while, up above the ever-dimming pastureland, the new arrival inconspicuously circled in the form of a black raven. When Corin left, he dove down, shape-shifting into his human form the moment he touched the ground.

A Turk, walking the earth for nearly three hundred years, he was a force to be feared. Taking several steps, his ankle-length suede coat brushed his pants as he moved in a serpentine manner. His frame was long and lean, his black, shoulder-length hair blowing loose around his face. He cocked his head and sniffed the air. "You are immortal." He rubbed one of ten amber buttons that adorned his coat between his fingers. Each prized piece contained a trapped insect or arachnid that he could move with his touch.

He'd seen Corin shape-shift from owl to human form while watching the girl at the creek, ran with him as a wolf in the woods, and now he'd witnessed him feeding from the beasts of the field. Yes, Corin von Vadim was indeed a nightwalker.

5

One Last Time

Jordon Black had no guilt whatsoever over deceiving the front desk man at Black River Falls Inn. "I need to get another door card for room 244. I've locked myself out. I checked in earlier, I'm sure you remember."

Jordon had checked into the inn, but he'd been assigned room 131, not room 244, hoping the clerk didn't recall that fact.

"Thank you. I'll be more careful this time." Jordon took the card and hurried away.

Finding room 244, he slipped inside and shut the heavy, blue door behind him. Scanning the room, he found it cold and musky, reeking of an offensive, overpowering odor. This stink he'd smelled many times before—a very distinctive mark of the killer he pursued.

"You've been here all right." The stink dissolved any doubt of the killer in Jackson County being the fugitive he was trailing. "But where are you now?"

The room was clean, despite the odor, and no different from every other time the killer had chosen a motel room for refuge—the closet had been emptied, and its contents tossed in a pile to the left of the wardrobe, supplying a makeshift coffin.

Jordon scoured the room, finding no personal items. The wretch had already taken flight.

He cursed. "You knew I was getting close."

The killer was smart, knowing not to linger in one place too long. And Jordon, the bloodhound that he was, kept the fiend on his toes. He would never give up the hunt. At some point, the manslayer would slip up, and when he did, Jordon would be right there to nab him.

"I'm going to get you, rotter." Jordon headed out the door. "One way or another, Nightwalker, I will eventually get you."

* * * *

It was July twenty-third; a morning Angelique would never be able to drive from her memories. She and Tomes were laying Louisa to rest, and knowing he was agonizing over the thought of having to entomb his dead wife in the depths of the cold, dark earth made her sick to her stomach.

Since Louisa had no family to speak of, the funeral arrangements had gone relatively smoothly. Angelique and Tomes had only one estranged uncle, and a couple of distant cousins scattered far and wide about the country, or beyond. They had no list of family connections since no one had cared to stay in contact over the years. Angelique doubted she'd even recognize a blood kin should she ever meet any of them on the street.

The service was simple, conducted at Louisa's

gravesite beneath a partially enclosed pole-tent that barely fit beneath the outstretched limbs of an old oak.

Angelique and Tomes sat in the first of four rows staring at the pearl-colored coffin laid out before them, adorned with a wreath of white roses. Several other flower arrangements sat on either side of the casket, sent by friends and neighbors. A sorrowful hymn, "In the Garden," played over a portable CD player, followed by a song Louisa had always loved, "Angel Band." Both more than befitting such a time of mourning.

A handful of friends and acquaintances paid their respects. They made polite appearances—rather expeditious with their condolences. Because she and Tomes were being portrayed as suspects in Louisa's killing, she was surprised that any of them had bothered to show up at all. Still, she'd have been lying not to admit being spurned didn't hurt—some of them lifelong neighbors, people she'd considered their closest friends. But at least she and Tomes had each other for support, and their tie was strong.

"Pamela sure made a fast getaway." Tomes glowered.

"Well, with everything that's been said about us on the news, they probably don't know what to believe. We're the talk of the town," Angelique replied.

"Real friends would have stuck around. Take a look, sis." He nodded. "As you can see, there's no one left sitting here but us...just you and me."

Angelique glanced back at the rows of empty chairs. Everyone was gone. "They're most likely scared of getting involved."

She blamed the media for slathering their unfortunate experience, along with insinuating speculation, across every news-broadcasting network and newspaper in the area. There was no escaping the injustice. And to make matters worse, the murder had now taken on national exposure.

"A lifetime here, and we can't count on anyone in this town." Tomes sounded resentful...indignant.

With the service ended and all attendees gone, the funeral director approached, ready to conclude the proceedings, but Angelique asked for a little more time.

She and Tomes sat in silent mourning, gazing on the casket. Neither said a single word for several minutes, each submerged in their memories of Louisa.

"I want to see her," Tomes broke the silence, his desire unexpected.

"What?" Angelique shot him a questioning glance.

"You heard me, Angel. I want the casket opened so I can see her," he persisted while standing and motioning for the director who stood at the back of the tent.

Angelique rose to her feet as the overweight, balding man hopped into action, a severe expression masking his face.

"Sir?" he responded.

"I want this lid opened so I can view my wife one last time."

"Oh, sir, I w-wouldn't recommend it," the director discouraged, shaking his head, his thin lips stretched tight.

"I did request that you not seal the casket until services were completed. It hasn't been sealed, has it?"

"No, no sir, it hasn't. It's just that, well, you may wish to remember her as she was, due to the circumstances...you understand."

Angelique understood the director's meaning. Louisa had undergone a complete autopsy, including the head and organs, and she would probably have little resemblance to the woman they'd known and loved. Horrific images flashed in her mind of a stitched together *corpse bride,* filling her with dread.

"Tomes, maybe he's right...the autopsy," she reminded him, not wanting either of them plagued by nightmares for the rest of their days. At present, they had fond memories to hold onto of the beautiful woman she'd been in life. "I really don't think you should." Angelique tried to deter her brother from making what she feared would be a mistake.

"How many times do I have to say it, Angel, I want the casket opened." Tomes was determined.

The director started to protest again, "Sir, I really—"

"Either you open it, or I'll do it myself," Tomes snapped.

The director looked at Angelique, biting the tip of his thumb nervously. She knew he was hoping for further support, but Angelique offered none. Despite her fears, she had no right to interfere in such a personal matter regarding her brother. If Tomes needed to see Louisa one last time for closure, who was she to stand in the way of that?

"Please open it," she told the director. "My brother needs to see his wife...say goodbye."

Angelique heard the director release a grumble beneath his breath.

"All right, just one minute," he muttered, hustling over to the east side of the tent and lowering the wall flap, leaving only the west side of the shelter open.

Angelique didn't understand the purpose of the director's actions. The interior was already dim, and the sun had reached a position where it cast no bothersome rays, leaving her to conclude that he must have been attempting to darken the space in hopes of cushioning the terrible shock to come. She shuddered at the thought, wondering just how butchered Louisa was. Unable to stop herself, once again Angelique imagined the worst of conditions—an autopsied nightmare.

Tomes stood next to the casket while the director unlatched the top. Angelique, standing alongside, held tightly onto his arm for support, just in case her knees should grow weak. Taking a deep breath, she squinted while the director raised the left portion of the lid, exposing the upper body. Awaiting the harsh impact, she stiffened. When Louisa's face came into view, a cold chill swept up her spine. She exhaled and took a staggering step back, looking down on her sister-in-law in astonishment. The autopsy marks were hardly noticeable, as if she'd been stitched back together with the utmost precision and care by a master surgeon.

"She's beautiful," Angelique whispered, looking up at Tomes, unable to believe how calm he remained. However, she couldn't say the same about the director, who stood with mouth agape, his shocked expression telling her that he, too, had expected much worse. Till this point, she'd assumed he'd been the one to prepare the body for burial, but by his reaction, she realized someone else must have done the job.

"I'll give you some privacy." The man backed away and returned to his previous position at the back of the tent.

Angelique stared at Louisa and quivered inside at the pristine condition of her body, looking so healthy it was haunting. Instead of seeing the pieced-together *corpse bride* she'd envisioned, an angel lay there in that silk-lined casket, clothed in a feminine blue dress. A double strand of white pearls wrapped her neckline, a gift from Tomes on their first anniversary. She was a vision to behold, far from the condition one would expect of a four-day-old autopsied corpse. Angelique couldn't help worrying that Louisa might open her eyes, sit up, and speak at any given moment, shocking all three of them into heart failure. And with that thought, Angelique grew lightheaded and had to sit down.

"Are you okay?" Tomes helped her to a chair.

"Just a little overwhelmed. You take the time you need to say goodbye. I'll be fine right here," she assured him.

Tomes stepped back over to the casket and took Louisa's hand. He leaned in close and spoke to her in a soft, loving voice.

"I feel you with me, even now, inspiring me from beyond the grave. You must know you were cherished. You didn't deserve this...not you."

He wiped his cheeks, unable to hold back his tears.

"You will always own my heart." He gently rubbed her fingers. "Forever...I will love you forever. You'll live on in my heart and in my memories. You'll never be forgotten. I just wish... I wish that...." He stumbled with what he wanted to say. "I wish you were with me now, that we had more time. I wish I knew why this happened. I wish so many things."

Angelique watched through swelling tears as Tomes placed a soft kiss on Louisa's lips. She wondered how their lives had made such a drastic turn, leading them to this point, with Tomes standing over Louisa's casket, saying goodbye to the woman he had planned to spend the rest of his life with.

"I love you, bright eyes," he whispered. "I was going to leave you with the words of our song, *To Me*—the one we played at our wedding and a thousand times since. But this morning when I was dressing to come here, a Bonnie Tyler song came on the radio, "Total Eclipse of the Heart." And she had it right, bright eyes."

This should have been a private moment for Tomes, but Angelique didn't want to leave him alone. If he needed her, she meant to be there for him. But out of respect, she turned away, trying not to watch, but she couldn't help overhearing as he sang to Louisa in a hushed voice, his final serenade drawing her eyes back as her heart broke for her brother.

Tomes stared fixedly into Louisa's face as if willing her to live. Angelique felt his dark depression and fearing for his state of mind, for his life, she mumbled a prayer to God, that He might comfort Tomes and be a light to guide him through this dark, dismal time.

She'd seen Tomes suffer before, with the loss of their parents, but never to such a critical degree. She knew better than anyone how much he loved Louisa, but she had to make him see that life does go on and somehow deter him from continuing down his current path of self-destruction. He had barely slept or ate since the murder, and the strain was evident in his physical appearance. She could only hope that the old saying was true, and time really did heal all wounds.

The director coughed, prompting Angelique to glance back. Seeing him fidgeting, she rose, stepped over to Tomes, and placed a hand on his shoulder. "Are you ready?"

"I'll never be ready to leave her. How can I?"

"She's in heaven now. This is just her earthly body...an empty shell."

"You really think she's in heaven? You truly believe that?"

"Of course, where else would she be? Louisa was a good person. She was well loved, Tomes, by you and by me. And we'll be with her again one day, on the other side."

With that said, Tomes kissed Louisa one last time, let go of her hand, and backed away from the casket. Angelique motioned for the director to close the lid, finding him quick in performing the task. Although, she had to admit relief at having it once again closed, for the sight of Louisa lying there, a sleeping beauty, was utterly disturbing. Something didn't feel quite right, but she never would have revealed her fears to Tomes.

Before leaving, Angelique took one of two white roses and laid it atop the casket. "Rest in peace, Louisa." She released the stem.

Passing the second one to Tomes, he kissed the velvety tip before laying it across the first rose. "Goodbye, my love," he whispered, and a tear trickled from his right eye, trailed down his cheek, and dropped onto the casket.

Angelique grasped Tomes's arm, and they turned away. As they left Louisa to her final resting, the words to *Angel Band* weighed heavily on her mind, the melody, from this day forth, forever to remind her of this sad, sad day.

* * * *

Corin awoke with a start and crawled out of his hollowed crypt forged into the earth along the back wall of the dark room—a lion emerging from his lair. He cocked his head while sniffing the air. A steady rumble emanated from the depths of his throat. Someone was in the house!

Sensing the presence growing nearer, he quickly took cover behind some stored furniture. Within seconds, the door above him creaked open, allowing the light of day to penetrate the recess. He looked up and squinted, able to make out the form of a man standing in the doorway.

"Corin," the intruder called out. "Are you down there? What am I saying? Of course you're down there. Where else would you be?"

Recognizing the voice, Corin stepped out of hiding. "Shut the door...please," he yelled up to Tomes, shielding his sensitive eyes.

"I'd be happy to accommodate, but unlike you, I

can't see in the dark. There's a light switch here. Can I flip it on?"

"No, I've got it down here." Corin lit a lantern that cast plenty of light for Tomes to find his way.

"I know you wouldn't want me to fall and break my neck," Tomes remarked snidely.

"Of course not," Corin responded. "And if this visit is about Angelique, you have nothing to be concerned about."

"Not entirely." Tomes shut the door and started down the narrow staircase. "You know, you should consider installing an inside lock on the door. You're vulnerable down here. Anyone could bust in on you, and they may not all be as nice as me."

"Nice...are you sure you know the meaning of the word?" Corin threw back with a deriding laugh.

"Of course I do, von Vadim." Tomes was smug. "But why waste manners—"

"On the likes of me?" Corin finished.

Tomes didn't deny it. "So, this is how a creature of the night spends his days." He stopped at the foot of the stairs and scanned the basement. "And you sleep there?" He motioned to the crypt. "Befitting, I guess. An animal in a cave."

"A nightwalker in his bed." Corin tried not to let Tomes's loathsome remarks agitate him. "And it's who I am, Tomes. You know that."

"It's quite a mess down here, a mixture of storage space, tomb, and some semblance of a bedroom." Tomes moved further into the room. "Musty too. A couple of air vents wouldn't hurt...or a window. But the light would shine in and what, burn you to a crisp?"

Corin sighed. Tomes's offensive, tiresome yapping was growing old.

"Seriously, though, you're down here in a hole, sleeping in pitch dark, breathing stale air. You're like a—"

"Don't say it!" Corin cut him off.

Tomes was obviously trying to rile him, and it was working. His patience was beginning to run thin. He did have his limits, after all, and Tomes had dished out just about all the insolence he could stand for the moment.

"You don't care for being compared to animals, huh? But you don't mind living like one down here in this heap," Tomes braved one more comment.

"How about you just tell me why you're here. What's so important that it couldn't wait till evening?" Corin bit his bottom lip, striving to control his rising temper, for Angelique's sake. He would do just about anything for her, and he knew how much she loved her brother.

"You know why I'm here. I want to know what you've learned about the nightwalker."

"Nothing yet, I'm sorry to say."

"We can't let him get away. Isn't there anything I can do to help? I can't just sit around doing nothing. I'll go crazy."

"There is, actually. I was trying to find out if anyone purchased any local properties over the last few weeks, but the real estate offices close by the time I get around to them. Maybe you could make some inquiries, taking special note of any larger homesteads. Any place that would offer a nightwalker the seclusion and privacy he'd require."

"I can do that. I take it you think this nightwalker might be planning on sticking around?"

"It's just a feeling...a place to start."

"Okay. I'll get right on it."

"I have something that might help." Corin fetched his wallet, pulling out a business card, giving it a quick glance before handing it to Tomes. "I was at Purcell's Garage, and he passed along this agent's card. Her name is Sandy Darnell. She's with Brookside Realty over in Black River Falls."

"I know the place."

"Good. I tried to reach her several times at the cell number listed, but she never answered. Maybe you'll have better luck."

"I'll head on over there and see what I can find out."

"You know, Tomes, you could do with a little rest," Corin remarked. "You look like hell."

"I put my wife in her grave this morning," Tomes replied somberly. "I won't rest until the demon that killed her pays, and pays good, with my kind of justice."

Corin understood Tomes's pain, having endured his own share of losses over his long years of walking the earth. More, in fact, than he'd ever care to remember.

"When we catch this monster...then I'll rest." Tomes rubbed his eyes, wiping away gathering tears before they had a chance to fall.

"We do have to catch up with him, and soon, because he'll kill again." Corin knew the insatiable hunger of the creature, what such a craving could do to one's sanity, something he fought every fall of night. "It takes a strong will to fight the thirst."

"You haven't forgotten that when the time comes, this nightwalker is mine, have you?" Tomes reminded Corin. "Like I said, I'll do the serving, and it'll be my kind of justice. The Bible says, 'eye for eye, tooth for tooth, hand for hand, foot for foot,' and before that it clearly states, 'life for a life.' I am due my right of retribution, and I'm warning you, Corin, if you get in my way, I'll do you in without a second thought."

"We need to know what we're facing before taking any action, and we know nothing about this newcomer."

"It makes no difference to me who or what he is. Louisa will get her justice. I know there's no love lost between us, but I need your help to find this monster. And when we get him, I'll take my vengeance."

"I'll work with you, Tomes, only because I don't wish to see you dead. Despite your disdain of me, we do share a connection. Your father was a friend, and I cared too much for him not to look out for you now."

Corin meant what he said. He would look out for Tomes, but he labored with uncertainty over the matter of the nightwalker. He had no intention of killing the newcomer if he was merely passing through the area, doing only what it was in his nature to do—feed. However, if the nightwalker did plan to linger, Corin would make one thing clear to the immortal, that his community and the people in Hixton were, without negotiation, off limits. But in order to confront the nightwalker, he first had to find him, a task he knew would be a feat in itself.

Tomes left, eager to get to the real estate office and make inquiries. Corin blew out the light and settled back down in his crypt, hating deceiving Tomes but knowing the man would never accept his reasoning when it came to the newcomer.

I need to know more.

Conflicted, he felt a natural sympathy for his own kind, but at the same time, his community was at risk, and that included Angelique. This, alone, made it dire for him to find the newcomer and determine whether he'd be making peace or joining Tomes in combat. He could only hope that with the coming night he'd learn the newcomer's intentions and finally ascertain which action to take.

Needing rejuvenation, Corin closed his eyes and returned to his slumber, but his mind continued to reel, even in sleep, pondering the critical matter at hand.

* * * *

"We seem to have a real epidemic on our hands, Sheriff. Her name's Sandy Darnell. She was a real estate agent over at Brookside Realty," Deputy Rudy informed Sheriff Pierson, who'd just arrived on the scene. "It's basically the same MO as the first murder—except this killing was carried out in a much more brutal fashion."

"Blood drained too. And by the look frozen on her face, I'd say she was terrified," Pierson remarked on the marred corpse of the woman. "We should rule out a sexual attack."

"I agree," Deputy Rudy replied. "There's something else here you ought to see, Sheriff."

"What is it?"

"Take a look at these marks." Rudy knelt and pointed out one of several jagged areas of punctured, ripped flesh.

"What on earth!"

"I think they're animal bites," Rudy gave his opinion.

"Wolves?" Pierson speculated.

"I wouldn't think so, but if not, what else could it be?"

"To tell you the truth, I don't know what to make of any of this. Well, there's no sense standing around gabbing. We have a job to do. Let's get this area taped off, and get on the horn with Forensics. We need them out here ASAP—pictures, labs, the works," he ordered.

"I'm one step ahead of you. They're en route."

"Good." Pierson pulled out his notepad and laid a few notes to paper. "We also need to notify the medical examiner."

"I'll take care of it, Sheriff. Do you think we have a serial killer on our hands?"

"It sure looks that way, two women, both drained of

blood. We need to do a real thorough job here. I don't want to miss anything."

"I'll make everyone aware of that."

"When Forensics gets their job done, have them send the body over to Black River Falls Memorial for an autopsy," he instructed. "And one last thing, Rudy, has her family been contacted?"

"Not yet."

"Have someone contact them. We need to inform the husband. She's wearing a wedding ring, so I presume she's married."

"I'll see to it." Rudy nodded. "Right away."

"I want to get a handle on things before the media shows up."

"Understood." Deputy Rudy went straight to his duties.

Sheriff Pierson squatted next to the body, examining the perplexing marks, looking up when a black Dodge Charger arrived on the scene giving rise to a profane word. This was just what he didn't need, that blasted egotistical marshal getting under his skin like a bad itch.

Sheriff Pierson hated collaborating with the man. He certainly hadn't requested any outside assistance and didn't relish the idea of having some arrogant know-it-all coming into his county implying that they were doing an insufficient job. He appreciated Black's position—trying to determine if there was a link between the Jaffler murder and the fugitive he was tracking—giving him the right to full access to the case; however, without hearing from a higher official or the Wisconsin U.S. Marshal, he wasn't about to hand Black the reins. This was his county and case. He may have had to work with him, but he was by no means outranked.

I don't trust you.

Thinking back to his first encounter with Black, he couldn't imagine a federal lawman withholding evidence, something the sheriff still believed the marshal had done, sure the man had slipped evidence from the Jaffler crime scene. He just didn't know how he'd managed the vanishing act, wishing he'd searched him at the time.

Pierson bridled his temper as Jordon approached with a "higher than thou" attitude, his long hair and appearance indicative of his attitude. The sheriff would have liked nothing more than to knock that smirk right off his face, but resorting to physical aggression was something his badge and position prevented him from doing. However, nothing could stop him from fantasizing about it, and with a mental image of his fist against the marshal's jaw came a possum grin of his own. A nice, stretched out grin.

6

The Challenge

Arriving at Jaffler Farm, light from the barn that sat beyond the farmhouse cast a hazy glow in the night. Corin followed the light, finding Angelique brushing down a sorrel mare.

"Corin." She was surprised to see him step through the open doorway.

"I'm glad you're not out roaming the woods in the dark." He strode toward her.

"Not tonight. Tomes and I have both been neglecting our duties. Understandable, though, under the circumstances."

"Tomes, is he's around?"

"No. He went into Black River Falls."

"When I saw the light out here, I thought it might be him."

"Sorry to disappoint." Angelique continued brushing the horse. "Is there something I can help you with?"

"You could never disappoint, Angelique. I just have a little business proposition I thought I'd run by him." Corin couldn't tell her the truth, that he and Tomes were working together, hunting a nightwalker. She had no idea such creatures even existed. But he was prepared with what he thought to be a convincing cover.

"What business could you possibly have with Tomes?"

"I hear he's quite the skilled contractor. I was hoping he'd consider doing some work for me at the estate."

"I'll let him know, but he's going to need some time to get past his loss."

"Of course. There's no rush. And, you know, it might be good therapy...help get his mind off things."

Pretending to hire Tomes would hopefully douse any suspicion that might arise over his sudden and unexpected association with her brother.

"Are you sure about hiring Tomes? From what I've seen so far, he doesn't take too kindly to you," she pointed out while putting her grooming supplies away.

"Yes. He does seem to have some negative issues with me. He's made that perfectly clear. But we're going to be neighbors for a long time to come, and someone has to take the first step. Be the bigger man. Might as well be me."

"You're a good person, Corin." Angelique brushed off her jeans and moved toward him. "I think I'm done here. Would you like to join me for a walk to the creek? It's turning out to be a beautiful night."

"I'd love to, but I can't tonight." Corin hated declining her invitation, but it couldn't be helped. He groaned under his breath, cursing himself for causing such a look of disappointment on her face, knowing she felt rejected. "How about tomorrow...a twilight walk?"

he quickly proposed, hoping to rectify the situation. "If I didn't have some pressing matters to take care of, believe me, I'd be all yours."

"I understand." Angelique's face lit up again. "Tomorrow, after sunset, then. I'm looking forward to it."

"And no going out alone tonight."

Until the newcomer was found and confronted, he didn't want her going anywhere alone, especially after nightfall.

"I could find my way through these woods blindfolded."

"I have no doubt about that. I just worry about the wolves, not to mention what happened to your sister-in-law. You shouldn't even be out here, alone in the barn. Not until the killer is caught."

"Nothing's going to happen to me, Corin."

"I'm sure your sister-in-law thought the same thing. I'm sorry if that sounds harsh, but I just want you to be safe."

The look on her face showed surprise at his genuine concern.

"No. It's okay. You're right."

"Just promise me that you'll be extra cautious until whoever killed Louisa is no longer a threat."

"You'd better be careful yourself, Mr. von Vadim. I'm beginning to think you really do care," she teased.

Corin flashed a devilish smile. If she only knew how deep-rooted his feelings for her truly were.

He helped her close up the barn and escorted her to the front door of the house before leaving. Climbing in the driver's seat, he pushed in a CD of mixed rock tunes and set a course for Black River Falls to track down Tomes, hoping his cohort had made some progress in obtaining the information they needed from the real estate office.

"He's the only man in the civilized world who doesn't carry a cell phone," he griped, aggravated that he had to physically track Tomes down.

Starting along I-94, Corin caught sight of a dusty-blue Camaro for the third time since leaving the farm. Changing direction, he exited the interstate onto a side road. And just as he suspected, the Camaro followed. He was being tailed.

Reaching a perfect standoff point, a dead zone just past a large curve, he hit the brakes, stopping crossways in the middle of the road. Blocking both lanes, he opened his door and got out of his car, ready to confront the spy who'd just rounded the curve and squealed to a stop about fifty feet in front of him. Corin stood dauntless, staring into the window of the Camaro, trying to make out the driver hidden behind dark tint. Enraged, the look on Corin's face told whomever was sitting behind the wheel of the car that he would not be intimidated.

The driver responded by revving his engine, further vexing Corin.

Who is this clown?

Something critical then dawned on Corin. He couldn't sense the driver's presence. The cad was sitting right in front of him, but just like the situation in the woods, he couldn't detect him.

There's something different about you.

Since becoming immortal, Corin had never met another creature—mortal or immortal—whom he couldn't sense.

The driver revved his engine three more times, pausing several seconds between each roar, sending out a clear challenge. But Corin kept his cool, not letting the stranger provoke him, determined to maintain control.

The Camaro's loud V8 engine rumbled and roared,

threatening to charge forward, but Corin held his gaze on the black windshield. A small flicker of light became visible through the glass, and he furrowed his brow in an attempt to make it out, realizing it was the flame of a lighter. He believe what he was seeing. They were in the middle of a standoff, and the SOB was lighting a cigarette. The brazenness of this guy irked Corin to no end, but the arrogant act had afforded him one benefit—a silhouetted view of the lower portion of the man's face.

"What are you up to?" Corin wondered why the stranger lingered with the light next to his mouth.

What the devil! What kind of a game are you playing?

The maggot dared to toss him a menacing grin, flashing a wretched rack of teeth.

"You don't know who you're dealing with." Corin was not going to let this stranger's childish tactics unnerve him, and having had enough of the game, he advanced toward the Camaro, reaching only half the distance when the car accelerated in reverse with tires squealing. Corin scanned for a tag as smoke barreled from beneath the vehicle in its 180 spin, but he wasn't able to make it out through the cloud of dust left in the wake.

Swearing, he rushed back to his car, but it was too late to pursue. The Camaro had already rounded the curve. Cursing again, he slammed his hands against the steering wheel and took in a deep breath, letting it out with a growl.

"So, Nightwalker, you have no intention of being cordial, I see. Testing your grounds."

It was now clear the newcomer was an aggressor—more apt to wage war than make peace. There was also the matter of not being able to sense him. Alarming how the stranger possessed a unique power that Corin had never encountered before in any other nightwalker.

"How do you hide your presence?"

The newcomer's advantage was unsettling, for what kind of odds could he expect to hold against an ancient whom he couldn't sense? And something else giving rise to concern was the nightwalker's knowledge of who and what he was, proving he'd been spying, and that thought made Corin angry. However, their brief encounter on that deserted roadway had afforded him at least one answer to his many questions. He no longer had to struggle with uncertainty over which course of action to take against the newcomer. He now knew, without a doubt, he'd be conquering.

* * * *

Corin found Tomes slumped over at a two-seat table in a dark, smoky bar with several glasses scattered in front of him. A large, neon sign cast a blue glow about the room, creating a gloomy atmosphere.

"I'll have a brandy," Corin called over to the bartender, before taking a seat at the table with Tomes. "I thought I might find you here."

"Yep." Tomes raised his head just long enough to acknowledge him. He then dropped it back down with a thud.

"I think you've had more than your share of liquor tonight."

The bartender approached with Corin's drink, and Tomes managed to raise his head again, demanding another Scotch.

"I told you, sir. You're cut off. You can't chug whiskey like that. I'd be happy to bring you something alcohol-free, but no more liquor."

"Oh, forget it," Tomes grumbled.

"We're good here," Corin told the bartender, holding

their conversation until he left. "What's this?" He observed a folder marked Brookside Realty, half-hidden beneath a newspaper on the table. "Is this the information?"

Tomes managed a nod. "Be my guest."

Corin reached for the folder. "I guess this means you met with Sandy Darnell. She gave you the information?"

"N-not exactly." Tomes's voice was dry and raspy.

"What do you mean?" Corin was growing irritated with Tomes in his drunken state.

"She's—she's dead. That's what I mean!" Tomes blurted out his reply without any thought for others in earshot. Luckily, the room was nearly vacant, save the bartender, another worker who came and went from behind the bar, and an older man who'd just stumbled in, appearing to be in no better shape than Tomes. "Just like Louisa, killed by that blood...bloodsucking monster!"

"Keep it down," Corin quieted him. "Are you sure?"

"It's in the paper. Take a look for yourself." Tomes slid it his way, the article front page. "He dr-drained her dry too."

Corin knew that the new arrival would keep taking lives. He'd now seen, firsthand, the immortal's antagonistic ways, labeling him a nightwalker who reveled in the hunt. So long as he lingered in the area, no one in or around Hixton was safe.

"I've had a run-in with the nightwalker." Corin leaned toward Tomes and spoke in a hushed voice. Glancing over his shoulder, he caught the drunk at the next table eavesdropping on their conversation.

Tomes raised his head and looked at Corin, his eyes red and glazed. But from his expression, Corin knew he fully comprehended what he'd just been told.

"The nightwalker?" Tomes blurted, drawing the

bartender's attention. "When?"

Corin shot the bartender a warning glare to mind his own business, also tossing the drunken eavesdropper a cautionary growl, prompting the man to get up and move.

"On the way here," Corin answered. "He was tailing me."

"Following you?"

"That's right. So, I made a little detour to confront him. We had ourselves a standoff. He was challenging me. He knows who I am...what I am."

"Did you get a good look at him?" Tomes grilled, as if instantaneously sobered.

"I wish I had, but he never got out of his car—a dusty-blue Camaro with dark tinting. Even with my night vision, I couldn't make out much of his facial features through the glass. But for a moment, when he lit a cigarette and the lower portion of his face became visible, he flashed me one insolent grin. Finally, having had enough of his game, I started for his car, but he took off."

"Do you think he's out to get you b-before you get him?"

"I'd say that's a feasible assumption. He's testing the waters, and unfortunately, he's several steps ahead in the game. He knows all about us, but we know nothing about him."

"We know he's a killer."

Corin flipped through the real estate folder. "What do these green stars mean?" He placed a finger on one of the marked addresses.

"Those are properties with acreage, l-large places, all sold over the last month. There are five," Tomes slurred. "Another agent, um, Lauren N-Nanner, at Brook—Brookside Realty was kind enough to assist me. I led her to believe I was interested in selling, and she was happy to oblige, giving me recent c-comparable sales."

"I'm glad she didn't recognize you from the news, she might not have been so accommodating."

"It wouldn't have mattered. A sale is a s-sale."

Corin pulled the sheet free from the folder. "I'd best get moving and check these out. Time's wasting."

"Oh no. No, you don't. I'm coming with you," Tomes insisted and attempted to push himself up from the table with wobbly legs struggling to hold his weight. "I told you, this guy is mine!"

"I understand your anger, Tomes, but look at you. You're in no shape for a fight. Besides, even if I'm lucky enough to find the nightwalker's hideout tonight, I still need to learn more about him before initiating any sort of altercation. There's something unsettling about this one, something I've never come across before. I'm not going to make any rash moves, not without more details on what it is I'm facing."

"He's a killer! W-what more do you need to know?" Tomes shouted; his voice full of hostility. The outburst drawing back the attention of the old drunk and the bartender.

"I need to know how powerful he is." Corin leaned in close. "Let me make this clear. You are not coming with me tonight."

Frustrated, Tomes knocked over several glasses.

"Sober up and go home. The best thing you can do right now is stay close to your sister. I've tried to impress upon her that it isn't safe to go out alone, but it would help to hear it seconded by her brother."

"I want you to keep your distance when it comes to Angel." Tomes huffed and slammed his palm down on the table, rattling the glasses.

"Is there a problem?" The bartender didn't look pleased.

"Everything's under control," Corin assured the man who kept a safe distance.

Tomes leaned toward Corin in an aggressive manner. "I thought I made things c-clear to you before. You keep away from her. I will not have her p-pursued by a—"

"Monster," Corin finished. "You're lucky I understand your protectiveness."

"She d-deserves the best life has to offer. And you aren't even human."

Tomes took in several deep breaths. "I don't want her exposed to that sort of madness. She doesn't even know your kind exists outside of tales and f-folk—lore."

"On this we agree, Tomes." Corin got up and pushed his chair in, saying nothing more on the matter. "Now, have some coffee and sober up before you head home. I'll touch base with you later."

Corin paid the bartender on his way out, with a little extra for the tension he and Tomes had caused. Exiting the bar, he bit his bottom lip so hard it bled, something he had to do when dealing with Tomes Jaffler.

"For Angelique," he reminded himself, just as he had every other time Tomes got under his skin. The man needed a serious attitude adjustment, but Corin understood the fire driving him.

Cursing to himself, he hated admitting that somewhere along the line he'd started to develop a genuine fondness for the confounded man.

* * * *

Angelique wrote a note to Tomes and left it on the kitchen table.

Tomes,
I made you an appointment for tomorrow

morning, 9:00 a.m., here, at the farm. Client's name is Louis Gomez. He's looking to renovate.
  Angel

She recalled meeting Mr. Gomez earlier that evening at the local grocery store, having literally run into him while strolling down aisle three, veering, by accident, into his oncoming cart. To make matters worse, his cart then hit a display of jarred gravy, knocking it over and creating quite an embarrassing scene.

"I am so sorry," Angelique apologized, completely humiliated. "I should have been paying better attention...stupid of me."

"Don't worry about it. Accidents happen." The man, very polite, spoke with a scintillating accent.

They both laughed, trying to reposition the jars in a somewhat orderly display.

"I hope we're not banned from the store." Angelique's lips drew into a thin line.

"I don't think we're deserving that harsh a punishment." He smiled. "By the way, I'm Louis. Louis Gomez."

"Angelique Jaffler," she reciprocated. "You know, I think one of these jars has gone bad. Do you smell that?" She couldn't ignore a lingering odor.

Before Mr. Gomez could respond, a store employee hustling over. "You folks go ahead with your shopping. I'll take care of this."

Angelique and Louis Gomez moved to the end of the aisle and continued their conversation. He'd claimed to be new to the area, telling her how he'd just purchased an older home and planned to renovate, currently looking for a contractor.

"That is so uncanny," she expressed. "My brother, Tomes, is a contractor, the best around. He does jobs on the side."

"Seems it was a lucky thing I ran into you. But what do you mean 'on the side?' Does he have another occupation?"

"We own a thoroughbred farm—Jaffler Farm," Angelique told him. "But I have no problem running it alone when he has other work."

"Do you think he'd be interested?"

"I know he would, if you wouldn't mind waiting a few weeks. We just suffered a death in the family, and he needs a little time...to get back on his feet."

Angelique hated pushing her brother back to work so soon, but their previous season had been a slow, dismal one, and they were drowning in debt...real financial trouble. Without some much-needed cash flow coming in soon, their future wasn't looking too bright. She'd hoped to line up some events or races, or if it became necessary, even a sale, but to date, they had no shows to speak of, and a bleak bottom line just grew bleaker.

"I'll give you our number." She opened her purse in search of a business card.

"I'd rather meet with him," Mr. Gomez told her. "How about tomorrow, just to go over the particulars?"

"I didn't expect...."

"I'd just like to run some ideas by him. Maybe get an estimate on the cost...a ballpark figure."

"Okay. Why don't you come by the farm in the morning? Say nine?" Finding a card, she jotted down the directions on the back before passing it to him.

Parting ways with Mr. Gomez, she moved on with her shopping, suddenly remembering Corin's interest in hiring Tomes. But she didn't fret over the matter, uncertain if Tomes would even work for Corin, considering his attitude toward him. And this way, they had a backup.

I'm asking too much, too soon. But our home is at

stake.

She felt guilty soliciting work for Tomes, knowing his heartache. Life had struck them an awful blow, but she had to trust they would find a light somewhere at the end of that dark tunnel they were lost in. Their lives had been torn apart and they were in danger of losing the only thing they had left...their home. She couldn't let that happen. With things as they were, she had no choice but to step up and save her brother, their farm, and both of their sanities.

Tomes's well-being weighed heavy on her mind. She was terrified for him, seeing nothing but an empty shell of the warm, loving man he had been before the murder. It was all so despairing, worrying that neither of them would ever recover from this matter of murder, praying they weren't doomed to walk in the darkness forever.

7

The Midnight Hour

Boldor Enescu metamorphosed the second his talons touched the ground. His ebony hair and overcoat blowing in the breeze, he stood at the back of the stately house, gazing with dark-brown eyes on the impressive structure. Shape-shifting once more into a small, gray rodent, he wiggled his way through a crack of deteriorating mortar, wormed his way along the interior of the wall, and squeezed under a loosened baseboard. Inside, he shed the fur and took back human form.

A small black spider crawled up his leg and onto his coat, stopping on one of the amber buttons. The gem liquefied to a sticky resin, the arachnid melting into the large stone as if sinking into a spoon of honey. Bound inside until called upon again, he rubbed the now solid button.

Scanning the room, his eyes narrowed. With help

from his little spy, he knew Corin wasn't there, so he moved about with ease, sizing up the place, examining his subject's accumulation of wealth.

"Not bad, von Vadim. I see you're from ages past," he remarked.

Boldor was by no means dimwitted, knowledgeable in many fields of study and excessively passionate when it came to the fine arts, which he believed defined points in time. And the history pouring out from the exceptional pieces hidden away in the mansion told him quite a lot about his rival.

After touring every room on the first floor, Boldor made his way up the elaborate staircase to the second level where he found the library. He took a comfortable seat in one of two brown leather-bound chairs sitting near a non-burning fireplace and propped his feet up on an accompanying ottoman.

"I could get used to this...a king in his castle."

His gaze trailed the room, stopping on a silver-etched cigar box lying atop the mantle. Unable to resist a good smoke, he snaked over and opened it, finding the box filled with Monties.

"Very good choice." He ran one of the beauties under his nose, breathing in the unique aroma. Eager to try it, he pulled a lighter from his pocket, bit the tip off the cigar, and lit it while settling back down, enjoying the moment, envisioning himself master of the estate.

After satisfying his fancies there, he slinked through the remainder of the second floor before venturing up to the third level. Seeing that it hadn't been occupied in what appeared to be ages, he returned to the main floor and found the basement, knowing that would be Corin's place of rest. Creeping down the narrow staircase into the cold, damp hollow below, he sniffed the air, his heightened senses overcome by Corin's distinct scent permeating the room. Von Vadim had inhabited that basement for a very long time.

"You have it all, don't you, von Vadim."

Walking over to the crypt forged into the back wall, he ran his hand along Corin's bed. He jerked the linens back, exposing a thick liner separating the bed from the earth. Lifting it, he reached down and scooped up a handful of Corin's native soil and raised it to his nose.

"Hungary." He identified the origin with a grunt.

Boldor allowed the grains to sift through his fingers, falling back onto the earth. He dropped the liner and repositioned the linens before turning his attention to the contents of the room.

"What is this?"

He slithered toward a dark-finished antique dresser, aimed for a gold pocket watch lying on its top, along with several other personal items. He picked up the piece and dangled it before him from an affixed chain. Standing there, examining the timepiece, a wicked smile stretched across his face as a beastly idea struck him. All of this could be his. He could become von Vadim and have it all—the wealth, the estate, the ease of life...everything.

Generating a low, malevolent chuckle, he slid the watch, along with a small pewter figurine of an owl in flight, into his pocket. He headed for the stairs, knowing he should depart before the master of the estate returned home and caught him in his lair. Besides, he had a scheme to devise—a plan to get that blasted marshal off his trail once and for all, and at the same time, set himself up in comfort for a long time to come. He pictured it all in his mind, relishing the idea of obtaining a new identity, one where he wouldn't be prey on the run from the relentless hunter, Jordon Black. Yes, a fiendish plan was developing, and if he played his cards right, he could pull it off...take over

Corin von Vadim's perfect life. Pirate that he was, he had only one motto, *Whatever Boldor wants, Boldor takes.*

He could see no downfall to his plot, other than having to maintain restraint in feeding on mortals. Unlike von Vadim, he loved the kill, especially the sweet, arousing taste of a woman in her prime. But he could exercise some control and learn to survive on the blood of beasts, just as von Vadim did, to keep his existence here secure. He could discipline himself...get by with just an occasional splurge of the good stuff. Oh yes, he had a grand plan in the making, and soon the old timer wouldn't know what hit him.

* * * *

Angelique leaned against a twisted old oak several feet in front of Louisa's grave. Something had compelled her to drive to the cemetery at that late hour—nearly midnight—as if Louisa were summoning her from beyond the grave. Not a believer in the supernatural, she discerned it was nothing more than a delayed reaction to her loss. Things had been so chaotic since the murder. She hadn't had time to just stop and grieve. So, in the night, she sat there amid the dead, and she cried.

The cemetery glowed under the light of the luminous moon, bringing to mind *The Legend of the Midnight Hour*—a story pertaining to that very place. She recalled the tale from her childhood. Set during the revolutionary war, it gave the account of a young man who'd been sent out in service of his country, leaving his new wife to await his return. Unfortunately, this brave soldier fell in battle, a casualty of war, his lifeless body returned to her by a fellow soldier.

Devastated and full of misery, the grief-stricken

widow couldn't go on in life without him. At the midnight hour, weeping upon her beloved's grave, she drank a vial of poison, vowing to reunite with her lost love in death. Taking her last breath at precisely three minutes past twelve, the spirit of the young soldier rose from his grave and took her in a graceful dance, enchanting the cemetery forevermore.

According to the legend, each night at the exact moment of her demise, the inhabitants of the cemetery rise from their graves and dance under the night sky in honor of the lovers. Beyond death, she found life again, proving love really does conquer all.

Angelique didn't believe the tale, but she loved the romance of it, a sorrowful but beautiful story of two souls fated to be joined forever, never to be parted, not even by death. And the thought of the spirits resting there, beneath that sacred earth, rising from their graves and dancing amid the stones was enthralling. She could picture the ghostly scene in her mind.

She looked up at the moon ruling the night sky and imagined it pulling the dead from their resting places, calling them forth to dance under a massive sea of lights, all in honor of eternal love. Angelique had to admit to wishing the tale was true, but she wouldn't hold her breath. Yawning, she looked down at her watch. It read 12:10 a.m.

"I guess there'll be no dancing spirits tonight." She pushed herself up, figuring she'd best head home, not wanting Tomes to find her gone and send out a search party.

Angelique left the cemetery with the intention of heading straight home, but when she came to a small bridge that spanned one of many creeks running through the hilly, wooded area, she had an inclination to stop. Pulling over, she got out without the tiniest bit of apprehension—she had no fear of being out there all alone—making her way down a slope to the rushing water below. The bank lay blanketed in darkness beneath the cover of the overhanging trees. The movement of the water cooled the air as it rolled along practically unseen, flowing into some imperceptible black void. Very little light hit its surface, but where it did manage to dapple through, it sparkled like melted silver.

She walked along the bank, away from the road. The scene reminded her of a black and white movie, with everything appearing in shades of gray. She took a seat on a large rock at the water's edge and stared into the endless depths of rippling water. Examining the reflections, she found her own dim, distorted outline.

Falling deep into her thoughts, she sat motionless, until the sound of crunching leaves caused her to jump and turn back. She wasn't alone. Not knowing what to expect, Angelique searched the ground for a limb or rock, anything she might use to defend herself. Her heart pounding fast and hard, she grabbed a branch, gripping it tightly to face the unseen intruder.

"Who's there?" she called out in a shaky voice.

A tall male figure stepped out from the shadows; his outline just visible. A chill swept through her as he approached. "Who are you?" She stiffened in fear, and with wide eyes, prepared to release a scream.

"It's okay," the man finally spoke.

"Corin, is that you?"

"Yes. It's just me."

Seeing his face come into view, he almost didn't look real, the sight of him the only color in an otherwise somber scene.

"I think you enjoy sneaking up on me. What are you doing out here?"

"I should be asking you that question. I saw your car by the road and thought something might be wrong."

"No. Nothing's wrong."

"You shouldn't be out here all alone so late at night. It's after midnight. You don't listen to anyone, do you?"

"I've taken plenty of nighttime drives before. This isn't the first."

"We've been over this. What if I'd been the killer?" Corin argued.

"No lectures...please." Angelique dropped the limb. "I get enough of that from Tomes. Besides, I've always felt so safe in these woods. This is where I find my solace. I'm drawn to the wilderness at night. I guess you could call me a *Vampira Pocahontas*." Angelique laughed.

"Being drawn to the night and wilderness is something I completely understand. As you plainly see, you're not the only one out wandering the deserted roadways after midnight."

"So that's what you're doing out here, succumbing to the call of the wild?"

"For the most part. The night is my time."

"Yes. I know that about you. I don't think I've ever seen you out during the day."

Angelique looked up as an owl called out from the dark canopy above them, impressed when Corin returned its call.

"Amazing. You sound just like it."

"We creatures of the night share a common language." He stepped closer and claimed her hand.

His dark, enigmatic eyes drew her in. She was powerless to resist, although resisting was the farthest thing from her mind. Taking in a quick breath, his touch was merely a tease, sending a sensation of pins and needles rushing through her, making her yearn for more.

"The night, it's full of life. It stirs while the rest of the world lies sleeping," he said. "Close your eyes and listen.”

Angelique shut her eyes and the sounds became clear—the rushing of water, crickets and frogs, the whistling of the wind blowing through the treetops. The night birds calling to one another from distant branches further added to the beauty of the symphony, creating a soothing melody that could lull her to sleep. Everything was separate, yet perfectly blended.

“It’s incredible.” She opened her eyes and looked into his dark stare.

“You see, I do understand your attraction to the night, probably better than anyone else could. She’s the queen of seduction—a true siren. Like you, I am just another of her many captives. But as tempting as it may be, you have to be careful right now.” He leaned toward her and inhaled, lingering several seconds. “Forgive me.”

Stepping back, he released her hand.

“There’s nothing to apologize for.” She was disappointed he’d pulled away, wishing he had kissed her.

She had wanted him from the very first time she’d laid eyes on him a month earlier, recalling the evening. Night had just fallen when he came along, finding her trying to catch a stubborn mare that had slipped through the gate. She was a short distance past the farm on Old Denaud Road, attempting to coax the horse to her with a bucket of feed. Seeing her predicament, he’d stopped to help, and to her surprise, had the mare eating right out of his hand in a matter of minutes. Standing there with him now, she found herself in the same position as that lulled mare—ready to take whatever he had to give.

* * * *

Corin stood on the bank, struggling against his desire to take Angelique's enticing, rosy mouth to his.

"The night is a seductress, she puts her spell on us all," he said.

"You really are a night owl."

Corin allowed a slight laugh to escape. *If she only knew how right on the mark she was.*

"I didn't hear your car," she mentioned. "The creek's so loud."

"I could have been anyone. I'll say it again, Angelique, you shouldn't be wandering off alone."

He understood that he couldn't pin down her free spirit—one of the many things he loved about her—but he had to open her eyes to the danger existing there. He couldn't bear to lose her, especially not as food to a nocturnal hunter.

"I love how you worry about me." She twirled a long tendril of hair around her finger.

Corin turned away, fighting his compulsion to take her in his arms and have his way with her, something he knew he shouldn't do...could not do. Struggling against his animal urges, he'd managed to control his desires until she wrapped her arms around him from behind, sending a rage of heat through his loins.

His restraint weakening, he turned and faced her. She was enticing as the night, a force whose pull he could not resist. Peering into her eyes, she initiated the first move, taking both of his hands in hers and stepping so near he felt the warmth of her skin. Her scent was arousing, her face so close to his jawline that her breath moistened his neck.

Expelling a groan, he seized her slender waist, unable to resist her pull any longer. Giving in to desire, he brushed his lips over the top of her sable head, silently cursing himself for his weakness. His hands traveled up her seductive body, stopping when he reached her face, where he placed two fingers under her chin and lifted her gaze to meet his. He saw her want, her need, pure hunger in the depths of her gaze, sending his blood surging—molten lava—through his veins.

"We shouldn't be—" he started to protest their actions, but Angelique hushed him.

"It's okay," she whispered, as if knowing his struggle.

He brushed his thumb over her lips and ran his mouth down the side of her face, to her neck, lingering at her jugular, momentarily seized by the intensity of her racing pulse.

"Kiss me, Corin," she whispered.

Those three words were all it took. He sought her mouth, besotted by the pure rapture of their kiss. He'd never wanted anything more. The line was crossed, and he didn't want to revert. But in the midst of passion, he suddenly pulled back, and let her go. He had to let her go.

"I can't do this." He wanted nothing more than to satisfy his burning urges, but for her sake, he had to stop himself. "This shouldn't be happening."

"What's wrong?"

"Your brother's right. You deserve the best life has to offer," he mumbled.

"My brother? What is it with you and Tomes?"

He could see her agitation. He'd lifted her to a heightened state of arousal, only to pull away.

"We have an understanding...and a common interest." He gave her a vague reply.

"Why don't you clarify for me whether you two are friends or enemies, because from where I'm standing, it's impossible to determine."

"We are both, I guess...and neither." By her reaction, Corin could tell his response had only infuriated her more.

I'd have been better off saying nothing at all.

"Friends who are enemies. That clears everything right up. And no one forced you to kiss me, Corin. But don't worry, you're off the hook. I just wish you could be truthful with me."

"You have no idea how much I wanted to kiss you, Angelique. I wish things were different...that Tomes wasn't so disapproving."

"I think it might be best if we leave Tomes out of the equation, whatever that may be. If it were left up to him, I'd be single till the day I die. He'd be happy to see me an old maid."

"He's just looking out for your best interests. He wants to make sure you're safe and happy." Corin defended Tomes's intentions.

"Yes, well, he needs to realize I'm not a child anymore. I'm an adult with all the needs and wants of a grown woman."

Angelique stepped closer to Corin and stroked his face with her fingertips.

"You see that, don't you? I wasn't mistaken, was I?"

Corin took her hand in his and placed a gentle kiss on the inside of her wrist. "No, you weren't mistaken. But for your sake, let's just slow it down a bit. We don't have to move so fast."

Corin knew she had doubts, thinking maybe he didn't share her interest. But she couldn't have been further from the truth. He wanted her more than he'd ever wanted anyone before, but he had to control his wants and desires, for her sake. He just wished he could make her understand why it couldn't happen...what was at stake. But telling her the truth was something he couldn't do.

"Are we still on for our walk tomorrow evening?" Angelique turned and moved along the bank, in the direction of the road.

"I haven't forgotten. But I was thinking, maybe you'd rather accompany me to the county fair instead. It's in Black River Falls this week."

"You mean...like a date?"

"Yes, it would be our first official date." He smiled.

"Don't you need to check with Tomes first," she needled. "Get his approval?"

"Ouch. I deserve that. And we both know your brother would never give me his approval. But after tonight, I'm having second thoughts when it comes to him. I think you're right, from now on let's just leave him out of our relationship."

"Agreed. And the fair...I'd love to go."

Reaching the car, he opened the door, and she climbed in.

"What do you say I pick you up at nine thirty? It's a little late, but the lights will be nice after dark." he proposed.

"At the farm? Tomes might be there."

"I can handle him. No worries."

"I'm sure you can. I'll be ready."

Corin leaned in and pressed a tender kiss to her lips, disregarding all the boundaries he'd previously set for himself.

"I'll give you an escort home."

"That's not necessary."

"I'm headed home as well, so being my neighbor, it's the only neighborly thing to do." Corin winced at the sound of his corny attempt at wit.

Following her to the farm, he was glad to find Tomes's truck parked in front of the house. Then, tossing a wave of his hand, he drove on, plagued by the taste of her kiss, the sweet traces still lingering on his lips.

Get you mind back on business.

Failing to reach his earlier destination, he made tracks toward the cemetery, but stopped several miles up the road. Pulled to the curb, he stepped out of the car cursing himself for going too far with Angelique.

What am I doing?

He looked up at the moon and released an anguished roar. The power of the midnight hour was strong. It took more to control his desire for her than it did to fight his craving for fresh blood—something he would die without.

* * * *

Corin laid his hands upon the earth, endeavoring to see Louisa's attacker, but the image was clouded. Detecting another presence, he looked over the cemetery.

Who is here?

Finding no one around, he left and headed home, met by a cold, empty estate, settling in the stillness of the night.

Pouring a glass of brandy, he stepped onto the lanai. He didn't require food or drink, but there were certain things he enjoyed, and brandy was one of those indulgences.

Looking over the back grounds at the woods lying beyond the wall, he contemplated taking flight, but decided against it. Something seemed out of sorts in the house, making him uneasy.

Pushing off the vexing feeling, he went back inside and busied himself with finances and tidying up the main floor, biding his time till dawn. Finally, the blessed morning came, and he retreated to the basement, leaving Tomes a note on the outside door that he'd see him at dusk. With the plan set in motion of Angelique thinking her brother was working for him, Corin figured he'd be coming around.

"Sometimes you do know what you're talking about, Tomes. At least this time." Corin slid a bolt lock into place, having taken Tomes's advice and installed it, realizing with the main gate open, he was vulnerable while at rest. And with the door secured, he headed down and started undressing, pulling his wallet from his pants and laying it atop the dresser.

"What?" His eyes widened, realizing something was missing.

He growled and sniffed the air, catching the faint trace of an odor wafting about the room.

No!

Anger overtook him. The fiend had been in his home...stolen his things!

With a vehement energy inspired by his craving to do nothing more than even the score, he cursed as he stormed the room.

"You've gone too far. No one invades my home and gets away with it. No one!"

He slammed his hand against the wall, creating a hairline crack that traced its way to the floor.

Corin wondered how the newcomer had managed it. When a home had been occupied for a duration of three consecutive lunar cycles, a nightwalker couldn't enter that residence without first being invited. This told him there could only be one explanation—he must have come into contact with this character at some point, but where? He thought back over the last several nights, pinning down the moment he'd encountered the demon, at a local establishment called Micky Joe's Bar and Grill. Corin often frequented the bar, not so much for the drink, but for the atmosphere, feeling a camaraderie with the tortured souls attempting to drown their sorrows in liquor. He recalled sitting at a table, obscured in the back of the room, when a foreigner had approached him in a friendly manner and initiated conversation.

"I was told you're von Vadim." The man spoke with a strong Turkish accent.

"You were told right. What can I do for you?" Corin wondered who had pointed him out.

"I heard you have a fine collection of classic cars. I'm a collector myself."

"Is that so?" Corin wasn't too sure of the individual.

"I might be willing to take a model or two off your hands if you're interested in parting with any of your collection."

"I don't know who you've been talking to, but I have no interest in selling...sorry."

"I completely understand. I would never part with any of my own. But you can't blame a man for trying. I know the dedication it takes to restore those vehicles to their original glory, not to mention the time and money. In the process, they kind of become a part of you."

Corin took a sip of his drink, still trying to read the stranger. He had an odor attached to him that just didn't fit—an odd, moldy stink that even a generous dousing of aftershave couldn't mask. This was an odor Corin would typically have associated with the undead, but he sensed no other immortals in the room. And after listening to the man's endless rambling about several cars he'd restored, Corin finally concluded the foreigner to be just what he claimed to be, merely a fellow enthusiast, albeit lacking hygiene, but harmless. And disregarding his initial reservations, Corin found himself engrossed by their conversation, a topic he knew a lot about.

"I can't believe you have a fully restored 1958 Lister." The man was impressed. "I would really love to see it."

"I don't drive it much. But I'd be glad to show it to

you sometime." Corin proceeded to invite him to von Vadim Estate to view the Lister, along with the rest of his collection that he referred to as his "pride and toys."

Corin drew his thoughts back to the present, slamming a hand down on the dresser. He had been played...duped.

"So, that's how you did it."

One brief invite was all the newcomer needed to gain access.

You shielded yourself. How?

Corin's biggest challenge lay in not being able to sense the clever nightwalker. He could only imagine the degree of power the immortal possessed, enabling him to shield his presence from other nightwalkers in such a way. This left Corin wondering if he might be from an age-old clan, or even from an unknown race of immortals possessing powers far superior to his own. Nevertheless, learning the newcomer's lineage or what powers he possessed would change nothing at this point. The fiend had now made this fight personal. Disadvantaged or not, Corin intended to see it through to the bitter end. But at present, there was nothing more he could do till sunset. So, in his perturbed state, he proceeded to undress, climbed into the crypt, and slept within the comforting confines of the earth. His rest would not be peaceful, but it would be productive. He needed to be at his peak, mentally and physically, prepared for anything that the nightwalker might throw at him. This newcomer had deceived him, invaded his domain with cruel intent, and stolen from him.

May the best nightwalker win.

8

Boldor Enescu

Boldor Enescu had been walking the earth for nearly three hundred years. Although not the ancient Corin was, he was still well versed in his species. Holding an unfair advantage over other immortals, he had the ability to shield his presence, disguise what he was. He possessed this power by means of a charm he'd obtained through thievery. While using the name Karlot, he'd infiltrated the Order of the Clythguard—a special league of nightwalkers—with the aid of a partner associated with the society. Together, they'd devised a plan to gain the trust of the Order, all in a malicious scheme to steal the mystical relic right out from under their noses. It was a phenomenal feat, and to date, his proudest achievement.

Boldor had made many enemies over his lifespan, human and otherwise, for it was his nature to cheat, steal, and kill. He even prided himself on his abhorrent talents and abilities. Chased out of his homeland of Turkey more than fifty years earlier, he fled to the lands of the Americas where he found a bountiful reservoir of fresh blood for the taking. Boldor could have sought refuge in any of several bordering countries, but he figured that in this new "land of opportunity" he could start over with his freedom intact, and more importantly, with his head remaining right where it needed to be, resting safe and secure on his shoulders.

Boldor had never managed to acquire the worth and means Corin had built over the last several hundred years. Unlike von Vadim, he didn't have the patience to wait for his wealth to accumulate over time, finding it easier to just take what he wanted rather than work for it. So, he robbed and stole his fortunes, filching from unsuspecting prey, his wanton acts keeping him on the run. He had been considerably fortunate at various aspects of his life, but was never apt to hold onto his riches, always squandering the bounty away.

Once upon a time, Boldor had even been an aristocrat, but when he'd murdered a fellow Turk over a simple dispute, he'd been stripped of his title and thrown into prison. However, possessing abilities that enabled him to pull a convenient disappearing act, he'd escaped from his cell before dawn. And today, he was still running, only now it was from the tenacious Marshal Jordon Black. Unlike other lawmen before him, the marshal had a special talent for tracking, not allowing Boldor a moment of peace in the past two years. Staying ahead of Black wasn't always easy, the man was a bulldog, and Boldor knew there was no way he would ever give up the chase.

* * * *

Where were you last night, Angel?" Tomes probed.

"I was restless, so I took a drive." Angelique offered no further details.

"Well, I found your note, and I've been waiting for this Louis Gomez fellow for over an hour. I don't think he's going to show."

"Oh, that's right." She spooned a teaspoon of sugar into her coffee. "Weird. He seemed so interested in hiring you."

"He must have changed his mind."

"Maybe, but he could have at least called."

"I wish he had. I've wasted time I could be putting to much better use. Where did you meet this guy, anyway?"

"In the grocery store."

"Well, if I'm reading this situation right, I'd say this Louis Gomez fellow was probably more interested in obtaining your services than mine."

"Tomes, you're such a child. And it wasn't like that. We had a minor mishap. I accidentally ran my cart into his, which led to conversation—him telling me how he'd just purchased an older home and was looking to renovate. He was a complete gentleman. Honestly, I don't know about you sometimes," she groused.

Tomes laughed, and she loved hearing it.

"But all jokes aside, I thought he'd be here."

"Well, it's too bad he didn't show. I was looking over the books this morning, and our account's running a little low."

"That's an understatement. But I don't want you pushing yourself. I told him it would be a couple of weeks before you could start. Till then, we'll get by."

"Thanks, Angel. But we both know we're slowly sinking. If it gets any more critical, we'll be forced to sell a couple of the foals sooner than expected. We might even have to let go of one of the mares. Dale Wickerton, over at Little Water Ranch, has had his eye on Dixie Long for quite some time."

"No, Tomes, not Dixie Long. I'd hate giving her up," Angelique protested. "She gives us our best foals. And Wickerton is our biggest competitor. That would really hurt us in the long run."

"I know. And trust me, letting her go will be a last resort," he assured her. "I'll go later today and enter us in next month's show. In the meantime, I do have some work lined up with von Vadim."

"He told me he was interested in hiring you, but I wasn't sure you'd take him up on it."

"Well, work is work. And beggars can't be choosers. Who knows, maybe this Mr. Gomez will still get in touch. What sort of person was he?"

"He was nice, I'd guess around thirty. Dark features. Tall and thin. He talked with a foreign accent."

"Where was he from?"

"I didn't think to ask. If I had to guess, I'd say he was European. You would have liked his car. When I was leaving, he waved to me in the parking lot while getting into a nice-looking blue Camaro." She remembered admiring it.

"A Camaro?" Tomes's voice grew serious. "What color blue? Was it light, dark, what?"

"Not too dark. I'd say it was sort of a grayish-blue color."

"Dusty-blue...did it look dusty-blue?" Tomes pressed.

"I guess you could call it that."

"And dark tinting?"

"Yes. Why? What is it, Tomes?"

"I want you to promise, Angel, that you'll let me know right away if this Louis Gomez does happen to call or come around. You need to stay away from him."

"I know he's new in town, but I really don't think he's the killer, if that's what you're thinking."

"I can't get into it right now, but he's not to be trusted."

"You're not going to tell me a thing, are you?"

"Just promise me, Angel."

"He seemed harmless, but if you're that worried, you have my word. I'll let you know if I hear from him again."

"Good." Tomes checked his watch. "It's almost ten thirty. I need to get over to the estate. The number's on the fridge if you need me for anything."

"About this job, Tomes, are you sure you're going to be okay with it...working for Corin?"

"It's just business, and we need the money. Besides, I never said I hated the man. I just don't like him making moves on my sister. And he knows why."

Tomes got up from the table.

"I don't think that's your decision to make."

"He's not the man for you, Angel, trust me. And I don't want to fight with you right now. Like I said, if you need me, the number's on the fridge."

Angelique held her temper, silently fuming as Tomes left the room.

What is really going on with you and Corin?

She suspected it was more than it first seemed. Much more.

* * * *

Sheriff Pierson paid a visit to Brookside Realty. Sitting in Sandy Darnell's office, he mulled over her desk calendar, trying to find a link, any link. He had just received a call on his cell phone from Dr. Berg, informing him that Mrs. Darnell's blood type was altogether different from the first victim, Louisa Jaffler, ruling out the possibility of the killer being in dire need of specifically "O positive" blood type.

The receptionist, Ginger, walked in. "Can I get you some coffee?"

"No coffee, thanks," he replied. "But if you have a minute, I could use a little help deciphering Mrs. Darnell's handwriting." He pointed out the area of interest—the activity from July twenty-second. Something written in that square might very well be vital to his case.

"Drop the car off at Purcell's Garage." Ginger interpreted the first note. "Sandy took her car there the day before yesterday. I remember her mentioning how it was stalling."

"Can you think of anyone who might have had any grudges against Mrs. Darnell? Possibly a real estate deal gone wrong, or anything in her personal life you might know of?"

"No, sir. Everyone loved Sandy. And business was good. I can't imagine anyone wanting to harm her."

"What about these other two appointments, can you tell me anything about them?"

"This one is Mr. Glynn Kensington, the new principal over at the high school." She pointed out the name. "He's a client. An eccentric one."

"What do you mean?"

"Well, it took him the longest time to decide between two properties in his price quota—a very nice ranch that's been sitting vacant for some time over in Hixton, and a home with substantially less acreage in Northfield. After much debate, he decided on the smaller residence in Northfield, which didn't make much sense to me. For the same price he could have had the larger ranch house with way more land, not to mention a shorter commute to and from work."

"Did he say why?"

"He claimed that something didn't feel right with the ranch house in Hixton. He had a wild notion the place was haunted. Isn't that crazy? You wouldn't think such an educated man would be so superstitious. Anyway, we all got a good laugh out of it."

"What about this other appointment an hour later?"

"Oh, that was with Charlotte Mitchell from the title company. She handles all of our closings. Sandy was getting the ball rolling with Mr. Kensington's purchase. Another one of our agents, Lauren Nanner, is finishing up his transaction now. In fact, she's taken over all of Sandy's clients. I think she's in her office if you'd like to speak with her."

"That won't be necessary." He jotted down a few things in his trusty notepad.

"I'll know where to find her if anything arises."

Just then, to Sheriff Pierson's dismay, a very unpleasant voice drifted through the open doorway. It was none other than Jordon Black rudely calling for assistance from the outside counter, repeatedly dinging the service bell. Ginger excused herself and rushed out to attend him.

"What a pompous ass." Pierson followed her out, wanting to confront the arrogant marshal. The man continually proving his insolence with scenes like this one, strutting around with his uppity attitude. It couldn't have been more obvious if he'd plastered a banner across his chest saying, *I am the man.*

"Can I help you, sir?" Ginger asked in agitation, bumping a ceramic cup containing several pens and knocking it over.

Sheriff Pierson knew Black's tactics—aiming for intimidation—and it irked him. He didn't care for bullies.

"Is there a problem?" Pierson made his presence known.

"Why, Sheriff Pierson, fancy meeting you here. If we're going to keep running into each other this way, maybe we should team up...save us both some footwork," Jordon spouted wryly.

Over my dead body.

"No need for all that disturbance. I'd hate having to haul you down to the station for belligerent behavior."

"No belligerence here, Sheriff, I assure you." The marshal held his hands up, palms out. "Just trying to get some help. No one was around."

"Just stay out of my way, Marshal Black," Pierson warned.

"I am authorized to be here, like it or not," Jordon reminded him.

Sheriff Pierson turned to Ginger and thanked her for her assistance before heading out the door. He figured he'd better leave before his temper got the better of him. He'd never been so tempted to just shoot someone before. Frankly, he was surprised someone hadn't already attempted it, but for all he knew, maybe they had. He certainly couldn't imagine the man having many friends, visualizing, rather, a whole slew of enemies just waiting for a chance to take him out.

Sheriff Pierson left the real estate office and drove over to Purcell's Garage where he found the garage owner working on an older model Ford truck. He climbed out of the pit, half covered in grease, wiping his hands on an old rag.

"I thought you'd be coming around. I assume you're here about Sandy?"

"That's right. Sandy Darnell. I was informed you did some work on her car the day before yesterday." Pierson went straight to his questioning.

"Yeah, she was here."

"What was the problem with her car?"

"Nothing major. She just needed a new fuel filter. She left it and came back later in the day and picked it up."

"Was anyone with her?"

"I remember her saying that someone was waiting, but I'm afraid I didn't see who it was. I was busy on another job at the time and didn't notice. Although...."

Purcell paused. "I think it was a client. She mentioned coming back for her car after showing some properties."

"How about the vehicle? Did you happen to get a look at it?"

"Sorry, Sheriff, I wish I had paid more attention. Sandy was a loyal customer of mine for years—a real fine lady. It makes me sick thinking what happened to her."

Sheriff Pierson wondered why there was no mention of a meeting marked on her calendar. He decided it must have been spur of the moment.

"Is there anything else you can think of pertaining to Mrs. Darnell that you might consider relevant in any way?" Pierson hoped he might jog a memory.

"No, I don't think so, except...." Purcell's voice trailed off. "It's probably nothing, but I did give one of Sandy's business cards to a chap named von Vadim. He just inherited the large estate over in Hixton."

"I know him," Sheriff Pierson told him.

"Well, he asked me if I knew anything about the real estate company down the street. I couldn't tell him much, except that I knew Sandy. And since the office was closed, I passed along one of her cards. I have a stack of 'em inside, on the counter. We had a little agreement, Sandy and me, to recommend each other's services. I thought I was doing her a real favor with him being loaded."

"When was he here?" Pierson probed.

"Night before last. I remember because it was the same day Sandy had been in with her car, I think it was the twenty-second." He counted the dates back. "Yeah, that's right, the twenty-second."

"Mr. von Vadim was here the same night Mrs. Darnell was killed?" Pierson confirmed, jotting down another entry in his notepad. The wheels in his mind were turning at an alarming rate, spurred by the sudden intake of new information. "Don't you close up shop at six, Purcell?" Sheriff Pierson motioned toward the sign taped on the door showing his hours of operation.

"I can be flexible. Besides, he called ahead to let me know he was coming. I did business with that young man's uncle, Victor von Vadim, from the time I started my garage, more than twenty years back. He was my best customer. Like the young heir now, he preferred to conduct his business after hours."

"Why after closing?" Sheriff Pierson wanted to know.

"I asked him once. He just said he didn't get around during the day. Besides, he paid me plenty for the inconvenience. Lucky for me, the heir seems to have inherited his uncle's enthusiasm for restoring antique cars. That'll keep the dough rolling—lots of parts needed. His uncle did a great portion of his own labor. I don't know if that'll be the case with this young man, but he's equally generous when it comes to compensation." Purcell admitted he'd been bought.

"As they say, money talks," Pierson remarked. The estate owner had more wealth than any one man ought to have.

"You know, I feel bad about ratting out a customer. If it was anyone but Sandy, I wouldn't have. I don't think anything will come of it, though. He just doesn't fit the MO."

"And what do you know of a killer's MO?" Sheriff Pierson was curious to hear Purcell's reply.

"I know I'm no expert. He just doesn't strike me as

the murdering kind."

"Looks can be deceiving."

"True," Purcell agreed. "Very true."

"What service did you provide for Mr. von Vadim that night? Was he also having car trouble?"

"No. He just came by to have some spark plugs changed on his Harley. Look, Sheriff, I wasn't accusing him of any wrongdoing. Like I said, I dealt with his uncle for years, and he was a decent man."

"But this isn't the uncle we're talking about; this is the nephew who is nothing more than a stranger. You did the right thing, telling me about the card. Think of the two unfortunate women that were killed, and what they must have gone through. It's imperative that every possible connection gets checked out, no matter how insignificant it may seem."

"I know you're right, Sheriff, I just wish I felt better about it."

"I think we're done here. I'll go and let you get back to work." Pierson handed him a business card. "If you think of anything else, give me a call."

Leaving Purcell's Garage, his next destination was von Vadim Estate. The sheriff's visit with Purcell had pushed the wealthy estate owner right to the top of his suspect list. Von Vadim's arrival in Jackson County certainly coincided with the start of the murders, making Sheriff Pierson all the more suspicious.

9

The Tape

Tomes answered the door dressed in a pair of tattered jeans and a green, plaid flannel shirt. His wide-open blue eyes widened even further when he saw Sheriff Pierson.

"Sheriff, what can I help you with?" he greeted.

"Mr. Jaffler. I didn't expect to find you here. I was hoping to see Mr. von Vadim. He's home, I presume?"

"No. He's out right now." Tomes couldn't tell Sheriff Pierson that Corin was actually down in the basement, asleep in a crypt.

"I had no idea the two of you were friends."

"He's only been here about a month, but we're getting acquainted. He's also hired me to do some work on this old place."

"And he gives you free reign to his home while he's out? As you just pointed out, he hasn't known you long."

"I'm trustworthy, Sheriff. It's not like he picked me out of the yellow pages. I'm his neighbor."

There was a brief silent pause before Pierson continued.

"Since I've found you here, Mr. Jaffler, I'd like to ask you something about your wife. Did she happen to have an illness?"

"No. Why do you ask?"

"There were some irregularities in her blood work."

"She was sick and didn't know it? What was wrong with her?" Tomes wanted to know.

"I can't answer that for you yet. Forensics is running a more thorough analysis. I'll let you know the results when I get them. It'll most likely be several days."

"Be sure to do that."

Pierson nodded. "Tell me, do you know anything about a woman named Sandy Darnell?"

"Only that she's the real estate agent found murdered over in Black River Falls. It's breaking news. You can't turn on the TV or radio without hearing about it."

Pierson silently cursed, hating the media. "I've recently discovered that Mr. von Vadim acquired one of her business cards from Purcell's Garage the very night of her death, mere hours before her murder. Would you happen to know what interest he might have had in meeting with her?"

"I'd assume it was concerning real estate. What else could it have been?"

Tomes shifted nervously, the business card in question tucked away in his wallet, a flaming ember burning in his back pocket.

"That's what I'm trying to discern, Mr. Jaffler. So, you don't know if he ever made contact with her?" Sheriff Pierson continued to probe. "If he did, it's very likely he was the last person to communicate with her before the attack."

"Sorry. I can't help you. But I'll let Corin know you were here."

"Mr. von Vadim has become a person of interest, and he shouldn't avoid me."

"If you think Corin had anything at all to do with that poor woman's death, you're way off base," Tomes stated.

"And you know this for fact? A man you've known for only a month, and you can defend him so wholeheartedly?"

"He didn't do it, Sheriff."

"I hope you're right, Mr. Jaffler."

"You should be out there hunting down the real killer, instead of wasting your time here, harassing the innocent. My wife lies dead in her grave, and you're standing here, making false accusations."

"We're following every available lead, I assure you, one of which led me right here, to this very door."

"Well, you've apparently missed a trail somewhere along the way, because you're sniffing in the wrong place. Corin didn't kill my wife, or that real estate agent."

"How do I know the two of you aren't in this together?" Sheriff Pierson threw the accusation at him.

"I didn't kill my wife. Louisa meant everything to me. I would have given my life for her. And if I find the SOB that did kill her before you do, Sheriff, you'll be collecting him in pieces," Tomes declared, his voice rising with emotion.

"You can't go taking the law into your own hands. That's not the answer," Pierson warned him. "You may see it as justice served, but it would be murder. I have enough to worry about without adding vigilantes to the list."

Tomes held his tongue, knowing he'd already said

too much. He'd allowed his emotions to get the better of him.

"Well, I'll be on my way." Sheriff Pierson handed him a card. "Let Mr. von Vadim know I'll be waiting for his call."

Tomes took the card and watched while Sheriff Pierson sauntered to his SUV.

He turned back before getting in. "One other thing, Mr. Jaffler, what job did you say you were doing for Mr. von Vadim?"

"I didn't say, Sheriff. But to answer your question, at present I'm doing some repairs on the south wall. There's some stone damage and roof leakage I'm attending to."

"Very good." Pierson waved, got in his vehicle, and departed.

Bothered by the visit, Tomes, was more anxious than ever for the day to pass so Corin would awaken. Earlier, when he'd arrived at the estate, he'd headed for the basement, finding Corin's note on the door. Even though he had news, he'd decided to let him rest, knowing there was nothing he could do till nightfall.

* * * *

Sheriff Pierson received a call from the station. Patricia Watson was there requesting to see him.

"I'm really sorry, Sheriff, but she says it's urgent," Officer Traci Keller told him. "She insists on waiting."

"It's okay, Traci. I'm on my way back from Hixton as we speak."

When Sheriff Pierson arrived, he found Ms. Watson in an anxious state.

"Ms. Watson," he greeted. "What is it you're needing to see me about?"

"Please, Allen, I wish you'd call me Patricia," she

said.

"My apologies, Patricia, I'll remember that."

"I have something to show you." She caught hold of his arm, whispering as if it were top secret. "Is there someplace private we can view a tape?" She revealed a VHS tape tucked away in her oversized purse.

"Come with me." Sheriff Pierson led her to a small conference room containing a rectangular table, ten accompanying chairs, and a TV and multiplayer system set up on a rolling stand.

"You don't see these too much anymore. What's on it?" He took the tape and inserted it into the player before joining her at the table with the remote control in hand.

"It's a surveillance video from the hospital blood bank. And you're not going to believe what we've caught on it. I can hardly believe it myself."

He started the tape, listening to Patricia explain what they were viewing. He observed a nurse entering the blood storage room by use of an access card, where she collected two bags and then left.

"Keep your eyes on the screen." She motioned with a wagging finger. "This is it."

Sheriff Pierson watched with heightened interest as a male figure suddenly appeared in the room, materializing right out of thin air.

"Where did he come from?"

"That's what we can't figure out. And you see, he's leaving with several bags of blood," she pointed out.

"Maybe he was already in the room when the nurse entered," the sheriff proposed. "Hiding somewhere."

"No. The camera picks up every inch of it."

"How many employees have access cards?" He moved closer to the screen.

"Quite a few—doctors, nurses, and others. You can't get into the room without one."

Sheriff Pierson was stumped. He rewound the video to the point where the nurse entered the room to view it again, pressing pause when something of interest caught his eye.

"What do you make of that?" He indicated what appeared to be a faint foggy vapor moving in behind the nurse.

Patricia scooted next to him. "The tape's so fuzzy, it's hard to tell what it is. Could it be a shadow?"

"I don't think so." He let the tape play on. "It slips in behind her, takes a turn to the right, then lingers against the wall until she leaves? And look, it's that same vapor that materializes into the man. It has to be a trick, but for the life of me, I can't figure it out."

"I wish the tape was clearer. You can't make out his face. We'll never be able to identify him with this picture."

"The room's too dark. Fix the lighting, and you'll have a better picture next time. You might also consider a higher resolution camera and going digital."

"The budget won't allow for a new system right now. What we're using was pulled from storage," she told him. "And hopefully there won't be a next time."

"There has to be a logical explanation. People don't just magically appear out of thin air." Sheriff Pierson refused to accept the possibility of paranormal activity.

"I know I'd certainly feel a whole lot better if you could clarify this one for me."

"I wish I could," Pierson said. "He moves strangely for a man, don't you think?"

"He wriggles side-to-side—snakelike." Patricia watched as the thief tucked the bags of vital fluid beneath his full body length overcoat.

"That coat he's wearing should help with identifying him. It's certainly different. The buttons stand out, even with the picture blurred. I think someone would have noticed it."

"It's hard to be certain, but they look like cabochon gems," she agreed. "Far from ordinary. I'll ask around the floor...see if anyone recollects."

And what's that, a necklace?" Sheriff Pierson drew her attention to a shiny object hanging in the upper vicinity of the man's chest.

"Yes, I believe it is, maybe a dark-colored stone. He seems to like his gems. You really do have a trained eye, Allen."

"It's not much to go on, but every little bit helps." That he'd impressed her made his day. "I'll send this over to the lab. Maybe they can clean it up, give us something more to identify him by." He stopped the tape and got up to retrieve it.

"The blood...what do you think he took it for?"

"I have no idea, but he's definitely getting added to my suspect list."

"You mean for the murders? You think our burglar could be the killer?"

"It's a strong possibility. You should tighten security until we get a handle on things," he suggested. "And you should be careful yourself."

"This is all a bit disturbing. But I feel better knowing you're handling things," she told him. "Say, Allen, would you care to join me for a late lunch, or have you already eaten?"

"No, matter of fact, I haven't. I could use a little something."

"Wonderful." Patricia smiled. "Let's go."

Heading out, Sheriff Pierson handed the surveillance tape marked "urgent" to Officer Traci, along with implicit instructions for the lab regarding its cleanup.

"Have a nice lunch." Traci tossed him a teasing wink.

Sheriff Pierson hustled Patricia out, attempting to thwart any further attempts by the officers to share potentially embarrassing remarks. He'd tried not to be so transparent, but he knew he wasn't fooling anyone, least of all himself. He might have been embarking on a somewhat official outing with Patricia, but there was no mistaking the chemistry.

* * * *

Angelique stood at the fence line, a distance behind the barn. Two foals frolicked in the pasture, running and kicking up their heels while the unaffected mares grazed on the fresh grass of the newly opened field. Startled by a hand grabbing her shoulder, she whirled around with an accompanying yelp. Finding herself staring into the face of a stranger, she cautiously backed away from him.

"Sorry if I scared you. Ms. Jaffler, I presume?"

"Yes. Who are you?"

"I'm Marshal Jordon Black." He held out a badge. "I'm here investigating Louisa Jaffler's death. I was hoping to ask you a few questions, if it's not too inconvenient a time."

Angelique hesitated, wary of the man despite seeing his badge. With his faded jeans and long hair pulled back in a ponytail, he wasn't at all what she expected a marshal to look like. And uncomfortable with the way he'd wandered onto their back grounds, she figured he was most likely snooping, thinking no one was around.

"I guess I can spare a few minutes," she finally said.

"Let me just get to it, then. The victim was your sister-in-law?"

"Yes. Louisa was my brother's wife."

"Your brother, Tomes Jaffler," Jordon confirmed.

"That's right, Marshal. Isn't all of this on record?"

Angelique, suddenly reconsidering the questioning, moved into defensive mode. She had been through this same ordeal several times now and didn't care to repeat the "twenty questions routine" yet again.

"Yes, it is, Ms. Jaffler, but if you don't mind, I just want to make certain nothing was overlooked. You're not a suspect, if that's your concern. I assure you."

"And my brother, can you say the same about him?"

"I'm not here to accuse you, or your brother, of anything. I just want to ask a few questions. People often recall things in the aftermath of a tragedy that they'd initially blanked out or thought little of at the time. Shock can also do strange things to the mind."

"I've thought about that night a thousand times. There's nothing more, trust me. I wish there was."

"What about earlier in the evening? Would you mind telling me what you do remember?"

Angelique gave in and proceeded to tell him all she recalled.

"That's pretty much what I reviewed in your initial report," he said after hearing her account.

"I told you there was nothing more."

"How about your brother, is he around? I should review this with him as well."

"Is that really necessary? He's been through so much."

"I know it's a rough time, but there's a murderer on the loose. I'd think your brother would be obliging, glad to know we're doing everything in our power to catch his wife's killer."

"I'm sure you're right, but he's not here at the moment. He's doing some work for a neighbor—Corin von Vadim."

"Von Vadim?"

"He owns the large estate neighboring ours. Over two thousand acres."

"Maybe I can catch him there. I guess I'll find the entrance on up the road?"

"You can't miss it. There's a large gate."

"I'll be on my way, then."

"Before you go, Marshal, since you're insistent on questioning Tomes, you should know...he truly loved Louisa."

"I'm sure he did," Jordon replied. "And I do sympathize, but I have a job to do. If I tiptoed around every sensitive situation, I'd never get anywhere," he stated bluntly.

"Just take it easy on him. That's all I'm asking. He's been through a lot."

"I understand." Jordon bid her good day and headed away, his boots throwing up a light powdering of dust behind him.

Angelique watched until he disappeared around the side of the barn, knowing he'd be making a beeline for von Vadim Estate. She wished now she'd kept her mouth shut about her brother's whereabouts, but lying had never come easy to her. However, despite her name, she was no angel, and if it became necessary, she could conjure her dark side and do whatever she had to do in order to protect her family from the evils of the outside world. That included law enforcement.

"Tomes," she whispered her brother's name, thinking of what he was going through. He was an ever-changing man since Louisa's death, bringing the story of *Jekyll and Hyde* to mind. Like Stevenson's character, he seemed to be fully transforming into his own sinister alter ego. Angelique feared if things didn't change, the good side of Tomes might be lost forever.

10

In the Fog

Tomes cursed as he walked across the living room toward the front door. He contemplated not answering, but his truck was parked outside, evidence that he was there.

Jordon Black introduced himself. "I'm sorry to bother you, Mr. Jaffler, but it's essential that I learn all I can about the murders if I'm to have any success with catching this killer."

"No, it's all right. I understand." Tomes stepped outside, leaving the door open. "Nice car. A Charger, huh?"

"Yeah, for the horsepower." Jordon moved to give him some space.

"What do you need to know?"

"Tell me what happened the night your wife was murdered."

Tomes cooperated, reviewing the last evening he'd

spent with Louisa, not wanting to raise any suspicions.

"Your recollections are an exact match to your sister's." Jordon looked past Tomes and into the house.

"We were both there, experiencing the same things," he responded. "Is something wrong?" He wondered what had caught the marshal's attention.

"Just admiring the place. Very old, I suspect."

"Yes. It is. If there's nothing else, I should get back to work. I wouldn't want the owner to come back and find me slacking," he joked.

"Well, thank you for your time, Mr. Jaffler." Jordon looked past him yet again before turning to go.

Tomes shut the door and visually scanned the room wondering what had given rise to the inquisitive look on the marshal's face.

The man couldn't possibly suspect vampires...could he?

Tomes shook his head. *He couldn't possibly know.*

Alone again, Tomes poked around the estate grounds while the day crept to an end, the longest Tomes thought he'd ever endured. After dwindling on and on, the sun had now lowered in the western sky, making the transition to twilight.

Tomes stood on the lanai observing a mysterious bank of fog moving in, an eerie phenomenon unlike anything he'd ever seen before. Fearing that the strange occurrence was a forewarning of things to come, a bone-chilling sensation enveloped him.

Was there something wicked lurking in the dense, rolling fog, coming to devour them all?

Tomes shook off the feeling and stepped inside the house. He headed for the basement door to alert the slumbering nightwalker that it was time to rise and shine, but before he reached it, Corin burst out.

"What's going on?" Tomes heart skipped a beat.

"He was here!" Corin stared Tomes dead-in-the-eyes, the savage look on his face reminding Tomes that he was far from human. Releasing a menacing growl with teeth gnashed, he fully depicted the notion of a vampire—a monster out for the kill.

"If you're talking about the sheriff, he was here all right. And a marshal also came by—said his name was Black. I'm not sure what to make of him. He seemed suspicious of something."

"Not the police. I'm talking about the nightwalker," Corin clarified.

"He was here?"

"The wretch sneaked in while I was out last night," Corin explained. "He took some personal things of mine from the basement."

"What? What did he take?"

"A gold pocket watch and a pewter figurine from my dresser."

"That's it?" In his opinion, the items weren't very valuable when compared to the many priceless treasures filling the house.

"That's all he needed to take. Don't you get it, Tomes? This is all a game to him. He wanted me to know he was here, in my home. And both items he took have more worth and meaning to me than a vault full of gold. They're priceless in sentiment. I haven't lived my long life without forming several close attachments, and those two small things he dared to steal from me, well, they are symbols of two cherished memories."

Corin's genuine emotion surprised Tomes. It made him seem almost human. He thought it strange how he went from being a raging monster one minute, ready to tear out his adversary's throat, to the sentimental, nostalgic being presently standing before him. He just hoped that the sullen nightwalker didn't burst into tears, 'cause there was no way in Hades he was comforting him. At that thought, he gave his head a good shake, tossing out the horrid image.

"Maybe we can get them back."

"Oh, we're going to get them back all right. Then, I'm going to teach that good-for-nothing a lesson he'll never forget!" Fire flashed in Corin's eyes as he clenched his fists and paced the floor. "He has deceived me, challenged me, and now stolen from me. There will be no more games. It's time to get serious."

"I found your note on the door this morning. I wish now I hadn't suggested that lock. I've been waiting around here all day."

"I sensed you in the house, but I needed to restore my energy. I knew if it was urgent, you'd let me know."

"Well, something else has happened."

"What?"

"Angelique said she met a man at the grocery store last night who wanted to hire me for renovations, and you won't believe what he was driving. A dusty-blue Camaro."

"That miserable.... He's gone way too far."

"He told her his name was Louis Gomez and set up an appointment to meet with me at the farm this morning. But he didn't show, of course, not with the sun rising and all."

"Did he touch her?" Corin demanded to know.

"She's fine. He didn't do anything to her," Tomes assured him, hearing the rage behind his words, surprised by his height of emotion over Angelique. He didn't care for Corin's reaction regarding his sister, but this wasn't the time to confront him about it. "So, I take it you're pretty sure it was the nightwalker?"

"It was him. And like I said...it's time to get serious."

* * * *

Patricia Watson's watch read 9:50. She'd put in a long

day in preparation for a board meeting, and the effects from the extra hours had left her with a kinked neck, and an aching back.

"Time to call it quits." She shut down her computer, grabbed her purse, and headed out. She had a bad feeling as she started across the nearly abandoned lot, aiming for her car parked quite a distance away. To make matters worse, a heavy fog had moved in over the area, adding to her apprehension.

Moonlight cast a silvery-blue tint onto the misty blanket of fog, giving it a buoyant glow. The sound of her shoes hitting the pavement echoed as she moved across the black asphalt. Halfway to her car, she glanced back, intuition telling her that something wasn't right. Disregarding her instincts, she continued on, drawing in a quick breath when she heard someone else's footsteps trailing her own. She stopped, turned back again, and gave her surroundings a quick scan, but the thick, creeping fog diminished her view.

"Pa-tri-cia." A menacing voice sounded from the depths of darkness causing her to release a slight yelp. She slapped her hand against her chest to calm her racing heart. It was impossible to determine what direction the call had come from for it emanated from all around her.

"Who's there?" she called out to the unseen presence; her voice shaky.

She stood frozen in place as her eyes darted in all directions, trying to ascertain who could be tormenting her in such an inhuman way.

"Pa-tri-cia." The creepy, drawn-out voice came again, giving her gooseflesh, along with a nauseating feeling of dread.

Frantic, she made a mad dash for her car. Reaching it, she cursed, realizing her keys were in her purse. Huddled against the hood of the vehicle, she tried to control her nerves. Desperate to find the keys, Patricia unzipped the bag, fumbling for them. Lost in her panic, a sharp pain in the back of her head took her by surprise. She dropped forward onto the hood of the car as darkness enveloped her.

Patricia awoke to find the contents of her purse scattered on the pavement next to her. "Nooo!" she cried.

Searching the pavement, she fought the terrible pain ripping through her skull. She had no idea where her attacker was, but she knew that if she was to survive, she had to find her keys, and fast, before he finished her off.

"Peek-a-boo. I see you Pa-tri-cia."

She was easy prey—exposed and vulnerable. With dimming vision, she struggled to hold onto consciousness. She squinted; her eyes clouded with tears. Her blouse, wet and sticky, clung to her back. Wincing, her head throbbed so intensely she thought it might split in two. Yet, despite her weakening condition and growing nausea, she forced herself to continue.

"I. Will. Not. Die." She tried to control her panic. The stalker was playing cat and mouse—viciously toying with her. "Thank you, God." She felt the cold impression of the keychain against the palm of her hand.

She pressed the buttons, relieved to hear the click of the door lock. It was a struggle to pull herself up. With her body weak and her legs uncooperative, she could scarcely hold her own weight. Half leaning onto the hood of the front driver's side, she shuffled toward the door, running her shaking hands along the side of the car until she located the handle. She opened the door and slid her weary body inside.

"Please, God, don't let me die. I need your help," she

prayed while searching the door panel for the lock.

Hearing it click, she attempted to place the ignition key in the starter, but in her trepidation, dropped the ring on the floorboard. Reaching down, she found it difficult to control her trembling body and feared she was going into shock. Growing faint, she lowered her head onto the steering wheel. Even if she did manage to retrieve the keys, she didn't know how much longer she could remain conscious.

"Pa-tri-cia." The horrifying voice prompted her to dig deep for the will and energy she needed to continue her search.

Managing to locate the keychain again, she focused on placing the key in the starter. Despite her uncooperative fingers, she finally accomplished the task. She turned the key, and the radio blasted on. Reaching for the power button to shut the racket off, a flicker of movement drew her gaze to the stalker's silhouette through the front windshield. The fog had shifted, outlining his position.

Did he have the ability to part the fog at will?

Patricia screamed at the unearthly sight of the dark figure standing there. Her heart pounded so fiercely she thought it might explode or stop altogether. He seemed to be wearing a long coat, making her think of the blood bank thief, but she couldn't see any detail. Facing her, he stood motionless for several seconds before withdrawing into the fog. Her vision dimming, she dropped her head onto the steering wheel.

"Patricia. Hey, Patricia." A familiar voice drew her back to consciousness.

Looking out her driver's side window, she saw the shape of a woman approaching. She recognized Jessica—a surgical nurse who worked on the orthopedic floor.

"Is everything all right?" Jessica leaned down and

looked into the car, releasing a gasp when she saw Patricia covered in blood. "Oh God." She yanked the handle. "Unlock the door," she urged through the glass and ran to the opposite side while calling out for help.

Barely conscious, Patricia tried to unlock the door but pressed the window control instead, lowering the passenger's side window.

"Get in, J-Jessica, it's not, not s-safe," Patricia warned her friend. "He's in the f-fog." She motioned toward the front of the vehicle where her attacker had stood a mere moment earlier.

Jessica reached in to open the door. "Where's the lock, Patricia? We've got to get you to Emergency."

Patricia didn't respond, her vision fixed on an area about ten feet behind her friend. The fog was parting...a figure emerging. She opened her mouth in an attempt to warn Jessica that her attacker had reappeared, but the only word she could manage to muster from her paralyzed lips was "no—"

Seeing the terrified look on Patricia's face, Jessica slowly turned around to face whoever, or whatever, was there. The last thing Patricia remembered hearing before passing out was a snarling sound, like that of a vicious dog, and Jessica's bloodcurdling shriek of utter terror ripping through the air. The latter, a sound she would never forget.

* * * *

Sheriff Pierson received a call from the station informing him of another killing at Black River Falls Memorial Hospital. Hearing that Patricia Watson had been attacked, he couldn't get to the scene fast enough.

"What do you know?" he asked Rudy, who met him on arrival, the deputy wasting no time rambling off his report.

Approaching the body, he let out a long breath, relieved to see it wasn't Patricia, but another unfortunate woman who lay dead at the hands of the killer roaming his county.

"Do we know who she is?"

"She's been identified as Jessica Daniels, a nurse here at the hospital," Rudy informed him. "It's not certain what happened. We'll know more when the other victim, Patricia Watson, regains consciousness."

"About Ms. Watson, do you know any details about her condition?" Sheriff Pierson tried not to be too obvious about his concern for Patricia.

"She's alive, but sustained trauma to the head. That's really all I know."

"Who found them?"

"A doctor. Michael Simmons. He'd been called in on emergency and was pulling in to park when he spotted Jessica Daniels's body lying on the pavement. According to him, when he rushed over to assess the situation, he discovered Ms. Watson, unresponsive in her car. I'd say she's mighty lucky the doctor came along when he did."

"But not soon enough to save this poor woman," Pierson said with remorse.

The loss of life was tragic.

"Well, you know the drill, Rudy. Get Forensics out here, and when they're done, the body will go for autopsy just like the other two before her."

"Yes, sir." Rudy went straight to his duties.

With Rudy in control of things, Sheriff Pierson headed for the hospital entrance to inquire on Patricia's condition.

"She's still unconscious, but stable. She was just taken to radiology for testing," a nurse updated him. "We'll know more once we get those results."

"When will that be?"

"An hour, maybe two."

"Take good care of her."

"You can rest assured, she's in the best of hands. I'm worried too. I've known Patricia for years. If it weren't for her, I wouldn't have this job."

The moment the nurse walked away, a woman who'd been standing nearby approached him.

"Sheriff Pierson?"

"Yes," he responded.

"I couldn't help overhearing your conversation. My name is Ann Tinley. I'm Patricia's sister."

"Oh. Allen Pierson." He shook her hand. "Nice to meet you."

"You know, I've heard an awful lot about you from Patricia. It seems you've made quite an impression on her."

"Yes, well, the feeling's mutual," he replied, somewhat abashed, wondering what Patricia had said about him. "Do you think she's going to be okay? I don't suppose you know anything more about her condition?"

"I was told the same thing, that they're running tests."

"The waiting, it's always the hardest, isn't it?" He nervously wrung his fingers.

"She's a strong woman. We just have to believe she'll pull through. And a little prayer wouldn't hurt."

"I haven't been to church in years," Pierson said.

"God won't hold that against you." Ann smiled.

"I hope you're right. Well, I should get back to the crime scene. Would you mind keeping me informed?" He pulled out a business card and handed it to her, pointing out his cell number.

"The moment I hear something, you'll be the next to know," she assured him.

Sheriff Pierson thanked her and went back to the

murder site to see how the investigation was progressing. Looking down at the corpse lying on the cold, black pavement, drained of blood, he thanked God it wasn't Patricia. He'd never thought it was possible to fall in love at first sight, but he couldn't deny the bond already present. Smiling, he recalled their first meeting, knowing she'd hooked him from the start. He just hoped he wouldn't be left to live out the rest of his days wondering what might have been.

11

The Fortuneteller

Corin shut the lid on the toolbox in the back of Tomes's truck and climbed into the cab. "It's a good thing you had a fuel filter on hand."

"It started cutting out on me a week or so ago, but with everything that's happened, I never got a chance to change it." He pulled onto the road. "Ol' Bonny wasn't going any further tonight, though."

"Bonny, huh?"

"It means good-looking."

Corin laughed. "I'm not sure the name suits her, but at least she's running good now."

Several minutes later, Tomes turned into a wooded area Corin indicated and parked near a pasture line. They got out of the truck, and Tomes followed him over to a barbed wire fence, waiting while he slipped into the field and chose an animal to feed on. The beasts went so willingly to Corin, as if wanting to give themselves freely, to please him. Tomes knew the animal was being charmed, but that fact didn't make the event any less amazing to watch.

Trailing Corin's silhouette until he sank his fangs into the upper neck of the animal, Tomes diverted his eyes, finding it hard to watch the nightwalker's revolting act of feeding. The thought of drinking blood from another living creature—man or beast—nauseated him.

"What is this?" Tomes glanced past Corin, observing the same spooky fog that he'd witnessed earlier at the estate. It seemed to turn at will, possessing a supernatural nature. Creeping in and devouring entire areas, with no obvious rhyme or reason, it would suddenly withdraw and change course.

Tomes whistled to Corin, alerting him to the oncoming mass. He shivered as a chill traced his spine, afraid of what lurked within the confines of that haunting mist.

Corin closed the wound on the cow's neck and hurried back to where Tomes waited.

"This isn't good, is it?" Tomes watched the fog move closer with each passing second, as if it were in pursuit of them.

"I'm not sure what it means. It is odd."

"Creepy, I think is the right word. You can't tell me this isn't a bad omen."

"You may be right," Corin agreed.

Retreating to Tomes's truck, they pulled back onto the road, narrowly missing a small silver car as it flew around the curve and passed, nearly sideswiping them in the process.

"What the...." Tomes recognized Angelique's car.

Red taillights popped on as it slowed to a stop.

Tomes got out and stormed toward her driver's side door. "What in devil's hell, Angel. You can't be driving like that!"

Corin followed him over but kept his remarks to himself.

"I've been looking for you." She ignored her brother, fixing her attention on Corin.

"We're just checking out some areas for hunting," Tomes lied.

"According to my watch, Corin, it's long past nine thirty." She stood, holding open the car door. "I tried your cell phone, but I didn't get an answer."

"Crap. I must have left it back at the house."

"Isn't there something else you've forgotten?" She appeared annoyed by his loss of memory.

"Come on, Angel?" Tomes said. "If you have something to say, just say it."

By the fiery look in her eyes, he could see she was livid—a volcano on the verge of eruption.

"We had a date tonight, or so I thought." She gave Corin a "what happened?" look. "You were supposed to pick me up an hour ago."

"The fair!" Corin slapped his forehead.

"A date?" Tomes glared at Corin. "I thought we understood one another."

"Tomes, please." Angelique intervened before turning her focus back on Corin. "I take it you must have a good reason for not bothering to call?"

"Something came up, and it did slip my mind."

"Something came up," she repeated his words and looked at Tomes. "Well, since I was dressed, I decided to head on over." She started to get back into her car. "You two can just go on with whatever it is you're doing."

"Wait," Corin said. "I know you must hate me right now, but we can still make our date. I'd like nothing more than to spend the evening with you."

Tomes didn't know how much more he could stand

to hear. He was frustrated, but he contained his anger, not wanting to add to his sister's upset.

"I don't hate you, Corin." She looked at him. "I'm just disappointed."

"Then give me a chance to make it up to you."

The edge of her mouth curled. "You make it impossible for me to stay mad at you."

"We can go on from here. We'll just have to take your car, since I rode with Tomes."

"That's not a problem. I'll even let you drive." She stepped his way. "You'll just have to settle for sitting behind the wheel of a fifteen-thousand-dollar vehicle tonight instead of that expensive 'Vette of yours," she teased. "But I see that Tomes is already bringing you down to the lower levels of living, driving you around in that rust-bucket he dares call a truck."

"Don't be raggin' on my ride," Tomes threw back. "And Corin, you know how I feel about this. I don't want—" Tomes started to protest again, but Angelique quickly silenced him.

"I'm getting so tired of this childishness, Tomes. You have to stop trying to control my life."

"Angel, I'm only looking—" Tomes tried to defend his actions, but she didn't give him a chance, heading to the passenger's side of her car without another word.

Corin followed and opened the door for her to get in. He looked over the top of the vehicle at Tomes who returned his stare and pointed his index finger in an unmistakable warning.

"I'll catch you later," Corin responded and nodded.

Tomes hated the situation, but without telling her the whole truth, his hands were tied. He knew his sister was falling for Corin, and for her sake, he had to put a stop to their developing relationship before it was too late.

* * * *

Driving into Black River Falls, Angelique apologized once again for Tomes's bad behavior.

"I don't know what Tomes's problem is." She had no idea why he was so averse to Corin.

"He's just looking out for you."

"You're sticking up for him again? Look at the way he treats you. I can't believe you put up with it."

"I've told you before, we have an understanding."

"That's right...friends who are enemies. I guess I'll never understand you two and your dysfunctional friendship."

"You look nice tonight."

"Thanks," she replied, pleased with the compliment.

She was aware of his intent to sway the conversation to something other than Tomes, but she had put extra effort into looking good for him, and the fact that he'd noticed definitely scored him points.

Approaching the fairgrounds, the lights from the larger rides came into view. Pulling in, they parked and headed for a long admission line, not surprised to find the fair packed. The Jackson County Fair, after all, was one of the biggest highlights of the year.

Passing through the gate, the smell of funnel cakes and smoked pork wafted in the air, making Angelique's mouth water. Unable to resist the tempting aroma, she purchased a funnel cake and soda to enjoy while they strolled the grounds, sizing up the sights and rides. The place was perfect pandemonium. The racket pouring out from each attraction so loud Angelique thought she'd go deaf, but oddly, it didn't affect her interaction with Corin. When he spoke, his voice rang clear, while everything else faded into the background.

"You should help me eat this." Angelique offered him some of the funnel cake.

"No, thanks. I'm afraid I'd have trouble digesting it later. Sugary muck doesn't agree with me."

"Well, I love sugary muck." Angelique took no offense, noticing again how his voice magically floated above the blaring music and commotion. She compared it to walking in the eye of a storm—there was chaos all about them, but they strolled along in the calm center.

"What do you think of the Ferris wheel?"

"It's my favorite ride." She hoped he could hear her over the noise the way she was able to hear him.

"I'll get some tickets, and we'll ride."

Corin left her sitting on a bench behind the ticket booths to finish off her funnel cake. A minute later, Louis Gomez appeared in front of her.

"Mr. Gomez," Angelique acknowledged with surprise.

"How are you, Ms. Jaffler? I confess, I'm a bit embarrassed about missing our meeting this morning. You must convey my apologies to your brother. Something came up that prevented me from showing."

"No harm done." Angelique looked into his dark eyes, not entirely sure of his sincerity. She didn't mention how irritated Tomes had been, thinking he had purposely stood them up. "You have our number. Just give Tomes a call when you're ready to reschedule. He's flexible. Or, if you're out our way, you're welcome to stop by the farm. I can't guarantee you'll catch him home without a call, though. He comes and goes a lot."

"I have a rather unusual schedule myself," he replied. "So, are you here alone?"

"No, my date is getting tickets. He'll be back in a minute." She motioned toward the booth, bringing her hand back to her nose as a rancid smell floated her way.

Thinking that Louis Gomez might be giving off the odor and not wanting to offend him, she pretended to scratch an itch before lowering her hand. Her gaze then drifted past him to a trashcan sitting a few feet away. She supposed the smell could be emanating from there.

"Since you're in good hands, I'll be going. And I'll be sure to get in touch with your brother real soon," he told her. "Have a great evening."

Angelique observed his odd manner of walking as he left—practically slinking. Watching as he gradually blended in with the crowd around him and faded out of sight, she couldn't help thinking him a phantom...not a man at all.

* * * *

"Angelique." The sound of Corin's voice caused her to jump. "Is something wrong?"

"No. At least...I don't think so," she responded. "It's strange...I just saw a man I met last night—Louis Gomez. He had expressed an interest in hiring Tomes. He was just here. We talked while you were getting the tickets."

Corin turned and scoured the area for any sign of the brute. The fact that the nightwalker had dared to make contact with her yet again vexed him to no end. It was apparent that the immortal knew of his affection for Angelique, and that made the rival a real threat to her.

"Tomes told me about him. What did he want?" Corin took a seat next to her.

"He apologized for missing his appointment this morning. And I even hate to say this, because I know it's going to sound crazy, but I'd swear he just disappeared...literally."

"I imagine you lost sight of him in the crowd. There are a lot of people here tonight." Corin couldn't tell her she was right, that the nightwalker had probably dissipated into vapor. "Did he say anything else?"

"Only that he's still interested in hiring Tomes. I told him he could call to reschedule or just stop by the farm if he happened to be out our way."

"You gave him an open invitation?"

"I'm not interested in the man, Corin. I'm just trying to ensure some work for Tomes. "The farm hasn't been too productive as of late, and Tomes needs the job."

"I had no idea. If you need—"

"We'll get by. We always do."

"I just want you to be careful when it comes to dealing with this guy. I don't trust him."

"You sound like Tomes. I think you two have been spending way too much time together. Although, even I have to admit that there is something peculiar about him."

"I want you to promise that you'll call right away if he does happen to show up at the farm."

"I've already made that promise to Tomes. But should he come around, I'll call one of you. Odds are I'll probably reach you both with one call anyway. You're practically joined at the hip lately."

"He is working for me," Corin reminded her.

"Don't get me wrong, I'm glad he's doing something, keeping busy. It's good for him. And about Mr. Gomez, why don't we put him, and everything else, out of our minds and just have some fun. At least for tonight." She took Corin's hand and pulled him up. "The Ferris wheel awaits."

Getting in line, Corin kept an ever-watchful eye out for the nightwalker. He knew the fiend was there somewhere, watching their every move, no doubt following him since sundown. The clever creature spelt danger with a capital "D."

When they got on the ride and reached the top of the first turn, the immortal suddenly revealed himself in the crowd below, knowing Corin couldn't do anything while trapped in the air with Angelique. And just as he'd suspected, the newcomer was the foreigner he'd met at Micky Joe's Bar and Grill, only now he wore a long coat, showy, something Corin would have remembered.

You were playing me.

The immortal could have disguised himself, but he didn't. It was obvious he wanted Corin to know who he was, instigating another challenge.

Their eyes locked and time slowed to a crawl. A sneer contorted the nightwalker's face while people moved around him in rapid time.

"You're not scared of heights, are you?" Angelique asked.

"No, I'm fine." Corin pulled his eyes away from his adversary to respond. But when he looked back, his opponent had vanished.

Where are you?

Exiting the ride, Corin stayed mindful of their surroundings as they rejoined the crowd, spending the next two hours hopping from attraction to attraction. Claiming to have a worrisome knee, he avoided the funhouses and the many mirrors accompanying them, knowing that it might prove difficult to explain why he cast no reflection. Finally, with their tickets used up and satisfied that they'd seen everything, they headed for the exit. But just before reaching the gate, Angelique spotted a fortune-teller tent set back off the fairway, half-hidden in the background.

"Look." She pointed, insistent on having her fortune read.

Corin, not caring for psychics, tried to persuade her otherwise, but she was determined. He followed her inside. It was quiet with no other fairgoers present. The interior, though open, was muffled and dim. He rotated a shoulder, feeling oppressed, as if someone had suddenly strapped a weight to his back. His gaze, drawn to the back of the tent, settled on a woman sitting at a small, round table. Half-shadowed, she stared their way. Her hair, long and white, was not synonymous with her visible age of no more than forty.

"I am Madam Monicca," she announced. "I am a seer. You have come for a reading?"

The woman peered at Corin causing him to shift with unease. Her chilling eyes contained very little color, the lightest blue he'd ever seen. Her blank expression made him wonder if she saw beyond his façade—knew he wasn't mortal, but rather, the living dead.

* * * *

"I would like a reading." Angelique stepped toward the fortuneteller, pulling Corin along. "And my friend as well."

That must be a wig and contacts. Angelique couldn't pull her eyes off of the woman who appeared fixated on Corin. But when Madam Monicca's gaze suddenly shifted and met her stare, Angelique nearly jumped out of her skin.

"I will read only you. I have nothing for your friend." Madam Monicca offered no explanation.

"What?" Angelique started to protest, but Corin stopped her.

"It's okay. I have no interest in this nonsense. You go ahead, and I'll wait outside." He backed out of the tent, leaving Angelique alone with the fortuneteller.

Uncomfortable with the negative atmosphere, Angelique muttered that she'd changed her mind and started to follow Corin out, but Madam Monicca called to her, prompting her to turn back.

"Wait! I do have a reading for you."

"No thanks." Angelique waved. "I told you, I've changed my mind."

"There will be no charge." The woman stepped out from behind the table and moved toward her. "Listen to me, child, I see things you cannot." She now stood close enough to touch. "Let me see your hand."

Angelique, having had enough, wasn't cooperating, prompting Madam Monicca to reach down and forcibly seize her right hand regardless of her unwillingness.

"No charge," the fortuneteller said again. And turning Angelique's palm face-up, she traced the lines with her two middle fingers. "Yes. This is what I sensed. You are being drawn into a world of eternal darkness. I see you standing on the brink of a fall. Very soon you will be forced to choose between the day and the night."

"What?" Angelique wished she'd listened to Corin and bypassed the tent altogether. Attempting to pull her hand away, the woman tightened her grip.

"You may be fated, but a soul thrives within you, so hope remains. You walk with danger, but you will be given a choice. Just remember, my dear, that once lost, the light can never be rekindled. When the darkness has fully claimed you, it will be for all time. The day will become a thing of the past, and you will be left to walk forever in the night."

With that eerily spoken warning, Angelique jerked her hand away and rushed out of the tent. Spotting Corin leaning against a nearby fence, she hurried over to him and clutched his arm.

"You're upset. What happened?"

"I'm not sure what to make of it. I tried to leave right after you did, but the fortuneteller stopped me, saying she'd do my reading for free. The next thing I knew, she was standing right in front of me. She grabbed my hand and babbled absurd gibberish that gave me the creeps."

"She really unnerved you." Corin looked back at the tent seeing the fortuneteller standing in the entrance, staring their way.

"She said something about the darkness claiming me. Having to choose between the day and the night. It was disturbing."

Corin ushered her toward the gate. "I'm sure it's all just part of her act. Don't let this foolishness ruin your night."

"If that's her act, I'd recommend a new one, effective immediately. It's terrible to go in thinking you'll get a fun, entertaining reading, only to have something so disturbing thrown at you. I just hope it doesn't give me nightmares tonight."

Already a restless sleeper, that was the last thing she needed. Shuddering, she wasn't certain what Madam Monicca had intended, but after tonight, there would be no more fortunetellers in her future. That she was certain of.

* * * *

Back inside the tent, Madam Monicca took a seat at the table, grabbed her deck of cards, and did a reading while traces of the girl's essence were still fresh.

She laid several cards out on the table, drawing back at the horror they revealed. It was even worse than she'd feared. The girl was being overtaken by darkness, but in that world of eternal night lurked not only one monster, but two.

"God help this child."

With eyes fixed on the cards, she fell into a trance-like state, overcome by a vision if two beasts facing off in a great hall adorned with precious metals and fine jewels. One was light in color. The other dark.

The dark monster snarled and lashed out with large claws and sharp teeth dripping in blood, revealing him to be a savage killer. Sharing a connection with him, Madam Monicca could taste blood in her own mouth and feel his insatiable thirst for more.

Monstrous roars echoed as the two beasts turned on each other, engaging in a fierce battle. During this time, a young, dark-haired woman appeared in the hall, dressed in a pure white gown, a representation of innocence walking blindly into the midst of evil.

The monsters ceased fighting upon sight of her and backed away, allowing her free passage between them. Each beast crouched low to the ground in the manner of bowing to royalty. But then, with no rhyme or reason, their actions suddenly changed, and they turned into hunters stalking prey. Much like a naïve lamb wandering through the blood-strewn gate of a slaughterhouse, she was heedless of the danger. However, before either had a chance to lunge, an apparition of a large wolf appeared at her side, protecting her from attack.

"I am not afraid," the young woman told the apparition and placed her right hand on its back, fading away with the phantom.

The hall grew dark—a pit of doom. The monsters bellowed and resumed their fight, the clamor so intense that the structure fissured, raining down dust and stone in its collapse. Growing fainter and fainter, the scene then faded, and the vision ended.

Madam Monicca dropped her head on the table, physically and mentally drained by the episode. She hated the unsettling trepidation that always followed such prognostic visions, but it was a gift she'd been born with and not something she could switch off at will.

"Dear child, I must find you...warn you of the dark

one I've just foreseen."

The sound of a customer walking in prompted her to lift her head. Her pale-colored eyes grew wide, falling on the tall, dark form of a man coming toward her. Only this was no ordinary man.

"The dark monster," her words escaped on a choked breath.

"You see too much, witch."

Madam Monicca released one horrifying shriek before he reached her, then all grew silent. Dead silent.

12

The Staker

Gordy leaned on the service counter. "I'm sure this could come in handy." He handed Tomes a reengineered, battery-operated nail gun, along with wooden nails custom made from blackthorn. "Now, be serious, what in the world do you plan on doing with the thing?"

"Believe me, it's better you don't know."

"You're probably right, especially if it's something illegal. But, I'm paid, so it's all good. Be careful though, that thing has some force behind it. The way it fires them nails out, they'd cut right through someone."

"That's what I'm counting on." Tomes was even more pleased with the item after hearing it had the potential to be lethal. "How many nails will it hold at a time?"

"It'll hold eight."

"You do fine work, Gordy. Real fine work. When can

you have some more of these blackthorn nails ready for me?"

"You have fifty there."

"Well, I'm going to need another fifty," Tomes informed him.

"I'll see what I can do. I may have enough blackthorn left to do one more batch. Just keep in mind, this stuff isn't easy to come by, so you'd best not waste 'em."

"I hear you. And the second batch, you think you can have them ready by tomorrow?"

"Jeez, Tomes, nothing like laying the pressure on," Gordy griped. "But if it can't wait, I guess I can have Carl work on it. He's pretty good with the machine."

"Great." Tomes acted as if his demands were no bother at all. Of course, he and Gordy had been friends for a long time—since they were children.

"I've been meaning to tell you how sorry I am about missing Louisa's funeral. It couldn't be helped. Are you holding up okay?"

"The best any man could after such a blow. I have Angelique and the farm."

"Tell your sister hi for me."

"I'll do that." Tomes turned when the bell on the door alerted them of a customer. "I'll let you get back to work."

"Drop by tomorrow, sometime after two. The nails should be ready."

"Thanks for doing this, Gordy."

The man pretended to be shocked by his gratitude.

"Very funny." Tomes waved him off, heading out with his new weapon in hand.

Since he and Corin had made no headway in locating the nightwalker's lair, catching the immortal unaware in a daytime staking wasn't likely. But with armament, he now had the means to face the monster at night, and maybe even live through it to see another day. The nails wouldn't kill him, but Tomes was optimistic, anticipating the blackthorn would weaken him. He could then finish the newcomer off by the most error-proof means of death for a nightwalker—decapitation. So, with this devil it would be off with his head!

Following Louisa's murder, Tomes had grown obsessed with researching nightwalkers. He'd spent hours on end roaming the Internet, discovering all he could about the creatures. The information he'd dug up from the far reaches of the World Wide Web—and a few other unexpected places—he'd compiled in a green expandable folder. He kept it tucked away in the bottom drawer of his desk, pulling it out every available chance he had, in his preoccupation with the material. Educating himself—learning the nightwalkers strengths and weaknesses—would give him a greater chance of success when it came time to face the nightwalker.

Tomes had been lucky enough to make contact with a professor of mythology, Dr. Nathanial Roberts, one night while checking out a new chat room he'd come across. He was unquestionably a believer in vampires and all things paranormal. There was something in his manner of speech that had led Tomes to trust him. He seemed to possess first-hand knowledge of the creatures.

Discovering the professor lived less than three hours from Hixton, Tomes had set up a meeting, glad that the many hours he'd spent hunched behind his eye-boggling seventeen-inch screen had finally paid off. He needed guidance in the matter of facing his vampire foe, and Dr. Roberts was just the expert to give it.

Tomes's mental image of the man was spot on. Of latter years, with bushy white hair, a neatly trimmed beard, and black wire-framed glasses resting midpoint on a slender nose, the professor invited him to have a seat at a table in the dining room. The doctor passed along some very insightful information during their lengthy, in-depth conversation regarding walkers of the night. They'd put their heads together and voilà, a new weapon was born—a device Tomes decided to call the "staker." Luckily, Tomes had the means to make it happen—Gordy.

After leaving the shop, Tomes headed to von Vadim Estate to wait for Corin's return. He parked in the garage, at the back of the mansion, not wanting Angelique to know he was there when she dropped Corin off. With the way things were progressing, he wanted to keep her out of the loop, and hopefully, safe.

Having some time to spare and eager to test the staker's performance, he set up a target outside the lanai using an old sheet of plywood he'd found in the garage. He loaded the weapon with eight nails and fired them off, surprising himself by the accuracy of his aim.

"Wow." He whistled. Gordy was right—the gun had some force behind it, completely slicing through the quarter inch panel from twenty feet away.

He had just reloaded when the sound of a vehicle approaching captured his attention. Recognizing the distinct whine of the engine, he knew it was Angelique's car. And quickly slipping around the side of the house to spy, he watched, unseen, from the shadows.

"Next time we'll take my car." Corin opened the passenger door and escorted Angelique to the driver's side.

"Are you saying you don't care for my car, Corin von Vadim?" She slid behind the wheel.

"Not at all. But it's no Corvette."

"I'll give you that. Honestly, though, you forget our date...criticize my car. I'm almost afraid to ask what comes next. It leaves me wondering if there's anything you like about me at all."

"I like everything about you, Angelique." He bent down, giving her a tender kiss on the lips.

Angelique held onto him, prolonging the moment, running her fingers through his mass of blond hair.

At the side of the house, Tomes fumed. He raised the staker, boiling with anger and disgust, taking aim at Corin with an itchy finger twitching on the trigger. It was hard to find restraint, but he didn't shoot. He wanted to, but he needed Corin's help to find the nightwalker. Without him, he may never avenge Louisa's death. But he wouldn't sacrifice his sister to make that happen. He had warned Corin numerous times to stay away from her, and if he didn't back off, next time he might not have any qualms with using the staker on him. No qualms at all.

* * * *

Sheriff Pierson received a call from Ann Tinley. Patricia was awake and asking for him. Breathing a sigh of relief, he rushed to see her, finding her alert and comfortably settled in a room. When their eyes met, several seconds of poignant silence passed between them.

"I'll give the two of you some privacy," Ann excused herself and patted Sheriff Pierson on the shoulder as she left the room.

"How do you feel?" He took a seat next to her bed. "I see they have you all bandaged up."

"I guess I won't have to worry about my hair for a while."

"Are you sure you're up for talking right now?" She looked weak.

"I need to tell you what happened, Allen. I was so scared," she spoke through building tears. "I knew he was there to kill me. If Jessica hadn't shown up when she did, I'd probably be dead. I know I'd be dead." She broke down. "And Jessica.... That should have been me. I couldn't even help her. I was barely conscious."

"You can't blame yourself for what happened to her. You are both the victims of a sadistic killer."

"I just can't believe it happened...that she's dead."

"I hate to question you right now, but I need to know if you can give me a description. Did you get a good look at him?"

"I couldn't make out much, his features were blotted out, and there was a lot of fog. He appeared tall, thin, and it looked like he was wearing a long coat. It made me think of the man on the surveillance tape."

"You think it was the same person?"

"I can't be certain. I only saw his silhouette for a moment when the fog parted. He hid in the fog, calling out to me. He knew my name." Her heart rate spiked, and she pressed a hand to her chest. "The sounds...like an animal."

"Animal?"

"I heard what I thought were growls. And Jessica's scream. How can I ever get that out of my head?" She buried her face in her hands.

"That's enough for now." He knew how hard it must be to relive the horrifying incident.

Her mention of animal sounds piqued his interest, along with the fact that the killer knew her by name, giving him something more to contemplate.

"I promise you, Patricia, I'm going to get this guy." He took her trembling hand in his. He couldn't stand seeing this vital, confident woman, whom he'd come to admire and care for, reduced to such a weak and fragmented state. "I have to leave now, but I'll be back to see you soon."

Sheriff Pierson called Ann back in and returned to

the crime scene. Profanity rolled off his tongue when he saw onlookers and reporters buzzing the site. And to make matters worse, his least favorite person—Jordon Black—was right in the middle of everything, poking around vital homicide evidence.

"I hope you're not planning on stealing evidence from this murder site too, Marshal." Sheriff Pierson still believed he'd taken something from the first crime scene at Jaffler Farm regardless of his lack of proof.

"You insult my professionalism," Black countered. "Just like you, I work strictly by the book."

"By whose book?" Sheriff Pierson scoffed.

"The same book you use to regulate your county, Sheriff, the good book of laws and ethics?" Jordon tossed back.

"We do know how to follow proper protocol here, despite what you think of us, Black. And look at what you're doing, hindering our investigation by clomping all over the crime scene. Contaminating evidence. You need to move back behind the tape with the rest of the spectators," Pierson ordered. "See to it you stay out of the way of my team. And that's not a suggestion."

"How many times do I have to remind you, I am authorized to be here."

"This is my jurisdiction and I will handle things in whatever manner I see fit. And if you're still insistent on arguing, Marshal, I'd be more than happy to pass that information along to your superiors," he threatened.

"I'm not here to work against you, Sheriff." Jordon backed down. "I'll get out of the way and let your crew do their job."

Sheriff Pierson wasn't fooled by a word coming out of Marshal Black's mouth. In fact, he got the distinct impression his intent was to prevent him from calling the agency.

Could he have something to hide?

With that thought, Sheriff Pierson jotted down a reminder on his list of priorities, *check out Black's credentials.* Until he knew the marshal was on the up and up, he was cutting off his access to the cases.

Looking down at the body of Jessica Daniels, it was evident the killer was targeting women. A duplicate of the second killing, she had suffered a cruel death, the proof in the numerous bite marks covering her body. Sheriff Pierson recalled his conversation with the medical examiner that morning, regarding the previous victim's autopsy. In Dr. Berg's study of the bite marks on the body of Sandy Darnell, when comparing his tissue findings with Forensics' lab results, it was conclusive that canine saliva was present. However, in spite of the findings and the sudden increase in wolf activity, Sheriff Pierson found it hard to believe that the animals alone were responsible for her death. Besides, Patricia had encountered the killer, and her assailant was human. But she had heard growls.

He speculated that canines may have perhaps been employed as trained killers or used as a cover for the true cause of death—the chronic loss of blood. At any rate, with the animals linked to the killings, questions were bound to arise about the possibility of a wild pack of wolves endangering the county. So, just to cover all bases, he proceeded to alert the department of a potential threat.

Stepping around the body, he flipped through his notepad. Inconsistencies between the first and latter two victims irked him. Each drained of blood, showing a definite connection, yet Louisa hadn't sustained any bite marks whatsoever, only two small punctures found on her neck. All three women were attractive, of similar build, and in their prime of life. So, what was he missing?

"The blood irregularity," he remembered, wondering if that could have had something to do with it.

Sheriff Pierson sighed. He had too many questions and no answers. The thought of facing family members empty handed twisted his guts. These victims were much more than just case files. They were mothers, sisters, wives—women who didn't deserve having their lives snatched from them by some nefarious killer. He could only hope something would point him in the right direction, because, if nothing else, the families were due justice.

Pierson knew Dr. Berg would be exasperated to find another body on the way, but it couldn't be helped. Even though the doctor was exhausted, he refused to pass any work to a colleague. Seeming haunted, he'd labored 24/7 since receiving the corpse of the second victim, Sandy Darnell, for autopsy.

His odd behavior left the sheriff to speculate the gossip floating around to be true—that he and the deceased had been involved—lovers. Both married, this information was, of course, of a sensitive nature. Knowing the situation now, Pierson could only imagine how hard it must have been for him to perform the postmortem examination.

Patricia came to mind; he'd come close to losing her at the hands of this murdering psychopath. He wanted nothing more than to make the killer pay for all the suffering he'd caused these poor women, and the people who loved them, and not necessarily in the legal way. He might have been sheriff of Jackson County, but he felt more than capable of turning rogue cop and throwing that book of "laws and ethics" right out the window.

"Sheriff, we've found something." Rudy held up a gold pocket watch with a latex-gloved hand.

Sheriff Pierson slipped on a pair of gloves and

examined it closer.

"There's an inscription on the back."

Sheriff Pierson read it aloud, "For my prince of the night. Miralanya."

"The chain's broken," Rudy pointed out. "I think the victim might have grabbed it during their struggle, ripping it off her attacker."

"I'd say that's a strong possibility," Pierson agreed. "Where did you find this?"

"Under the victim's car." Rudy showed him the exact spot.

"Do you know anyone locally named Miralanya?"

"No, I don't. It's not a very common name, is it?"

Sheriff Pierson shook his head. "No. It isn't."

"I could run a search and see what pops up."

"That's a good idea." Pierson passed the watch off to another officer with orders to bag and tag it. "And Rudy, let me know right away if you come up with anything."

Repossessing the evidence, disregarding procedure and his own better judgment, the sheriff started to slip the watch in his pocket but halted his action when he caught sight of the marshal watching like a hungry hawk.

Mumbling an obscenity, he reconsidered the undertaking, knowing evidence wasn't supposed to leave the crime scene due to the possibility of tampering. It had to follow proper channels to guarantee holding up in court. But being the sheriff, there had to be a clause written somewhere in that doggone book of laws, excluding him from having to abide by the same rules.

"Holding the title of Sheriff ought to count for something." He shoved the bagged evidence in his pocket. "I'll deal with you tomorrow, Black. We'll see then, if you are who you claim to be."

Contacting the agency and confirming the marshal's credentials was definitely going to be his next order of business.

13

The Cemetery

Tomes confronted Corin, gripping the staker so tightly his knuckles turned white.

"I thought we were clear about Angel."

"I won't hurt her."

"You know there's nothing you can offer her. She has no idea what you are. It isn't right, or fair to her."

"I know that, Tomes. And regardless of what you think of me, you can trust me when I tell you her well-being will always come before my own."

"That doesn't sound like you intend to keep away from her."

Corin moved past Tomes, taking a seat in a high-backed, burgundy-colored chair. "We have more pressing matters to focus on at the moment."

"We're not finished with this. You know I want the nightwalker, justice for Louisa, but I will also do whatever it takes to protect Angel."

Glaring into Corin's dark, wide-open stare, he searched for a soul apparently lost to the immortal.

"As will I. And right now, the newcomer is her biggest threat. Tonight, when I left her alone tonight to buy tickets, he made contact with her again."

Tomes lowered the staker.

"He knows we're after him."

"Yes," Corin agreed. "You've cut your face...must have caught a thorn on the bougainvillea while spying from the side of the house."

Tomes scanned the room for a mirror to examine his injury. "That darn bush ought to be cut down." He wiped blood from his right cheek with the sleeve of his left arm. "I forgot; you have no use for mirrors."

"The soul reflects who we are, and since I have no soul, I cast no reflection," Corin explained. "So, no, I have no need for mirrors. But I do keep one in the guest bath for the sake of visitors. You know where it is, just down the corridor, second door on the right. Any others would be in storage on the third floor. Out of sight is out of mind."

"It bothers you to look at them?" Tomes asked with interest.

"It's only a reminder of what I've lost."

"I see your point." Tomes picked up a picture frame, holding it in a way that showed the reflection of the room behind him. He saw the chair where Corin was sitting, but not Corin.

"It's true." Tomes whirled to face him. "How do you keep people from noticing?"

"I'm careful when I'm out in public. Over the years, I've developed a talent for hiding certain things." Corin swung his right foot onto his left knee. "What is that weapon you have?"

"This little baby is what I call a staker," Tomes said with pride. "I had it specially made. It's a nail gun converted to shoot these wooden nails, or small stakes, ergo the name." Tomes held one up. "They're made from blackthorn."

"Cleverly thought out. You've done your homework. But I hope you weren't planning on using it on me just now."

"I confess, I thought about it...pissed as I was."

"Well, I'm glad you didn't. Blackthorn would no doubt give a good sting."

"Oh, I'm pretty sure it would have given you a little more than a sting. This thing packs a punch. Would you care for a demonstration?"

"Not if I'm to be the target."

"I have a board set up out back." Tomes led the way to the back yard where he took position, aimed, and fired a shot into the panel.

"I think you really have something with this, what did you call it, a staker?"

"That's right." Tomes could see that Corin was impressed.

"It might just come in handy."

"My thoughts precisely." Tomes fired off a second shot.

"I was thinking we should take a look around the cemetery again. When you found me there four nights ago, I had no idea what we were dealing with.

Discovering that I can't sense the newcomer, he may very well be taking shelter there during the day. It's more likely he'd choose an abandoned building, but it's worth checking."

"No better time than the present. We'll take my truck. I parked in the garage."

"Taking over the garage now? You're getting rather comfortable in my home." Corin followed him out.

"I didn't want Angel to know I was here," Tomes explained.

Corin climbed into the passenger's seat of the oversized vehicle in desperate need of a paint job. A sharpened machete lay on the floorboard.

"Like it?" Tomes observed him eyeballing the weapon. "I'm sure you have a good idea what it's for."

"Yes. I think I do."

"If I take the nightwalker's head, I've taken his life."

"That's one way to go about it. Sever an immortal's head from his body, and he won't be coming back to the world of the living."

Tomes reached for the machete. "Which is exactly why I'm keeping this close." He secured the weapon between them and backed out.

"You're turning into a dangerous one, a real commando."

"A hunter on a mission." Tomes flipped on the radio, catching the latest report on the hospital murder.

"A third killing now. We've got to catch a break at some point."

"Maybe we're on the right track tonight," Tomes replied. "The cemetery is a perfect hideout."

When they reached their destination, Tomes parked just outside the gate and pulled a flashlight from the toolbox in the back of the truck. The moon was full, hanging low in the sky, but Tomes felt he needed some additional light.

"Take this." Armed with the staker, he passed the machete to Corin.

"I have to carry this?"

"I need the flashlight. Just bring it." Tomes was going in prepared for a fight. "What are we looking for?" he spoke in a whisper as they entered the cemetery, looking over the scattered gravesites.

"There's an above ground family vault, dating back many generations—the Chesterson crypt—he might be utilizing. We should check there first. There are also several partially-raised vaults that would meet his needs.”

“You’re familiar with the place, so lead the way.” Tomes motioned.

The headstones appeared florescent in the night, in combination with shadowed bases, casting the illusion of floating inches above the ground.

“It’s creepy out here.” Tomes stayed close to Corin with his finger twitching on the trigger of the staker.

“You’re not going to get spooked and accidentally shoot me in the back with that contraption, are you? Maybe I should walk behind you.”

“If I shoot you, Corin, believe me, it won’t be an accident.”

“That certainly evokes confidence.”

“I aim...to please.” Tomes snickered at his own lame joke.

“This is it.” Corin approached a large crypt with “CHESTERSON” etched across the top of the stone door. “I’ll take a look inside.” He shoved the blade of the machete into the earth, dematerialized into mist, and disappeared beyond the door. Returning a moment later, he materialized where he’d previously stood. “It’s uninhabited—by anyone living, anyway.”

Disappointed, Tomes cursed.

Corin raised a hand. “Wait.” He turned and scanned their surroundings.

“What’s wrong?”

“I’m not sure. I don’t sense anyone, but I feel as though we’re being watched.”

“Could it be the nightwalker?”

“I don’t know. It could be nothing more than an animal eyeing us from a distance beyond my range of detection, but stay alert, just in case.”

Corin grabbed the machete and moved on to the partially raised vaults. He pushed back each slab, peering down into the black caverns, finding them all undisturbed.

"Another dead end." Tomes frowned. "Despite the cliché—you know, vampires and coffins—looking here made perfect sense. I just wish it had panned out."

"Don't get discouraged. We'll just have to keep looking. He can't hide forever."

"I can't rest till we get him."

"We both have scores to settle."

Heading toward the gate, Tomes stopped and faced the newer section of the cemetery.

"What is it?" Corin turned back.

"I want to see Louisa's grave while we're here."

"I understand." Corin shifted direction, guiding them through the maze of headstones and slabs.

"No." Tomes rushed toward the gravesite, discovering that someone, or something, had unearthed her grave. "What's happened!" He peered into the dark cavity, shining the flashlight beam onto the casket. "The latch and seal's been broken." He slid into the hole and raised the lid. "This can't be." Louisa's body was gone! "What the devil is happening?"

"I never thought he'd go so far."

"What do you mean?" Discombobulated, Tomes's voice was loud with outrage. "You can't mean the nightwalker."

"I'm afraid so."

"What has he done? What has that mongrel done with her?" Tomes exploded, unable to control the rage boiling within him.

"I'm so sorry, Tomes, but it looks like he's brought her back."

"Brought her back?"

"Yes, from the dead. Turned her...immortal," Corin clarified.

"No. This cannot be happening!" Tomes collapsed

against the wall of earth, knocking dirt onto his head and shoulders. He didn't know how much more torment he could stand.

"God help her," Corin spoke under his breath. "Nightwalker, what have you done?"

* * * *

It had been a busy night for Boldor, committing two murders, the first for food, and the second a necessity to guard his secret. He'd shared the fortuneteller's vision and had no other option but to dispose of her before she had a chance to become an obstacle in his plan. Her gift was her downfall. She'd seen too much.

His plot was coming together nicely, but he thought it wise to enlist a little aid. He needed someone to serve his needs when the sun was up, prompting him to drop in on the funeral director, Jerry Fulner. The man was lowlife, but his lack of morals and his greed made him the perfect choice.

Working late in a back room of his small funeral home, Fulner, a man in his fifties, pudgy and balding, was embalming a corpse. It had arrived only hours before—a poor bloke in his forties, struck down in his prime by a massive heart attack. The director hovered over the naked body lying on the slab.

"Director." Boldor caught him unaware, speaking out from the shadows.

"Boldor, I thought our business was complete." Fulner's voice quivered. "I didn't embalm the girl, just as you'd instructed."

"I'm well aware of that." Boldor stepped out of the shadows and snaked across the room, his eyes glancing over the corpse.

"Rather disgusting job." He ran a finger along the embalming tube.

"Someone has to do it. It might as well be me."

"True. Are we alone?" He knew the director employed two men, one tended the gravesites, and the other performed the cosmetology work, since beautifying the dead wasn't one of Fulner's strong suits.

"I work alone at night. I prefer to take care of cremations and embalming after hours."

"I'm sure you're wondering why I'm here. I want to propose another deal...a more permanent arrangement this time."

"What sort of deal?"

Fulner appeared afraid, but Boldor suspected his greed would overpower his fear.

"You know what I am, Director. And with circumstances what they are, I may require assistance during the daylight hours. I need to have someone at my disposal." Boldor trailed his long index nail across the corpse's chest leaving a cut behind. He looked into the director's face with a cold, piercing stare. "You will be paid quite generously for your services."

"So, I take it you're planning on sticking around?"

"I believe I will."

"And if I refuse?"

"Bravery's a real achievement for you, Director, but I'd suggest you think twice before refusing me," Boldor warned in a low, chilling voice.

"Hold on. I didn't say I was refusing," Fulner quickly clarified. "What kind of payment are we talking about?"

"A thousand per week for now...more later. And I'll need you to continue here as undertaker, even though I'm sure you'd jump at a chance to rid yourself of this miserable profession." Boldor stroked a button on his coat as he talked, waking the trapped insect sleeping within. "In addition, it's imperative you maintain control of the local cemetery."

"I enjoy running my business. I'm proprietor,

mortician, and director of my own parlor. I wouldn't want to give it up."

"That's why you'll make the perfect collaborator. You're accustomed to dealing with the dead...even take pleasure in it. And you've proven you don't mind getting your hands dirty."

"How does the cemetery fit into your plans?"

"Let me just say, you never know what might arise."

Fulner swallowed hard. "You don't mean more vampires?"

* * * *

At the cemetery, Corin grabbed Tomes's hand and pulled him out of the grave.

"What has he done to her?" Tomes squeezed his head in an attempt to control the building pressure.

"He's turned her, Tomes, but the chance of her transformation being a successful one is slim. Such foolhardy and risky attempts rarely are... something any sound-minded nightwalker would know."

"What do you mean?" Tomes didn't want anything held back, no matter how hard it might be to hear.

"You have to understand, because of the autopsy, her body would have had to undergo extensive repair. The more injury there is to heal during transformation, the longer it takes, resulting in less mentality of the former self remaining when the change is complete. The infected body draws energy from the mind as it is turned," Corin explained.

"You're saying she won't know who she was?"

"Not only that, but she might very well be mad. There's a fine line between the monster we subdue within us and the human part remaining of the person we were in life. And in Louisa's case, I'm afraid she may turn out to be more monster than human. I've seen it happen before."

"Did you have any idea he might do this?"

"I had a suspicion," Corin confessed. "Louisa wasn't attacked in the same brutal fashion as the second victim, and now the third. I can only assume he wanted to preserve her beauty, not considering that an autopsy would be performed."

Tomes release his anger on a tree standing near the open grave, stomping in rage, kicking at the mound of dirt, his storm of emotion raining a shower of rock and sand into the cavity. "I don't know how much more I can take. Why didn't you warn me? We could have stopped this from happening."

"What would you have done? Staked her in her grave?"

"To save her from this hell...yes!"

"Maybe you're right. But I never dreamt he'd still attempt a transformation knowing she'd undergone that autopsy. He was crazy to think the change could be successful, knowing the strain even a healthy body must endure. Sometimes it's just too late, too much damage. He's taken a great gamble on what he'll end up with, not to mention the agony he's put Louisa through."

"I can't stand this." Tomes pressed his face into his hands. "He has to die. I have to kill him."

"I'm sorry if that sounded insensitive. I don't mean to be so blunt about all of this, but you must prepare yourself."

"No, it's okay. I want to know the truth, no matter what."

"When the sheriff came by the estate, he asked me if she had been ill. He said there were some irregularities in her blood work."

"It was the virus. And that's what they'll eventually surmise it to be—an unidentified virus. It's our curse...what changes us."

"Why didn't the doctor who performed the autopsy know she was still alive?"

"She wasn't. The attacking virus carried her beyond the brink of death. She died before being reanimated as an immortal—the living dead," Corin explained. "With all the risk, I still can't believe he did it. I've never encountered another quite like him. He's a real devil."

"And now he has Louisa." Tomes choked back emotion. "At the funeral, she looked so peaceful...beautiful. Angel and I were amazed by her appearance."

"You saw her?"

"I had the funeral director open the casket. I wanted one last look before she was gone forever."

"And he opened it? Going through transformation, when the top was raised and her flesh was exposed to the sunlight, it should have burnt her."

"Besides having the shade from the tree, we were under a partially enclosed tent. But before opening the casket, the funeral director lowered a third flap. It was dim. There was no direct sunlight. Thinking back now, he acted so strange...reluctant." Tomes was struck with a sudden realization. "He knew, didn't he?"

"It certainly seems so. The funeral director must be working for the newcomer. That explains why Louisa was never embalmed, and therefore, able to be changed."

"What do you mean she wasn't embalmed?" The thought had never crossed Tomes's mind.

"Her transformation would never have been possible if she had been."

"I should have known something wasn't right. Her scar lines were barely visible. She should have been all marked up from the autopsy. I just didn't want to see it."

"You can't blame yourself, Tomes. You couldn't have known."

"She was like an angel lying so peaceful in that casket," Tomes remembered. "Isn't there a chance she might be okay?" He wanted to believe Louisa would once again be the woman he'd known and loved.

"There's always a chance. And by what you've said about her appearance, her body seemed to have been doing a good job of regenerating itself. But as for her mind, well, that will be the determining factor, something we won't know until we find her."

"When do you think he took her from her grave?"

"Very recent. It looks like he just called her forth and claimed her tonight."

"What do you mean 'claimed her'?" Tomes didn't care for the way Corin had linked those words together.

"They are now joined. By blood. She's now part of him."

"Are you saying that if by some miracle she survived her transformation, she'll still never come back to me?"

"We all have our own will, influenced by both our past and present identities, but our ties with our creators are strong. Only death will ever completely sever it. There is no escaping the bond, but distance helps, and with time the pull does lessen. However, the fact that he has made her immortal, tying her to him, is something we can never change."

"He had designs on her from the very beginning...wanting her as a companion?" Tomes hated the thought of Louisa being trapped by the nightwalker.

Corin diverted his eyes, the silence telling Tomes all he needed to know. The horror his life had turned into was unfathomable. How would he ever survive this, knowing his wife had been brought back to life only to be joined with someone other than himself? Regardless of the circumstances, mortal or immortal, he couldn't accept it. And looking down on the empty casket, he vowed to do whatever it took to save her from that vile nightwalker, even if it meant ending both their lives.

14

A Surprise Visit

Sheriff Pierson stepped into Patricia's room. "I hope you don't mind me stopping by so late."

"No, I'm glad you're here." Her voice was drowsy.

"How are you feeling?" He took a seat next to her bed.

"The pain medication is doing an admirable job, but it leaves me fuzzyheaded. Tell me about the investigation. How's it going?"

"Forensics is still gathering evidence. It's not a speedy process."

"You look tired. You could use some rest."

"Oh, don't you worry about me. I'm just fine," he assured her.

Patricia pushed herself up into a more comfortable position. "I wish I were home in my own bed."

"You'll be heading home before you know it." Pierson repositioned her pillows. "I've been meaning to ask, how would you feel about joining me one night for dinner and a movie, when you get back on your feet? It's been years since I've been to a movie. We're not too old for that, are we?"

"Absolutely not. It sounds wonderful. That gives me a goal to work toward."

"It's a plan then." Pierson sat down.

"Dr. Krieger, my neurologist, wants to monitor me over the next forty-eight hours, but I'm hoping he'll let me go tomorrow. It's just standard procedure after this type of head trauma. He'll be around again in the morning, and I'm sure I'll get a favorable prognosis."

"Are you getting everything you need?"

"I'm being well cared for. Ann's here. And being the hospital administrator, the staff's been showering me with plenty of special treatment."

"That's good to know."

"Allen, about my attacker, the more I think about it, the more certain I am of it being the blood thief from the surveillance tape."

"His features weren't detectible," Pierson reminded her.

"It was the outline of a long coat. Something tells me it was him. Maybe we could take another look at the tape."

"I'll get it, but I'm afraid the police lab wasn't able to clean it up much. They proposed the subject to be a thin-framed male, standing at an approximate height of five feet ten, having dark-brown or black shoulder-length hair—an obvious deduction. And the pendant, they ascertained it to be a large, dark-colored gemstone, confirming what we'd already concluded ourselves."

"If that's the best clean up job those tech experts can manage, maybe they ought to be cleaning with brooms instead."

Pierson laughed. "You might be right."

"I can't stop thinking about it. What could he want all of that blood for?"

"God only knows. It's like the 'Twilight Zone' has settled over the county." Sheriff Pierson remembered the evidence he'd brought with him and pulled it out. "Before I forget, I want to show this to you. We found it at the crime scene. Have you seen it before?" He held the bag containing the watch in front of her.

"No. I haven't. Do you think it's his?"

"It's very likely." Pierson turned the piece over and showed her the back.

"There's an inscription, *For my prince of the night. Miralanya.*"

"Romantic. And a lovely name—Miralanya."

"But not very common."

"True. I can't say I've ever heard it before. It's unique."

"I have Rudy checking for any county matches. He's pretty topnotch when it comes to all that hi tech know how. Hopefully, he'll come up with something. There's a lot riding on this find. We need a solid lead. The people are counting on me for answers—good ol' Sheriff Pierson."

"Just be careful out there. The man who attacked me and killed Jessica, he was sinister. Pure evil."

"Making it a dire situation. The devil walks among us. No one will be safe until he's caught."

* * * *

Corin and Tomes slipped, unseen, to the back door of the funeral home. Peeking through a small glass insert centered in the upper portion of the door, Tomes could see the director in the room.

"He's working on a body." He reached for the

173

doorknob and slowly turned it. "It's unlocked."

"Good. Let's pay him a visit."

Tomes nodded, counted to three, and threw the door open. Both men barreled into the room, sending Fulner stumbling back from the slab, grabbing his chest as if they'd nearly given him a heart attack.

"Surprise, surprise." Tomes sang.

Corin took a stance behind him.

"Mr. Fulner, isn't it?" Tomes could tell the undertaker was trying not to show fear, but sadly failing in his attempt.

"That's right, Mr. Jaffler. Jerry Rinnert Fulner. Are you here about the funeral? I thought you were satisfied with our services."

Tomes's eyes narrowed. "Services never performed; I believe that is more accurate."

"I'm sure you know why we're here, Mr. Fulner." Corin stepped forward, staring him down. "Do you know who I am?"

"No. I d-don't b-believe so, sir," Fulner stuttered and grasped the edge of the slab for support.

"I am one of them."

"Corin—" Tomes interceded, afraid Corin was going to reveal his secret.

Corin held up his hand, halting Tomes. "It's okay. Mr. Fulner has a right to know with whom he's dealing."

"And who am I dealing with?" Fulner asked.

Instead of giving a verbal answer, Corin shapeshifted into a large, white wolf. He snarled at the man, his canine face and neck enhanced with a hint of brown detail.

"I believe you've made your point." Tomes watched wide-eyed as Corin took back his human form. Amazed by the metamorphosis, he wondered why immortals were granted these magnificent capabilities.

"That should answer your question." Corin told Fulner. "Now, from her on out, I'll be doing the questioning. Do we understand each other?"

Fulner nodded, clearly terrified.

"The other nightwalker, are you working for him?" Corin moved around the slab, where Fulner stood.

"I don't know what you're talking about." Fulner backed away.

"You're not a very convincing liar. I'd hate for this to get ugly."

"I'm not lying. I swear it," Fulner declared.

Corin allowed his fangs and nails to lengthen. "What do you think, Tomes?"

"He's lying."

Corin grabbed Fulner by his throat and lifted him a good foot off the ground. Suspended like a puppet, his feet dangled beneath him. Maintaining a firm grip with his right hand, Corin's extended talons punctured Fulner's flesh just below his jaw line.

"Please." The director whimpered, blood trickling down the side of his neck from the wounds.

"Corin—" Tomes started to protest his actions, thinking he might actually kill the man, but Corin turned his head in a way that concealed his face from Fulner and winked.

Relieved that Corin had no intention of harming Fulner, not fatally anyway, Tomes played along with his scare tactics.

"Maybe I'll just have a little drink." Corin caught some of Fulner's blood on two talons of his free hand and held it out for him to see before placing it in his mouth. He glared icily. "Or maybe I should just finish you off and be done with it."

Tomes couldn't help being taken aback by Corin's bestial appearance. Even though it was all an act, the image he portrayed was real—a bloodthirsty creature no man in his right mind would ever dare stand against. Act or not, it sent a chill racing up his spine.

"Please, wait!" Fulner pleaded, beads of sweat forming along his brow and running down the arch of his nose. "You don't understand. He'll kill me!"

"Or I can do that right now." Corin, baring his fangs, emitted a low-pitched growl and drew the sniveling man closer.

"Okay, okay. I'll tell you what I know."

Corin relaxed his hold on the man's throat and lowered him to his feet. Grabbing a fistful of his shirt, he held him in place.

"He calls himself Boldor." He coughed several times before blabbing out information like a tattling child. "He paid me to skip the embalming on Mr. Jaffler's wife. I couldn't say no to him. He isn't the sort to take no for an answer."

"I suppose he's paying you well," Corin said.

"For the trouble, I've made out pretty good," the louse admitted.

"You son of a—" Tomes flew at Fulner in a flash of rage, but Corin held him at bay with his free hand.

Tomes fought against Corin's block. "This worm doesn't deserve to live."

"Taking his life won't solve our problems, pleasurable as it might be," Corin reasoned.

"If he'd done his job, embalmed Louisa, she'd be resting in peace right now instead of suffering at the hands of that monster."

"He is scum—the worst excuse for a man—but he's not the one we're after. And because of him, we now know the nightwalker's name—Boldor."

Tomes reluctantly backed off, endeavoring to control his anger. Oh, he still wanted to rip Fulner's head off, but he knew Corin was right, and this despicable man's only crime was being an immoral git.

He'd never been a violent person, but the unfortunate circumstances life had thrown at him had turned him into someone unrecognizable—a different sort of monster—the human-out-for-vengeance kind. Yet, despite the dark changes in him, there was still one thing separating him from the real monsters roaming the earth—his blasted conscience. Still, there was a big difference between taking the life of a bloodthirsty nightwalker and taking the life of a human, and he knew when the time came, he'd have no problem severing the fiend's head.

"Where is he taking refuge?" Corin demanded.

"I don't know," Fulner sniveled. "He didn't tell me."

Corin twisted the undertaker's shirt, pulling it up to his throat. "You expect me to believe that?"

"It's the truth. I swear it is. He said he'd contact me when my services were needed."

Corin stared into Fulner's face, obviously trying to decide whether or not to believe him.

The director whimpered. "If I knew, I'd tell you. I swear I would."

"For your sake, I hope you're telling the truth. I do not react well to liars." Corin relinquished his hold and stepped back. "I'd hate to have to come back and let eager Tomes, here, finish you off."

"It's all I know," Fulner insisted, rubbing his stinging neck, smearing blood that trickled from the puncture wounds.

"Let's go." Corin aimed for the door.

Tomes followed, but not quite finished with the man, he turned back before exiting. "Something tells me I'll be seeing you again real soon."

"Not if I can help it," Fulner responded.

"You helped that monster turn my wife into God knows what, and I won't forget the part you've played."

15

Tape Number Two

Louisa, her mind left maddened by the transformation, was wild as a rabid animal. Boldor eased toward her, cautious with his movements, knowing she was capable of inflicting damage.

Unlike her demented mind, her body had regenerated itself to a pleasing degree. It wasn't flawless, but considering the extent of damage present prior to her change, it was a miraculous transformation. Any visible evidence of the autopsy she'd undergone was nearly undetectable, leaving her with only very faint scarring.

"I think I'll call you my little firecat—red flaming hair, and eyes green as a wild feral." Boldor reached out to stroke her soft strands, fully expecting counteraction.

Her wavy locks, falling in mad disarray about her creamy, porcelain face, in combination with her cat-colored eyes presented a striking vision.

Responding defensively, just as he'd suspected, she laid a fast and fierce bite to the top of his hand. He snatched it back with a growl and ran his tongue over the wound before sealing it with a pass of his fingers. This was a power of the nightwalkers—the ability to instantly heal small wounds—regenerate the flesh. However, if the injuries were substantial, healing would require placing themselves in a deep sleep while the body repaired itself. Very little could permanently afflict them, making the immortals practically indestructible.

"It looks like I'll have to do some taming." Boldor gave a displeased gnarl. "But in time, you will come to trust me."

Louisa snarled back and flew at him in a starved attack.

Boldor, ready for her charge, spun her around and pinned her arms behind her back. "Lesson one, don't bite the hand that feeds you." He shoved her to the ground, demonstrating his dominance.

Louisa whirled back and hissed.

"You're starving, I know." Boldor remained calm.

The rodents he'd supplied her thus far just weren't enough to satisfy her ravenous appetite. He had to get her some human blood, and once fed, he hoped she might settle down enough for him to work with her, make a little progress in gaining her trust.

When he'd called her from the grave and realized her demented state, he'd placed her in a trance, releasing her from his control only when they reached his hideout. Knowing he couldn't watch her every minute, he'd installed a lock on the outside of the basement door, allowing him to leave her alone with confidence.

Although she showed no hint of civilized demeanor

whatsoever, Boldor refused to see her as a failure. He believed that with his guidance, she would calm down, and in time, learn to cope on her own. Regardless of her damaged mind, she was his masterpiece—his Goya—a woman well worth the trouble for the enjoyment she brought him.

"I won't be long." Boldor secured the door, taking a direct route to the hospital for a quick withdrawal.

Hospital blood banks were the perfect solution when in need of a quick feed. In Louisa's unmanageable state, he couldn't take her out to feed without placing her in another trance, which would be too draining for him. Besides, he had to lay off hunting for a while. The bodies piling up were drawing too much attention to von Vadim, all due to his clumsiness.

He reprimanded himself for losing the gold watch he'd taken from the estate while feeding on his kill in the hospital parking lot, something that wouldn't have happened had he satisfied himself with several bags from the blood bank, or as his opponent did, fed on cows. But when he'd spotted such easy prey, the meal had been too tempting to pass up. But from this point on, he was determined to be more careful, because too much attention on von Vadim would soon mean too much attention on him when he stepped into von Vadim's shoes.

* * * *

Noticing the desk calendar was a day behind, Sheriff Pierson turned it to July twenty-fifth. The night before had been utterly exhausting. Not only did he oversee the crime scene investigation at the hospital, but he'd also been called to another murder that occurred at the Jackson County Fair, bringing the total number of killings in his county to four.

180

The latter victim was a fortuneteller, discovered murdered in her tent, the same MO—chronic loss of blood. Two murders in one night was almost too much to fathom. It left him wondering if the killing was ever going to stop.

Pierson yawned, impatiently tapping his pen as he waited for a return call from the U.S. Marshals Service. Even with everything weighing on his mind, the matter of checking Jordon Black's legitimacy hadn't escaped him. In fact, it ate at him, stirring his insides. Scanning over the files, thirty minutes later, the call finally came.

"Sheriff Pierson, hello, my name is Wayne Purrant. I'm Head of Administration for the District of Arizona. I've been informed you wish to check Marshal Black's credentials. I hope he's not giving you too much trouble. He can be a bit unconventional."

"So, he is a legitimate marshal, then?" Pierson hated hearing the affirmation.

"Yes, he's legitimate all right. He's part of a special department that deals with major criminal cases...selective. They work closely with the FBI, hunting down the most dangerous offenders," Mr. Purrant informed him. "I assume you're calling with a complaint?"

"Funny you should say that. Marshal Black and I have definitely rubbed each other the wrong way."

"I suspected as much. He's the best at what he does, but he can be hard to take at times. I've warned him about abusing his authority, overstepping his boundaries with other officials."

"He has one heck of an ego, and a personality to match. And he doesn't mind using his pull, making it clear that *every* jurisdiction is his jurisdiction."

"Believe me, yours isn't the first call I've received regarding his 'not so pleasant' demeanor. I'm well aware of his personality flaws. I've threatened to pull the plug on him more than once. I don't know, maybe it's time I quit throwing idle threats at him and finally take some real action. He's been so obsessed with a longstanding case he's working on, I'm sure he could use a rest. It would certainly give him time to reflect...gain a little perspective. Maybe brush up on a few social skills, even a little etiquette to boot."

"I don't think you'd be so lucky." Sheriff Pierson laughed. "He's certainly not my favorite person in the world, Mr. Purrant, but I don't think such a harsh course of action will be necessary. I wasn't looking to get him thrown off his case, I just wanted to confirm that he was indeed part of your organization and authorized to be reviewing my files and getting under my skin."

"When I get these calls, I try to remind myself how hard it must be for the marshals in that sector of the agency, pursuing psychotics all over the country. They sacrifice their own lives for the safety of the people," Mr. Purrant rambled on. "It's a dedicated group of individuals, the job dominating their whole life. Most new recruits can't handle the sacrifice, but those in the ranks of Black, they hang in there for the long haul. I admit, I have cut him a lot of slack, but I justify it with the knowledge that he's doing a dangerous job, risking his life on a daily basis, in service of us all."

"You make it sound un-American not to have respect for what he does."

"I know it's not what you wanted to hear, Sheriff, but he is one of our best."

"I take it he's solved a lot of a cases?"

"He's handled more than his share. To be truthful, our Marshal Black has a reputation here at the agency for being the king of unsolved cases. And I'll let you in on a little secret, he also turns in the most 'presumed dead' reports, all perfectly explained, mind you. Now, I know that might sound a little cruel, but you have to remember, these marshals are chasing down the worst criminals and killers."

Had he heard the man right? Was Mr. Purrant saying that it was okay to kill if you were killing a killer?

"Black's current case is a prime example—a serial killer we call 'The Vampire.' He leaves his victims, typically women, drained of blood," Mr. Purrant further disclosed. "I'm afraid if Marshal Black can't eventually catch him, no one ever will."

"Well, after talking to you, I think I now understand him a little better. I hate to admit it, but he might be onto something here in my county. We've had four murders, all women, and all drained of blood."

"It sounds like he may have followed The Vampire right to your door. It's a good thing you have him there."

"You might be right."

"He should be kept informed; however, I'll make sure to reemphasize that he's to work *with* your department and not try to take over or get in the way of your investigations."

"I'd appreciate that," Pierson said. "You've been very helpful, Mr. Purrant. Thank you for returning my call."

"You're welcome, Sheriff, and don't hesitate to call again should anything else arise."

Sheriff Pierson hung up the phone with a curse rolling off his tongue. But at least he now knew a little more about Marshal Jordon Black—the king of unsolved cases—a real vigilante. However, under the circumstances, with the number of victims rising in Jackson County, maybe having him there wasn't such a bad thing after all. If it meant catching the killer, he could stand him awhile longer.

Pierson pulled out his notepad and flipped through

pages of memorandum, glancing over everything he'd taken down since the first murder. There had to be something he was missing, some vital clue hidden between the ever-expanding lines. His gaze stopped on the name Mr. Glynn Kensington—the new principal at Black River Falls High—taking special notice of a notation he'd placed in brackets mentioning his superstitions. He recalled the real estate office receptionist, Ginger, telling him how Mr. Kensington believed a property in Hixton to be haunted. The man was also part of a very short list of people who had contact with Sandy Darnell prior to her murder, and that couldn't be ignored. Sheriff Pierson didn't really suspect him of being the killer, but it was something he should check out. So, with that in mind, he headed over to the high school where he met with a very cooperative Glynn Kensington.

"Sandy Darnell was showing me a ranch over in Hixton. I really liked it—twenty acres of the finest wooded land you could ask for. The house was in pristine condition, but there was something disturbing about the place. Don't get me wrong, I'm not into the supernatural, but I'd swear that place was inhabited by something, or someone."

"What makes you say that?" The sheriff was curious to hear what strange notions the man harbored.

"Well, first of all, the menacing apprehension was just overwhelming, literally making me sick to my stomach. And there were noises coming from below the house. Something was moving around in the basement."

"It was probably just mice. Did you go down and check it out?"

"Not a chance. What I heard wasn't mice. Trust me. It was something else. I'd bet my life someone was down there."

"Did the real estate office look into it?" The sheriff was concerned that a drifter might have taken up temporary residence there.

"I was too embarrassed to mention it. The agent already thought I was off my rocker."

"Maybe I'd better take a ride over to Hixton and check the place out for myself. With the property sitting vacant, vagrants could have moved in, and that could pose a danger for the sales agents."

"I'd hate to see anything bad happen to any of the other ladies over at Brookside Realty."

"That makes two of us." Pierson got up. "I'll be on my way. You have a school to run."

Done there, the sheriff pulled out of the parking lot with his cell phone to his ear, attaining directions to the ranch house from Ginger. He thanked her for her assistance, ended the call, and started up I94, en route to Hixton. A minute later, he received a call from Patricia informing him that the hospital blood bank had been robbed again overnight. She also had another surveillance tape she wanted him to view, and by the urgency in her voice, he knew the camera must have caught something interesting. He took the next turnaround and set a new course for the hospital. The ranch house would just have to wait.

He found Patricia with her secretary, Rhonda. They were viewing what he assumed was the surveillance tape on a small, thirteen-inch TV, set up at the foot of the bed.

"You can go, Rhonda. I'll get in touch with you in the morning."

The woman gave Sheriff Pierson a courteous nod as she exited.

"These last few hours sure have made a world of difference." Pierson was pleased with the progress of her recovery.

"I'm getting better by the minute. Dr. Krieger won't release me today, but he should in the morning."

"Wonderful. Now, tell me about this tape."

"Yes, tape number two." Patricia motioned for him to take a seat in the chair next to her bed and rewound the tape. "He's struck again, Allen, the same guy."

Sheriff Pierson watched the events play out pretty much the same as they had on the first tape. A foggy vapor followed a hospital worker into the room and materialized once the worker left. The man then took several bags of blood, tucked them beneath his coat, and walked right out.

"You're right. It is the same guy." Pierson observed the thin-framed man wearing the same gem-buttoned overcoat, and there was no mistaking the unusual sway present in his movement, more of a slither than a walk.

"You can see him a little better this time. I took your advice and had my secretary arrange for additional lighting. The electrician got right on it, installed them yesterday, just in time to catch the thief on camera."

"It's an improvement, but his face is still blurry. Without that coat, I don't think he could be picked out in a lineup."

"I know. But the overall picture is clearer than before, and now, it is plain to see that he just appears out of nowhere. I want you to explain to me how this could possibly be a trick."

"You can't be saying you actually believe he just formed right out of that foggy vapor like...Count Dracula?" He voiced his skepticism, not quite as willing to accept such preposterous notions.

Sheriff Pierson was a logical man, but all expression dropped from his face when he recalled what Mr. Purrant told him regarding the case Jordon Black was working on, the one he referred to as The Vampire. But that was just a name attached to a serial killer, a man, not a vampire. Such creatures didn't exist outside the realm of folklore and fairytales. No. What he and Patricia were seeing on the tape had to be a very clever trick. The thief was apparently a skilled magician. Pierson refused to concede to the prospect of reanimated corpses and would need a whole lot more proof to ever consider it.

16

A Person of Interest

Officer Traci waved a stack of messages at Sheriff Pierson the moment he walked in the station. "And Rudy wanted to see you, Sheriff, but he popped out for a bite. He should be back any time."

"Thank you, Traci." He checked the time—7:37. "Radio and let him know I'll be around awhile," he instructed and continued on to his office.

Rudy arrived twenty minutes later smelling of burgers and onions.

"Come on in and have a seat." Pierson motioned. "What do you have for me?"

"About the watch, I did some checking on the inscription and discovered that a woman did live in Hixton by the name Miralanya."

"Why does that sound past tense?"

"Because it was sixty-five years ago," Rudy told him.

"I take it she's deceased?"

"Yes, sir."

Pierson lit a cigarette. "I sure was counting on something more."

"Wait a minute now, let me finish. I haven't told you the most interesting part. Her last name was von Vadim. Miralanya von Vadim. Interesting tidbit of information, huh?"

"Very." Pierson blew out a whirl of smoke. "She lived at the estate?"

"That was the address on her death certificate."

"Check with the lab and see if they found a date on the watch."

"I'm ahead of you, Sheriff. They did find a date on the inside watchcase. It's marked 1926. They also lifted a couple of prints, but there was no match in the database."

"That's unfortunate. The time period doesn't fit the late uncle—Victor von Vadim. It would have been the estate owner before him. Does the death certificate show a relative? She must have been a wife or sister."

"There's no spouse or family member listed, and since there's no previous records, we can't be sure."

"It's curious that the murders started not long after our young von Vadim heir arrived at the estate," Pierson said.

"You're right. He moved in about a month ago."

"He's high on my list of suspects, but the only thing I have linking him to any of the murders is a business card he picked up at Purcell's garage. It was Sandy Darnell's, the second victim."

"It's certainly looking like his arrival corresponding with the start of the murders might be more than coincidence. But we don't have strong enough evidence to justify bringing him in. Having an inscription matching a distant relative's first name won't suffice. We can't prove it belongs to von Vadim, and there's no way of verifying that the Miralanya who inscribed it is even the same Miralanya von Vadim who lived at the estate all those years ago."

"I'd bet my life it's his, inherited along with everything else in that estate. You're right, though." Pierson grimaced, "we do need something more solid. It's ironic, yesterday, I stopped by the estate hoping to question Mr. von Vadim and found Tomes Jaffler there."

"The first victim's husband?"

Sheriff Pierson nodded.

"What's their relationship?"

"Neighbors, for one, and he claims to be working for von Vadim." Pierson checked the time. "You know, it's not too late. I still have a while before dark. I think I'll grab a burger myself and head over to Hixton. Try my luck again. Besides, there's something else I need to look into while I'm there. I can knock out two birds with one stone."

"What's that?"

"I received, on good authority, a report of noises heard in the basement of a vacant ranch house. Mr. Kensington, principal at the high school, declined purchasing the property, thinking the house might be haunted." He rubbed out his cigarette.

"You're joking, right, a haunted house?"

Sheriff Pierson laughed and stood up. "Things couldn't get any weirder, could they?" He moved toward the door and gave Rudy a friendly slap on the back as they exited his office.

"I certainly hope not, sir. This is Jackson County, not Transylvania."

* * * *

The sun had just fallen below the horizon when the

doorbell prompted Corin to crawl out of his crypt. It was quiet for a moment before it rang out again with three consecutive chimes. Wondering who the persistent visitor was, he pulled on his pants and made his way up the stairs. In the twilight, he was able to leave the protection of the darkened basement and walk in the dim light that came before the fall of night.

"Sheriff," he acknowledged upon opening the door, concealing his surprise and dread.

"Mr. von Vadim. I hope I'm not disturbing you."

"Not at all." Corin made an effort to put forth a friendly front, inconspicuously blocking the light, as his eyes had not yet adjusted.

"I was hoping to have a word with you, if you don't mind. It won't take long."

"Of course, please, come in." Corin shut the door the moment Pierson entered. "Please, have a seat." He motioned to a Victorian-style sofa displayed in the living room.

Corin sat across from the sheriff in a high-backed chair, waiting for him to divulge the purpose of his visit.

"I came by yesterday. Tomes Jaffler was here. I assume he informed you of my visit."

"Yes. He told me. I was planning to contact you. He thinks you might be considering me a suspect."

"Let's just say...a person of interest. About Mr. Jaffler, you'd do well to keep an eye on him. If I'm to believe the dramatic execution he gave, I'd say he's treading down a dark and dangerous road. The last thing I need is a vigilante to deal with."

"Tomes is in good hands. And I guess he was right about you suspecting me."

Corin was careful to maintain the appearance of a man at ease, with nothing to hide. He knew Sheriff Pierson was carefully observing his reactions, no doubt surmising him and Tomes to be conspirators.

"A person of interest," Pierson reiterated.

"If you don't mind my asking, just what is it about me that's sparked such interest?"

"To be truthful, Mr. von Vadim, a couple of things have led me to your door." Pierson pulled his notepad from his pocket and skimmed his notes. "It's curious how the murders started just after your arrival here in Jackson County. Then there's the matter of Sandy Darnell. You were supplied one of her business cards when having some spark plugs changed on your Harley at Purcell's Garage, the very night of her murder."

"Yes, I don't deny it. But I was never able to reach her," Corin told him the truth of the matter, knowing the man had done his homework.

"So, you're alleging that you never made contact with her by phone, or otherwise?"

"I neither spoke to nor saw her," Corin affirmed.

"With this large estate, I don't understand why you'd be looking to purchase more real estate."

"Just seeing what's available on the market for investment. I don't believe there's any crime in that."

Pierson moved on with his questioning. "There were two murders last night, one in the parking lot of Black River Falls Memorial Hospital, and the other at the county fair. I'm sure you've heard. It's been all over the news."

"Yes, I heard."

"I don't suppose you'd know anything about either of those murders, would you?"

"Nothing more than what's been broadcast." Sheriff Pierson's accusatory demeanor irritated Corin, but he kept his cool.

"At the hospital murder site, we found a gold pocket watch. The chain was broken, we presume yanked off during a struggle between the victim and her attacker."

"That's all very interesting, Sheriff, but I don't understand what any of this has to do with me."

"On the back of the watch there's an inscription, *For my prince of the night. Miralanya.* Would you know anything about this particular timepiece?"

"No. And I don't know why you'd suspect I would."

"I should tell you, Mr. von Vadim, we did some checking and discovered that a woman named Miralanya von Vadim resided in this very house, sixty-five years ago."

"I won't dispute that I had a past relative named Miralanya, but come on, Sheriff, it's preposterous to think the watch you found belonged to her. Anyone having that same first name could have inscribed it."

"True. But it's a rather uncommon name. No other records match it in the county. So, let's just suppose for a moment that Miralanya von Vadim did inscribe the watch we found and gave it to one of your relatives as a gift. It was dated 1926, so presumably, whoever resided here before your late uncle. And if that is the case, it would mean the watch came from this house, which is now your home, Mr. von Vadim."

"But you are only speculating, Sheriff. And I assure you, I know nothing about such a watch."

"If you're telling the truth, you shouldn't mind coming down to the station for fingerprinting. We lifted some prints from the piece, and if they prove not to be yours, that will put you in the clear. What do you say?"

"I always aim to cooperate with the law, but something tells me I should speak with my lawyer first. How about I have him get back with you on this fingerprinting issue, and we'll go from there." Corin didn't give an inch, irritated by Pierson's attempt at coercion, assuming the man lacked necessary legal grounds to enforce compliance.

"Fair enough, I can't force you to comply...yet."

I thought as much.

"I guess I'm not under arrest, then?" Corin got up, remaining cordial, despite the imputation.

"No, you're not being charged with anything at present. However, I could bring you in on suspicion alone," Pierson threatened.

"Suspicion of what?" Corin asked with all seriousness. "There's no proof I've committed any crime."

"If you're innocent, why refuse fingerprinting? What are you afraid of?" Pierson countered. "Something tells me I should bring you in right now."

"But I don't think you'll do that, Sheriff. In turn, I'd have to sue the Jackson County Sheriff's Office for false arrest. I know people, and it wouldn't look good for you. Besides, I told you, I don't know anything about that watch, or the realtor's murder."

"So you say, Mr. von Vadim."

"It's the truth, whether you chose to believe it or not. But if you insist on hounding me, my lawyer is only a phone call away. A little forewarning...he's *the best* at what he does, always eager to rip into someone." Corin escorted Sheriff Pierson to the door, more than ready for him to go.

"Just don't plan on leaving town anytime soon." Pierson was adamant. "And that's an order, not a request."

"I just got here, Sheriff. I have no plans of leaving."

Sheriff Pierson's cell phone rang just as he stepped outside. "Hello." He turned and moved several feet from Corin to talk. "Yes, Traci, but it'll be a little while. I have a ranch house to check out while I'm in Hixton." Pierson took several additional steps. "I guess Rudy didn't fill you in." He silently paused. "No. I got a report of strange noises coming from the basement of a vacant property over on Hillman Road. I assume it's mice, but you can never be too careful. It could be vagrants."

There was a second silent pause.

"Okay. Just leave it on my desk, and I'll get to it later." Pierson slid the phone in his pocket and turned back to face Corin.

"I couldn't help overhearing, Sheriff. With night on the fall, you might want to consider putting that task off till tomorrow," Corin attempted to dissuade him, thinking Boldor could be the source. A vacant, secluded home would suit the nightwalker's needs perfectly. "I heard you mention Hillman Rd. I recently passed by that ranch, and the place is overrun with weeds and overgrowth. I don't think it's been tended to in months, not a place you'd want to check out in the dark."

"You might be right." Pierson started for his SUV. "Remember, von Vadim, don't leave town."

Corin watched as the sheriff drove away, then reentering the house, he met up with Tomes who was coming through the lanai door.

"When did you get here?" He'd been so involved with the sheriff he hadn't sensed him.

Corin had grown accustomed to Tomes coming and going. Having him in the house during the day while he rested beneath the mansion, gave him an ease he hadn't had in quite some time. The company was also nice, someone to break the cycle of loneliness associated with his dark existence.

"Oh, about an hour ago, give or take. I'm parked out back. I wanted to do a little target practice with the staker. I wouldn't want to miss my mark when the time comes. Anyway, when I started inside and realized the sheriff was here, I decided to lay low until he left."

"It's a good thing you did. He's suspicious enough."

"I couldn't hear much, but it looked intense."

"They found a watch last night at the hospital

murder site, where the woman was found dead in the parking lot."

"What's that got to do with you?"

"The watch they found is mine—the gold pocket watch Boldor stole from me. The miscreant either lost it during his attack, or he planted it, trying to incriminate me."

"How did the sheriff find out that it belongs to you?"

"He can't prove it does, and I denied it was mine, but there's an inscription on the back signed with the name, Miralanya, and they discovered that a woman by that name resided here, at von Vadim Estate, many years ago. He knows he's right, but there's not enough proof."

"If I were in his shoes, I'd be suspicious too," Tomes said. "It doesn't look good. You were already on his suspect list due to Purcell giving you the realtor's business card."

"Something else he mentioned."

"Jail isn't an option for you. Come sunup, you'd have to escape or, poof, become dust of the earth."

Corin groaned, but Tomes's words rang true. Being arrested was not an option.

"The killing won't stop until we find Boldor's hideout and rid ourselves of him once and for all." Corin talked as he headed for the basement door. "Something the sheriff might have just unknowingly helped us with."

Tomes followed. "What do you know?"

"When he was leaving, he took a call, and I overheard him mention a vacant ranch house over on Hillman Road. Something about noises in the basement. He was concerned it might be vagrants, and I think he probably right, except something tells me that the nomad lying low there won't be of the human kind."

* * * *

Boldor gave Louisa a packet of blood and stepped back while she fed. He knew she hungered for fresh blood, and with his attempt to satisfy that craving, he hoped to also gain her trust in the process. Now able to approach her, he reached out and stroked her hair without fear of losing a limb.

"You're all but impossible to handle, my little firecat, but you are a beauty." He talked to her, even though he knew she didn't fully comprehend what he was saying. "I'm going to leave you again, but I won't be gone long. If you call, I will hear. With our mental connection, I will know if you need me, and I won't go beyond a distance of detecting you."

She grunted, paying him no mind, ripping apart the bag with her razor-sharp teeth, determined to lick up every drop.

Boldor felt more confident about leaving Louisa alone now that her hunger had been temporarily satisfied, and he figured he'd better go out to feed and save the bags of blood for her, knowing she would need more soon. Furthermore, it was time to put a plan he had contrived into action. So, locking the basement door, he exited the house and shape-shifted into a raven, expelling a menacing caw as he leaped into the darkness of the night.

17

The Darkness Below

Jordon Black sat at a corner table waiting for his order. He'd been eating at the Black River Falls Diner on a daily basis since his arrival in Jackson County. The food wasn't half-bad, and the servers were easy on the eyes. When the waitress approached with his meal, she remarked on a partially concealed tattoo marking his right forearm—a half-skull, half-human design with a moon replacing the eye of the skull, and a sun replacing the eye of the man.

"Strange looking tattoo you have there."

"Just something I got when I was younger...and wilder." He casually repositioned his arm to cover the mark he generally kept hidden, along with a second seal—the Circle of the Morpar Kingdom—a much larger design centered on his chest.

"What does it mean?" she asked curiously. "Or is it just something you picked out because it was cool?"

"It depicts the eternal struggle between day and night, and how, despite their continual battle to overtake each another, they are forever bound together. There is no day without night, and no night without day."

"Very deep...and true. You could be a poet. Maybe you should consider taking up the pen."

"I don't think so." He laughed. "I have trouble writing my own name."

"Well, it's something to think about. Now, is there anything else I can get for you?"

"No. Everything looks fine."

"I'll let you get to your meal, before it gets cold." She rushed away in the busy manner of all the waitresses in the diner. The establishment was small, but the booths were always full.

Jordon reached for his fork, and the symbol showed again. He placed his left hand on the mark, allowing his thoughts to carry him to another world...his world. Jordon was not from Earth, or even human, he was an Indith immortal from the Eleventh Dimension—a diurnal immortal—a daywalker. He differed from nightwalkers in several ways, one being he did not require blood to survive. However, there were many similarities between the two species. Both were shape-shifters, and each possessed the ability to sense the presence of other immortals.

Indith immortals were a cross between humans and nightwalkers, only unlike humans, they didn't grow ill or old. From birth until their fifteenth year, they aged as mortals, then the aging process slowed to a crawl—one year to forty human years—until they reached adulthood, when it stopped altogether. Fully matured around four hundred and fifteen human years, Jordon was still considered a youth by his kind's standards, at just a little over two hundred years old.

He recalled an Indith warlord named Gaun who had almost led the Indithians to their ruin. Endowed with the Clyth—a charm forged by a demon from solid black diamond and granted to the warlord as a gift of his favor—Gaun had embarked on a quest to banish all but his own species from the face of their world.

Jordon's own father, Denlor Day Morrain, and his half-brother, Lake, had served Gaun. They stood behind their commander, savagely attacking unsuspecting human villages in the night and slaughtering every living thing in their path. But in the end, in their devout loyalty to him, they had fallen to their deaths, beheaded in the final battle at Kenijor.

Along with humans, nightwalkers had also been plagued by these savage attacks, caught unaware during the daylight hours with entire clans infiltrated and destroyed. Gaun's Indithian forces left nothing but death and despair in their treacherous wake.

Survival became a tie binding human and nightwalker. Side by side, they had managed to thwart the Indith attacks. The nightwalkers protected humans from incursions at night, and humans guarded against raids on the nightwalkers during the day. Finally, with the aid of a powerful sorcerer, they had managed to defeat him.

Jordon slid his sleeve back down covering the design that represented this epic battle of survival—the joining of night and day. Now a sentry, he wore the symbol with pride and honor, but it was imperative he kept it hidden, should he meet up with any fugitives from his world.

Thinking of his family, Jordon tried not to dwell on his dishonorable heritage. But the memories were there, forever lodged in his mind. He knew he wasn't responsible for the barbaric actions of his father and Lake, but left to bear their disgrace, he couldn't help feeling the need to make amends for all their past evils. This personal shame was what had led him to become a sentry—dedicating his life to hunting down criminals—and the driving force behind his many successful captures.

"Is everything all right? You look a million miles away. You haven't touched a thing on your plate." The waitress's voice brought Jordon back to the present.

"I've just been struck with a headache. If you wouldn't mind bringing a box, I'll take this with me. I don't have much of an appetite at the moment."

"I can sympathize. I'll get one for you." She hustled off, returning a moment later with a box and check in hand.

Jordon transferred his meal, paid the bill, and headed out of the diner. Thinking of his past had depressed him, but he had to shake it off and stay focused on his present mission. He had a rotter to catch, a nightwalker who didn't have an inkling of the ultimate power the charm he'd stolen truly possessed.

Jackson County was the closest he'd come to capturing the miscreant since they'd started their cat and mouse chase two years earlier. The nightwalker had broken his pattern. Something in this tiresome little county had allured him, and Jordon knew the key to catching him lay in finding out just what the attraction was.

* * * *

Corin fed before he and Tomes headed to the ranch on Hillman Road. Arriving close to ten thirty, they found Boldor's dusty-blue Camaro hidden behind the house.

"This is it." Corin recognized the car.

Tomes broke a glass pane on a French door at the rear of the house. "Shall we?"

"You didn't have to do that." Corin led the way.

Although pitch-dark inside, Corin had no trouble finding his way with his phenomenal night vision. A well-armed Tomes followed closely, carrying a flashlight in one hand, and the staker in the other. A strap ran from his right shoulder, diagonally across his chest, keeping his supply of blackthorn nails within easy reach. Additionally, his machete hung at his mid-back by a second strap and sheath, with the handle accessible by reaching back and over his shoulder.

Corin stopped. "This is the basement door."

"There's a slide bolt. Aren't they usually installed on the inside of rooms...for safety?" Tomes's flashlight beam settled on the lock.

"Yes, they are," Corin replied in a hushed voice, sniffing the air.

"Strange. If they wanted to keep people out, wouldn't they have used a padlock instead?"

"Shhh." Corin reached for the bolt, slid it back, and eased the door open. Listening with his acute hearing, he looked down into the dark recess.

"I don't hear anything," Tomes whispered. "Do you think he's down there?"

"He's not here. The door wouldn't have been locked from the outside if he were. He's most likely out feeding."

"That makes sense. So, I guess we won't find Louisa here either. If she's a nightwalker, she'd have to feed too."

"She will have to feed." Corin exercised caution as he descended the stairs into the unknown territory below.

Tomes followed, his flashlight beam bouncing chaotically as he went. Stopping on the bottom step next to Corin, he shivered with gooseflesh. "It's cold, damp, and stale. It feels like a tomb. And what is that horrific smell? It reeks down here." Tomes pressed the top of his hand beneath his nose. "The smell in your basement isn't nearly this offensive." He sniffed Corin.

"Knock it off! It's not me, it's his scent." Corin kept his voice low, knowing they weren't alone. "Although...." He paused to smell the air again, noticing the odor of death in the mix. "There's decay. Rotting flesh."

"Oh man, you mean he's left corpses down here?" Tomes scanned the room.

"I'd say it's the decomposing remains of animals—rodents. But I do detect human blood, only, not the smell of their decaying bodies...strange."

"I think I can solve that mystery for you." Tomes's flashlight beam revealed an empty blood bag.

"Of course." Corin recognized the hospital bags.

Tomes ran the beam over the room, holding his aim when the light fell on a pile of rodent carcasses in the far corner. "Man. This just keeps getting better and better."

"With this nightwalker, I think your term of reference 'filth' is more than befitting. I can't stand the stench down here."

"Well, at least we won't have to worry about running into any rats. I'm pretty sure he's finished them all off."

Tomes started past Corin.

"Wait!" Corin blocked his move. "We're not alone."

"What do you mean? Who else could—"

A figure sprang out at them from behind a stack of crates, releasing a piercing shrill.

Tomes stumbled back, but quickly regained his footing. Managing to catch the individual in the light's direct beam, he gasped. "Louisa!"

"Stay behind me, Tomes." Corin saw her demented state.

Stepping into the room, testing her mental stability, Corin extended a hand, but she hurled herself at him in a frenzied attack with fangs and claws elongated in pursuit of blood. He managed to shove her away, but in the process, she lacerated him with her long, curved talons, leaving four gashes across his left jaw.

"Louisa!" Tomes yelled out, and she spun back, her brow furrowed and eyes narrowed as if recognizing something in his voice.

Tomes pushed past Corin and eased toward her.

"Careful, Tomes, she's insane," Corin warned. "The transformation was too much for her mind to handle."

"I'm her husband. I can get through to her. She won't attack me."

"I know you want to believe that, but don't be foolish. All she knows is her insatiable hunger."

"Louisa, it's me, Tomes. Let me help you." He focused on his wife, speaking calmly while inching closer.

A low, guttural growl resonated in her throat. Holding a defensive stance, she watched, eyes locked on his every move. Then, grabbing her head and pressing it in her hands, she expelled a deafening cry.

"Tomes stop! Don't move any closer. I know you want to save her, but she's already lost. She's not the woman you remember."

"What's wrong with her?"

"Her mind is burning...torment."

"I can't just walk away...leave her like this. She's my wife."

"There's nothing you can do to save her now. She's little more than a wild, starved animal. Death would be a blessing." Corin knew his words sounded cruel, but he had to make Tomes see the truth. "Look at her, I mean, really look at her! This is not Louisa!"

"You're saying we should kill her, aren't you?" Tomes responded, his voice low, all the while keeping his gaze on Louisa. "I can't do it. I won't' kill her. And

I'm not leaving her here, either, in this reeking pit of death."

Corin knew there would be no reasoning with Tomes. He was a man looking upon a woman he'd thought was lost to death, who now magically stood before him alive and breathing, like a miracle from God. The wonderment had blinded him to the fact that her reanimation was far from a blessing, but rather a curse from hell.

Louisa settled down, gaping at Tomes. He stood silent, locked in her gaze, entranced by her peering green eyes. Tomes's love for her made him easy prey, enabling her to use her newfound witchery in an attempt to lure him to her.

Regardless of her madness, she possessed a natural survival instinct, an innate ability to utilize her nightwalker powers for the purpose of feeding.

"Tomes!" Corin yelled just as Louisa attacked.

Viciously catching Tomes's shoulder with her fangs, she latched down, drinking in his fresh blood. Tomes struggled to push her off, but she had the superior strength and overpowered him. She pinned him to the ground, her talons cutting into his flesh—scissors to paper.

"Louisa, no! Stop!" Tomes tried to fight her off.

Corin rushed to his aid and seized Louisa at the back of her neck. He punctured her flesh with his talons, causing her to cry out. Yanking her up, he dragged her away from Tomes before relinquishing his hold. She retreated to a back corner of the room, releasing a high-pitched shrill liken a hawk, calling her keeper—Boldor.

Hurrying to Tomes, Corin bent down and examined his injuries. It looked bad, but he didn't have time to attend him. Boldor would be responding to Louisa's call, if he wasn't already en route, having sensed her distress.

"We have to go." He lifted Tomes to a sitting position, all the while keeping a watchful eye out for Louisa whose sharp, piercing cries still echoed.

"Can you walk?"

"I think so," Tomes winced. "I can't see anything." He reached for his flashlight on the floor at his feet, the beam of light slicing the darkness, striking a bare area of wall. "The staker, I dropped it. Do you see it?"

Corin spotted the weapon and quickly retrieved it for him.

"What is she doing?"

"She's calling Boldor to her rescue, and we need to go before he arrives."

"This is our chance."

"No. Not now. You need attention. Our fight will have to wait."

Corin pulled Tomes to his feet and guided him to the stairs, but before starting up, the room grew quiet and Louisa spoke out, drawing Tomes's attention back with one single word.

"Hus-band." Her voice was hypnotic.

"She knows me." Tomes's light found her in the darkness. "She remembers."

"She doesn't remember you. "It's a trick, Tomes, only a trick. She wouldn't have attacked you if she'd had any past remembrance of your life together. She'll use any means at her disposal to pull you back. She sees you as nothing more than food."

"H-husband." She attempted to entrance Tomes again.

"Let me go." Tomes fought against Corin's hold, trying to go to her, but Corin restrained him.

"I won't let you do this. All she wants is food." Corin knew what he had to do to end the madness and slipped the staker from Tomes's hand. "Forgive me," he whispered.

Surrendering his hold on Tomes, he held a steady aim on Louisa, and when she lunged in attack, he pulled the trigger, striking her mid-chest. She dropped to the floor, gnarling and hissing, the blackthorn nail embedded in her body. And while she was down, Corin charged into action. He pulled the machete from the sheath hanging at Tomes's back and proceeded her way. Raising the weapon high, he came down with one powerful blow, severing her head from her body with a single strike. Her life ended, she instantly disintegrated, her remains crumbling to ashes.

"No!" Tomes wailed, coming out of his trance during the final moments of the slaying, but not soon enough to stop it.

"It is done." For Tomes's sake, this was how it had to be.

"You killed her. That was my—"

"It wasn't Louisa. And I had to make a choice—you or the monster." Corin had no regrets.

Tomes started to fall.

Corin rushed to his side and took on the brunt of his weight. Needing a free hand, he wiped the machete blade on his pants leg and slipped the weapon back in the sheath. Holding onto the staker, he half-carried Tomes toward the stairs and ushered him to the top.

Tomes looked back from the door, into the darkness below. A tear traced his cheek.

"I wish it could have been different." Corin could see Tomes's physical and emotional pain.

"I hate it, but I know she was already lost. I blame Boldor. He's the one who put her through this torture. One day, I'll have his head, even if it takes the rest of my life."

18

Deceived

Corin put Tomes in the passenger seat and headed for the estate. Settling him in a second-floor room, he tried to mend his injuries with his healing power but could only partially repair the damage.

"This is the best I can do for you; the cuts are too deep. But it should help speed up the healing process. It's going to take time for you to regain your strength after losing so much blood."

"I'll live," Tomes groaned. "You should tend to yourself." He pointed to Corin's jaw where Louisa caught him with her talons.

Corin ran his fingers over the gashes, and his flesh regenerated itself, making him good as new.

"Tomes, about Louisa, taking her life, I—"

"I know you had to do it. I wanted to believe she'd come back to me, but the monster down in that basement wasn't the woman I knew. The human part of her was gone. She nearabout killed me. If it hadn't been for you, I'm sure she would have succeeded."

"I'm sorry you've lost her twice."

"It's worse this time, worrying that she'll never be at peace. Monsters without souls don't go to heaven." Tomes sighed. "My only hope of ever seeing her again in the afterlife would be to live a wretched life and hope to join her in hell one day."

"You don't know for sure that she's in hell. There could be something more."

"I was raised in a Christian family, taught that after death we either go to heaven or hell. Being the undead, I would think you'd know what comes next."

"I've never felt driven to journey in search of those answers. I'd rather not know if all that awaits me beyond this life is a pit of fire and brimstone."

"But you believe in heaven and hell."

"Yes. I know they exist."

"Might God show mercy on her, Corin? Does He ever show mercy on your kind?"

"I try not to dwell on things that torment my mind, and more importantly, are beyond my control. But in my opinion, cursed is cursed." Corin moved about the room, worked up by the subject of conversation. "If it were so easy for a nightwalker to find favor in the eyes of God, I'd be the first in line repenting, making my personal request for salvation. Whether or not that means we're all marked for hell, I can't say for certain. Since we have no soul to offer, hell may not even want us...maybe just the monster we harbor."

"I hadn't thought of that. What becomes of your soul when you're changed?"

"Our mortality is taken prior to resurrection, and our human bodies die. During this time of death, our souls are collected by the Angel of Death. I encountered this dark angel in my brief but memorable fall into the afterlife during my change," Corin told him. "And when this angel comes, he knows who are cursed—possessed by the virus—and he treats them accordingly. Just as he collects the souls of mortal men, he also takes ours, but those of us afflicted with the virus—damned to immortality—are left with nothing but an empty existence along with the remembrance of who we were in life. I don't know, maybe this is supposed to be God's show of mercy on us, leaving us with our memories intact, but for me, it's more of an eternal affliction. It left me forever longing for what I'd lost—my soul, the light of day...heaven. I confess, I don't entirely understand how it's all accomplished, or what later becomes of our souls. All I know is that the angel takes them away, and we never get that precious part of us back. This gives you a little insight into how it is and always shall be for our kind." A hint of dejection sounded in his voice.

"I'm so sorry for you, Corin, and for Louisa."

"What's done is done. There's no sense dwelling on it."

"But I can't help dwelling on it, because of Louisa."

"If God were to choose to grant mercy on any of us, Tomes, it would certainly be Louisa. Now, you'd better get some rest while you can. Something tells me Boldor isn't too happy right now."

"You think he'll retaliate?"

"I suspect he will."

"I'll rest, but you have to let me know if there's any sign of him," Tomes stipulated. "Nothing, not even this aching body, will stop me from facing him."

"You're one determined man," Corin told him. "Now rest. I'll be close by if you need me."

Corin left the room, troubled by the unfavorable turn of events. He couldn't help feeling responsible for Tomes's injuries, knowing the threat Louisa posed.

He'd allowed his judgment to be clouded by sentiment, and the result only added more heartache for Tomes.

"I can't let anything like that happen again."

When it came time to take on Boldor, he had to be at the top of his game, and that meant no distractions. He'd promised the kill to Tomes, but with circumstances what they were, he didn't see how he'd be able to keep his word.

Tomes couldn't fight in his condition, regardless of his determination to the contrary. Corin knew it was up to him to face the nightwalker, and in order to ensure he would be the one to walk away victorious, he would have to stay focused. And that meant leaving his emotions and this one, lone human who'd managed to worm his way into his life, out of the equation.

* * * *

Boldor landed, shape-shifted into his human form, and thundered into the house. Rushing to the basement and finding nothing left of Louisa but her ashy remains, he released a loud, ferocious roar.

Sharing a mental tie since their joining, he'd felt her anxiety, even over the span of distance between them. But in her mental state, he'd thought nothing of it until hearing her cries for help. Unfortunately, he'd traveled too far to get back to her in time, and now he'd lost his chosen one...his beauty.

"I should have left a watch." He rubbed a button, the insect awaiting command. "For now, you have the upper hand, von Vadim. But I'll soon rectify that."

Noticing a trail of blood, he squatted and ran his middle finger through the fluid. "So, my little firecat got you, mortal, before you managed to take her out." He tasted the blood. "A little bitter."

Rising, his eyes narrowed under a tense brow. "Fair

is fair, von Vadim. You took my companion, so now, I'll have to take yours."

* * * *

At the farm, Angelique answered the door to a late-night caller.

"I'm glad you came by. But I didn't expect to hear from you tonight." She greeted Corin with a warm, inviting smile, motioning for him to come inside.

"Tomes said you two had plans and that he might not be back till morning. I figured hunting. Nothing's wrong, is it?"

"Everything's fine. I hope I didn't wake you."

"No. I was up, watching TV."

"I know it's late, but I wanted to see you."

"You're welcome any time, Corin, day or night. It seems we're both restless. I take it you walked here from the mansion?"

"I did."

"It's foggy out." She showed him to the living room.

"In some areas, but I had no trouble finding my way."

"That's good. You wouldn't want to get lost on your own land," she teased. "It's past twelve thirty. Did Tomes mention where he was going?"

"He didn't say." Corin ran his gaze over the length of her.

"I'm sure he's fine, I just have this gnawing feeling. I can't seem to shake it. But you know that brother of mine, he's probably over at Micky Joes getting plastered while I'm sitting here worrying over nothing."

"You have a strong bond." Corin moved closer to her on the sofa.

"He's always been there for me, no matter what."

"And you for him."

"I try to be. But I can't take away his heartache."

"He'll get past it." Corin leaned toward her, suddenly demanding possession of her mouth, snatching her with such aggression she pulled away.

His kiss was different, forceful, and his scent was harsh. An odor she'd smelled before.

"Did I do something to offend you?" He caught her stare.

"No." She wiped her mouth, trying not to be too obvious, but wishing she could wash it out. "You just caught me off guard."

"My apologies."

She scooted over, putting more space between them. Something wasn't right.

Where are you, Tomes?

"Why don't we take a walk to the creek...enjoy the night?" Corin suggested. "There wasn't any fog along the trail."

Angelique hesitated. "Let me get my jacket." She decided to go.

Heading out into the woods with Corin when she sensed something was amiss might not have been the smartest of choices, but at least it spared her from the pressure of making out with him on the sofa, a situation she couldn't believe she was relieved to escape. And outside there was plenty of fresh air, a welcome escape from the rank odor attached to him.

What had changed?

Angelique was usually comfortable with Corin, but at the moment, he made her uneasy. Everything about him was different, his smell, his touch, his kiss, the way he looked at her...his eyes. She even noticed a difference in his speech. Had she not known it to be impossible, she would have sworn that this man standing beside her, looking to be Corin in every physical way, was an imposter.

* * * *

At the estate, Tomes frantically called out for Corin from the second-floor landing.

Corin rushed in from the lanai, hearing the distress in his voice. "What is it?"

"It's Angel! She's in trouble. I woke up hearing her voice in my mind."

"You were just dreaming, Tomes." Corin started up the stairs.

"No. You don't understand. We're twins. We've always been able to sense when something's wrong with each other."

"You and Angelique are twins?" Corin was surprised, wondering how he could have missed that. But it certainly explained Tomes's possessiveness over Angelique. They shared a unique connection.

"What if it's Boldor? We have to go now! She needs us."

"I thought she'd be safer if we kept her out of this whole messy situation. It hadn't dawned on me that he'd go after her." While Corin was keeping watch over Tomes, there, at the estate, Angelique had been the one in danger. "But you aren't going anywhere." He halted Tomes's attempt to start down the stairs. "In your condition, you'd be lucky to make it to the bottom before collapsing. You get back in bed. I'll go." Corin helped him back to the room. "After more than an hour of no retaliation, I should have known he was up to something."

"She's all alone, Corin. Helpless. Forget about me, I'm fine. Just get to her!"

"I'll be back...with Angelique."

"I can't lose her."

"Neither of us can, nor will." Corin retrieved

Tomes's gear—the staker and machete—from a nearby table. "Keep these close."

Tomes took them. "Don't worry. If he shows up, I won't go down without a fight." He raised the staker in a practice aim. "I'll definitely leave him with something to remember me by."

*** * * ***

Corin tore out of the estate in the Corvette, needing transportation to bring Angelique back in. When he arrived at the farm, he found her car parked in the drive. Hoping to find her safe inside the house, he rushed to the door, getting no response after several knocks. Finding the door unlocked, he stepped inside and called out, cursing when he picked up a faint trace of Boldor's nauseating scent. The fiend had been there. Corin feared the measures he'd go, sure it would be right up his alley to draw out his revenge to the fullest.

Rocketing outside, Corin searched the grounds. After checking the barn, he shape-shifted into the form he often chose, a Great Horned Owl, and took to the sky, scouting the nearby woods. Following the trail to the creek, he spotted two dark figures on the path below, nearing the water. He rushed ahead of them, landing at the creek bed, and quickly took cover in the shadowy backdrop of the tree line to await their arrival. Glancing around, he was sure he sensed another immortal.

Why is it I can detect you now?

He didn't understand what had changed, but he had no time to consider the matter in length. Crouched in the underbrush, he watched as the two individuals approached.

"Is something wrong?" Angelique asked her escort, who'd come to a standstill.

"We have a spy in our midst."

"A spy?" Angelique looked around.

"Show yourself, von Vadim!"

Corin stepped out of the tree line, silhouetted in the night, his features undetectable. But he knew Angelique recognized him by the perplexed look on her face.

"It can't be," she muttered.

Corin turned his attention on Boldor, taken aback by what he saw—a duplicate of himself standing next to her. "What the devil!"

Boldor had assumed his form.

"I've observed you, what you wear, how you act. In fact, I think I'm an improvement, a better you than you."

In similar clothing, they appeared identical.

"Let's ask this little angel what she thinks. She's had a taste."

Angelique stumbled back in fear.

Enraged, Corin advanced on him with his fangs and talons lengthening, taking brisk, confident strides. "I'm going to kill you!"

Boldor made his own charge, catching him mid-distance, each taking the other to the ground in a fierce collision.

Hearing Angelique scream, Corin searched for her position. How would he ever explain away such an impossible sight to her? It couldn't be done. There was only one solution. He would have to tell her the truth, what he was...everything.

Boldor, still in Corin's form, rolled out of reach and bellowed in laughter. He then turned and went for Angelique who stood paralyzed, seized her by a fistful of her hair, and yanked her to him.

"I made the mistake of leaving my companion alone, as you did." He cast Corin a brazen glare. "You took mine, and now, I have yours." He ran his mouth along the smooth flesh of her neckline

"Enough, Boldor, she's not the one you want." Corin was afraid the demon might rip into her.

"I believe she will replace my little firecat quite nicely."

The sight of his filthy hands on Angelique burned Corin's blood, but he restrained his temper, waiting for the precise moment to make his move.

"This one doesn't have the lustrous fiery hair I so adored in the other female, but she'll do." Boldor tossed Angelique to the side and shape-shifted into his own human form.

Scrambling back, Angelique gaped as Boldor transformed from one form to another. "Louis Gomez. This can't be real."

Both immortals possessed impeccable strength and endurance, each proving to be a very skilled fighter. Catching Corin around the neck, Boldor managed to drag him several feet toward the bank. Corin unleashed a terrible roar as the fiend's talons ripped into his flesh, but he fought back, tearing through Boldor's shirt and leaving the hellion with a few marks of his own.

With part of his chest exposed, Corin observed a large, black stone hanging from Boldor's neck, just visible between strips of ripped material. Assuming it was a talisman, he attempted to seize it. Taking him down hard, he reached for the chain, but Boldor was fast, scrambling back to his feet with the stone still safely in place.

Corin started for him again, but a great, black wolf unexpectedly lunged from the shadows, standing between them. The creature snarled ferociously before shape-shifting into the form of a man, adding a third fighter to the mix.

"I've finally caught up with you, after all this time." The stranger glared at Corin before charging, then wrestled him to the ground with a force that rivaled his own.

"Who the devil are you?" Corin fought him off and managed to scramble free, placing a few feet between them.

"Don't play games with me. You know who I am. I knew I'd catch up with you sooner or later, 'cause Marshal Jordon Black always gets his man."

The marshal? Corin couldn't believe it. *An immortal?*

"You're a nightwalker?" Corin was trying to figure him out.

"Not exactly. You know what I want, so hand it over and maybe I'll let you leave with your life."

Amid the unanticipated turn of events, Boldor withdrew and disappeared into the cover of the woods, leaving Corin in the clutches of the lawman. A laugh echoed as he slipped away in the night.

"No." Corin started after him, but the marshal interceded, making a simultaneous move to block him.

"You've got the wrong man, Marshal."

"You've managed to stay ahead of me for a long time, but I knew you'd eventually slip up." Jordon stared him down. "Why did you want me to see you kill that girl tonight? What are you up to?"

"I know you think you've got this whole situation figured out, but you're wrong. I'm not who you think I am," Corin declared. *How could the marshal possibly know he'd killed Louisa?*

"Don't insult my intelligence by denying it, Nightwalker. My eyes don't lie." Jordon held his gaze. "So, I finally get to meet the fugitive I've been chasing all over this god-forsaken country for the past two years. You're not exactly what I expected."

"That's because I'm not the one you're after. Can't you see he's tricked you? How do you know about

Louisa? Did you follow us to the ranch house?"

"What ranch house? I'm talking about the girl at the Inn. I saw you kill her. You let me see you."

"I think I'm beginning to understand what's going on here. Boldor committed a murder while disguised as me, using my form to mislead you, just as he did just now, with Angelique. He's a clever one all right, placing you on my trail and off his. Think about it, Marshal. Has he ever let you get so close before? Purposely shown himself?"

Jordon seemed to be considering his argument.

"You said to hand something over. What is it you're after? If I can't reason with you, I should at least know what I'm defending myself for."

"I haven't quite made up my mind about you, Nightwalker, but I'll play your game. You stole a charm from the Order of the Clythguard. A black diamond. I've been after it for a long time. After *you*. And I'm not leaving without it. So, you can either hand it over right now, or die."

"What do I have to do to convince you that I'm not your criminal?" Corin held out his arms submissively. "Search me."

Jordon wasted no time taking advantage of the opportunity and cautiously approached Corin, patting him down. Taking in a waft of Corin's scent, the marshal's entire demeanor instantly changed, and with a heavy exhale, he backed off.

A profane word passed his lips. "You're telling the truth."

"I take it you know your prey's scent."

"You don't possess his stench. I was so close this time." He cursed in frustration.

"He was right in front of you, Marshal, but you went for the wrong guy." Corin was annoyed. "You're lucky I didn't take your head for attacking me."

"Take it easy," Jordon spoke calmly. "I made a mistake."

"At least you realize it now. Boldor has played us all for fools."

Suddenly remembering Angelique, Corin whirled in search of her, spotting her crouched in the dark tree line. Rushing toward her, she scrambled back in fear.

"Stay away!" she yelled.

"It's okay now, Angelique, I would never hurt you." Corin could see she was shaken and understandably confused by everything she'd just witnessed.

"How do I know it's really you this time?" She kept him at a distance. "I don't know what to believe."

"Take my hand and look into my eyes. You'll feel the difference...see that it's me." He knelt and reached out to her. "Trust me, Angelique."

A look of relief replaced her frightened expression, and she threw herself into his arms, falling against his chest in tears. "You're not human, are you?" She whispered from the safety of his hold.

"No, I'm not human," he replied. "I'm a nightwalker."

How could he ever expect her to love him now that she'd glimpsed the monster in his face and seen the fangs and talons extending from his body?

"A nightwalker?"

"Yes, a vampire," he clarified.

Corin paused, waiting for hysterics, but Angelique remained calm.

"It's like I'm trapped in a dream—a nightmare. If I could just wake myself up...."

"This is no dream, Angelique, this is real. I know I'm not the man you thought I was, but I hope you believe me when I say, man or monster, you can trust me."

19

Fated For a Vampire

Jordon accompanied Corin and Angelique along the trail to the farm, explaining the events that had led him there. Earlier, while resting in his room at Black River Falls Inn, his phone had woken him at 11:52. He'd lay perturbed for a moment before answering.

"Still chasing after me, Jordon Black?" a voice mocked. "Another night, another bite, another victim runs in fright."

This was the first time the nightwalker had ever made contact, leaving Jordon bewildered.

"Care to join me for a feast? Wondering where I am, Marshal? Hmm...things I see—a black Dodge Charger, a blue door marked 131, a man in bed wearing a gray t-shirt."

Jordon scrambled out of bed and scanned the room. He slammed down the phone, swatting at a spider that narrowly escaped up the wall and out a vent. Moving fast, he dressed, grabbed his wallet, badge, and gun, and stepped outside. Knowing it was most likely a trap, he still had to take the bait.

Finding the lot uneventful, he made his way around the side of the building in search of the fugitive. He stopped when he spotted the wretch in a back alley, finishing off his kill. Jordon recognized the young, unfortunate woman—a housekeeper at the Inn. The nightwalker looked his way with a sneer and dropped the corpse to the pavement. He stepped into the light at the corner of the building and wiped his mouth. Squatting, he retrieved something from the ground. Jordon thought he saw movement, but he was too far away to make out what it was.

You're purposely showing yourself. Why?

The nightwalker stood up, shape-shifted into a black raven, and took to the sky. Jordon transformed and followed, just as his foe had apparently planned. Moving around thirty miles per hour, the rotter led him to the Jaffler's farm.

"And you thought it was me?" Corin said. "He was using my identity."

"Yes." Jordon looked at Corin. "He landed in front of the house, took back your form, and headed for the door before I could move in on him. Ms. Jaffler answered, so I stayed out of sight."

"Call me Angelique."

"Thank you, Angelique." Jordon immediately noticed the displeased look on Corin's face. A hint of jealousy creeping out perhaps? "Anyway, I didn't want to put her in danger, so I just continued to follow and watch until your confrontation with him in the woods. He sure did a good job of setting you up, von Vadim."

"And it almost worked. Except, he didn't count on me showing up and foiling his plan. Tell me, if you were following him the whole time, how did you manage to go for the wrong guy?"

"Approaching the creek, I thought I sensed someone behind me, so I doubled back to check it out. I had no idea you were out there, ahead of us. I'm usually better with direction. When I returned, I found the two of you fighting, thinking you were my mark."

"I also sensed someone. It must have been you. At the time, I thought it might be Boldor. I've never been able to detect him."

"That's a lengthy story," Jordon told him as the farmhouse came into view.

"It will have to wait." Corin caught Jordon's shoulder and whispered to him. "I need some time with Angelique. Meet us at the estate. We can talk more."

Jordon took to the woods—a black wolf—leaving them alone.

Corin turned and faced Angelique. "You never told me you and Tomes were twins."

"It's no secret. It just never came up in conversation. Besides, you're one to talk. I'm sure there are still a lot of things I don't know about you."

"I just can't help wondering why, in all the time I spent with your father, he never mentioned it. I always assumed Tomes was a couple of years older than you."

"He is older, but only by a few minutes," she said. "Hold on, did you just say that you spent time with my father?"

Angelique exhibited a puzzled expression, and Corin knew she wanted answers, not only about her father, but also about him.

"We'll talk in the car." He held the passenger door open while she got in and then took his seat behind the wheel. "I know you have questions. Feel free to ask me anything."

"Okay. You said you're a vampire. Do you drink blood? Or is that even true."

"Unfortunately, it is. Without it I couldn't survive," he told her. "I also sleep during the day, when the sun's out, in the darkened basement of the estate house. I'm also immortal."

"The murders, you didn't—"

"No. It wasn't me," he assured her. "The other nightwalker, the one who deceived you, he's the killer. His name is Boldor, and he's a real monster in every sense of the word. He's actually deluded you twice. Now, under the guise of me, and before, as Louis Gomez."

"That's why you and Tomes both warned me to watch out for him. And speaking of Tomes, I suppose he knows about you."

"He does."

"Everything is so much clearer now, why he didn't want me seeing you—a vampire. But he treats you so horribly."

"And I can't blame him for it." Corin was glad she finally knew everything.

"He's your brother, and he's only protecting you."

"Which is why you put up with him."

"In the beginning, yes. And out of respect for the friendship I had with your father. Tomes can be hard to take, but we understand one another. We've actually been working together, trying to track down Boldor. Besides stopping the killing, I have my own issues with him, and Tomes wants revenge for everything the nightwalker did to Louisa. He won't rest until he gets it."

"I can't believe I was alone with him tonight. He had ample opportunity to kill me if he'd wanted, so why didn't he?"

"I'm not sure. I know he wants payback for what happened with Louisa."

"What do you mean? He killed her, what, six nights

ago?"

"So much more has happened. I won't go into every detail, but to give you the short of it, Boldor resurrected her, there were problems, and she came back insane. When we found her tonight, and she attacked Tomes, I was forced to end her life in order to save him. Insanity, combined with the insatiable hunger of a nightwalker, is a hazardous mix."

"Is he all right?"

"She cut him up, and he's weak from loss of blood, but he'll make it."

"I knew something was wrong with him earlier. I could feel it."

"He said the same thing about you." Corin found their connection fascinating.

"We should get to him," Angelique said. "I have a funny feeling now, but with him being hurt, that's most likely the cause."

Trusting her connection, Corin didn't waste another minute. He turned the key, and the 'Vette's engine purred. He shifted into drive and hit the gas, eager to get to Tomes.

"I have Tomes settled in a room, but he's a stubborn one. It'll be a miracle if he's kept to his bed."

Angelique burst out laughing. "You really do know him well. He's strong-willed all right. I'm afraid we're a lot alike in that respect."

"God help me," Corin teased. "But seriously, despite our differences, he's grown on me."

"He has a way of doing that." Angelique smiled. "One of these days, when he gets past this terrible time in his life, he's going to look back and realize he has more material to work with than he'll ever know what to do with."

"What do you mean?"

"I doubt he'd want me telling you this, but he's

always wanted to write a novel."

"You're kidding."

"Not at all."

"Well, he's just full of talent, isn't he—contractor, equestrian farm owner, and now a writer?"

"As his sister, I'm of course biased, but I've read some of his short stories and they're really good. There are many sides to Tomes. You wouldn't know it by his recent behavior, but he really is a sensitive guy. Some of his best work are pieces he's written about Louisa. You can feel the passion and love they shared jumping off the pages."

"I just can't picture Tomes writing a novel." Corin laughed. "But then again, I suppose I have a lot of different sides myself."

Angelique lips curved upward. "I can only imagine."

Corin was amazed at how accepting she was, despite everything she'd seen. Still, he couldn't help wondering if her feelings for him would now change. Could she care for him, knowing he was a creature of the night that drank the blood of the living?

"Something's wrong." Angelique suddenly straightened. "It's Tomes. Something bad."

"Boldor." Corin picked up speed. "I was afraid he'd go after him."

* * * *

Tomes heard a noise outside his room and pushed himself up in bed. Someone was there. Watching the door, the knob slowly turned to the left. Gooseflesh covered his body as anxiety flooded him.

He grasped the staker tightly in his right hand and took a deep breath. The door inched open, and his heart drummed faster and faster. An unpleasant smell seeped through the crack, confirming his suspicion—

Boldor. With that knowledge, he expelled his breath and raised the staker, aimed for the center of the doorway. He steadied his arm, figuring he'd probably only get one shot before Boldor reached him.

"Step through that door and I'll shoot," he called out. "And you can bet it'll hurt, Nightwalker. I know your weakness."

The door stopped moving. Tomes assumed Boldor was contemplating his next move.

"Confined to our bed, are we?" The intruder's voice floated from the hall.

The menacing tone chilled Tomes's bones, but he fought his fear and held his aim, prepared for Boldor to rush in at any moment. However, to his dismay, instead of the human form of the foe he'd expected, a vapory mist crept through the opening and into the room.

Tomes swore and scrambled to the opposite side of the bed. How could he shoot vapor? Penned in, he was weak and in pain, but his heightened adrenaline overpowered his physical ailments, keeping him on his feet. The vapor drew closer and closer until it passed right through his body, stunning him for a brief moment. And before he could react, Boldor had already shape-shifted and restrained him from behind.

"So, you say you know my weakness." Boldor's last word rolled on a hiss. "Did you know my little firecat's as well?" He pressed an arm against his throat. "Although, I have to say, it looks like she left this feeble, mortal body of yours with some rather deep wounds."

"I made the mistake of trying to reason with her. Believe me, I won't make the same mistake with you," Tomes spoke through clenched teeth.

Boldor laughed. "There is nothing to be reasoned. I kill you, and we're done."

"Are you afraid to face me, a mere mortal? You have

to kill me from behind, proving yourself a coward?”

“Afraid?” Boldor laughed again. “Of you?”

“Then face me,” Tomes challenged.

Boldor spun Tomes around. Holding him with one hand at his throat, he stroked a button with the other. The insect moved inside the gem, sending an icy wave riding Tomes’s spine.

“Von Vadim’s little lackey. I’m beginning to see why he keeps you around.”

Boldor ran a talon up the side of Tomes’s face. “I have to say, you’re nearly as good-looking as your sister.”

“I’ve always thought so. But I’m afraid you’re not my type.”

“Quite the brave little soldier, aren’t you? And a mouth to match,” Boldor responded with a calm but assertive voice.

“So I’ve been told.” Tomes kept in character, attempting to keep Boldor in conversation while he inched the staker up, aiming straight for his mid-section.

“I could rip your head off right now with little effort, mortal.”

“I’m not afraid of you.”

“You should be,” Boldor warned.

Silently counting to three, Tomes pulled the trigger, firing a shot into Boldor’s gut. The nightwalker ejected an unearthly cry and doubled over. Amid the frenzy, Tomes broke free from his hold and scrambled to the opposite side of the room.

“Blackthorn nails,” Tomes boasted. “Probably burning like fiery bullets.”

Boldor jerked uncontrollably, drool seeping from his gaping mouth as he emitted a low, steady rumble. Managing to insert his index and thumb talons into the entry wound, he dug out the nail. Pulling it free, he took several deep, ragged breaths before turning his glare on Tomes who still held a steady aim with the staker.

"Blackthorn. I've never experienced it before. It's tormenting, but I'm sorry to say, it won't kill me," Boldor informed Tomes, taking a step his way, teeth gnashing.

The immortal was ready to finish him off, but before he had a chance to play out his final move, the sound of someone racing up the stairs diverted his attack.

"Von Vadim," Boldor growled.

"I hope you're prepared to take us both on."

"We'll have our chance again, lackey." Boldor dematerialized.

Corin rushed into the room with Angelique at his heels, both inquiring about his well-being. Tomes clutched the weapon for dear life, barely able to stand.

"Man, talk about cutting it close. You got here in the nick of time. Boldor took off when he heard you coming. And let me just say, there's something to be said about this baby." Tomes waved the staker at him.

"You shot him?" Corin sounded surprised. He hurried over and helped Tomes to the bed.

"I sure did. He wasn't too happy about it either."

"I bet. Where is he now?"

"He turned to vapor and streamed out the door into the hall." Tomes motioned.

"I didn't see anything," Angelique said.

"I'm going to make sure he's gone. Stay here with your brother," Corin instructed before darting away.

"You're lucky he didn't kill you, Tomes." Angelique sat on the edge of the bed and helped him situate the bedding.

"He would have if I hadn't kept him talking," Tomes told her. "Engaging him in conversation was the trick to getting the shot in. He has an ego the size of Texas.

And thank God for that."

"I'm just glad you're okay." She kissed him on the forehead.

"Please, Angel. I'm a grown man," he whined. "What if Corin walks in and sees you babying me? I have a reputation to uphold."

"Sorry."

"You know, don't you...about Corin? You don't seem the least bit shocked by any of this."

"He told me everything. He had to."

"So, you know about the other nightwalker—Boldor? He's the one committing the murders, who killed Louisa."

"I know. And he told me what happened tonight. I'm so sorry, Tomes."

"I've lost her twice. But he'll pay."

"It's unreal, isn't it, a nightwalker living right next door, becoming part of our lives? But it explains so much, the changes in you, your attitude toward him."

"Now you know why you can't be together," Tomes told her.

"I trust Corin, regardless of what he is. He saved both our lives tonight."

Outside the door, Corin paused before entering, catching the last part of their conversation as he entered. "Sorry to interrupt. The house is safe," he informed them. "Boldor's gone...for now."

* * * *

Corin left Angelique and Tomes alone, figuring they could use some private time to talk. He headed downstairs and found the marshal waiting in the foyer.

"Is everything in order?" Jordon asked.

"For the time being." Corin showed him to the living room and poured them each a glass of brandy. "Boldor was in the house, but he's gone now."

"He gets around, doesn't he?"

"He has a score to settle. At the moment, I guess we all do."

Corin relaxed on the sofa, and Jordon sat in a chair across from him.

"Now, Marshal, about you?" Corin raised an eyebrow.

"The name's Jordon."

"Okay, Jordon. You're immortal. That much I know. But when I asked you earlier if you were a nightwalker your reply was 'not exactly.' Why don't you start by explaining to me what you meant."

"I'm an Indith immortal from another world called the Eleventh Dimension. I'm not a nightwalker, but a daywalker. The sun doesn't harm us, so we're not prisoners to the night as you are."

"But you have powers. You're able to change form."

"Yes. There are many similarities between us, but I don't require blood to survive. I eat the same as mortals—steak, fries, and everything in between."

"I've never heard of your kind, or of the Eleventh Dimension. How do I know you're telling the truth and not just making all of this up? The existence of another world isn't so easy to accept."

"Believe it or not, it exists."

"And you're after Boldor to retrieve a charm you say he stole?"

"A black diamond. It's called the Heart of the Clyth."

"You've been chasing him for the past two years?" Corin wanted to make sure he had the story straight.

"Two long and frustrating years. It's crucial I get the charm back in the safekeeping of the Order," he told him.

"It must be powerful."

"More powerful than you could imagine. The charm

is how he's kept ahead of me all this time." Jordon leaned forward. "You call him Boldor?"

"We got the name from a scoundrel he's employed."

"The Order knew him as Karlot. He's certainly skilled in the art of deception. Not many immortals could pull off what he did and live to tell the tale. If I may ask, what is his issue with you?"

"I'm not sure why he's targeted me, but whatever his reason, he's not going to get away with it," Corin stated. "He's probably been around a long time, but I bet I've been here longer. I'll turn him to ashes and smear him into the earth before I let him destroy my life, or the lives of those I love."

"I have no doubt of that, my friend," Jordon replied. "You know, in the two years I've been trailing him, he's never changed his pattern, not once, until coming here. Something has definitely attracted him to this place. Any ideas what it might be?"

"I haven't come to any definite conclusions yet, but I'm beginning to lean toward the assumption that it may be my life and fortune he's after. He's seen what a five-hundred-year-old nightwalker has forged here, and I think he wants it for himself. As you've corroborated, he's a thief who infiltrates and takes what he wants. Something tells me he's planning to settle, and Louisa was to be his first."

"His first?" Jordon's brow rose. "His first what?"

"The first of a newly formed clan," Corin explained his meaning. "With his twisted mind, he wouldn't be content living in seclusion, the way I have. I prefer to walk alone."

"Not a family man?" Jordon said coolly.

"I keep it simple. There's less chance of discovery that way."

Jordon nodded. "True."

"Boldor is a different story, he'd require followers,

others to lord over, those made from him that he could stake full claim to."

"A clan of his own lineage. He'd put himself in the position of a Godfather to them all. Although, on my world most nightwalkers do live in clans with heads of families." Jordon finished his brandy and set the glass down.

"And some do here too. But any family formed by this nightwalker will be ruthless."

"I have to agree. And if he's after you, you'd best stay on guard. He's crafty—a maestro of mayhem," Jordon warned. "Seriously, watch yourself."

They broke off their conversation at the sound of Angelique coming down the stairs.

"How's Tomes?" Corin stood as she approached.

"He's been through a lot, but I think he'll live." She took a seat next to him.

"Marshal," she acknowledged. "I know you're also a nightwalker."

"I'm a daywalker, but close enough. And the name's Jordon."

Angelique smiled and turned to Corin. "Thank you for everything you've done for Tomes. He told me you healed some of his injuries."

"I did what I could, but the deeper, more extensive wounds will have to heal on their own. He lost a lot of blood, and I'm sure he'll be weak for some time."

"Well, thanks to you, at least he'll live to see another day."

"In spite of my actions, he's a very lucky man. Things could have gone much differently."

"But they didn't." Clearly impressed by his heroics, Angelique took his hand and squeezed it gently.

Corin, catching Jordon's grin, quickly rose. "Angelique, you must be tired. I think you'll be comfortable in the room next to your brother. And,

Jordon, we can find a place for you as well," he offered, thinking it would be best for them to join forces for the time being.

Jordon nodded. "To catch my mark, it looks like I'll need to stay close to you. So yes, I'll be sticking around."

"It's been a long time since I've had company, so forgive me if I forget something. You're welcome to use any part of the house with exception of the basement. You should be able to find something suitable for consumption in the kitchen. I leave a few things stocked for show."

"To show who?" Jordon asked with a laugh. "You're a strange fellow, von Vadim. I've never met a nightwalker, a loner at that, who possesses such a yearning to fit in, or one so mannerly."

"Only in the company of a select few. I assure you, I am no saint."

"Oh, I would never mistake you for a saint. But you are no Boldor either," Jordon said.

Corin studied Jordon. He seemed safe enough to have around, but he remembered how it felt having the immortal as an opponent, bringing about second thoughts. He didn't sense any treachery in him, but he also didn't relish the idea of harboring the stranger in his home while having Angelique and Tomes in his care. However, if he was legit, joining forces was the wise thing to do. The immortal could prove to be an asset in their fight against Boldor. He just wished what he claimed wasn't so outlandish—the Eleventh Dimension? But then again, if vampires existed, couldn't other unimaginable things like other worlds exist as well?

* * * *

The estate shone silver under the magical, cascading light of the full moon. Angelique stood on the darkened lanai, gazing in the direction of the woods, immersed in her thoughts.

What is that?

A dark image captured her attention, emerging from the silhouetted treetops, coming her way. It appeared to be a large bird, its massive wings audible as it drew nearer and landed several feet from the lanai, its widespread wings spanning a good five feet from tip to tip. Her heart rate sped when it zeroed in on her position with wide-open eyes.

"What?" The creature unexpectedly shape-shifted into the form of a man—Corin.

"Are you appalled?" he spoke out. "At what I am?"

"Appalled isn't the word I'd use." She stepped toward the screened door, all apprehension faded away. "I'm more along the lines of, I don't know...amazed." She opened the door and joined him outside.

"I was afraid of what you'd now think of me, after seeing what I become."

"I see you no differently than I did before." She approached him without fear, trusting he'd never harm her. In her heart she knew he cared for her the same way she cared for him. "Beautiful, isn't it?" She looked up at the moon, in awe of its radiance.

"Yes. It seems so close tonight, larger and brighter than I've seen it in a long time."

"Maybe that means something." Angelique took his hand and leaned against him. "Do you believe it possesses power?"

"The moon is magnetic, its energy drawing us toward it." He wrapped an arm around her. "It reigns over the night, connecting with us on many levels. My powers are strongest when it's full, like tonight. So yes,

I believe it to be true." Corin pulled her in front of him and lifted her chin with his fingertips, looking into her hazel eyes. "I'm so sorry, Angelique. I should have never pursued you, but curse it all, I just couldn't help myself."

She smiled and laid her head against his chest. "Is it even possible for us to be together?"

"Physically, I can be with you in the same manner any mortal man can. Beyond that, as time passes, being mortal, you would age, but I would live on unchanged."

"Unless I too became a nightwalker."

"That isn't a decision to be made lightly. I could never ask—"

She pressed her fingers to his lips. "I know you care for me, and right now, all I want to do is savor every moment of this night. There'll be plenty of time to worry about the obstacles later."

Corin pulled her soft, warm body against him. He kissed her neck, his breath damp and electrifying, filling her with such heat and desire she thought she might pass out from the burning intensity.

"Take me to bed," a sultry whisper broke her lips.

He looked earnestly into her eyes. "Are you sure?"

"I couldn't be more sure. I need you."

He kissed her with a deep, passionate longing and swept her off her feet. Carrying her into the house, he took her to the basement, flipping a light switch at the top of the stairs before descending the staircase into his lair. Glancing over the space, she clutched him tight when her gaze fell on the crypt forged into the back wall.

"Are you certain about this?" He lowered her to her feet. "I would never take you against your will."

Angelique ran her hand down the side of his face, looking into his eyes—dark, endless pools. She could see the love he had for her—true, undeniable love. "I'm not afraid of what you are."

Corin caught her hand and held it to his chest, against his heart.

"This is where you sleep?" Angelique couldn't stop herself from staring at the crypt.

"Yes, my shelter during the light of day. It bothers you, the crypt?"

"It...interests me," Angelique said. "I told you, I'm not afraid. I want to be here, with you."

"I'm sorry the room is such a mess, but I am a bachelor." He pulled away from her just long enough to light several candles and turn off the annoying light at the top of the stairs.

"It's not so bad. It just needs a woman's touch."

"That it does." Corin made a detour to turn on some music, setting the stereo to a soft rock station. An old song by REO Speedwagon sounded out: "Can't Fight This Feeling." "This has to be a sign tonight's meant to be, because I can't fight it anymore." He climbed into the crypt and pulled Angelique into bed behind him.

Angelique quivered, his touch sending a powerful surge through her body as he repeated the words of the song, running his lips up one side of her face, across her forehead, and down the other side. He gently laid her back, and taking his time, slowly began relieving her of her clothing. She arched with pleasure, tormented with arousal, his hands exploring every bare inch of her flesh before shedding his own clothes and positioning his fit, muscled body over her.

Burying her hands in his mass of blond hair, she moaned as he suckled her breasts, daring to allow her touch to traverse down, along his torso, making their way to the rippling muscles at his abdomen. Arching again, his exploration tantalized her, teasing her in the worst possible way, until she thought she might die of pure delight.

Before going any further, Corin suddenly pulled back. "I love you, Angelique." He looked into her eyes. "You must know that this is more than just sex to me." He tenderly brushed several strands of hair away from her face.

"I wouldn't be here otherwise," she responded breathlessly.

"I would give you anything you desired." He touched his forehead to hers. "Anything in my power to give."

"Right now, all I want is you." She reached up and pulled him to her, wanting release, needing him to satisfy her own insatiable hunger.

Corin moved into position to fully take her and slowly entered her fiery heat. She wrapped her legs around his waist, holding him tight, running her hands along the contours of his back. He slid deep, each stroke further building the heat between them until it was a raging furnace. Finally reaching her orgasm, she reveled in the ecstasy, knowing he held back his own release.

"I'm just getting started." Corin proceeded to ravish her body while she rested.

He caressed and suckled until she could stand no more and then took her again, bringing her to another peak before seeking out his own fulfillment with a muffled growl. Completely sated, they lay together, basking in the aftermath.

"I will forever praise the fates for this." Corin traced his fingers along her shoulder. "Do you believe in fate?"

"I do." She nestled against him. "And it seems that I am fated for a vampire—fangs and all."

Corin laughed, holding her close. "Seriously, do you regret being with me?"

"I could never regret you, Corin. I've never felt so fulfilled. But I am a little afraid."

"What are you afraid of...not of me?"

"No. Of what happens now, I guess. You're a nightwalker. You live a life I know very little about. How do I know you won't tire of me tomorrow and walk away?"

"That's not going to happen. I love you, Angelique. I have for years."

"Years? What do you mean? You've only been in Hixton a month. And my father, you mentioned him before. How could you have known him?"

"I'm not the nephew of Victor von Vadim, Angelique, I am Victor von Vadim," he confessed. "You probably don't remember, but I even met you once as Victor, when you were a child."

"Are you serious?" She propped herself up with her elbow and looked into his face. "You're Victor von Vadim? But he was an elderly man and you, well, you're so young."

"I have the ability to make myself appear to age just like a normal, mortal man would. And when I've lived out a full human lifetime, I fake my death and return as an heir," he explained.

"Wow. I do remember meeting you years ago as Victor." A childhood memory suddenly resurfaced. "I must have been eight or nine at the time. You came to the farm one evening to see my father, and I answered the door. We talked."

"I still remember what you said to me that night. You said, 'Don't you like people'?"

"Yes. And you told me you weren't fond of company...private. You said you might consider leaving the gate open once in a while if you knew you'd be getting a visit from a new friend. You meant me. I can't believe this. But you never did open the gate."

"No. I was respecting your father's wishes."

"But you have now. Why now?"

"You, Angelique. You've bewitched me. But it was

also time for the chains to go. I was thinking I'd install an automatic gate system."

"That's a good idea." Angelique loved the feel of his cool, firm body.

"Something I've been thinking of doing for a while, that should have been done a long time ago."

"So, you've always been here? For how long? Just how old are you exactly?" Angelique couldn't hold back the burst of questions.

"I've been walking this earth for over five hundred years."

"Five hundred years?" She could hardly believe it. "That's hard to fathom. The portrait in the corridor, the one I noticed on my first visit, it is you, isn't it?"

"Yes," he admitted.

"I knew it. The eyes gave it away. Your eyes," she told him. "Intuition was signaling me, but I chose not to listen."

"You were led to ignore it," Corin corrected. "I hated lying to you."

"I certainly understand, but I'm glad I now know the truth...about everything. And none of what I've learned about you could ever make me love you any less," she assured him. "It's amazing though."

"What?"

"That I just made love to a five hundred-year-old vampire." She smiled and stroked a finger over the dimple in his left cheek, feeling right at home with him in his crypt.

"Yes, well, I guess there's no accounting for taste," he quipped. "But I think I look rather good for my age."

"No argument there." Angelique gave him a warm, tender kiss before snuggling back against him.

"You do know Tomes is going to kill me if he finds out about this." He wrapped her in his arms, sliding his fingers through her long tendrils. "I had to hold in what should have been a thundering roar just because I knew he was upstairs. Oh man...."

"What?"

"He'll probably come after me with that machete of his."

Angelique giggled at his wit. "He'll get over it."

"I wouldn't count on it. He's been perfectly open about what he thinks of me and my kind."

"He can't make my choices for me. In time, I do think he'll come around." She leaned over Corin. "Speaking of my brother, I should check in on him soon."

"I'll do that in a little while; besides, you'd know if something was wrong. That connection the two of you share." Corin suddenly wondered if he'd sensed their lovemaking. "You don't suppose—"

"No." Angelique knew what he was thinking. "Tomes won't know we've been together. We only feel each other when something's wrong. Pain. Extreme fear. That sort of thing. I don't know why it happens."

"That's a relief. I'd prefer to keep my head."

"Let's not talk anymore about Tomes. I know how he feels about you, but it really doesn't matter what he thinks. It's my life, my choice, and I've chosen you."

"It would be nice to have his approval, but I won't hold my breath."

"Mortal or immortal, human or nightwalker, in my opinion, there's no one better. And look what you've done for him. You've risked exposure, not to mention your own life to help him."

"I love the way you see me. And I promise you, Angelique, I'll do everything I can to protect you, your brother, and our town from Boldor. I won't allow him to destroy us."

Angelique knew he meant every word he said. But in spite of everything he'd revealed to her, there remained a mystery about him, leading her to believe he still harbored many secrets. He had lived many lives and no doubt loved other women, something she'd have to accept. Five hundred years was a long time. But maybe the fates were waiting for her—his other half—to find him in life. She truly believed they were meant to be together, and walking trustingly into his world, she was certain of only one thing, that she was in love and fated for a vampire.

20

The Eleventh Dimension

Corin left Angelique sleeping in the crypt and slipped upstairs to look in on Tomes, glad to find him resting peacefully. Deciding to check the safety of the house, there was no indication of trouble, but he couldn't shake a nagging feeling of being watched. Not able to sense Boldor agitated him. The nightwalker's ability to conceal his presence posed a continual threat to them all.

Satisfied there was no danger, he drifted to the lanai and took a seat in the darkness, gazing out at the silvery landscape. Wolves howled in the near distance, a curious occurrence. In recent years, he was accustomed to hearing one from time to time, but never so many.

His thoughts trailed to his late wife and an old hurt pierced his heart, bringing tears to his eyes. She had been his friend and consort, and since her, there had been no one else, until Angelique.

Corin had met Miralanya when he'd lived as Nevin von Vadim. He'd shared her lifespan with her, loving her for nearly fifty years, using his power to give himself the appearance of aging. Allowing them to grow old together made the situation easier for her to accept. However, with her mortality, death eventually came. Losing her was hell, leaving him to endure the terrible heartache that he still felt all these years later.

His thoughts turned to Angelique. Could he do it again? Could he ever bear losing her the way he had Miralanya? Angelique was a blessing, his angel of light. She lit the darkness of his dismal existence, and without her, he feared he'd forevermore be incomplete.

He'd lived too many lifetimes and endured too much suffering, but he'd accepted his fate—his curse—long ago. But at times like these, the cruelty of what immortality really meant came flooding back. He knew that in a human lifespan times of joy typically outweighed those of sorrow—two things he had experienced many times over—but in his long life, the balance was reversed, with sorrow and loneliness overshadowing his existence. If only he didn't have to continue his eternal walk alone, wishing Angelique could continue with him as his immortal companion, but he could never ask her to give up her soul to be with him. It could not happen. He would not be the devil responsible for clipping an angel's wings.

* * * *

Sheriff Pierson couldn't believe he'd been called out for another homicide. All he could do was hope they'd find some solid evidence this time. He had Corin von Vadim pegged as the killer, but he had no firm proof. There was the watch, of course, but with it inscribed with only a first name, he had no way of proving it belonged to von Vadim. And with nothing else tying the estate owner to the murders, he couldn't build a case against him.

Rudy had searched every accessible database, digging up all the information he could find on the man, but what he'd discovered, or rather the lack of, was perplexing. He'd found the usual driver's license and social security records, but not much more beyond that. There were no birth or school records, nothing showing he'd ever existed as a child, which was odd, making Sheriff Pierson even more suspicious.

A mass of media had descended on the crime scene at the Black River Falls Inn. With this the fifth killing in a lengthening string of murders, there was no way of avoiding them. The *Jackson County killings*—as the murders had been dubbed—were quickly becoming nation-wide news.

Rambling off a prewritten statement to the many TV cameras and reporters gathered before him, Pierson grimaced when he spotted Robert Darnell—the husband of the second murder victim, Sandy Darnell—amid the crowd. He had been hounding the station since his wife's murder, demanding action and throwing about accusations of inadequacy toward him and his investigative team. Pierson understood his need for justice, but slandering the law certainly wasn't the way to go about achieving it.

The sheriff tugged his left ear, that ol' twitch revving up. His green eyes focused on Mr. Darnell. And just as he suspected, the man made his move, lifting a megaphone to his mouth and confronting the sheriff, creating a spectacle.

"What have you done to catch this killer, Sheriff? How many more women must die before the department finally takes some real action?"

"What is your response?" a reporter called out,

instigated by the drama.

"I assure you, we're following every available lead," Pierson replied. "But I can't divulge any particulars for the good of the investigation." With national exposure likely, he was careful with his words.

Sheriff Pierson tried to finish his statement, but Mr. Darnell's constant interruptions prompted him to skip ahead to his closing. He quickly offered his condolences to the families of the victims and reassured the public that his team was hard at work, giving one hundred percent to each case. He then backed away from the microphone and worked his way through the swarming media who had been stirred up by the public display. Mr. Darnell had certainly succeeded in creating quite a chaotic scene, turning what should have been a well-controlled media update into an outright protest, yelling out, "We want action. Show us action," and convincing a group of others to join his chant.

"Do you have any suspects, Sheriff?" One reporter managed to get close enough to shove a microphone in his face.

"Like I've already said, at present we are unable to disclose any information for concern of impairing our investigation." He pushed past the crowd with the help of two officers and made his way around the building to the taped-off crime scene in the back alley. "Let's move this perimeter back another hundred feet," he ordered. "I want this area kept clear."

Pulling an officer aside, he gave instructions to charge Mr. Darnell with creating a public disturbance and impeding a police investigation if he continued his protest. He knew the charge wouldn't stick, but all he was looking to do was settle things down so he could take care of business. This was a crime scene, after all, not a circus.

* * * *

At von Vadim Estate, Jordon stood at his bedroom window looking toward the woods, listening to the wolves howling in the night. They were too close for comfort.

Plagued by their doleful wails, he couldn't rest and made his way downstairs to the first floor, sensing Corin's presence. Moving toward the lanai door, he spotted the nightwalker's position right away, having exceptional night vision.

"Mind some company?" Jordon asked.

"Have a seat and tell me a little more about yourself." Corin welcomed the company.

Jordon pulled out one of three available chairs and joined Corin at the wrought iron patio table.

"The wolves are relentless tonight. Do you have them where you come from?"

"There used to be a great many wolves in my world. But they're now pretty much extinct, having been hunted and slaughtered by the nightwalkers."

"What a shame," Corin expressed with lament. "I find it strange how we immortals assume their canine forms more often than any other animal."

"It's always been that way, especially with clans, running as packs. But it's also a common choice for daywalkers. As you know. Although, the animals don't seek us out the way they do your kind."

"Why do you think that is? Why do they seek us out? Disclose our whereabouts?" Corin mused.

"I'd like to say it's because you are kindred spirits—creatures and hunters of the night—but the greater likelihood is they sense your bloodthirsty nature and are gathering for a feast of leftovers."

"Rather morbid theory."

I suppose, but they are hunters."

"Why did the nightwalkers wipe out the wolves on your world?"

"They had no choice. During times of war, the animals gave up the nightwalker's positions to their enemies. So, as you can understand, it came down to a matter of survival."

"Your world seems so much different from ours."

"It is, in many ways, and much the same in others. We're not as technologically advanced, stuck in a time similar to what you once called your Medieval period."

"Are there humans, or is it only immortals?"

"There are mortals. The population mostly consists of nightwalkers, daywalkers, and humans. However, contrary to Earth, humans aren't the dominant species. Here, immortals are viewed as monsters of myth, but in my world, we don't hide away in obscurity for fear of being discovered. We live free, open lives, right along with humans and other beings existing there."

"You all coexist in your world?" Corin was intrigued. "Mortal and immortal together...in peace?"

"Don't get me wrong, we are a far cry from being a perfect world. But at least in the Eleventh Dimension we each know of the others' existence. And even though Earth has far exceeded us technologically, we have managed to surpass you in several other areas, one example being a scientific breakthrough made by a nightwalker named Mirillow Traxl. He discovered a method of feeding that doesn't require taking blood from other living creatures. It's all in a pill."

"A pill?" Corin's voice held disbelief.

"Traxl created it from some newly discovered protein. But I'm no expert in the field of science, so don't go asking me to explain it to you. All I know is he made the discovery and it works."

"Imagine what that could do for my kind here, less killing, and no more feeding from beasts."

"Well, it's a fairly new find, and there's also the politics to contend with. We do have some who oppose it. Not every nightwalker is so willing to give up the traditional method of feeding."

"I sure would love to visit this world of yours. Has that ever been allowed?"

"You're immortal, so it could be arranged. I'd have to get permission from Council, but with me vouching for you, I don't think it would be a problem."

"How do you cross from world to world?"

Jordon could see Corin was fully engrossed, riveted by the deluge of information and wanting more. "There's an ancient passage called the Passage of Dimensions. It's been used since sorcerers ruled the divisions."

"Sorcerers? That must have been something."

"Sadly, today, only one sorcerer remains."

"You travel through this passage?"

Jordon nodded. "The Eleventh Dimension has ten portals that lead to ten other dimensions, with each of those other worlds connected to us by a single portal," he divulged. "We use those portals."

"So, each of the other worlds only have one portal that leads back to the Eleventh Dimension?"

"That's right. The Eleventh Dimension is the main world that all the others are tied to."

"Eleven dimensions. That says it all. Why your world is called the Eleventh Dimension." Corin's lips stretched as if amused.

You're skeptical. Jordon could tell.

"Amazing to think about. Multiple dimensions. And having the ability to travel between them."

"Not anymore." Jordon had more to tell. "The portals in the other ten dimensions have been blocked since the time of our ancient sorcerers and kept under the watch of supreme guardians."

"Why are they blocked?"

"In the beginning of our world, a supreme being, old as time, resided in the Eleventh Dimension. He favored the sorcerers, granting them discs that allowed them to travel through the portals to the other ten dimensions. It is believed that this supreme was actually the creator of the portals, and possibly the other dimensions as well." Jordon knew the events he told sounded more like a fairytale than truth, but he continued, hoping Corin would keep an open mind. "He gave the sorcerers knowledge of great things, but as they evolved, they became vain and unruly, placing themselves above all other beings, with the belief that they should rule over the other dimensions. Even daring to challenge him. So, in his wrath, the supreme destroyed all discs he had created and left the Eleventh Dimension to reside in one of the alternate dimensions known as Zarmeva—the Plane of Supreme Beings."

"That is some story."

"Not just a story. Our history."

"But if he destroyed all of the discs, how do you travel now? How did you come here, to Earth?" Corin held an inquisitive stare. "You also said that the portals were blocked."

"The portals are only blocked entering the other ten worlds," Jordon explained.

"But without the discs...."

"The sorcerers put all of their effort into recreating them and eventually succeeded. But when the supreme discovered their achievement, that's when he blocked the portals in the other dimensions and ensured their security by assigning supreme guardians, preventing anyone from entering the worlds. But the sorcerers didn't stop there and kept advancing the power of the discs, inadvertently developing a way of tapping into the wormholes to create new pathways capable of reaching other universes. Other worlds."

"Wormholes?"

"Yes, the portals are wormholes, but the Passage is partly engineered, controlled through a melding of science and magic. Discovering inhabitable worlds, the sorcerers could save the coordinates, enabling them to return by means of something they called a shalym disc, a sort of calling card. What we use now. The discs activate the passage for leaving and returning. They are our only means of getting back, so we guard them with our lives. Only those authorized to cross worlds are issued a disc. It is a great honor to be entrusted with one."

"Otherworld portals. Sorcerers. Supreme beings. With everything you've just told me, I don't know how you consider Earth technically advanced."

"We have no cars. No cell phones. No—"

"I get the picture," Corin told him. "But you cross worlds. Universes. Amazing, having that ability. I can hardly imagine it. The disc, do you have one with you now?"

Jordon pulled up his shirt revealing a quarter-sized disc secured by a piercing on his lower left abdomen. "I prefer to keep it out of sight in case I should happen upon others from my world." He pulled free the disc and lowered his shirt. "It's marked with ten interconnecting circles that surround a larger circle, representing the ten portals that lead from my world to the other ten dimensions." He allowed Corin a close-up look.

While leaning toward him, Corin observed a mark on the daywalker's forearm. "Your arm. Does that also have something to do with your world?"

"This is the mark of the Indith Sentry, a special force of trained hunters." Jordon replaced the disc beneath his shirt.

"And you're one of these hunters?"

"I'm proud to say I am. We're sent out in search of fugitives who have managed to escape our world, or in this particular circumstance, to recover a charm of great power and return it to its rightful place. That's why I hide the shalym disc and other markings I have, those being the only way others from my world can recognize me. With them concealed, they'll sense I'm an immortal, but that's all they'll know about me."

"You sure live an action-packed life. There's more to you than I would ever have imagined. A world-crossing Indith Sentry who masquerades as a U.S. marshal while chasing down otherworld fugitives."

"Deputy U.S. Marshal. And it's law enforcement. It's in my blood."

"I have to say, you'd make a great comic book character, fitting right in there with Superman and the others. But in all seriousness, you have quite a demanding job."

"I have a lot to make up for." Jordon didn't elaborate.

"So, I guess those from your world are rarely found out."

"You'd be surprised how many immortals in your world know of us. And now, you're one of them. Just remember that I'm incognito—Marshal Jordon Black. Being part of a special division of the Marshals Service, established specifically for capturing the most wretched offenders and killers, makes my job of hunting down fugitives from the Eleventh Dimension a lot easier."

"Is that your real name?"

"The first name, Jordon, but not Black. My true name is Jordon Day Morrain of Kordes."

"Jordon Day—a daywalker." Corin cocked his head.

"I know, very original. No jokes, please." He stopped Corin before he started. "It derives from diurnal immortals—what my kind are called," he explained. "I've also aged my appearance to fit my position. I'm over two hundred years old, but I'd only look around twenty in human years. Not old enough to get much respect in this line of work."

"I understand. I've aged my appearance many times," Corin told him. "About your work, how do you ensure you won't be assigned to other cases instead of those tied to your world? Do you have someone on the inside helping you out?"

"First, I create a case. Then—and I hate to own up to it—I use my powers to manipulate my way around the system," Jordon admitted. "I've even gone so far as to shape-shift into one of my higher-ups, and while assuming his form, specifically requested 'Jordon Black' for the case I needed to be assigned to."

"I'm surprised it hasn't caught up with you."

"Things tend to turn out to my advantage. I'm now presumed by my peers to be one of the top dog's favorites. It makes for good job security."

"You're diabolical."

"Hey, I only do what's necessary. And I'm not hurting anyone...except the bad guys." Jordon was feeling comfortable with Corin.

"Tell me more about the charm you're after. What power does it have?"

"It's one half of two parts. Boldor is in possession of the Heart of the Clyth—the center stone—giving him the power of concealment. But I don't think he's aware that it's actually one of two pieces. When joined with its counterpart, the Body, they form a charm of unimaginable power—the Clyth. This is information the Order of the Clythguard strives to conceal. Very few from this world are privy to the information."

"And you're telling me?"

"I'm breaking a sacred code, but I want you to

understand the vital importance of getting the Heart back. Over the years, Earthly immortals have been brought into the society—friends and spouses—but they are not members of the Order. However, several have proved themselves loyal and trustworthy. Like them, I believe you can be trusted."

"I told you, I'm no saint."

"You're different, Corin. There's something about you, about how all of this is playing out."

"Fate."

"I don't know about that."

"What makes you think Boldor doesn't know about the Body?" Corin asked.

"He was connected with another member of the Order who claimed she kept that information from him. Besides, if he knew it existed, I believe he would have made an attempt to steal it by now. Especially since he's endowed with the power of the Heart and can't be detected."

"You're probably right."

"The Order has always kept the charms separated for added security. When both halves are joined, the Clyth endows its wearer with the power to steal the life force of mortals and immortals alike. For a human, this would mean immortality, but for an immortal, much more—a step beyond immortality—the creation of a god. If it happened to fall into the wrong hands, it could mean the ruin of many worlds." Jordon went on to tell Corin about the demon who created the charm and of the evil warlord, Gaun. "Upon the fall of Gaun, the Order of the Clythguard—a special league of nightwalkers—was instituted for the purpose of guarding the charm. Their job is to ensure that it never fall into such destructive hands again, and for the good of all kind, they must never fail. That's why the charm was sent through the Passage of Dimensions and hidden away in another world. This world. Where the inhabitants know nothing of its existence. But cold and ruthless seekers followed, Indith immortals willing to go to any length to acquire the Clyth's formidable power. These are the worst of my kind, seeking the stature of a god, caring nothing of the vast number of casualties or of the many worlds that could be lost. But of all the immortals to come after the charm, not one from the Eleventh Dimension has ever succeeded in their mission. Yet, Boldor, an Earth-born nightwalker, even with his ignorance of the enormity of what he's acquired, has somehow managed to steal the Heart. He's certainly had luck on his side."

"Why not simply destroy the charm?" Corin suggested.

"I wish it were that easy. But only the demon who created it can destroy it, and he fled Zarmeva for the Endokyre Dimension, a world where a few of the darkest demons relocated to in order to separate themselves from the powers of light that dominate Zarmeva. We also do not know his name. Something Gaun never revealed."

"The other supreme beings, the good ones, won't act on your behalf? Help locate him?"

"With the darkest of demons—those with the power to cross dimensions—residing there, the powers of light avoid the dimension. Not to mention the prophecy."

"Prophecy?"

"Our world follows a prophecy, and in the latter days of that prophecy, a great dark power is mentioned. A power believed to be the Clyth. And with that being the case, the charm is fated to remain to the very end."

"The end of prophecy?"

"Apocalypse."

"Apocalypse. Prophecy." Corin repeated the words in a manner that indicated disbelief.

Jordon said nothing more about the prophecy, knowing that the slew of information he'd already thrown at the nightwalker was too much to digest.

"So, with the Clyth, all you can do is make sure that the power remains in trusted hands. For the sake of your world."

"And yours," Jordon added. "In bringing the relic here, endeavoring to save ourselves, we've selfishly implicated Earth in our plight."

"What's done is done. We're banded together. And now, I am one more soldier in the fight. From this night forth, we are allies."

"That's a union I am pleased to accept."

"Good. Now, you'll have to excuse me." Corin rose to his feet. "I have some things to attend to."

"The girl...Angelique?" Jordon knew what had transpired. "She's with you below?"

Corin tossed him a warning glare. "That doesn't concern you."

"No, it doesn't. Sorry. It's none of my business."

"Till tomorrow evening, then." Corin left.

Jordon went back to his room, hoping the wolves might move on soon. Lying in bed, thoughts of his home world weighed heavily on his heart and mind. With an urge to go back, if only for a few minutes, he pulled the shalym disc free from his side and placed it on his palm. The disc melted into his skin with the top still visible, similar to a coin pressed in a book. Then, outstretching his hand, he turned his palm outward as if halting someone from passing and said, "Ta marof beegha," meaning "take me home" in the ancient language of his ancestors. And with those words a wormhole appeared, providing him passage home.

* * * *

Boldor barged in on Fulner who lay sleeping on a cot in a back room at the funeral home. Startled, the director scrambled to his feet.

"It's nearly morning." Fulner glanced at a clock hanging on the wall. "What are you doing here at this hour?"

"I need shelter for the day. A casket and a room without windows will do. Two things I believe you can supply."

"You've come to the right place. Dealing with the dead and laying folks to rest is what I do best."

Boldor cast a blank stare, not humored in the least.

"I also have several jobs for you." Boldor got straight down to business. "The tasks must be done right away."

"What might these jobs entail?"

"First, I need you to fetch my soil from the basement of a ranch house I was holed up in and bring it to me. You'll find it beneath the bedding." He walked over to a table and took a seat, gesturing for Fulner to do the same. "I'll give you directions, but before you go, I want to go over my plan." Boldor rubbed a button on his coat, glancing down as the insect trapped inside shifted position. "Sit." He pulled his gaze back up, noticing the man was hesitating.

"I don't know if I want to—" Fulner started to protest.

Boldor cocked his head with a fearsome glare. "You should sit, Director. I haven't got time for this foolishness!"

Fulner didn't waste another second finding his seat.

Disregarding the director's momentary lapse in judgment, Boldor proceeded to go over his carefully laid-out plan. After instructing him on his duties, he picked out a very fine coffin and moved it to an adjoining storage room.

"Don't disappoint me," he warned Fulner as he left

the room to depart on his first task of retrieving the soil from the ranch house.

Boldor climbed into the coffin and retreated within its sweet confines for rejuvenation. He needed his soil, especially at this critical time. It wasn't necessary for survival, but lying upon native soil enriched a nightwalker, making him stronger—physically and mentally.

At this point in the game, he needed every advantage he could muster. His new life depended on him making all the right moves. There was no room for mistakes. He knew the night to come would be perilous, but if all went according to plan, he would soon be living a new life with a new identity—Corin von Vadim, Master of von Vadim Estate.

21

To Capture an Angel

Corin clenched his fists and cursed. "You've messed with the wrong guy, Boldor."

The cunning nightwalker had returned his pewter figurine to its rightful place atop the dresser in his basement. The fiend had no doubt slipped it back earlier when he'd attacked Tomes.

Boldor thrived on the thrill of the game and would undoubtedly make his next play soon. However, with two immortals now keeping watch at the estate, Corin didn't think the knave would dare to make another move here. It was now too risky an endeavor.

Corin's thoughts turned to Tomes, and a sigh escaped him. He recalled visiting Louisa's grave the night of her funeral where he'd attempted to see her attacker, but the image was clouded, or she hadn't seen the killer.

Boldor was the reason I couldn't see your

memories.

Corin now realized that the nightwalker's thoughts were already connected with Louisa, his chosen one, who was going through transformation in her grave. He had detected the faint presence of another being at the time, but finding no one around, he'd moved on.

It was Louisa I sensed. In her grave.

Pushing the disturbing thoughts aside, Corin lit a single lantern and left it burning atop a small table near the foot of the stairs. He climbed into the crypt and snuggled against Angelique, listening to the soothing rhythm of her heart, never wanting to let her go. Laying awhile in the silence, when dawn arrived, she awoke in his arms.

"How did you sleep?" he asked.

"It's very comfortable. I didn't wake once." She attempting to climb out of the crypt, but he grabbed her arm and drew her back.

"I'm not ready to let you go," he whispered. "Regrets?" He felt the need to ask again.

"Never." Her slender, naked body pressed against his. "I've never slept so well. And I dreamed of us."

"I hope it was a good dream."

"Wonderful. I was immortal, and we were together...very happy." She repositioned to face him. "You could change me...make my dream come true."

Corin scooted to a sitting position, agitated by her proposition.

"I'm not afraid, Corin."

"No. It's out of the question."

"I thought you'd want us to be together." The sound of her words told her disappointment. "I thought—"

"I will never love anyone else the way I love you, but you don't realize what you'd be giving up. Immortality comes at a great cost. Your soul would be forever lost." He tried to make her understand, looking earnestly into her questioning eyes. "I will never ask that of you—take that from you."

"You're not asking, Corin, I'm giving myself freely. I'm choosing to make the change. Not just for you, but for us."

"You don't understand the magnitude of what you're asking." He tried to discourage her; she had no idea of the enormity of it all. "Love can blind you."

"Maybe so, but what better reason is there for such a sacrifice, than for love—a real love, devouring and passionate. Isn't that what we have?"

"Yes. I'd never deny it. But to infect you with this virus...this curse! What if you later regret your choice and find that love isn't enough? I told you before, once the deed is done, there's no turning back. And I couldn't bear knowing you were living with eternal hatred of me."

"That would never happen," Angelique declared.

"You say that now, but you can't tell the future, when you're still walking this earth hundreds, possibly even thousands of years from now."

"My love for you will never die. I'd never regret choosing to spend eternity with you." She ran her fingers through his wavy hair. "Love lifted me up and into your arms. This is where I belong, now and forever. Please don't deny me this. You said you would give me anything I desired."

"That's not fair, Angelique. My fear isn't just for the loss of your soul, but for what lies beyond immortality. I don't know what happens to us if we ever die. And yes, we can die by certain means. Please, just think on this awhile longer. Don't be so rash in choosing such a cursed existence."

"My feelings aren't going to change, but it would be best if I settled a few things beforehand."

"It would kill Tomes if I made you immortal." Corin

knew she was thinking of her brother. "You don't know his aversion to it all…to me. But I promise you, my love, if and when the time is right and you still want the change, I will give you immortality." He gave her his word. "Right now, though, let's just enjoy what we have."

"I can do that. And I love how you just said, 'my love'."

"That's what you are to me—my love. Man, we certainly give an ironic depiction of the angel bedding down with the devil, don't we?"

"You're no devil, Corin. I wish you could see yourself through my eyes, because looking at you now, I'm the one seeing the angel."

Corin laughed, despite her seriousness. "That just proves you don't know me nearly as well as you think you do. There's a whole other side to me, Angelique. An ever-hungry monster resides in me, a demon I subdue in the depths of my being. This beast is part of who I am, forever reminding me of the horrors I'm capable of."

"You're not joking, are you?"

"No. It's no joke."

"A real demon?"

"Yes. Real as you and I."

If I was changed, would I also have this demon in me?" she wanted to know.

"Yes, you would. With immortality comes the curse, and with the curse comes the demon."

"You're right. There is a lot to consider."

"By denying you immortality, I'm only protecting you from the evil of what you'd become. It would be wonderful having you with me forever, but it would be selfish of me. I would rather die than to be responsible for plaguing you with an eternal life of affliction and regret."

"I understand what you're saying, and I do love you for it." She gave him a kiss. "Now, I'd best get up." She pulled away and crawled out of the crypt.

"Where are you going?" Worried for her safety, he wanted to keep her close.

He had no idea what move Boldor might make next. The nightwalker was dangerous and unpredictable.

"I thought I'd take a shower before checking on Tomes. Then I'll see what I can find for breakfast in that nearly barren kitchen of yours. After last night, I have quite an appetite." She winked. "And Tomes needs to eat so he can get his strength back." She talked while dressing.

"He slept well. I looked in on him earlier."

"I think he's going to be okay. Thanks to you."

Corin loved her endearing smile. "Don't leave the house, Angelique. After what Boldor pulled, I—"

"Don't worry. I'll be perfectly safe."

But Corin couldn't help worrying. Until Boldor was out of their lives, there was no place safe enough.

* * * *

Angelique left the basement and showered, doing the best grooming job she could without having any of her personal things from home. Before heading to the kitchen, she peeked into Tomes's room, finding him awake and vastly improved.

"I can't believe you're up and dressed."

"I want to go downstairs, Angel. I don't like being cooped up."

Knowing there was no stopping Tomes once his mind was set, she helped him to the stairs. Taking steps one by one, it was a slow process, but they managed to make it to the bottom without any mishaps. Relieved, she settled him on the living room sofa, propped on several pillows.

"Stop mothering me." He shooed her. "Have you seen Corin this morning?"

Before she spoke, Jordon entered the room.

"Good morning," he said cheerfully.

Angelique couldn't have been more thankful for his impeccable timing, his arrival giving her an escape from her brother's question.

Keeping things from Tomes wasn't something she was particularly proud of, but she couldn't confess to spending the night with Corin, in a crypt of all places. Tomes would blow a gasket. And she wasn't ready for him to know, considering what he would think of her.

"I'm going to see what's in the kitchen." She hurried away, hoping to find something palatable for breakfast.

Plundering through the cabinets, she managed to put together some oatmeal and canned fruit.

It'll have to do.

Hoping that Jordon had now steered Tomes's thoughts in another direction, she returned to the living room.

"You're looking so much better this morning." She handed Tomes a bowl.

She could breathe easier now, knowing he was on the mend. She couldn't stand the thought of ever losing him. He'd always been her rock.

"Thanks to Corin." He poked at his not-so-appetizing breakfast.

"What are these, peach slices?"

"It's all I could find." Angelique told him and turned to Jordon. "It's not much, but would you care for some?"

"Yes, please, if there's enough."

"You might regret that," Tomes chaffed.

"Knock it off, Tomes." She felt as though she were reprimanding a child. "And Jordon, there's plenty. I'll get us both a bowl."

Angelique returned several minutes later, a bowl in each hand, and passed one off to the immortal.

"I'm a lot better. Thank God for Corin's healing ability." Tomes immediately cut his eyes at Jordon.

"It's okay," Jordon responded. "I know what he is."

"Angel told me about you. That she saw you change form. So, you're not human either."

"I'm an immortal, similar to Corin," Jordon confessed.

"But you walk around in the daylight, so you can't be a nightwalker."

"I'm a different species—a diurnal immortal—a daywalker. The sun doesn't burn me, and I don't drink blood. For our first fifteen years of life, we develop as you do, but then our aging slows and eventually stops."

"That's amazing." Angelique said.

"At this point, nothing surprises me." Tomes made it clear he wasn't as impressed. "Are you even a real marshal?"

"You don't trust me." Jordon took a bite. "I can't blame you. I am, after all, nothing more than a stranger to you."

"Exactly." Tomes didn't try to be cordial. "How do I know you're being truthful?"

"You don't. But Corin knows who I am, and he trusts me."

"I'll be verifying that for myself, if you don't mind."

Jordon lowered his bowl and looked toward the foyer. "Someone's here," he announced.

A second later, the doorbell rang out, deflecting the tension in the room to the prospect of who the unexpected visitor might be.

"I'll get it," Angelique volunteered, happy to escape the animosity between the two men.

"Careful, Angel, it could be the sheriff." Tomes put

his bowl down.

"I shouldn't be seen. It might prove difficult explaining why I'm here." Jordon hustled out of sight.

"Mr. Fulner, isn't it?" Angelique was surprised to see the funeral director.

"What is it you want here, Fulner?" Tomes called out. "The scumbag's involved with Boldor, Angel. He's nothing but trouble."

Jordon stepped out of hiding, making his presence known.

"Now boys, don't go killing the messenger. I have something for you. Boldor's orders." He held out an envelope with a shaky hand.

"Bring it to me, Angel," Tomes instructed.

The moment her fingers touched the envelope, Fulner rushed away, like a rabbit running from a fox.

"That guy's a weasel." Jordon viewed the pudgy, balding man through the open doorway.

"I see him more as a worm," Tomes said. "He's working for Boldor."

"I guess that's not surprising. He'd need some greedy louse degrading enough to do his daytime devilries."

"He fits the bill." Tomes took the envelope from Angelique.

"Open it. See what it says." She was anxious to know.

Tomes tore it open, slid the note out, and read the three words aloud, "It's your move."

Angelique looked at Tomes, then Jordon. "What does it mean?"

"It's for Corin. Boldor's letting him know he's waiting for him to make the next move in this demented game of his," Tomes told her. "That's how he sees all of this, as one big, sordid game."

"I've been after this nightwalker for a long time, and

believe me when I say we'd best tread carefully," Jordon warned. "He doesn't play nice, or fair."

"And he's after Corin?" Angelique was afraid for him.

"Yes, he is, but with me, Corin, and now Jordon teamed up, our odds aren't looking too bad. It's three against one," Tomes said encouragingly.

"Four, including me."

"You need to stay out of this, Angel. Boldor's a killer," Tomes protested.

"I don't want to argue with you, Tomes. This involves all of us." Angelique retrieved her bowl and stormed from the room, returning a moment later to find both men silently gazing her way as if in anticipation of what she would say next. "I'm going to borrow your truck, Tomes, and make a quick run to the farm."

"No," Tomes objected. "You're going to do no such thing."

Jordon tried to suppress a laugh.

"What's so funny?" Tomes cut his eyes at him in irritation.

"You have to love her sass. She won't stand for being controlled."

"Someone has to feed the animals." Angelique moved toward the stairs. "Besides, I need to pick up a few things."

"You shouldn't be going off by yourself, not with Boldor out there."

"What harm can he do during the day? He's a nightwalker. He can't come out in the sunlight. So, I think I'll be safe enough." She stood her ground. "I won't be more than an hour."

"She's right." Jordon surprisingly backed her up. "We should all be safe till nightfall. And I'd be happy to tag along," he offered.

"Thank you, Jordon, but I'll be fine."

"I think it would put your brother at ease."

"You are so bullheaded, Angel," Tomes harped.

"Please, you guys, give me a little breathing room." She made her way up the staircase and fetched Tomes's keys from his room. Coming back down, she found Tomes stooped against the lower banister, struggling to follow.

"What are you doing?" She rushed to his aid.

"He wouldn't accept my help." Jordon stood at the foot of the stairs.

"It's okay, Jordon. He's stubborn." Angelique helped Tomes back to the sofa. "Ploys like this will do no good, Tomes. I'm still going."

"I know I can't stop you. Just be careful, Angel. If anything looks off to you, anything at all, you head straight back here," Tomes instructed.

Angelique started for the door. "I'll feed the animals and get the things I need. I won't be long. And don't worry about your truck, Tomes." She dangled the keys. "I'll be gentle with Bonny."

* * * *

Tomes had a bad feeling, fearing something had happened to Angelique.

"You're just worried. She'll be okay. Boldor's resting right now," Jordon assured him.

"She's next to impossible to deal with." he grumbled with frustration. "Stubborn as they come. I could argue with her till I'm blue in the face and still make no difference."

Jordon laughed. "She's a looker, though. Really hot. A woman with a mind of her own."

"Watch it! That's my sister you're talking about."

"Sorry." Jordon raised a hand. "But it's hard not to

notice."

"Well, she's off limits to your kind. I want her to have a normal life, meaning a human life with a human partner."

"You might want to make Corin aware of that fact," Jordon told him.

"Corin knows. We've discussed it."

"Maybe so, but it's not always so easy to abide by the rules, especially when emotions are involved. You'd have to be blind not to see the connection they have."

"It will never happen!"

"Well, good luck to you there, buddy." Jordon stood. "I'm pretty sure it's already out of your hands. Sometimes it's just meant to be."

Jordon left the room leaving Tomes alone. Contemplating the immortal's words, Tomes knew Angelique and Corin were attracted to each other, but he had to stand between them in order to save his sister. He would do whatever it took to protect her, even if it meant saving her from herself.

Waiting for her return, he listened to the clock tick, seconds turning to minutes and minutes eventually reaching an hour. Weighted with anxiety, still having a bad feeling, twisted knots his gut.

Something's not right.

"Tomes—" The sound of Corin's voice calling out from the basement door jolted him. Pushing himself up, he eased his injured body in Corin's direction.

"Where is Angelique?" Corin talked through the cracked door, careful not to let the sunlight strike his flesh. "I don't sense her presence in the house."

"She went to the farm. I couldn't stop her."

"What!" Corin bellowed, his shout startling Tomes. "Knowing the danger, you allowed her to go out alone?"

"She wouldn't listen. You know how she is. I swear, she's bound to turn me old and gray before my time."

"I can't believe this."

"Jordon didn't help matters any, saying she'd be okay since Boldor can't do anything till nightfall."

"I'm surprised by his lack in judgment. He, better than anyone, should know how resourceful Boldor is—that he can find a way to get his jobs done day or night."

"You might be right. I'm worried. She should have been back by now." Tomes wished now he'd put up more of a fight and not given in to her stubbornness.

Tomes suddenly buckled over, struck by an overwhelming flash of anxiety and dread. He could feel Angelique's panic.

"What is it?"

"Angel." He grabbed the edge of the door to steady himself. "She's in trouble!"

Jordon rounded the corner, having heard Corin's outburst. "What's going on?"

"Angelique's in trouble. You have to go after her," Corin told him. "You're the only one of us who can."

Jordon peered through the narrow opening. "How do you know she's in trouble?"

"There's no time to explain." Tomes knew something was happening, and it wasn't good.

"Hold on. I'll be right back." Corin rushed down the stairs and returned in a flash. "Here." He shoved a set of keys at Jordon. "Take the 'Vette and get moving," he barked. "Get to the farm and find her. Don't waste another minute."

Jordon rushed out without further delay, leaving Corin and Tomes to worry and wait.

"I almost forgot." Tomes handed Corin the message Fulner had delivered.

"It's your move." Corin read the words and cursed. "This was just a diversion to make us think we were safe. And it worked."

Corin flew down to the basement and paced the floor. Tomes could hear his rant as he thrashed about the room below him, knowing it was best to leave the nightwalker alone for the time being.

Hobbling back to the living room sofa, he sat and watched the movement of the clock, its sound amplified as the hand crawled past each second, as if time had slowed to a crawl. It felt like an eternity had passed when Jordon finally returned nearly half an hour later...alone.

"You couldn't find her?" Tomes followed him to the basement door, where Corin met them.

"The truck was parked in front of the house, but she wasn't there," he informed them.

"You checked the entire grounds?" Corin wasn't satisfied. "And the creek?"

"Yes, I remembered the creek. I was very thorough. I'm so sorry. I thought she'd be safe till nightfall."

"He has her, doesn't he?" Tomes already knew the answer, his worst fear becoming reality.

"Yes. He has her." Corin struck the wall. "Fulner. It had to be Fulner."

"Someone's outside," Jordon alerted them to another arrival a moment before the bell rang out.

"You'll have to get it, Tomes," Corin said.

Jordon reclaimed his previous position, remaining out of sight while Tomes hobbled to the door.

"Mr. Jaffler, so we meet again."

"Sheriff. Back so soon?" Tomes stepped outside alongside the official.

"If I didn't know for a fact you lived at the farm, I'd swear you'd taken up residence right here with Mr. von Vadim."

Tomes grimaced, not quite sure what he was implying, but having no time to elaborate. What unbelievable timing this guy had. This was the last thing they needed, a snooping sheriff hanging around the front door, when his sister was out there somewhere in trouble.

"What brings you 'round, Sheriff," Tomes asked.

"What, if I may ask, happened to you, Mr. Jaffler? Were you in an accident?"

"Oh, yeah, I-I took a spill off the ladder. I was way up there, too. But as you can see, I survived it. I got lucky and some rocks broke my fall," Tomes joshed.

"I see. Well, I'm here to see Mr. von Vadim, if he's around."

"He's not, sorry Sheriff." Tomes hoped he'd just leave but knew he wouldn't get off that easy.

"He's gone a lot."

"I don't question what he does. I just work for the man."

Sheriff Pierson looked at him skeptically.

"With his kind of money, he can afford to take off and do anything he pleases without having to answer to me or anyone else." Tomes held onto the edge of the door for support.

"Not exactly anything he pleases. The rich must abide by all the same laws as the rest of us."

"Of course. I just meant he has the means to do whatever comes to mind without having to worry about cost, a job, or even family. He has nothing tying him down and millions to spare," Tomes explained.

"It's hard to relate, since I do have a job to worry about, and what money I have, I've had to earn."

"You're not alone there, Sheriff. Most of us are in that same boat."

"Still working on the north wall?" Sheriff Pierson asked.

"It's the south wall," Tomes corrected. Pierson was obviously testing him. "And yes, I am. But Corin's now hired me as his estate manager," he added, thinking it would be a perfect cover.

"You have time for that with a farm of your own to run?"

"I make time. I also have money to earn. Bills to pay. Now, Sheriff, if there's nothing else, I do have things to attend to."

"In the shape you're in, it's surprising you're working."

"I can do a few things. I bounce back fast."

"Let Mr. von Vadim know I was here. I have some more questions. I'd like to ask him about one of the murder victims, a Madam Monicca."

"He's not the killer," Tomes declared.

"You've defended him before. There are five women dead now, your wife being the first. What if you're wrong?"

"I'm not wrong," Tomes maintained.

"I don't understand how you can be so certain of a man you hardly know. He must be paying you well."

"Now wait just a minute, Sheriff. You're way off base with that one."

"You're right, Mr. Jaffler, I was out of line," Pierson quickly apologized for his remark.

"Yes, you were. I think we're done here."

"For now." Pierson headed away.

Waiting till the SUV was out of sight, Tomes hurried back inside, rejoining Corin and Jordon at the basement door.

"He's gone."

"We heard," Jordon said. "I have to give you kudos for that performance."

"That man gets under my skin," Tomes griped. "Did you hear, Corin? He wants to question you again about one of the murders. He said a Madam...something. I don't remember the name."

"The fortuneteller from the county fair." Corin's

voice floated from the darkness behind the door.

"He's definitely still got his mind set on you being the killer." Tomes told him.

"We'll have to deal with him later. Right now, Angelique is first priority," Corin made clear.

"So, what's the game plan?" Tomes was in full agreement.

"We know Fulner has to be behind her abduction," Corin said. "If we find him, you can bet Angelique won't be far off."

"They're probably holed up at the funeral home." Jordon figured.

"My thoughts as well," Corin agreed. "Boldor would have shelter there."

"You don't think he'll kill her, do you?" Tomes worried for his sister's safety.

"I don't think so. He needs leverage to use against me. Although, he has threatened to change her—make her a replacement for Louisa."

The possibility of that hadn't occurred to Tomes. "We can't let that happen!"

Just then, the phone rang, jolting Tomes from his nightmarish thoughts.

"I don't get many calls," Corin said. "It may be about Angelique."

Tomes answered, wishing he could climb through the line and rid the world of the person on the other end, sleazy funeral director, Fulner.

"Where's my sister?" Tomes demanded. "If you touch—"

"Threats won't get her back," Fulner cut him off. "Put von Vadim on the line."

"You hurt her and you're dead." Tomes pressed speakerphone on the handset before shoving it through the cracked door to Corin.

"You tell me what you've done with her." Corin's

tone was fearsome. "I'm in no mood for games."

"Now, now, I believe we're the ones holding all of the cards."

"What does he want in exchange?" Corin growled.

A moment of silence passed.

"What is it you want?" Corin's temper flared.

"Haven't you figured it out yet, von Vadim?" Boldor's voice came on the line. "I want everything you have. I want your life—your identity, your estate, and your millions," he stipulated. "By the way, what did you think of my little message?"

"You didn't give me my move," Corin told him. "This wasn't a fair play."

"One doesn't stay ahead in the game by playing fair. And now I've won a prize. Just look at this little angel I've captured. Isn't that what her brother calls her, Angel? To save this luscious, little mortal, I think you'd probably give up your life. Am I right?" He released a sinister chuckle. "I do believe I've found your weak spot, von Vadim."

"I'll take your head for this." Corin snarled.

"I have the upper hand here."

"You think you have me all figured out?"

"I know I do." Boldor's voice remained calm. "Take a listen to the card I have to play."

Angelique cried out, a sound that ripped through Tomes's heart. "Corin!" he yelled, experiencing her pain, her fear.

"I could snap this precious little thing's arm right off if I desired." Boldor made his point. "Now, enough of this. The deal is your life for hers. Understand?"

"I understand." Corin hit the wall with a thundering force. "Just name where and when. I'll be there."

"Tonight. After the fall of night. Center of the cemetery." Boldor rattled off the location and ended the call.

Corin threw the phone to the floor. "I can't stand the thought of that filthy wretch's hands on her." He struck the wall again.

Tomes wasn't altogether sure how to react to Corin's behavior, wondering the same thing he'd asked himself several times now—just how close had he and Angelique already gotten?

In spite of it all, he had to push his disapproval of their relationship aside and focus on getting his sister back, something he needed Corin's help to accomplish. At the moment he was dependent on him, trusting that together, they would save her from Boldor's clutches.

22

The Green Folder

Boldor shoved Angelique into a closet and secured the door. No match for his strength, she still continued to fight back, banging against the inside panel.

"Give it up, princess." He shielded himself from the faint light entering the back room. "You'll get out when I let you out. Now mind your manners, and maybe I'll let you live."

Angelique gave up and slid onto her knees. Boldor could hear her whimpering and laughed.

"I want you to keep an eye on her while I rest," he instructed Fulner. "Remember, if she vanishes...you vanish." He slithered back to the room containing his casket to rest within its dark confines until nightfall.

It was going to be his night to seize riches. He would set everything in motion by killing von Vadim, thus, putting himself in the position to take over his role. He'd then get rid of everyone involved, that short list including Tomes Jaffler, the marshal, the little angel in the closet, and the director. They'd all have to be terminated in order for his plan to go without a hitch. With von Vadim and these four dead, he'd be free to step right into the nightwalker's shoes.

* * * *

Sheriff Pierson decided to pay a visit to Jaffler Farm, hoping he might manage to manipulate some information out of Angelique Jaffler. Involved or not, she seemed to be the person closest to both Tomes Jaffler and Corin von Vadim.

Pulling up the drive, he stopped in front of the house where two vehicles sat—a car and a truck. Shoving the shifter into park, he got out and went to the front door, finding it ajar.

"Hello?" he called out, receiving no response.

Pushing a hand against the door, a light shone in a back room. Stepping inside, he called out again, but there was clearly no one around.

Backing out of the house, he walked around the building to the back lawn and checked the barn, finding the farm deserted. He rubbed his left ear. Things didn't feel right, and that worrisome quiver was going at it full speed, something it had done a lot this last week.

Returning to the front door of the residence, he decided to go back inside and check the house, justifying the act with the thought that the lady of the house might be in distress, or worse, a victim of foul play. An understandable concern considering the murders in the county.

"Ms. Jaffler," he called out as he meandered the living room, glancing over an array of photos and décor, observing a large, white Bible displayed on a small, oval table near the window.

Moving on through the home, he saw no sign of mischief and backtracked to leave, but he halted when he passed by an office where a desktop computer sat atop a compact desk.

You have no legal right to snoop, Pierson.

But unable to resist, legal or not, he took advantage of the opportunity and slid open the top drawer of the desk, finding pens, clips, and other typical office items. Nothing of consequence. Traveling to a lower drawer, his luck fared better, discovering a green folder lying atop several reams of paper.

Interest piqued, he skimmed its contents. "What on earth?" The extensive research someone had applied toward such a foolish matter surprised him. "Vampires," he mumbled. "Ridiculous notion."

Coming upon a handwritten page, it appeared to be a theory of Louisa Jaffler's death, leading him to presume, by the manner of writing, that the folder belonged to Tomes Jaffler.

What? His eyes widened with disbelief as his gaze locked on a single line written in capital letters, a conclusion at the bottom of the page.

VON VADIM IS A NIGHTWALKER.

Pierson contemplated taking the folder with him for further study, but he'd be committing theft. Knowing it was wrong, he reluctantly placed it back in the drawer. Besides, such nonsense couldn't be of significance to him in regard to the murders. Yet, that nerve behind his left ear was signaling him otherwise, giving rise to second thoughts, and to date, it had never steered him wrong.

"You have no search warrant." His conscience was working on him—a devil on one shoulder, an angel on the other. "You're the sheriff, for Pete's sake. You need to do this by the book."

The pitchfork winning out, he went against his own

better judgment and grabbed the folder, tucked it under his arm, and made a rapid exit. If he had to take a few detours off the straight and narrow in order to get to the bottom of the murders, then so be it. He never claimed to be perfect. He was no different from every other man in the world...just human.

Leaving the farm, he thought over the connection between Corin von Vadim and the Jafflers. First of all, the two siblings' farm connected to von Vadim's estate, making them neighbors. Secondly, Tomes Jaffler worked for von Vadim at his estate, and thirdly, Angelique had been seen out on a date with the estate owner, spotted by the very reliable Officer Traci Keller while visiting the fair with her young son the night before last. *They looked pretty cozy with each other*, Pierson recalled her exact words.

He was slowly building his case against Corin von Vadim, and the Jaffler siblings were all tangled up in the man's life. He didn't have a motive yet, but he was sure if he kept digging, things would start coming together. Reviewing his links, what he had so far was the second victim's business card acquired by the heir from Purcell's Garage the very night of her murder. In addition, there was the gold pocket watch found at the murder site of the third victim, Jessica Daniel's, inscribed with the name Miralanya, matching a past relative of von Vadim. And now, Officer Keller had placed both him and Angelique Jaffler at the fairgrounds where Madam Monicca, the fortuneteller, was murdered. However, other than being a neighbor of the first victim, Louisa Jaffler, he didn't have anything connecting him to her murder, or to the latest victim—the maid at the Inn. But he had no doubt that something would eventually arise as it had with the others.

Unfortunately, what information Sheriff Pierson had

was all circumstantial, not enough for an arrest. He needed something concrete to turn over to the DA that would get an indictment. This pushed him to the next step, setting up a stakeout to keep twenty-four-hour surveillance on the suspect, hoping that at some point, von Vadim would slip up.

Von Vadim Estate was without a doubt the primary headquarters of whatever was going on. He just had to be patient until the man made another move. And this time, God willing, the law would be there to catch him in the act.

* * * *

In the basement of the estate house, Corin, antsy as a nervous cat, paced to-and-fro. He cursed the clock, the world moving around him in slow motion. Continually rebuking himself, he questioned how he'd ever allowed this to happen, wishing he'd never let Angelique out of his sight. Filled with rage and worry, the sting of helplessness ate at him. He'd never loved anyone with such heated desire and passion. She was not only in his heart...she owned it.

Corin could hear Tomes hobbling about the room above him, no doubt full of turmoil and feeling the same helplessness he felt. A beloved sister's life was at stake, a twin whom he'd shared everything with since conception. They were connected in a way very few could understand.

"Corin," Tomes called from the doorway above. "Do you mind if I flip on the light?"

"I'll get it down here." Corin lit the lantern near the foot of the stairs. The softer, dimmer light was easier on his sensitive eyes. "Careful with your footing. I don't want to be responsible for you taking a nasty spill down the stairs and further debilitating that already abused body of yours."

"I'm not coming down." Tomes shut the door and took a seat on the top step.

"You should be resting. You need to heal."

"I'm a good eighty percent there, I'd say." Tomes looked down at him.

"Have you come up with a way to get her back?" He was hoping to hear that Tomes had a rescue mission all planned out.

"I don't want to put her in any unnecessary danger. He wants me, and he'll take nothing less." Corin resumed pacing. "But that leaves me with a dilemma. If I give myself up in exchange for Angelique, in the end, you can bet he'll still come after all of you despite my sacrifice. In order for his plan to work, he'll have to eliminate everyone who knows of it. Other than the director, that includes me, you, Angelique, and now Jordon, since he's joined our little band of misfits."

"Lucky guy," Tomes said. "Speaking of Jordon, he took off. I heard him slip out, so I watched from a front window and saw him shape-shift into a wolf. He headed for the woods and disappeared near the stone wall. What do you think he's up to?"

"You don't trust him."

"I don't know him. So no, I don't," Tomes confessed. "And you do?"

"I believe he's legit. He has his own motivation for catching Boldor." Corin stopped pacing and looked up at him with a serious expression. "I'm not sure you'd believe me if I told you the truth about him."

"I don't think much would shock me now, Corin. A year ago, I never would have imagined nightwalkers to be real, but look at me collaborating in a darkened basement with the very thing I always thought was make-believe. I'd really like to know what's so extraordinary about him that's enabled him to win your trust."

"Okay, I'll tell you. He's from another world—the Eleventh Dimension. He calls himself an Indith immortal and claims to be after Boldor to retrieve a powerful charm he stole from a special order of nightwalkers."

"Wow. I'm almost sorry I asked. Other worlds and magical charms—it's as if I've been sucked into a children's fantasy book."

Corin paced. "I told you it was unbelievable."

"That's an understatement. Impossible is the appropriate word. This couldn't be more ludicrous. I'm partnered with a nightwalker, and now an immortal from another world."

"Maybe so, but because of what we are, Angelique just might stand a chance. That is, if this infernal day would ever end. I need to feed."

Tomes took a deep breath, already having accepted that it would take an immortal to defeat the nefarious nightwalker. As much as he wanted to be the one to take the killer's life—revenge for Louisa—he now had to think of Angelique. At this juncture, the nightwalker and the alien immortal were her best hope.

* * * *

Sheriff Pierson leaned back and stretched. Parked on von Vadim's land, he couldn't have created a better stakeout position if he'd tried. Well concealed behind a group of large trees, not far from the gate, he had a near-perfect view of the mansion from where he sat.

"What the..." he sprang forward. Choking on a mouthful of salty chips, he fumbled for a diet cola growing warm in a center console cup-holder. Taking a large swallow, he washed down the lump.

What he'd just seen had left him flabbergasted.

"It can't be." He brushed crumbs off his shirt while clearing his throat. He stared in bewilderment at the driveway leading to the mansion. "No, it has to be some play on the eye."

He tried to convince himself, as he'd done with the surveillance tapes, but this time he knew better. This was no trick, or illusion. What he'd just seen with his own two eyes was disconcertingly real.

It was illogical to believe that a person could transform from man to animal, but he'd just witnessed the phenomena all the same. There was no mistaking what he saw—Marshal Jordon Black shape-shifting into a rather fierce-looking, dark-colored wolf.

Sheriff Pierson had never believed in the supernatural, but after what he'd just observed, he found himself reevaluating his beliefs. Seeing the marshal change form had made an impact, something he hadn't expected, but couldn't ignore.

Eyeing the green folder lying on the passenger's seat next to him, he reached for it and flipped it open. Skimming through the sheets, he stopped on a page he'd seen earlier titled "shape-shifting." He pulled the sheet out and ran his eyes down the length of it.

"No. It's not possible...vampires?" He laid his head back, letting the shock soak in.

It would certainly explain Corin von Vadim—an odd man, never home during the day, only seen at night—but when it came to the marshal, it didn't fit. He had seen him out in the daytime. Nevertheless, vampire or not, Marshal Black was no normal human man. Pierson wasn't sure what the blazes he was.

He hated to admit it, but the infernal reporter, Terry Phillips, just might have been on the right track after all when he compared the first killing to the myth of the vampire. He recalled the title, "Man or Monster."

"Talk about hitting the nail on the head. Is this why

you were avoiding me, Mr. Phillips?" He recalled attempting to see the reporter, without success. "Maybe your informer wasn't quite as human as the rest of us?" he speculated.

Pierson had always been a levelheaded man, but he now found himself forced to reconsider a bizarre possibility—that the Jackson County killer could actually be a real life, shape-shifting, blood-sucking vampire. Or was he simply losing his mind?

<h1 style="text-align:center">23</h1>

Lehndra

Wearing his cape and black Stetson, tilting the brim down to shade his face, Corin headed for the garage even though the sun was still setting, making the slow transition to twilight. He moved quickly, gripping his collar to minimize exposure.

Tomes followed, lagging behind, not yet recovered. Corin had tried to persuade him to wait at the estate, but to no avail. Moreover, with Angelique in danger, he understood Tomes's need to do something.

"If she died and I didn't do all I could to save her, I'd never forgive myself." Tomes made it to the garage and climbed into the car. "She's at the mercy of a killer. You know better than anyone just how fragile she is in his hands. Your kind are the hunters, and we're the prey. Rabbits to wolves."

"Drop the negativity right now. She's not going to die." Corin tore through the gate, unable to stand the thought. "We know what he wants. We just have to figure out how to use that knowledge to our advantage."

"When he had me cornered in the room, I got a good look at the buttons on his coat. They're stones with insects and spiders trapped inside. When he touched one, it moved, like it was alive."

"There could be something distinctive about the source of the stones."

"A gift from the devil?" Tomes figured the probability likely.

"I'd imagine something along those lines. Maybe a spell. Just reaffirming it's a demon we're dealing with."

Corin drove to one of his feeding spots and pulled the 'Vette off the road, parking out of view of passing traffic.

"I won't be long." He got out and slipped into the pasture to feed. Now twilight, the sun had dropped below the horizon, waiting for the veil of darkness to fall.

With the setting of the sun came the eerie fog, moving in again as it had the two previous nights. Corin, experiencing déjà vu, stopped feeding and gazed on the ominous wall of mist rolling toward him from a distance across the pasture. He quickly resumed feeding, wanting to finish before the fog reached him, not comfortable with the trepidation it brought, seeming to be an augury of misfortune. Then, sensing they weren't alone, he closed the wound and hurried back to the car.

"I think someone else is out here."

"It could just be a hunter."

Corin nodded. "Maybe. But we can't be too careful."

* * * *

Unbeknownst to Corin and Tomes, Sheriff Pierson was following, staying far enough behind to prevent detection. With no traffic on the desolate road and his familiarity with the area, he drove without headlights, an expert in the art of tailing a suspect.

Leaning forward in the driver's seat of his SUV, he clicked his tongue against the back of his front teeth, wondering why they'd pulled off the road into a secluded, wooded area. Figuring they were less than a quarter mile ahead of him, he eased closer and pulled into the edge of the woods. He grabbed his night vision goggles from the back seat in case he needed them in the dense territory and moved in on foot, keeping to the shadows at the tree line. Reaching the area he was sure they'd turned into, he pinpointed the opening—a path cleverly cloaked by overlapping lines of woods—running several feet at a left angle and then making a sharp turn back to the right, just wide enough to accommodate a vehicle. Starting up the avenue, he spotted the Corvette in the path ahead of him and quickly took cover in the woods. Making as little noise as possible, he detoured around the car, observing Tomes sitting in the passenger's seat with the window lowered.

"Where are you, von Vadim?" He was careful with his footing, creeping deeper into the woods in search of his suspect.

Pierson kept his eyes wide open as he moved beyond the ended path to the backside of the woods, where he came upon a pasture. His gaze traveled into the field, catching sight of von Vadim's silhouette latched onto a cow.

"What the devil?"

Caught off guard, he took in a sharp breath, disgusted by the thought of drinking fresh blood from a living animal.

It's time to go.

Not wanting to chance being detected, he doubled back, slipped past the car, and returned to his vehicle.

"Vampires." Pierson climbed into the driver's seat. "Either Corin von Vadim really is one of the undead, or I'm going crazy."

Needing reassurance that his sanity was intact, he pulled his phone out and called Patricia who was still in the hospital, but well on the mend. He knew he shouldn't involve her in this madness, but he couldn't think of anyone else open-minded enough to call.

"You're saying you saw the marshal shape-shift into a wolf?" she repeated what he'd told her.

"You wouldn't believe the strange things going on around here, Patricia. Things I never imagined possible. I think they're vampires. As we speak, von Vadim is feeding from a cow. I'm afraid the whole county might be swarming with the leeches," he rambled in agitation.

"Allen, listen to me. The first thing you have to do is calm down. This doesn't sound like you. You've been working continuously since the murders started. Sleep deprivation can be detrimental to your health. Why don't you call it quits for the night and head home?"

"This isn't sleep deprivation, Patricia. Of all people, I thought for sure you'd believe me. You know how skeptical I am, but I can't deny what I've seen tonight." A single profanity escaped under his breath. "It was real!"

"It's not that I don't believe you, Allen. I'm just worried. If what you're saying is true, and you really have encountered vampires, you shouldn't be out there alone. Can't you at least call for some back up?"

"They'd think I'm nuts. Besides, I don't want to get any of my deputies involved in this mess. It would be equivalent to leading unsuspecting sheep into a den of lions." He spotted the lights from Corin's 'Vette. "I have to go. They're on the move again."

"Be careful, Allen," Patricia implored.

"I will, don't worry." He ended the call.

Allowing them a good head start before pulling back on the road, he followed at a distance, having little fear of losing them on the deserted route. Nearing Cemetery Road, where they eventually turned off, he rolled to a stop, unable to follow them down the dead-end avenue without risk of being seen.

Why are you heading to the cemetery?

He watched the headlights of their car bounce between the scattered trees as it moved along the single-lane road that ran about two miles amid aged, mossy oaks until meeting up with a cemetery. Pierson had been there on several occasions. It was a secluded area, the graveyard nestled amongst a fortress of thick, entangled woods.

"I'll have to wait you out." He backed up and pulled off the road. Until he figured a few things out, he wasn't going anywhere.

* * * *

It was a fitting night for a standoff with the cemetery lying half-hidden by the mysterious, creeping fog. But the obscured view was no obstacle for Corin, he knew the grounds well, having visited the deceased there often.

Moving at a slow pace, he and Tomes maneuvered through the multitude of graves, to the center of the cemetery where Boldor had instructed him to go. He thought it strange how the fog moved and shifted around them in a haunting, unnatural manner. He could see Tomes's anxiety, the man sticking close by his side with the staker gripped tight, prepared for an attack. He'd become inseparable from the weapon, keeping it with him at all times, the staker proving to be an invaluable commodity, having saved his life once already.

"This seems vaguely familiar. Me leading the way while you follow with that thing aimed right at my back," Corin whispered. "Just watch your trigger finger."

"I'm not going to shoot you. I know how to handle the staker."

"That's a load off my mind." Corin tossed the words at him with a hint of sarcasm.

After taking several more steps, Corin reached back and halted Tomes. A short distance in front of them, in the misty fog, a form was taking shape. It was Boldor.

"Where is she?" Corin demanded to know the moment he'd completely solidified.

"She's here." Boldor offered no details.

"Show me she's safe, or no deal."

The area between them was clear, giving Corin a direct view of his opponent who retreated to a large oak tree and disappeared beyond it. Reappearing a moment later with Angelique bound and gagged, he dragged her like a rag-doll.

"Fulner." Corin snarled, seeing the louse traipse behind Boldor, carrying what appeared to be a large sword and a length of rope.

"Angel!" Tomes called out and started toward her, but Corin placed a firm hand against his chest, holding him back.

He understood how Tomes felt, because he wanted nothing more than to tear Boldor apart, but for now, they had to play by the devil's rules.

"Just tell me what you want," Corin called out to Boldor.

"What I want is your head on this gravestone." He

pointed it out. "You do that, and I'll send this little angel over to her brother."

Boldor glared at Tomes who stood with the staker aimed at him, uttering a deep, rolling growl.

"How do I know I can trust you?"

"You don't. But it's all you have, isn't it?" Boldor sneered. "I should have taken her life for what you did to my little firecat, but after getting a closer look, I decided it would be a waste. She's willful, but beautiful."

Corin struggled to control the monster rising within him.

"Enough talk! Sacrifice yourself, and the girl goes free. Try anything, anything at all, and she's mine."

Boldor grazed his fangs along the side of her face, and Angelique tried to pull back, but he yanked her to him, causing her to cry out.

"Okay, I'll do it." Corin moved toward the gravestone.

Boldor snarled. "I thought you'd see things my way."

"No, Corin! Don't!" Angelique yelled, but Boldor quickly silenced her with a slap across her face.

Corin started for him, but Boldor's words quickly halted his charge.

"I'd kill her before you ever reach me." Boldor snatched her close.

Corin backed off and continued to the headstone, watching as Boldor passed Angelique to Fulner in exchange for the sword and rope. The fiend then snaked his way with the weapon gripped tightly, so eager to have his head he was salivating.

"I can't believe you're giving up your life for this one insignificant mortal. No woman is worth that high a sacrifice, mortal or otherwise."

"She's worth a hundred of me and more," Corin declared. "Now, I've done what you asked. Give her to her brother."

"First, I want you on all fours."

"Corin, please!" Angelique cried out again, but Fulner muffled her, placing his hand over her mouth.

"The director knows what to do should you refuse to cooperate," Boldor warned him.

Corin dropped to his knees, but stopped there. "You'll have me on all fours when you let her go. Give her to her brother, or I'll end this now."

A smug grin plastered Boldor's face. Corin could see his hunger for the kill. The devil was sure he'd already won the game.

"On your knees and still spouting orders. I do admire the fight in you." Boldor made his move. Grabbing a fistful of Corin's hair, he snatched his head back. "But I'm in charge here. When you're bound, then I'll send her, not before." He tied Corin's hands behind him, pulling the ropes so tight they sliced into his flesh. "I need some insurance. You understand." He shoved Corin down, forcing his head against the upper edge of the stone. With him bound, he pressed his knee into his mid-back to hold him in place.

"Corin," Tomes called to him.

"Just get Angelique," Corin responded through gnashed teeth.

"Take her to her brother," Boldor instructed Fulner. "But don't release her until I give the word. This one might try something if we give her up too soon."

Corin choked, the stone cutting into his throat. This was to be his guillotine. An ironically fitting ending for one of the walking dead.

He managed to turn his head just enough to see Fulner dragging Angelique toward Tomes for the handoff. But just as they'd reached half the distance, a vapory fog unexpectedly appeared between them. A phantom in the night, the entity took the form of a woman.

"It looks like I'm just in time." The female immortal slashed Fulner across the left side of his face with one quick motion and seized Angelique.

Fulner cried out and ran, disappearing into the darkness.

"Let her go!" Tomes yelled, but he kept his distance when she tossed him a warning hiss, revealing her long fangs.

Angelique struggled against her, but the immortal was strong, keeping her in place with little effort.

"So much commotion over this mortal?" She scanned everyone around her.

"Lehndra," Boldor acknowledged.

"It seems the blow of my arrival has sunk in." She cut her piercing eyes his way. "I bet you never expected to see me tonight, or any other."

"It is a shock, yes. You look ravishing as always," he wheedled.

Her hand shot up. "You can save the flattery, Karlot. You forget, I know you. There is no chance of your charms having any effect on me. Those times are long past. I'm here for one reason only. You have something that belongs to me, and I'm here to reclaim it."

With Boldor preoccupied with the female immortal, Corin took the opportunity to scramble free from the chopping block. The nightwalker tried to seize him, but Corin was too fast.

Swearing, Boldor tore after him, taking several swings, just missing with each strike.

Finding the right moment to shape-shift, Corin assumed the form of a wolf, white with brown detailing. The ropes fell free from his wrists as the smaller legs of the animal replaced his own limbs. And giving a vicious bark, he took a stance, prompting Boldor to back off.

The fog, held at bay till that moment, suddenly

shrouded them in a sea of mist, making it impossible to see the others' positions.

"Corin!" Tomes called frantically. "She's on the move with Angelique."

Corin reverted to his original form and searched for their locations, finally finding Tomes when he called out a second time.

"Did you see where they went?" Corin's fangs had emerged.

"The fog moved in too fast.," Tomes told him. "I couldn't shoot. I was afraid I might hit Angel."

"Stay here, I'll check the car." Corin darted away, but the 'Vette squealed off before he reached the gate. Not knowing where Boldor might be lurking, he made tracks back to Tomes.

"I heard the car," Tomes said. "Go after them."

"I can't leave you out here alone. Not with Boldor still out here somewhere. He'll kill you, Tomes."

"Don't worry about me. Angelique comes first."

"We'll get her back. I believe the immortal has a score of her own to settle with Boldor. Something tells me she's planning to use Angelique as a bargaining chip."

"I pray you're right, 'cause if you're not—"

"I'll get her back," Corin proclaimed. "Even if I have to move heaven and hell to make it happen."

Corin thought about how vexed the female immortal seemed with Boldor. It was apparent they shared a past relationship. He recalled what she said to him: "*You have something that belongs to me, and I'm here to reclaim it.*" He assumed she was referring to the charm, the same one Jordon was after, the Heart of the Clyth.

Corin's thoughts shifted to Angelique. He would never admit it to Tomes, but not knowing anything about the female immortal, he, too, had his doubts. If he was right, and she was planning to use Angelique as a bargaining chip against Boldor, it was only a matter of time before she discovered the fiend could care less whether her captive lived or died. When that happened, Angelique would be useless to her, and at that point, done for. Corin could only hope the immortal had another plan in mind.

* * * *

Boldor, in the form of a black raven, landed a few miles away, on the bank of a narrow, swiftly running creek. He shape-shifted into human form and squatted next to the water.

How did she ever catch up with me?

He had met Lehndra more than two years earlier in New Orleans during the Mardi Gras while under the identity of Karlot Delacruse. They had eyed the same victim, finding a sordid humor in cornering an unfortunate woman at the same moment. Both impulsive, and a perfect match, they quickly forged a partnership and became lovers.

Lehndra, affiliated with a special order of nightwalkers, had brought him into her secret society. He could never be a member, but the Order had granted him permission to reside among them. But, like him, Lehndra was corrupt, and it didn't take long for them to concoct a plan to steal a powerful charm from the sect. Lehndra had set up the heist, and when the Heart of the Clyth was in their possession, they'd fled with their prize. However, Boldor decided he didn't want to share the power, not even with Lehndra and skipped out with the charm. Heartless and selfish, he left her to face the wolves alone.

"You seek revenge." He rubbed an amber button, and the insect squirmed, bringing to mind how he'd stolen the stones from a witch more than two hundred years ago, using her the same way he'd used Lehndra.

The witch, Suna, had placed a spell on ten amber gemstones, imprisoning specific insects and arachnids inside each stone for the purpose of calling them forth when she needed them to be her eyes and her ears. Several words and a potion connected her to the immortalized creatures through touch, allowing her to care for and control them, just as he did now. Obeying his command, they seeped free of the gems when he summoned them, returning when their tasks were done. They were his personal miniature agents, playing a large part in achieving his goals. He couldn't have stolen the charm from Lehndra without them. A secret asset, he trusted no one with the knowledge of the stones. No one. As far as anyone ever knew, they were merely a prized collection.

"Lehndra," he groaned. "I'll have to deal with you."

The female immortal's arrival had put a damper on things—an inconvenient and unforeseen turn of events—forcing him to come up with a new game plan, and fast. But the game was far from over.

* * * *

Lehndra, having commandeered Corin's Corvette, fled with Angelique to Jaffler Farm.

"Home sweet home. This is probably the last place they'd expect me to bring you." The immortal grinned as she pulled up to the house.

"How did you know where I live?"

"I got lucky and came upon your nightwalker, von Vadim, and his mortal friend the night before last in the cemetery. I've been watching from a safe distance, careful not to be detected. When I saw that Jordon was sticking close to all of you, I knew I was in the right place. He came close to spotting me in the woods, but I was barely in range and moved fast. That fight, between the immortals, answered a lot of questions I had about Karlot's agenda here, leading me to devise a plan."

"And what is your plan? What are you going to do with me?"

"Don't worry, I'm not planning to feed on you, yummy as you smell." She shoved Angelique onto the sofa.

The room was dark, and Angelique could only make out faint outlines.

"I saw the way that nightwalker was willing to give his life to save you. If I were to take your life, he'd hunt me till he, or I, was dust. And that could be a very long time."

"We're in love," Angelique told her.

"Oh, that's obvious." Lehndra moved through the dark room.

Angelique suddenly jumped, startled by a single, quick scratching sound. A tiny flame broke the darkness, allowing her to see the immortal holding a match to the wick of a candle.

"You're a nervous one." The nightwalker placed the candle on the coffee table in front of her.

It didn't offer much light, but it was a welcome escape from the suffocating darkness.

"Why not use the lights?" Angelique asked.

"A softer light is more comfortable on our eyes. Associated with a nightwalker, you should know this."

"I just recently found out about him—that he's an immortal."

"You're very lucky to have won the heart of such a man. Although, I find little use for the masculine sex." Lehndra moved aimlessly about the room.

"You prefer women?" Angelique wasn't sure of her meaning.

"Not exactly." Lehndra laugh. "I've just never known a trustworthy man, and I've been around a long time, almost two hundred years. I must say, I find myself a bit envious of your relationship with von Vadim. I've never had a man care for me with such a passion."

"Do you know Corin?"

"He's no acquaintance. It's merely observation." She found two more candles and positioned them in the room.

"But you do know Boldor."

The additional light offered Angelique a much better view of the immortal who was a stunning creature with unusually light-blue eyes displaying large, black pupils. Her hair, a beautiful shade of red, fell wildly along her back, the front dressed in braids, three on either side, running from her temples until blending with her loose, disorganized tresses.

"He called you by name. Len—"

"Lehndra. And yes, I know him," she admitted. "Karlot Delacruse. He played me for a fool. He took my heart, double-crossed me, and abandoned me. A terrible mistake on his part."

"So, you're here for revenge." Angelique observed the various pieces of jewelry adorning her body—a bold gem cuff wrapping her left wrist, and some erotic-looking body piercings.

"Amongst other things. He took something I want back. And I'm not leaving without it."

"How do I fit into your plans? I'll be of no use to you against Boldor. He was only using me to get to Corin."

"Yes, I'm aware of that. I figured I could use a little help from von Vadim in my own endeavors. From what I've seen, I think he'd do just about anything to get you back."

"So, you want to use me as ransom to force Corin into helping you take down Boldor?"

"That's about the gist of it," Lehndra admitted. "It worked for Boldor, or almost worked for Boldor," she corrected herself with a scornful snicker.

"You don't need to do this. We have the same goal. We could be working together, on the same side."

"That's not possible, my dear. Besides, I've seen you with Jordon, the Indith Sentry, and he and I will never be on the same side of anything. That diurnal immortal would sooner kill me than help me," Lehndra snapped.

"I don't know much about Jordon," Angelique told her, having no idea what she meant by Indith Sentry or diurnal immortal.

"He and I are after the same thing—a charm. But I plan on getting to it first. I risked my life stealing it, and I'm due my prize. If it wasn't for Karlot, I'd have it now."

"You're a thief, like Boldor."

"Never compare me to that odious cad!" Lehndra hissed. "I've never been able to stand the way he slinks about—the vermin. Always rubbing those insect buttons, as if getting some kind of perverted pleasure from it. He makes them move, and I hate bugs." She released a growl of repugnance. "I only resorted to thievery to further my cause. I'm a visionary, and with the aid of the Clyth, I'll be in a position to lead my world to greatness. I'll bring my people out of obscurity and into a new and advanced age. Under my leadership, no other worlds will compare."

"What do you mean by 'your world'?"

"I'm not from Earth, I'm from the Eleventh Dimension. It's a world lost in time, at a standstill in its current era, what you would consider in your history, the Middle Ages. Oh, there's been slight advancement over the years, but the pace of change is painfully slow. But with the Clyth, I can carry us forth into a superior age, transforming the Eleventh Dimension into a world not even Earth could equal."

Angelique couldn't help envisioning the female immortal as an animated mad dictator. Her scheme just sounded so loony. And the Eleventh Dimension, how was she ever to wrap her mind around the existence of other worlds when she'd just come to terms with the reality of vampires and immortals?

"The Clyth?" Angelique asked. "What is that?"

"You sure ask a lot of questions." Lehndra stared at Angelique. "I made a pledge to uphold the secrets of the Order, but I abide by my own rules. Besides, they've already sentenced me for treason, and what threat can you be?"

Angelique didn't know what she meant, but she listened silently.

"I'll quench your curiosity, if nothing more but to pass the time. The Clyth is a charm of great power. Boldor possesses one part of it called the Heart, a black diamond, and the imbecile doesn't even know the full value of what he carries with him. When we were together, I wasn't completely open with him. Intuition warned me to be cautious until he had proven his devotion, and luckily, I listened to that inner voice. Not even a week later, he abandoned me, disappeared with the Heart, leaving me to fend for myself against the Order—the guardians of the charm. Now, two years later, I've finally found him, still up to his old tricks." She pulled what appeared to be a large locket from her pocket and rubbed it between her fingers. "But I know what the Clyth can do, and with a little luck, the Heart and Body will soon be joined, and the power will be mine."

24

The Gathering

Corin and Tomes headed for the cemetery gate. "With no transportation, we'll have to walk. If you can make it to the main road, we might be able to catch a ride. Hopefully someone will come along."

"You should go and hunt for Angel. I'll be okay."

Corin shook his head. "I can't leave you out here alone. Look at you. You can barely get around. And with Boldor out for the kill, your chances of making it back alive would be slim to none. Right now, it's best we stick together."

"I just hope Angel's okay. This is all my fault. I insisted on coming with you. I should have stayed at the estate. We wouldn't be here, in this predicament, if I had."

"You can't blame yourself."

"Angel was so close. If I'd just done something, maybe—"

"That immortal would have ripped you to shreds."

Keeping a steady pace, they'd just passed through the gate and started up Cemetery Road, when Corin caught the sound of a vehicle nearing.

"Someone's coming," he alerted Tomes just before headlights appeared around the curve in front of them, and a vehicle came into view. "I think it's the sheriff."

"What on earth is he doing out here?"

"I have no idea, but we need the ride."

Sheriff Pierson rolled to a stop and lowered his window.

"What brings you boys out here this time of night, and without transportation to boot?" he asked.

"Oh, w-we had transportation, but—" Tomes attempted to supply a feasible response.

"I'll tell you what happened, Sheriff." Corin took over, catching Pierson's fixed, disconcerting stare. "This fellow here...." He pointed back at Tomes. "He went and royally pissed off his sister. She took the car and left us to find our own way back."

"I guess that was her I passed tearing out of here like a bat out of hell?"

"It was." Corin hoped the sheriff didn't question why they were at the cemetery, or how three of them had gotten out there in a two-seater car. "She's a spirited one."

"In your condition, Mr. Jaffler, that's surprising," Pierson told Tomes. "You're not looking too well. You ought to be home in bed."

"It's hard keeping this one down," Corin spoke for Tomes.

"Well, hop in and I'll give you boys a lift. Unless you think she might come back for you once she's cooled off."

"We're not counting on it." Corin opened the back door and helped Tomes get in.

Corin knew Sheriff Pierson was suspicious of them, but he had no choice but to accept the ride. Tomes wouldn't make it far in his condition.

"We appreciate you going out of your way." Corin climbed in the front seat.

"I wouldn't be a very good lawman if I left the two of you stranded out here, now would I?"

"You're a fine officer, Sheriff." Corin fastened his seatbelt. "Always on top of things."

"Should I drop you at the estate?"

"Yes. That would be great," Corin replied. "Tell me, how's the investigation coming along?"

"Funny you should ask that. I've been trying to track you down. I'm sure Mr. Jaffler has told you." He eyed Tomes in the rearview mirror. "I wanted to ask you a few questions about a murder that occurred at the county fair two nights ago. The victim was a fortuneteller—Madam Monicca."

"I don't understand how this concerns me."

"I believe you were there the same night she was killed, in the company of Ms. Jaffler."

"We were at the fair. Angelique and I were on a date. It's no secret," Corin admitted. *How did the sheriff know?* "Half the county was probably there."

"Well, I find it more than just a coincidence that your name keeps popping up in connection with all of these young women's murders." Pierson's tone was accusing.

"I'd be surprised if you had any real connections, Sheriff. I told you, I don't know anything about those murders," Corin spoke calmly. "But I don't think it matters what I say. It's obvious you've got your mind set on me being the killer. But you're wrong."

"So your friend back there keeps telling me." Pierson looked at Tomes again in the mirror.

"If you're so sure of my guilt, why haven't you

arrested me?" Corin asked outright. Although, he couldn't be certain that Sheriff Pierson wouldn't haul him in on some trumped-up charge, leaving him to count the minutes until sunrise. If that happened, he'd be forced to either let the daylight disintegrate him or disappear and leave Hixton for good.

"Something tells me there's more going on around here than meets the eye," Pierson said. "Unusual things. And I assure you, I'll figure it all out."

Corin glanced over his shoulder at Tomes whose eyes widened in return. Just what was the sheriff getting at? What did he know?

Enduring more questioning and insinuations as they rode, Corin released a sigh of relief when they reached the estate, eager to escape the interrogation.

"This is quite a place you've inherited." Pierson pulled through the gate.

"Yes, I'm very fortunate."

"Your uncle, I hear, was a recluse...rarely seen."

"Yes." Corin nodded. "He kept to himself—a rather eccentric man."

"Much like you, it seems he only came out at night." Sheriff Pierson's words were unanticipated, leaving both Corin and Tomes perplexed.

The vehicle rolled to a stop in front of the mansion.

"I need to get inside." Tomes groaned.

"Thank you again for the ride, Sheriff." Corin got out and helped Tomes. "You always provide stimulating conversation."

"Don't you boys get any ideas about leaving town now," Pierson said. "Understand?"

Corin shut the door. "We'll be around," he answered through the glass.

Sheriff Pierson drove on.

Tomes looked at Corin. "What do you think he knows?"

"I'm not sure. But I don't see how he could know I'm a nightwalker."

* * * *

The wind gusting through the tops of the trees gave a haunting moan. In an isolated clearing, the Order gathered in its formidable mission to seize and punish those who had betrayed them, and to return the relic to its rightful place in their guard. It was a remarkable sight. Some of the immortals moved in as phantoms, materializing from a vapory mist. Others shape-shifted from animal to human form, creating a unified circle. When they had all assembled, Jordon stepped forth from the multitude, into the center of the ring.

"I heard your call," he addressed the entire Order.

A nightwalker stepped forward and joined him in the circle. Appearing less than the age of thirty in mortal years, he was a tall and distinguished, yet imposing, figure, with jet-black hair and eyes to match. Jordon bowed his head in respect, and the immortal returned his gesture.

"Commander Mikhail," Jordon acknowledged.

"It has been too long, Jordon," Galvar Mikhail, the Commander of the Order, greeted. "Let us take a walk together." He motioned for two nightwalkers to part, allowing them passage outside of the circle.

"What's brought you here, Commander?" Jordon asked as they walked shoulder-to-shoulder away from the group.

"Must I always remind you to drop the title?"

"Habit," Jordon said. "I see there are only members with you. It must be serious."

"The Body has been taken," Galvar informed him.

"How is that possible?"

"Lehndra." Galvar sighed.

"Lehndra? I thought she was disposed of two years back." Jordon didn't understand. "Why is she still living?"

"She is of ancient Delghorlin blood. You know there are many of our kind who have pledged to preserve that nearly extinct lineage. We must always consider the repercussions of our actions, no matter how deserving of death one might be."

"It isn't right," Jordon disputed. "She's a traitor."

"I agree, but the Order, together, determined her fate by secret ballot, and the outcome has revealed that there are still several among our council who remain loyal to the lineage," Galvar spoke in a hushed voice. "I don't mean to say she went without punishment. We took into account her many crimes and transgressions and sentenced her accordingly."

"So, what was her punishment, a slap on the wrist?" Jordon barked in irritation. "It apparently wasn't banishment to a barren world. Otherwise, she wouldn't be here, in this one now, stirring up more trouble."

"It was imprisonment...in a sense. We stripped her of all privilege and free reign for a time of fifty years."

"Punishment indeed." Jordon mocked the miniscule penalty. "Forgive my disrespect, Galvar, but if it were up to me, I'd finish off that godawful Delghorlin line once and for all."

"Use caution, Jordon," Galvar responded to his rash remark, glancing back at the Order. "Repercussions can be disastrous. The lineage, I agree, is ruthless, but it is also the oldest of our race. The Delghorlin are our forefathers. You are diurnal, not nightwalker, but we are brethren, and we must all respect the ancestry of our world."

"I will never claim pride in such a merciless lineage. They have all been nothing more than demons. Lehndra is a prime example of the savage nature of that bloodline, continually betraying her own kind, which is the worst of crimes to be committed." Jordon spoke his mind regarding the female immortal, not caring if he was overheard. "I'm a sworn sentry. It's my job to track down these reprehensible culprits and bring them to justice."

"And none has done a better job," Galvar praised.

"How do I rationalize continuing with what I do if the criminals are never brought to justice? It makes my life's work meaningless."

"Lehndra is a special circumstance, Jordon, you know this," Galvar asserted. "You carry this beyond proportion."

"Do I?"

"What's done is done." Galvar's voice grew stern. "Let us get past this and move on to what presently matters."

Jordon nodded, knowing that very few immortals could talk to Galvar the way he just had and live to see another night.

"About Lehndra. Unlike Karlot, who possesses the power of concealment, we were able to track her here."

"Karlot is here as well, now calling himself Boldor," Jordon informed him.

"How has she managed to find him?"

"I suspect the recent news reports alerted her. Since obtaining the Heart, this is the first time he's stopped moving. He's become obsessed with another nightwalker residing here named von Vadim."

"Interesting," Galvar remarked. "Well, I need not tell you what will become of us all should Lehndra succeed in acquiring the Heart from him."

"With the Body already in her possession, it would be disastrous."

"We must find the Heart of the Clyth before she does," Galvar stressed, "for the sake of us all—our world, this world, and all others. We cannot fail."

25

No Ordinary Wolf

Inside the estate house, Corin and Tomes contemplated their next course of action.

"I don't feel anything from Angel." Tomes rested on the sofa. "That must be a good sign, don't you think?"

Corin didn't reply, pacing the room.

"She's not dead. I would know if she were," Tomes told him.

Corin nodded. "What you have with Angelique is remarkable."

"It can be a burden. She's been fighting me since the day we were born, probably even kicked my butt once or twice in the womb." He laughed.

"She is a true force—a magnificent force."

"Hey. I don't want to hear that from you. Nothing has changed when it comes to the issue of you two."

"Yes, you've made your position very clear."

Before an argument ensued, the phone rang,

averting their attention. Corin quickly answered, the caller being the female immortal.

"I think I have something of value to you," she told him.

"Just what is it you're after?" Corin spoke sharply.

"Boldor has something I want. I'm sure you know of it by now."

"The charm?"

"Yes," she confirmed. "The Heart of the Clyth. It belongs to me."

"To you, or to the Order?"

"There must be something unique about you, Nightwalker, to gain Jordon's confidence. But no matter, I know your only interest lies in getting this female mortal back. And she is so sweet, warm, and tempting...."

"You harm her, and you'll get nothing from me. Except my wrath." Corin's voice held a growl. "You'd best remember that."

"Oh, believe me, von Vadim, I know where I stand with you," she replied. "You get me what I want, and you'll get what you want. Bring me the charm, and she's yours, unharmed. You have my word."

"And how good is your word?"

"My acts, though they may seem illicit, have been carried out only for the betterment of my home-world. Karlot is nothing more than a common thief out to do whatever benefits him most. I'm just glad I didn't share my aspirations with him," she rambled on. "Even when we were together, I never fully trusted him. But he's not important. My vision is what drives me. My goal is to lead my world into a new age. Under my reign, and with the power of the Clyth, the Eleventh Dimension will become a more advanced and powerful world, surpassing all others."

"And what if those of your world don't wish to change and move into this new future you envision?" Corin wasn't sure what to make of the immortal, but the more she talked, the more he learned.

"There will be no choice given. They will follow, or die." Her response held no emotion. "In pursuit of greatness there are always casualties."

"You certainly have the makings of a true oppressor, forcing your people to either submit to your reign, or perish."

"We've gotten off track. You know the terms. I'll bring the girl to the estate in three hours for the trade. I suggest you get moving in search of your prey. Karlot's not an easy one to track, and the clock's ticking. Tick...tick...tick," she imitated the sound and hung up.

Corin slammed the phone down.

"What are her demands?" Tomes was eager to know.

"She proposed a trade—the charm Boldor possesses for Angelique. I have three hours to find him."

"It was next to impossible locating his hideout the first time," Tomes fretted. "He could be anywhere."

"I know, but I have no choice but to try. Angelique's life depends on it."

Tomes pushed himself up. "I'll come with you."

"I'm sorry, Tomes, but you'll just slow me down. This time, I'm going alone."

"You're right, you'll cover a lot more ground without me. Go. Do whatever you can to find him. I'll hold down the fort here."

"I hate leaving you alone, not knowing where he might be."

"Don't worry about me. We both agree Angelique comes first."

Corin nodded. "Do you still have plenty of those blackthorn nails left? I don't want to leave you completely defenseless."

"I have plenty. And I'll keep the staker close," Tomes assured him.

"See that you do."

"You better get moving."

Not wasting another minute, Corin exited the house through the lanai, shape-shifted into the form of a night bird, and took to the sky.

* * * *

"They sound really close, Angelique remarked on a pack of wolves howling from the nearby woods. "I've never heard so many at one time before."

"They know I'm here." Lehndra cocked her head, mimicking the way birds move their heads in quick, short turns. "The bloody things will give us away if I don't get rid of them."

"How do you plan on accomplishing that?"

"There's only one way I can think of to shut them up. First, I need rope. Where can I find some?" she spoke with heightened anxiety.

"Out back. In the barn."

"Let's go." Lehndra grabbed Angelique by the arm and yanked her up.

Angelique winced as the immortal's long nails bit into her delicate flesh, but she didn't cry out. When they reached the barn, she pointed out some rope hanging from a hook on a wall covered with tack.

Lehndra made haste in retrieving it. "This will do." She bound Angelique's hands and secured her to a stable rail.

Angelique attempted to squirm free, but it was a useless effort.

"You're only making it harder on yourself, my dear." Lehndra yanked the knot tight. "Now be a good little girl while I'm gone."

She turned and marched out the open doorway, her fangs and talons emerged, prepared for the hunt. Heading for the woods with only one mission in mind, she was going to seek out and destroy those whining wolves. Approaching the tree line, she shape-shifted into the form of a lioness, but just as she solidified, a lanky, dark-colored wolf burst forth from the shadows. This was no ordinary wolf. Transforming into his human form, with fangs and talons extended, Boldor was ready for a fight. Lehndra did the same, taking a defensive stance.

"Thought you could outsmart me, my lover? Out for a little taste of revenge?" Boldor looked her up and down. "I thought you'd be over me by now."

Lehndra played along with his assumption. Stroking his very large ego was her best bet for survival. "I loved you, Karlot, and you left me to the mercy of the Order."

"I go by Boldor now, and I haven't time for this. Where is the girl?" He grabbed her by the throat.

"The b-barn," she managed to say, knowing he wouldn't hesitate to kill her. "She's in the barn."

"You'd best not toy with me," Boldor threatened. "Not if you value your life."

"I'll t-take you to her." She gasped as he squeezed her throat with a firm, unflinching grasp.

He threw her out in front of him. "Lead on."

"How clever of you to use the wolves to draw me out." Lehndra rubbed away the lingering discomfort.

"Deceit is my specialty."

"I've come to learn that, Karlot, and believe me, I won't underestimate you again."

26

Same Deal, Same Place

Angelique gasped when Boldor slithered through the door. And catching a whiff of his vile scent, she wrinkled her nose in aversion.

"Back as my ransom again." He wore a menacing grin, swaggering her way. His eyes wandered over the length of her body, leaving her feeling dirty all over. "Nice to have things back in order, not exactly as planned, but still workable."

Angelique looked into Lehndra's face, observing the hatred in her eyes. It obviously hadn't been her plan to bring him into the picture, leaving Angelique to presume Boldor had caught the female immortal off guard.

"I just don't see it." Boldor squeezed Angelique's face, barely an inch between them. "Do you see it?" he asked Lehndra.

"I don't understand. See what?"

"A face worth dying for." He studied his subject.

"Beauty yes, that I see, but worth your life?" He released his hold with a huff. "No matter, von Vadim sees it, and that's what counts."

Boldor found another length of rope and bound Lehndra's hands before untying Angelique from the stall rail. Shoving them in the direction of the open doorway, he ordered them to the house. When inside, he pushed them toward the sofa.

"Take a seat." He kept close watch while he made a call. "Director, come to Jaffler Farm. I have another job for you."

It was apparent that the recipient didn't want to cooperate, making Boldor furious.

"There is no discussion to be had. I own you," he threatened. "We have an arrangement, and there will be no wriggling out of it. Now, the night draws on, so I suggest you come this instant! We have a lot to achieve before dawn. Get a move on, Director, or die at our next meeting," Boldor spat a final warning and ended the call, cursing the mortal.

"That sounded a little desperate," Lehndra braved the remark.

"Things are growing riskier by the minute. If I don't finish this tonight, I'll have to walk away from the score," he told her. "And I never walk away a loser."

While waiting, he took the time to pen a note to von Vadim, reading it aloud when he was done, Lehndra and Angelique his audience.

"Why are you doing this?" Angelique asked.

"Why not?" Boldor responded coldly, folded the sheet, and placed it in an envelope.

"What has Corin ever done to you?"

"Nothing. But he's going to do a lot *for* me." His top lip rose at the corners and stretched into a broad grin. "When he's gone, I'll take his identity. The security and wealth, it will all be mine."

"You'll never be the man he is," Angelique insulted the immortal. "Not even close."

"You might want to consider being a little nicer to me. Maybe I'd spare you...give you immortality."

"I'd rather die!" she declared.

"That could be arranged," Boldor growled.

"You should back off, my dear," Lehndra suggested. "His patience runs thin."

Angelique took her advice and said nothing more, watching Boldor slither about the room till Fulner arrived.

"Not much of an army, Karlot." Lehndra laughed when her eyes fell on the pathetic-looking man.

"She did this to me. The bitch." Fulner pointed to his bandaged face.

"We were all there," Boldor reminded him.

Lehndra laughed at the asinine fool, then hissed, sending him scampering closer to Boldor for protection.

"And I will do much worse than a few talon marks if you don't pay attention and do as I say." He shoved a sealed envelope at the man. "I want this delivered to von Vadim Estate without delay. It is to be placed in no other hand but his. Is that understood?"

"Perfectly." Fulner noticed the Jaffler Farm logo marking the upper corner as he started for the door, keeping a safe distance away from Lehndra.

"Wait, one other thing." Boldor aimed for Angelique and cut off a section of her hair with a pass of an extended nail. Then, ripping a strip of cloth from a nearby curtain, he secured the strands and handed it to Fulner. "Present this as well and tell him: Till death do us part."

* * * *

Tomes listened to the wolves howling in the surrounding woods, their forlorn echoes sending a shiver up his spine. Startled by the doorbell, he cursed, hoping it wasn't the sheriff. Making his way to the entry, he started to open it, but thinking he should be cautious under the circumstances, he called out to see who was there.

"Jerry Fulner, from the funeral home. I have a message for von Vadim."

Tomes unlocked the door and cracked it just far enough to view him, staker in hand. "Fulner," he acknowledged in an unwelcome tone. "Are you alone?"

"Yes. As I said, I'm here to deliver a message."

Tomes opened the door. "Adding a few more dirty deeds to your resume?"

"I told you before, don't shoot the messenger."

"Just hand over whatever it is he's sent."

"It's for von Vadim. I was instructed to place it in his hand. Only his."

"Well, Corin's not here, so you're going to have to leave it with me or take it back to Boldor undelivered." Tomes gave him his options.

Fulner mumbled under his breath in indecision. "Okay, take it." He shoved the bundle at him. "Just see that he gets it."

"What is this supposed to mean?" Tomes recognized Angelique's hair.

"Till death do us part." Fulner took several steps back. "That's what he said to tell von Vadim."

"Why, you worthless.... Where is she?" Tomes reached for Fulner, missing by mere inches.

The director dashed for his car, and Tomes attempted to pursue, but his sore body refused to cooperate.

Stepping back inside, Tomes leaned against the inside of the door and tore open the envelope.

Checkmate, von Vadim. It seems I am back in the game. Your little angel has once again played right into my hands.

Same deal, same place. Come now, or her life is mine. Make haste, for we end this tonight. Come dawn, this game is over!

"Same deal, same place. The cemetery again." Tomes knew what he had to do.

He slapped the note down and gripped the staker. He'd lied to Corin about having plenty of nails, desperately wishing that weren't the case. Frowning as he opened the chamber, he counted the last of his supply already loaded in the weapon. *One, two...three.* Nearly a hundred nails dwindled down to a measly three. He'd wasted them all. But there was nothing he could do now.

What's done is done; what will be, will be.

Tossing the strap of the sheath holding the machete over his shoulder, he hurried over to the key rack and scanned the titles above each one marking the automobiles they matched. Deciding on the '66 Chevelle, he headed for a building just past the garage, where Corin housed his classic cars. Someone had to go after Angel, and he had no idea where Corin was, or when he'd be back.

According to the note, Tomes figured that come dawn, Boldor intended to kill her, or worse, change her. At present, he was her only hope. God help them.

* * * *

Sheriff Pierson watched the mansion from his previous stakeout position.

"I don't buy it for a second." He thought back over Corin and Tomes's story about Angelique leaving them stranded at the cemetery.

Only the two of them had been in the 'Vette when it entered the cemetery, yet a third person left in the car, racing out at a high speed, scarcely making the turn onto the main road. He'd attempted to follow, but a flat tire had ceased the chase.

After changing the tire, he'd climbed back in the driver's seat and headed down the narrow lane where he'd seen two figures walking toward him—Tomes Jaffler and Corin von Vadim.

"What were you really up to out there?"

Sheriff Pierson reached for his cup in the console and took a drink.

"Now what is this?" He saw a car leaving the estate.

Quick to follow, he soon realized that it was heading in the direction of the cemetery.

"Not again. I hope it's not rituals." The prospect seemed likely with vampires involved.

Thinking of the murdered victims, he couldn't help wondering if von Vadim fed on those poor women the way he had on that cow in the field. It was unnerving knowing immortals resided amongst them—hungry, bloodthirsty nocturnal creatures, preying on the innocent. The situation was turning out to be more of a vampire hunt than a homicide investigation.

Picturing a character in a comic book, he envisioned a caption, *And Super Lawman lost his mind.* With that came an image of himself gripping his head with eyes bulging out in lunacy.

"I need a cigarette." He groaned and attempted to shake the picture from his mind.

Pulling a pack of Marlboros from his front shirt pocket, he tapped one out, and lit it. He took in a deep, comforting drag.

"Get a grip, lawman, you're as sane as the next guy," he assured himself. But then again, that all depended on who the next guy was, didn't it?

* * * *

Boldor shoved Lehndra toward the truck while dragging Angelique at his side.

"Pity we can't take the 'Vette," he groaned, "but it won't seat three. This thing will have to do." He ushered both women into the cab of the work truck, placing Angelique next to him, keeping his meal ticket close. "Don't try anything," he warned Lehndra, expecting her to attempt an escape at any given moment.

Just as he'd suspected, about a mile from the farm, she made her move, suddenly dematerializing into vapor and slipping through the partially opened passenger's side window. Boldor screeched to a halt, but she was gone in a flash, fleeing into the fog-laden woods.

"Lehndra!" he roared, unable to go after her for fear of losing his ransom.

Swearing, he slammed his hands against the wheel, wishing now that he had killed her when he'd had the chance. He'd never been one for sentiment, and he didn't plan to start now. A few residual feelings wouldn't stop him from taking her out when the time came. And if she messed things up for him this time, he wouldn't just kill her, he'd make her suffer.

* * * *

Corin stood at the edge of a small clearing in his human form, contemplating heading back to the estate. He'd searched the woods and every unoccupied building in the area for Boldor, making no progress.

"Who's there?" He felt a presence and whirled around, finding a vapor moving in on him. It stopped about fifteen feet from him and took form. He could hardly believe his eyes—the female immortal. "What have you done with Angelique?"

"I'm afraid she's no longer my captive."

"What's happened to her? She's not—"

"Oh, she's alive." She cut him off. "But for how long, I can't say. Boldor has her. Didn't you get his message?"

"Since your phone call, I've been out searching for him, trying to get that cursed charm you demanded. But without being able to sense him, it's a useless endeavor."

"He certainly had no trouble finding me," Lehndra informed him. "Luring me right to him, using the wolves as cover. A dirty trick."

"And now he has Angelique again. What was his message?"

"He sent the one he calls 'Director' to deliver it to you at the estate. It said, *Same deal, same place. Come now, or her life is mine. And make haste, for we end this tonight. Come dawn, this game is over!*" She remembered every word. "He's on his way to the cemetery with the girl as we speak. I got away from him in the truck. He's planning to pick right back up where he left off earlier, before I arrived and screwed everything up for him."

"The miserable...." he cursed under his breath. "He just won't give up."

"There's something else. With the note, he also sent a clipping of the girl's hair. The man was to tell you: Till death do us part."

"He's telling me that this won't be over till one of us takes the other's head."

Corin shape-shifted and took to the sky as a Great Horned Owl, his massive wings beating the air with such ferocity that the sound trailed behind him.

"Oh, I'm not going to miss this." Lehndra's mouth

curled upward. "When he takes you out, Karlot, and I know he will, the Heart will be mine for the taking. I'll have my sweet revenge and both halves of the Clyth."

The female immortal transformed into a smaller night bird and followed a short distance behind, bound for the cemetery.

27

Fully Consumed

Tomes caught sight of a vehicle moving in the darkness behind him. Had it been any other color but white, he might not have noticed it following with no headlights. Not caring for being spied on, he set a trap, hiding just inside the gate and catching Sheriff Pierson unaware when he entered the cemetery.

"Why are you following me, Sheriff?" Tomes stepped into view just as Pierson passed, causing him to turn back in surprise.

"I should be the one asking the questions, Mr. Jaffler. I knew there was a good chance you'd spot me, but I had to know what's going on out here."

Wolves crying from the woods surrounding the cemetery momentarily captured both men's attention.

"Strange spot for hunting." Pierson eyed the weapon in Tomes's hand, along with the machete hanging behind him.

"Whatever it is you're thinking, I'm sure it's wrong."

Remembering the sheriff's prior comment suggesting that Corin only came out at night left Tomes wondering just how long he'd been watching them.

"I know what he is," Pierson said.

"What who is, Sheriff?" *Was he saying he knew about Corin...that he was a nightwalker?*

"Von Vadim. I've seen him. The marshal too. But why Black's able to walk around in the daylight stumps me."

"What is it you're saying?" Tomes didn't want to confess anything, still not certain the Sheriff knew they were immortals.

"Vampires!" Sheriff Pierson shot the words at him. "I've seen von Vadim feed on cows. And Black, I've watched him change from man to animal...into a wolf. I know what I saw. They're not human."

"You're right, Sheriff, they're not human, they're immortals. And Corin, he is a nightwalker. I take it you've been following us for quite a while?"

"Not too long. Your green folder, the one filled with all of the vampire research, helped me put things together. Not to mention everything I've seen with my own two eyes."

"So, you've now resorted to breaking and entering? That folder was in my desk...in my house. A place you had no right to be."

"Just doing what had to be done," Pierson admitted. "Sometimes the rules have to be bent a little."

"Or overlooked altogether?" Tomes retorted. "I'll need it back. I have plans for that research. It's going to make one gripping book...if I survive. But right now, you'd best prepare yourself, Sheriff, because there's more going on here than anything in that folder could ever tell you. Angelique's been captured by none other than your Jackson County killer, and before you ask, yes, he is a nightwalker."

"What is your involvement with von Vadim? Why do you cover for him, the killer who murdered your wife?"

"Corin is not the killer. It's another nightwalker called Boldor, and he's a nasty one. In fact, he's targeted Corin, holding Angelique hostage, using her as a bargaining chip," Tomes explained. "Without Corin, we'd probably all be dead right now. It's taken me a while to accept it, but his feelings are still very much human. Just like us, some immortals are good, and some are bad."

A vehicle approached and Tomes pulled Sheriff Pierson into hiding. Crouching in the shadows behind some overgrowth, they watched it barrel through the gate.

"That's my truck!" Tomes caught a glimpse of Angelique as it passed. "All hell is about to break loose, Sheriff. If you value your life, I'd suggest you get out of here while you can."

Tomes started into the cemetery in pursuit of Boldor.

"I'm not going anywhere, Jaffler." Pierson rushed to catch up with him.

"It's your neck." Tomes put no effort into stopping him, knowing it would be a waste of energy.

Fog lingered over the area, thick, lying low to the ground. Cautious with their footing, they worked their way toward the center of the cemetery. Tomes noticed that the wolves seemed to be growing nearer, their howls now echoing out from the boundaries of the cemetery, closing in on them.

"I've never encountered this kind of fog before," Pierson said. "I can't even see the ground. And what's with the wolves?"

"Quiet." Tomes hushed him. Squatting behind a headstone, he motioned for him to do the same. "It's

Boldor." He pointed out the fiend's position a short distance in front of them.

Boldor retrieved the sword he'd dropped earlier, turned, and peered their way. "I know you're here," he called out.

Tomes took a deep breath, stood, and stepped out from behind the gravestone.

"You're not alone." Boldor gripped the sword. "I sense another."

Pierson followed Tomes's lead and revealed himself, but with his pistol drawn and aimed at the nightwalker's chest.

"That gun won't do you any good," Tomes told him. "He's a nightwalker—the undead."

"I don't care. I feel better knowing I have it." Pierson refused to lower his aim.

Boldor laughed. "Brought the law with you, lackey? Planning on making an arrest?"

"I have other things in mind tonight." Tomes showed no fear. "Angel," he called out to his sister, "are you okay?"

"I—" she attempted to answer but released a yelp when Boldor yanked her head back.

"Lay off!" Tomes took several bold steps forward.

At that moment, a large owl soared in, its wings spread wide, landing a few feet from Tomes, where it shape-shifted into Corin. Lehndra, not far behind, touched down a short distance to their right, and reclaimed human form.

Witnessing the immortals' transformations, Sheriff Pierson stumbled backward, nearly dropping his pistol.

"Like I said, Sheriff." Tomes looked at him. "All hell is about to break loose."

* * * *

Corin faced Boldor, fire flashing in his eyes. "Same deal, same place."

"Yes." Boldor's gaze caught Lehndra. "Taking sides with the enemy?"

"I'd side with Satan to see you pay, Karlot."

Boldor snarled. "I'll take care of you later, my lover. And it won't be painless." He then shifted his focus back to Corin. "I'm glad to see you made it, von Vadim. I was beginning to wonder if you'd sent these two pathetic mortals in your place."

"I fight my own battles."

"Same deal as before." Boldor pointed to the headstone. "When your head hits this stone...you know the drill."

Corin looked into Angelique's face, conveying the love he felt for her in an unspoken whisper. Then, seeing the pain in her eyes, he forced his gaze away and proceeded to the gravestone. With no hesitation, he dropped onto all fours and lowered his head over the top edge of the stone, ready for execution.

"No, Corin!" Angelique cried out, but Boldor gave her a firm yank.

The nightwalker writhed toward Corin, pulling Angelique along with one hand while eagerly gripping the sword in the other. She fought against his hold, creating a diversion, but when Corin attempted a maneuver, Boldor turned the blade to her throat.

"Keep your place, or it's her head instead," he threatened.

"Don't hurt her." Corin fell back into place, his eyes locking with Angelique's tearful stare.

"Please, Corin. I won't let you sacrifice yourself for me," she sobbed. "I could never live with that."

Corin looked away, unable to bear her heartache. "You'll have to let her go to finish the job," he told Boldor, cocking his head to focus on the devil's thin, miserable face, knowing he'd need both hands to make the strike. "Go ahead. Take your swing!" he pressed, wanting him to release his hold on Angelique.

"Wait! Don't—" Tomes called out.

"Stay out of this." Corin cut him off. "Now take your swing!" He fixed his attention on Boldor. "Take it before I change my mind!"

Making his move, Boldor shoved Angelique away from him, raised the sword high, and came down with a powerful strike, but the blade intended to sever Corin's head missed him by millimeters and struck nothing but stone.

"Run, Angel!" Tomes saw she was dazed from striking her head against a statue and rushed toward her.

"I'm okay." She met him halfway. "We need to help Corin."

Corin motioned to Tomes to get her to the sideline.

"This is his fight, Angel. I think he can handle it."

"Your swing wasn't quick enough, Boldor. Unfortunate...for you." Corin turned the tables on the nightwalker. "And now, as you said, we end this tonight."

Boldor allowed his inner monster to emerge as he advanced on Corin, swinging again, striking another headstone with such force that it snapped the blade in half. Enraged, he threw the weapon to the ground and zeroed in on Angelique's position.

Corin, knowing Boldor planned to go after her, flew at him with superhuman speed. With fangs and talons lengthening, he aimed for the charm hanging around the fiend's neck, managing to grab the chain and snatch it free with a powerful yank, sending the piece hurling away from them.

"Oh, I sense you now," Corin told him. The sensation was strong. "Without that charm, you have nothing to hide behind."

Boldor let out a thundering roar and retaliated, ramming Corin with all the force he could muster, his fangs tearing into Corin's right shoulder.

The battle was on! Till death.

* * * *

Tomes tried to stop Angelique, who rushed to claim the Heart. But she was determined to beat the female immortal to the mark, and being closer, succeeded.

"Hand it over, sweetness," Lehndra demanded with eyes locked on the charm.

"Careful, Angel," Tomes warned while aiming the staker, ready to fire.

"I'm only asking once more, girl. It means nothing to you," she growled.

"I don't think so. If this is the charm you told me about, it should be returned to the guardians you stole it from."

Lehndra's demon emerged. "Then you leave me no choice."

She assailed, fast and furious, thrusting her talons deep into Angelique's chest, the charge happening so fast no one had time to react.

"No! God, no—" Tomes cried out.

"Sorry, my sweetness, but you did force my hand." Lehndra pulled her talons free, allowing Angelique to collapse like a puppet whose strings had just been cut.

Sheriff Pierson fired several shots into the immortal, but the bullets only had a momentary effect on her. Unhappy with his attack, she tossed him a warning hiss before bending and claiming the charm from Angelique's clasped hand. And now in possession of her long-awaited prize, she retreated, but was forced to stop a short distance away to tend her wounds.

"What on earth?" Pierson watched in disbelief as she repaired the damage with healing hands.

Tomes rushed to his sister's aid, sharing her pain, fearing the severity of her injury. Lifting her into his arms, she gasped, struggling to breathe.

"Angel. No, this can't be happening." He could feel her slipping away, her life force fading.

"I c-can't b-breathe." Her body trembled as shock overtook her.

Angry and blaming himself for not taking a shot at Lehndra when he had the chance, Tomes went for the immortal who remained in sight, distracted by the charm. Slipping up behind her with the staker raised, he now stood close enough to see that she was in possession of not one, but two charms, and was attempting to connect the pieces. Whatever she was planning, he knew it wasn't good.

For Angel.

He held a steady aim and fired off his three remaining blackthorn nails into the immortal's back. Expelling a horrific screech, she buckled over in agony, unable to pursue him.

"I hope they're killing you." Tomes took his revenge and rushed back to Angelique.

Even though he knew blackthorn was a terrible agony to nightwalkers—a fiery torment burning them from within—it didn't seem enough.

The charms.

Tomes caught sight of both pieces hurling from her hold as she flung about in a violent fit, trying to rid herself of the searing nails. Crying out, she used an index talon in an effort to extrude a nail by pushing it on through her body, but before she could finish the job, a great, black wolf lunged in attack.

Tomes clutched Angelique close, not knowing whether the canine was friend or foe, relieved when it went for the female immortal. It took her to the ground and pinned her down with a ruthless growl before shape-shifting into Jordon.

"Thank God. Jordon, I need you here!" Tomes called for the daywalker's help. "It's Angel. She's been stabbed. It's bad!"

Jordon left Lehndra huffing and squirming and rushed over to examine Angelique's injury.

"Can you heal her?"

Jordon ran his hands over Angelique's chest, but the small amount of healing he was able to offer made only a minor difference. "The wound is too severe."

"Why won't it work?"

"We can only do so much with mortal's injuries. I'm afraid there's nothing we can do for her now."

"I can't accept that." Tomes fought back tears. "I won't."

"Corin should know." Jordon observed the two nightwalkers engaged in a fierce battle.

"Yes. Corin." Tomes looked at Jordon, realizing their only hope. "There is a way to save her." He knew what had to be done, and lowering Angelique, he stood and sought Corin's position. "Corin, it's Angel. She's dying!"

* * * *

Corin whirled, the words striking him like a bolt of lightning. Releasing a hellish wail, the evil entity dwelling within him crawled forth from the depths of his being and overtook him. Transmuted beyond nightwalker to that of a full-fledged demon, he was more monster than man.

"W-what power is this?" Boldor stammered and backed away. "I've never seen this kind of change before."

"I'm going to send you to hell." Corin's voice

deepened. "We end this now!" He charged with a deafening roar, taking Boldor down with demonic force.

Boldor's bones cracked beneath his weight as they hit the ground, rendering him immobile long enough for Corin to flip him face up and straddle him.

"You are no ordinary nightwalker," Boldor uttered.

Corin's mind burned as he glared into his opponents eyes, not able to control what he was becoming. He felt himself turning savage, thirsting for blood...for the kill. All humanity was fading, leaving nothing but the demon. Until this moment, he had never allowed his monster full release, only now discovering the full magnitude of the hellish entity he harbored.

"You." He clutched Boldor's head in his hands, still retaining enough of himself to know he wanted the nightwalker dead. "To hell!" His voice was unrecognizable...fearsome.

Boldor struggled, but he was no match for Corin's demon. "You win, von Vadim. Don't kill me. I'll walk away, and you'll never see me again."

"Too late." Corin slowly rotated Boldor's head, and in one barbarous movement, decapitated him with a strength he never knew he had.

Boldor's remains instantly disintegrated. Their fight was ended. Once and for all, the morbid game was finally over.

During the final moments of the battle, the Order of the Clythguard had moved in—a pack of wolves—their howls echoing as they encircled the cemetery. Shape-shifting into their human forms, they were an impressive-looking group of immortals.

"You've been fully consumed. You must bring yourself back." Galvar rushed toward Corin. "Regain yourself, before it's too late."

"Angel needs you, Corin," Tomes called out to him.

"We're losing her."

Even though his human part had plummeted to the darkest depths of his being, he heard his friend's words, and comprehending what it meant, fought to take back control. Collapsing forward, he thrashed about, engulfed in an internal battle to climb to the surface.

"Fight harder," Galvar yelled. "Take back control."

Finally, overpowering the demon, he bridled the evil and confined it deep inside.

"You play a dangerous game." Galvar leaned over him. "Your physical changes were frightful. The demon you harbor is one to be feared. The strength it took to sever that head with nothing but your bare hands...a powerful monster to behold."

Corin breathed hard, lying motionless, exhausted from the fight.

"We each carry our own monsters within us that arise from time to time, but yours is of a different rank—a match for the devil himself." Galvar pulled him up to a sitting position. "Take my advice and keep it caged. You may not be able to bring yourself back next time."

"I'm all right now." Corin pushed himself up. "Angelique." He rushed toward Tomes who called out once again. Right now, she was all that mattered.

* * * *

With the immortals focused on Corin's possession, Lehndra managed to slip into the woods, valuing her existence over her aspirations. However, with her body still searing with the embedded blackthorn nails, she found it difficult to concentrate and therefore couldn't shape-shift.

Needing to do something fast, she grabbed a sturdy stick, and with one strong thrust, rammed it through one of the wounds, pushing the nail out through her back. It was pure agony, but she withheld her cry by sinking her teeth into her arm, muffling any sound that might escape. Then, doing the same with the two remaining nails, she finally freed herself from the tormenting fire and regained the ability to shape-shift. Without hesitation, she quickly turned to vapor and fled before anyone became aware of her escape. She was once again on the run.

28

Changed

Corin fell to his knees alongside Tomes and took Angelique from his hold. He pulled her close and looked into her ever-dimming eyes.

"Do you s-see him?" she said through gasps.

"See who, my love?" Corin brushed away a tear trailing her right cheek.

"The a-angel." She struggled to talk, her body trembling. "He's h-here."

"What is she talking about?" Tomes looked at Corin.

"It's the Angel of Death." Corin couldn't bear her suffering. "She's teetering on the brink, and Death is here to collect her soul."

"I'm so sorry." Jordon knelt next to Corin, placing a consoling hand on his shoulder.

"You all act like there's no hope, but she can be saved," Tomes said. "Corin, you can save her."

"The only way would be to change her—make her

336

immortal," Corin told him. "And I won't damn her to that fate."

"We can't just stand by and watch her die. God forgive me for this, but I'd rather have her changed than snatched through death's door."

Tomes's words surprised Corin, knowing how he despised the undead. He'd fought so hard to save his sister from the very thing he was now asking for.

"You saw what I was just now, Tomes, how can you ask me to condemn her with such a curse?"

"With you, I know she'll be fine. You haven't lost your humanity, and she won't either. I know what she means to you, Corin. What you mean to her."

"Yes." Corin caressed Angelique's face with the back of his fingers. "I don't want to let her go."

"We don't have to lose her," Tomes pleaded.

Corin couldn't deny wanting to keep her with him. But the Angel of Death stood among them, lingering, ready to collect her soul and guide her to her afterlife. Heaven awaited. A beautiful heaven. And if he changed her, she'd never see that paradise.

"I would be robbing you of the light...of heaven," he whispered to her. "Of your soul."

"Ch-change me, m-my love." Angelique made her own request in a faint voice. It's w-what I want."

"I promised you anything. Anything in my power to give."

With those words he lifted her and sank his fangs into her neck. Jordon backed away, giving him space, pulling Tomes with him.

Corin released his bite and lowered her to the ground, making a cut across his left wrist with an extended nail. "Drink of me." He pressed his bleeding wrist to her mouth, stroking her throat, making sure she swallowed enough for the exchange.

Tomes turned away. "Forgive me, God, but I

couldn't bear to lose another loved one."

Corin sealed the slash on his wrist, then leaned down and pressed a gentle kiss on her lips. "I'll be waiting." He swept his hand over her eyes, helping her fall into a trance.

"She won't come back like Louisa, will she?" Tomes feared.

"Her body isn't damaged to the extent Louisa's was due to the autopsy. I believe the transformation will take nicely. But only time will tell."

"How long will it take?"

Galvar stepped in. "Some say seventy-two hours, but the metamorphosis actually differs from person to person. It can take longer, but the quicker the better."

Tomes reached for Angelique's hand. "What will happen to her now?"

"With the virus upon her, she will face Death," Galvar continued to explain. "The angel will take her soul, but in the end, she will retain the memory of who she was in life. With the miracle of transformation, her body will undergo repair, and she will eventually awaken, immortal."

"I won't be able to rest until I know she's Okay," Tomes agonized.

"Nor will I," Corin said. "Forgive me, Tomes."

"I asked you to change her," Tomes reminded him.

"Not Angelique. Boldor. I promised you vengeance, and I took the kill from you."

"There's nothing to forgive. Just as you were consumed by that monster, I was overcome by my own rage. Besides, in my condition, I couldn't have taken him on and survived it. I'm satisfied and grateful that you avenged Louisa for me."

With Corin and Angelique settled, Galvar turned and addressed the Order. "What do we know of the charms?"

"The Heart has been recovered, but the Body was not found." A nightwalker stepped forward with the Heart of the Clyth and handed the charm to Galvar. "Lehndra must still be in possession of it, and she's gotten away."

"Unfortunate, but we have the Heart, and it will never leave our watch again," Galvar declared.

"What about these?" An immortal approached with the amber gemstones Boldor had possessed. "They didn't disintegrate with Karlot."

"They are charmed." Galvar held one up and viewed the insect inside. "We will take them. They may be of use to us."

"You should know, Galvar, I disclosed the secret of the Order to Corin," Jordon confessed.

"This was a special circumstance. And because of this immortal, the Heart is returned to us. But I suppose I shouldn't let you go without punishment, something to fit the crime—Lehndra."

Jordon groaned. "With her on the run, I guess my job isn't finished yet."

"You still have work to do," Galvar replied.

"I suppose the fact that she's of ancient Delghorlin blood is still an issue, even after all of this?"

"Everything remains the same. She mustn't be killed, only captured," Galvar stressed. "Leave her fate to the Order, Jordon. Remember what I told you about repercussions. Think of the consequences before you act."

"I can't say I'm happy about it, but I understand."

Galvar pressed a hand against his shoulder. "Keep us informed."

Jordon nodded. "I'll report soon."

Galvar called out to the Order. "Prepare to depart as we arrived—wolves." The immortals shifted, but the commander held off changing form. "My friend," he spoke to Corin, "the monster inside of you is a rare power, but remember, your human side has proven to be stronger."

"The girl will give him all the strength he needs," Jordon said.

"Yes." Galvar nodded. "Love is a mighty power in itself. Use that."

Standing next to Jordon, Corin extended a hand to the leader of the Order. "I will."

Galvar shook it. "Good life to you."

He then bid them farewell, transformed, and took his place at the front of the pack. Releasing a howl, he led the Order of the Clythguard into the woods, gone as quickly as they'd arrived, a passing wind in the night.

"Who were those guys, anyway?" Sheriff Pierson emerged from the backdrop, the manner of his question triggering laughter from Tomes, Corin, and Jordon. Amid all of the chaos, they had completely forgotten about him.

Jordon approached him with a slap to his back. "Those were the good guys, Sheriff, and they were with me," he bragged. "It took two years, but I finally got my man. I always do."

"I think Mr. von Vadim got your man, Marshal Black," Pierson busted his bubble.

Jordon cut his eyes at Corin with a wry grin. "If we have to get technical."

"Since the agency doesn't seem too concerned with the measures you take when it comes to getting your man, I suppose all of this will just be added to your growing list of 'presumed dead' reports," Pierson said.

"What other kind is there?" Jordon boasted.

"I sure wish I knew how I to explain this one," Pierson fretted. "I don't even have a body to produce."

"There's no explaining the truth, Sheriff. Don't jeopardize your position by spouting stories of immortal shape-shifters. Just make something up. Create a death. Have him burned up in a fire or lost in that black river of yours," Jordon suggested.

"It's hard to believe you work under the jurisdiction of the U.S. Department of Justice. You make it sound so easy."

"After two years of hunting a killer, this is the easy part," Jordon told him.

"I'll come up with something. I have no choice." Pierson looked at Angelique. "Is she going to be okay?"

Corin nodded. "She'll go through transformation and will awaken immortal."

"Well, I'd best get moving." Jordon faced Corin. "I don't want my new assignment to get too far ahead of me."

"Can I ask that you show me your true appearance before you go," Corin requested.

"Why not." Jordon's age melted away revealing a younger version of himself.

"What the.... You're just a kid!" Pierson exclaimed.

"Precisely why the aging is necessary," Jordon said to Corin.

"Will we see you again?" Corin asked. "I'm interested in learning more about your world. Maybe even make that visit we talked about."

"When this job is done, I'll drop in for a little RNR. I'm sure I'll need it after dealing with Lehndra."

"I'll look forward to it." Corin let him know he was welcome. "Don't you have a car? Do you need one of us to pick it up?"

"I'll have someone take care of it."

"I didn't think you had anyone on the inside helping you out." Corin caught his stare.

Jordon smiled slyly. "I never said that." He didn't elaborate.

Corin nodded.

With everything in order, Jordon shape-shifted and took to the sky.

"We'd best be going ourselves if we plan on making it to the estate before dawn." Corin lifted Angelique from the ground and headed for the truck. "Hopefully, Boldor left the keys."

"You go ahead." Tomes motioned. "I'll walk out with the sheriff. I have the Chevelle parked at the gate."

"My fully restored 1966 Chevrolet Chevelle Super Sport?" Corin said.

"The one and only, and she handles like a dream," Tomes razzed.

"It ought to with all the time and money I've put into it. Just remember, you're sitting behind a bundle. I'd best not find a scratch," Corin warned, making haste with Angelique, knowing sunrise wasn't far off.

* * * *

"Vampires, wolves, decapitations, it's certainly been interesting A night to remember." Pierson walked alongside Tomes, en route to the gate. "Does it still feel a little disturbing out here to you?" He felt the twitch behind his left ear, concerned things might not be quite as wrapped up as they believed them to be.

"There's nothing to worry about. Boldor's dead. And he's not coming back."

Pierson rubbed his ear. "I'll tell you one thing, after tonight, I'll never look at a cemetery the same way again."

"I know what you mean, Sheriff. This past week has completely changed my life."

Nearing the gate, Corin drove by, tossing a wave as he passed.

"Where are you parked?" Tomes asked.

"Behind those trees." Pierson pointed out the spot.

"You go ahead. I'll manage just fine."

"Okay. I'll see you soon, Sheriff." Tomes turned back. "What about my folder?"

"I'll get it to you." He wanted to do a little more reading before giving it up.

"All right, Sheriff." Tomes moved on. "I know where to find it."

Pierson went to his SUV and climbed behind the wheel, glancing at Tomes who left with a blow of the horn.

"Alone at last." He lit a Marlboro and flipped on an inside light.

With everyone cleared out, he reached in his jacket and pulled out a charm that resembled a large locket. A wide grin stretched across his face as he examined the relic. He wasn't at all the bumbling, backwoods simpleton the others thought him to be. Not by a long shot. Tonight, they were the ones royally duped.

Pierson had no idea what power the charm possessed, but he intended to find out. Since learning of the reality of immortals, how could he be content with living such a short life—a mere eighty years if lucky? Knowing what he now knew, he wanted what they had...the immortals. He wanted to live forever, and one way or another, he was going to make that happen.

* * * *

Three nights later, Tomes stirred about the mansion while Corin remained with Angelique, emerging from the basement only long enough to feed.

Falling asleep on the sofa, he woke just before sunrise and stepped onto the lanai. Collapsing in a chair, he thought about Louisa, plagued by her memory. She was gone, but he'd never stop loving or

343

missing her.

Watching the sky growing brighter by the minute—the sun rising to a new day—his thoughts transferred to Angelique.

"You will never see this again, Angel."

"I will see it from this day forth through your eyes, brother." He heard her voice in his mind, sending him scrambling to his feet in bewilderment.

"I hear you, Angel. By God, I hear you." He laughed, then cried.

With Angelique now immortal, he figured the telepathy was possible due to their twin connection, and her new powers. Nevertheless, all that mattered was his cherished sister, whom he dearly loved, was still with him. She was no longer mortal, but she would always be his Angel. And walking with Corin—an immortal he was now proud to call his brother—she would be happy.

EPILOGUE

Tomes sat at his computer and started typing, his fingers flying over the keys as he transposed his memories into words. His story would be both terrifying and incredible, telling of two destined immortals—Corin and Angelique—who reside in a small town called Hixton, located in Jackson County, Wisconsin. There, they inhabit a secluded, sprawling estate, claiming their isolation, hiding the fact that in the day, they rest within the dark confines of the earth, and after the fall of night, they walk, for they are nightwalkers.

It all started one stormy night. Corin von Vadim walked amid the stones....